THREE KINGDOMS

A GABRIEL WOLFE THRILLER

ANDY MASLEN

TYTON PRESS

For Michelle Lowery

'An oppressive government is more to be feared than a tiger.'

Confucius

AUTHOR'S NOTE

Gabriel Wolfe is fluent in many languages, including Mandarin, Cantonese and Russian. To save the reader trouble, I have written the dialogue throughout in English.

1

HONG KONG | PRESENT DAY

Gabriel Wolfe grasped the heavy cleaver. He adjusted his grip on the wooden handle, worn smooth from many hands before his. Looking down at the body stretched out beneath him, he picked his spot, ignoring the dark eye staring up at him.

One clean blow just behind the head. That was what the triad boss standing beside him had advised.

"And aim for the block beneath, not the surface of the skin. That way your cut is clean and you remove the head without needing more than one blow."

He twisted the blade so that it caught the blue-white light from the overhead neon tubes, which flickered constantly, plinking in the silence. Then he raised the cleaver high overhead and brought it down, fast and hard. He felt the crunch as the razor-sharp edge met skin, muscle, bone, and the scarred wood of the chopping block. The sound, a trebly *chack*, slapped back off the white tiles. Blood sprayed upwards, hitting him in the face. He held on tight until the shuddering spasms beneath his fingers ceased.

Smiling, he turned to the gangster and to the man standing a respectful half-pace behind him.

"How did I do?"

Fang Jian, the boss of the White Koi triad, nodded, then turned to the second man.

"Well, Master Lo, would you take him on as your apprentice?"

The man, short, thin, with wrinkled brown skin like a weathered apple, grinned.

"He removed fifty dollars' worth of meat along with the head. The cat-food factory will get it now. He needs more practice."

Fang laughed, throwing his large, blocky head back and showing a mouthful of gold-filled teeth.

"You hear that, Gabriel? You wasted good tuna, clumsy boy."

Gabriel smiled back, laying the bloody cleaver alongside the four-foot-long fish, its silver scales streaked scarlet, a pool of translucent blood forming around the sliced-off head.

"Maybe I'll stick to human targets, Master Lo. But thank you for allowing me to learn from a true master."

Lo bowed slightly and Gabriel returned the bow, much deeper as befitted his age relative to the older man. Fang laid a beefy arm around Gabriel's shoulder, forcing him to adjust his stance if he was to avoid buckling under the pressure. This close, he could smell the gangster's aftershave and beneath that his garlicky sweat.

"Come, my friend. Let's leave the man to his work. We'll enjoy the fruits of your labour out front."

Fang led Gabriel out of the kitchen, with its spotless stainless-steel surfaces and hanging racks of ladles, fish slices, tongs and long-bladed knives, to their booth in the corner of the restaurant. As they made their way through the other tables Gabriel glanced around the room. He found what he was looking for a couple of tables from the front door.

Two young women, dressed in white leather outfits, were eating from plates of rice, fish and bright-green pak choi. Both wore their hair up in sleek, glossy buns. Both were attractive, with scarlet lips and large brown eyes with cat-flicks of eyeliner at their outer corners. Both were capable of relieving a man of his life at a snap of their boss's stubby fingers, with or without a weapon. Jian never travelled anywhere without a pair of bodyguards. And although Gabriel had once heard, if not seen, an English freelance assassin named Sasha Beck kill an earlier pair, he knew Jian placed great faith in the women he called his "lotus blossoms".

One of the women looked up and caught his glance. Stared back. Inclined her head fractionally. Gabriel nodded a greeting in return. This was Wei Mei. *Beautiful Plum*, in Cantonese. Their last encounter had been eventful, to say the least. Between them, they had killed three Colombian cartel members in the Moscow dacha of a Russian crime boss. Then Mei, after aiming her Uzi submachine gun at Gabriel, had fired into the ceiling and sent him diving for cover before disappearing.

Other diners looked up as Fang led Gabriel to the coveted corner booth. A few smiled greetings to the thickset man, a couple scowled, others looked hurriedly away. Friend, foe or cautious bystanders, all seemed to know the identity of this sharply-dressed man with a boxer's build and tattoos of koi carp peeking from the golden cuffs of his dinner jacket.

Once they were seated, and a bottle of champagne ordered, Gabriel spoke.

"You said you wanted something from me, Mister Fang. Please, tell me. I am in your debt."

Fang laughed.

"I told you once before. Call me Jian. You are not my employee. Nor one of those corrupt Party officials we all have to deal with nowadays."

Gabriel nodded as he spread the gleaming white napkin over his lap.

"Jian, then. Though it feels disrespectful to me. How can I help you?"

"By doing what you do best."

"Meaning…?"

"Well, not cutting up tuna, that's for sure, eh!" Another roar of laughter that drew a few more curious glances. "Ah, here is our champagne. Thank you, my dear."

The waitress, dressed in a red sheath dress with a high collar, removed the bottle's yellow cellophane wrapping with a crackle. She ripped the gold foil away then deftly untwisted the wire cage before squashing it and secreting all the debris in a hidden pocket in her dress. She twisted the bottle in her right hand while holding the cork steady in her left. The cork came free with a hiss and Gabriel watched as a wisp of vapour escaped. Heavier than air, it curled over the lip of the neck and flowed downwards, a spectral version of the sparkling wine that issued forth a second later.

She filled Fang's coupe glass, then Gabriel's, before scrunching the bottle into a floor-mounted ice bucket and laying a red cloth across its exposed upper surface. With a slight bow and an even slighter smile on her red lips, she withdrew.

Fang picked up his glass, waited for Gabriel to clink rims, then drained it. Belching loudly, he refilled his glass. Gabriel took a mouthful of the champagne. Fang had ordered the most expensive bottle on the menu, a Louis Roederer Cristal. It tasted of apricots, hazelnuts and, oddly, Danish pastries, though Gabriel preferred his own, and Winston Churchill's, favourite, Pol Roger.

Fang set his glass down carefully on the starched white tablecloth.

"Now, Gabriel. We have, what do you English say, wetted our whistles? Here is my problem. I have a new contact from the mainland, though he is based here now. A very important man. As in, *extremely* important. You can guess his occupation?"

Gabriel took another sip of the Cristal while he thought. Fang rarely asked a question unless it tested the person answering in some way. Fang had mentioned corrupt officials only a few moments earlier. Party officials.

"CPC?"

Fang's deep-set eyes widened for a fraction of a second, giving Gabriel a glimpse of their dark-brown, almost black irises.

"Exactly. The Communist Party of China. Although, quite honestly, what that lot have to do with Communism is beyond me. Poor old Mao must be spinning in his grave."

Reflecting that "poor old" wasn't quite the phrase he would use for a dead dictator with the blood of tens of millions on his hands, Gabriel confined himself to another sip of the champagne.

"More billionaires than any other country except the US," he said.

"And half of them with copies of the Little Red Book on their nightstands. Anyway, it's all good business for us."

"And your contact has a business problem?"

Gabriel was envisaging some other heavy mob putting the hard word on this Party high-up, threatening blackmail or worse.

"No! His business interests are perfectly all right. No," Fang repeated, shaking his head and knocking back the rest of his champagne before refilling for the second time, "he has a public relations problem."

Gabriel frowned. Fang surely knew it was a long time since Gabriel had been engaged in anything existing even vaguely under the umbrella term "public relations". These days, the idea that the public might catch even a whiff of what he and his fellow assassins at The Department got up to would be the occasion for a UK-wide media blackout rather than the crafting of a press release. It reminded him of one of his boss's catchphrases. "If we let the hyenas smell blood, we'll have to pack up our toys and vanish, old sport."

"What kind of public relations problem?"

"I will let him explain. He is coming out here tomorrow to meet you. Now, drink up!"

Gabriel drank some more champagne, wondering what sort of PR challenge a Communist Party official would have that he could possibly help with.

2

A MISSILE BATTERY, NORTHEASTERN CHINA

Colonel Na kneels at his altar to perform his devotions. For the ceremony, as always, he has changed out of his People's Liberation Army uniform, which now lies, in a neatly-folded olive-green pile, on the chest of drawers in his bedroom. In its place, a priest's robe, sewn by a village woman to a design of his own devising. Purple for immortality and divinity. Black for death and destruction. Around his considerable waist is tied a gold sash, from which a gold silk purse dangles. The purse bulges, and it rattles when he moves. It's the knuckle bones inside that make the noise. No longer than the nail of his little finger, the tiny cylinders are bleached to a whiteness that makes him think of winter snows.

The village woman is dead long since. She was his first. A sweet old lady. And even though he resisted initially, the experience taught him a valuable lesson. The ancestors would not mind if he took baby steps at first, just so long as he complied with their wishes.

They are gathered around him now. Shuffling, whispering, urging him on to ever greater acts of devotion. They made their wishes clear to him a long time ago. He must unite the three kingdoms. Of Heaven, of Earth and of the Underworld, where the demons reside. With sufficient sacrifice, he may achieve their goals, and, at that point, ascend into Paradise. They have warned him what will happen if his efforts are *insufficient*. He tries to avoid thinking of that.

His altar has grown more complex over the years. Once, a simple lacquered bowl holding a few white blossoms sufficed. Then the ancestors let it be known that he should begin the process of unification by including materials from living creatures. He had started with dead beetles and snail shells, bird skulls and feathers, little tokens gleaned from his walks into the countryside around the village. But although these pacified the ancestors for a few weeks – or was it months? – they hungered for more. Always more.

Mice and voles, then rabbits and foxes, ducks and wild geese: all fed the flames. Growing tired of his pathetic attempts to please them, the ancestors, in the person of his Great-great- grandmother, made themselves perfectly clear.

"It is *people* you must bring us, little Keng. You must spill their blood on the ground and then you must unify yourself with them. Only then will you become pure enough to bring together the three kingdoms."

Na rocks back on his heels then forwards again until his broad forehead touches the gold cloth in front of the altar. A fan of rib bones extends outwards from the base like the rays of the setting sun. They draw in energy towards the centrepiece, a female pelvis in which nestles a screw-topped jar containing a child's heart suspended in rice spirit.

The eyes are there to help him see clearly. Eight pairs, floating in more rice spirit, arranged according to the principles of feng shui – facing north, east, south and west – for good luck and spiritual balance. A skull, perfect in every way except for the starred bullet hole between the eyes, sits atop the altar, gazing out and, from time to time, issuing instructions to Keng.

And behind the altar, forming a watchful backdrop to his morning and evening prayers, more skulls, set with lime mortar into a six-foot-high wall, each empty socket housing a shell, or a second, tiny skull, or a ring, a tooth, a dried ear, or a gold coin, or a fragment of a Party card or a lock of a child's hair.

He intends to add to the altar. The ancestors must be placated. He must pay another visit to the village. He stands, turns and leaves the temple. Outside, the temperature has plummeted to an unseasonal five degrees Celsius – some freak of nature, or else *they* have commanded the weather to change. Na shivers as biting specks of cold rain sting his cheeks. The latest captive, a monk on pilgrimage, slumps in his bindings, his bald head hanging down on his saffron-robed chest. His plait descends like a greasy black rope from a point at the base of his skull.

Na looks around but all the doors are barred and the windows curtained. If his subjects are peeking, they are being extremely careful not to let him notice. But he sees them, nonetheless. He sees their hungry faces, their red-rimmed eyes glowing with that crimson inner fire that Great-great-grandmother possesses.

He marches over to the unconscious monk and hauls his head up by his plait. Slaps him. Hard. Across the cheeks, left, right, left again.

"Hey, monk!" he shouts into the man's face. "Wake up!"

The monk's eyes flutter open, revealing whites spotted with red where the tiny blood vessels have burst.

"Please, don't kill me, my son. Whatever evil you have done here, I promise I won't say anything. Just let me go."

Na grins into the monk's face, wondering whether the chattering teeth please the ancestors or if they merely find them irritating, as he himself does.

"I have to kill you. They want me to. There is no other way."

Na draws a ceremonial knife from a scabbard concealed in a fold of his robe. The monk's eyes open wider until Na can see white all the way round the irises.

"Please," the monk begs.

Na grabs the plait and winds it around his left fist. He presses the knife against the monk's throat. Pauses for a moment. Then, as the monk screams from a stretched mouth, draws the long curving blade steadily from left to right in a backhand motion, severing the thick, ropy muscles, tendons, veins and arteries, and the gristle protecting the windpipe and oesophagus.

The monk dies with a gurgle and a hiss of outrushing breath. Blood spurts out in thick scarlet jets, splashing Na and soaking into his robe. The contrast in temperature between the scalding liquid and the icy-cold air makes him laugh. He saws at the dead monk's neck until he reaches the spine. Finding the cartilaginous disc between two vertebrae, he slices hard through the tough, fibrous tissue until it parts around his blade. A few more sawing cuts are all that he needs to separate the head from the shoulders. The body falls back. Na throws the knife to the ground, where it sticks, point-first, in the earth.

He turns to the ancestors, all of whom have gathered in a semicircle around him and are now smiling and nodding their approval. He holds the head aloft by the plait, so that it swings left, right, forwards, backwards, like a divining rod. They applaud politely, tapping their left palms with three fingers of their right hands.

A lid bound with iron bands covers the wooden vat he uses to clean the bones. He pulls it towards him and lets the heavy disk fall to the ground where it spirals slowly like a clumsily spun coin before coming to rest. Na peers into the acid, which suspended particles have turned cloudy. He intones a prayer.

"O ancestors! Grandmothers and grandfathers, great-grandmothers and great- grandfathers, all you who have honoured me with your trust, hear my plea. Tell me when I have done enough to unite the three kingdoms that I may join you."

Then, suppressing a giggle, which he feels is inappropriate to the sacred task with which they have entrusted him, he lowers the head by the topknot into the acid, which fizzes on contact with the exposed raw flesh of the neck. Just before it disappears below the foamy surface, the head rolls upwards and the monk's sightless, filmy eyes point directly at his own. Na stares back, wondering if the monk will blink first. He does not, but sinks, instead, into the blackness.

Na returns to the wooden post and yanks the knife from the cold embrace of the kingdom of the earth. He sets to work.

———

Later that evening, after he has eaten, he opens his Party-supplied laptop, protected, as all PLA units are, by a specially developed rubber case, and types out an email.

Esteemed Comrade Tan,

Morale on the base remains at above-optimal levels, as mandated by the Rules for Party Military Commissars, Section Seven, Sub-section Nineteen. I inspected the missiles this morning myself and found them to be in 100% operational order, ready to repel any attack by our enemies.

No disciplinary matters to report. Missile Battery Command #371 functions at peak readiness, and ideological purity is unsullied by Imperialist Western infiltration.

Colonel Na Keng

Commander and Party Commissar

People's Liberation Army Missile Battery Command #371

114th Division

Xinjiang Province

Eastern Theatre

3

HONG KONG | 1983

The two kidnappers observed the diplomat's house. They were dressed from head to foot in slate-grey: hoods, face masks, cotton outfits and plimsolls. Only *gweilo* – westerners – thought black gave the best concealment in dim light.

Both men were low-level members of the Four-Point Star triad. One was thirty, the other still in his teens. One was happy to spend his days beating people up or sitting around drinking and smoking dope. The other, ambitious for more, envisioned himself running the group one day. And if not the Four-Point Star, then another triad. The Coral Snakes, perhaps.

Despite the difference in their ages, the younger man was in charge of the operation. The seventeen-year-old had graduated from running fifty-dollar bags of weed all over the city to more serious crimes. In the process, he'd dropped his old nickname, which he now considered silly. He much preferred his new handle: "Snake". It fitted his ability to slither and slide his way through impossibly narrow or improbable entrance-points. And, he liked to think, his cunning and his ruthlessness.

His partner in this piece of wickedness, a man he'd picked for his brawn and not his brains, went by "Donkey". He'd earned the soubriquet for his braying laugh, though he told anyone who asked that it was for his devastating win chung kicks. Kick or laugh, neither man would be making a sound until the operation was concluded. Each was armed, not heavily, but with deadly intent, should force become necessary. They carried Chinese-made 9mm pistols, Norinco Type 54s, and daggers on their belts.

Inside the house, unaware it would be the last time she'd ever touch her daughter, Lin Wolfe finished nursing the five-month-old baby. She sat her upright and gently patted her back, just the width of Lin's hand, until she emitted a comical little belch that smelled of the milk she'd just swallowed. She settled her down in her pink-blanketed cot to sleep.

"Night-night, Tara. Sleep tight. Don't let the bed bugs bite. Not that we have bed bugs. Daddy would never allow it."

Lin crossed to the window and raised the sash by a few inches to let in some air. Her own mother had told her she'd never closed Lin's window all the way, even on the rare occasions when snow lay on the ground.

With the nursery bathed in a soft orange glow from a nightlight plugged into the wall, Lin tiptoed from the room, smiling at the sound of her daughter's snuffling breaths. At least Tara was a good sleeper. Sometimes Lin had to prod her to make sure she was still alive. She walked along the landing to her bathroom, where she took off her fluffy towelling bathrobe and stepped into the shower.

Emerging from the steaming water feeling refreshed and, for the moment at least, freed from her role as nursing mother, she dried herself then entered her dressing room, which she could also reach from the master bedroom. Pants and bra, into which she slid nursing pads to prevent any embarrassing leaks at the reception later on, sheer black tights, then a beautiful black watered-silk cocktail dress Gerald had bought her the previous month, specially made by a local seamstress to accommodate her new, post-pregnancy figure.

She slipped on a pair of black patent Ferragamo heels and sat at her dressing table to apply her makeup. Twenty minutes later, she descended the staircase in the rather grand house she occupied with her husband, two-year-old son, Gabriel, and new daughter.

Gerald was waiting for her in the drawing room, a half-full Martini glass in hand, its sloping sides beaded with condensation. He kissed her cheek before stepping back to appraise her.

"You look beautiful, darling," he said. "Absolutely beautiful. Drink?"

"Just a tonic water. God, I'll be glad when she's weaned and I can have a proper cocktail again."

They finished their drinks chatting about their respective days, he as a senior British diplomat discussing trade policy with the Chinese, she, well, she taking the children off the nanny's hands for half an hour for a walk, discussing meals for the week with cook, and inspecting the new rose bed in the back garden.

Gerald checked his watch, a Breitling he intended to give to his son on his admission to Cambridge.

"Five minutes, darling. Let's go and say goodnight to Gabriel."

Outside, the chauffeur was already waiting, the vintage Jaguar's engine purring at idle, the large headlamps throwing cones of yellow light onto the drive and the gates at its end. Gerald saw his wife safely into the back seat then rounded the rear of the black limousine to join her. The chauffeur eased the ageing transmission into Drive and the long, sleek car swept the two parents away to an evening of drinks and small talk with a visiting Malaysian trade delegation. Later, on the way home, they would joke about which was more numbing, the alcohol or the conversation.

———

Snake and Donkey watched the diplomat and his wife climb into the back of their absurd car. With its tall grille, swooping fenders and chromed noodle-bowl headlamps it looked as though it had been shipped out when the British first took control of Hong Kong.

Snake placed his binoculars in a daysack.

"Come on. It's time."

They descended the wooded slope and stood inside a fence that divided the vegetation from the pavement opposite the house. Snake tapped Donkey on the shoulder. Both men froze, looking down until a car passed them. They watched it disappear round the next corner, the glow from its brake lights staining the road blood-red.

A quick left-right-left glance, then they vaulted the fence, landing on the pavement on noiseless feet. They darted across the road to the diplomat's house. Ignoring the gates, they slipped along in the lee of the laurel hedge for thirty yards until they reached a narrow path that led between the house and the neighbouring property. At the rear of the house lay a vast garden, and more woodland beyond that. The chain-link fence had been artfully concealed with honeysuckle, climbing roses and clematis, but they merely provided footholds for the two men, who were up and over the seven-foot fence in seconds.

Snake looked up at the rear elevation. One room showed light peeping from a crack in the curtains. This was the boy's room. The nanny slept next door to him. Her room was dark. She tended to read in the evenings, or watch TV in the separate sitting room they allowed her on the first floor. Weeks of observation had enabled Snake and Donkey to map with military precision not only the layout of the house but the routines of its inhabitants on weekdays and weekends.

The house was poorly protected. No guards, no barred windows, no security lighting. Their inside man, Ting, had said the British had sprung for a burglar alarm, but as the staff were inside, the alarm was turned off.

Snake and Donkey sprinted across the wide back lawn, flattening themselves against the wall between the drawing room windows and a door leading out from a hallway that ran the length of the house. They looked at each other. Nodded. Snake turned and began climbing a trellis that, until he placed his right foot into one of its diamonds, had been supporting nothing more dangerous than a bee-filled wisteria. Donkey's role was to keep watch for, and if necessary disable, anyone foolish, suspicious or simply unfortunate enough to take a walk around the back garden.

Snake's abilities, his "superpowers" as he called them, depended on a combination of agility, flexibility and strength. To fill out his slight frame, he'd built impressive upper body muscles through obsessive weight training. He clambered up the trellis effortlessly, barely panting by the time he reached the first floor. Now came the only truly challenging part of the operation. He must cross a six-foot gap between the trellis and the nursery window. At five feet seven, even stretching as far into a star-shape as he could manage – and he had practised for hours on a specially built mock-up in one of the triad's warehouses – his fingertips wouldn't even graze the edge of the sash-window's frame.

Instead, he had figured out a different way to reach the window. A leap, up and sideways, keeping as close to the wall as he could manage. He would fall beneath the window ledge but grab on, and, after absorbing the shock of his bodyweight with just his fingertips, haul himself up and onto the six-inch-wide strip of concrete. Eighty-eight times he had made the leap in the warehouse in Kwai Chung Container Terminal No.7. He had fallen on every single one of the first seventy-three attempts, landing on a thick pile of old mattresses and bouncing around for a few seconds before jumping down and trying again. He had succeeded on seven of the next ten, and all of the last five.

From a pouch at his waist he withdrew a handful of powdered resin bought three weeks earlier. The music shop's other customers might use the translucent amber blocks to ensure they produced a good tone from their violin bows; Snake had spent an hour milling them into a fine, sticky dust. Hooking his right arm around a thick section of wisteria stem, he rubbed his palms together and worked the resin onto the pads of his fingers.

He crossed to the left-hand edge of the trellis and brought his feet higher, so that his knees bent outwards, giving him the appearance of a tree frog, albeit a rather drab example, about to leap. Then, from below, Donkey imitated a sparrow's chitter. The signal for "stop"! Snake froze, barely breathing lest the expansions of his chest should rustle one of the thinner stems. He clutched the trellis tighter, flattening himself against the scratchy tangle. He felt a sharp jab in his side from a pruned branch and he grunted with the pain.

From below he heard footsteps. Light, so a woman's. The nanny, or maybe the cook. Donkey didn't mind killing women, but Snake hoped it wouldn't be necessary.

Not daring to turn his face away from the trellis, Snake had to make do with his sense of hearing to understand what was happening ten feet below him.

The woman took fifteen steps down the pathway laid out in stepping stones across the lawn. Then she stopped. Sighed deeply. He heard the quick whisper of something being retrieved from a pocket. Not a dragging sound as it would be if she were wearing jeans or trousers, so a skirt or dress. Silk, maybe or a light cotton like his own night-camouflage suit.

Flink! His straining ears registered the distinctive sound of the lid being flipped open on a Zippo lighter. A snap as she applied her thumb to the knurled wheel. A hiss and crackle as her cigarette ignited and she sucked smoke through the filter.

She sighed. And Snake permitted himself to exhale too, though silently. He prayed that Donkey would hold himself in check, content to hide, probably in a crouch, until the smoker had finished and returned to the sanctuary of the house's interior.

Snake counted slowly to sixty. Then again. Three more times. *Come on, just finish the damn thing. It's a cigarette not a three-course meal.* He could smell the intoxicating aroma of the Western tobacco as the smoke drifted towards the house in the still night air. Finally, just as he was changing his mind, and wishing Donkey would step out from the shadows and snap her spine with a twist of his massive hands, he heard the sandpapery rasp as she twisted her toe on a stepping stone. He visualised her picking up the ground-out butt and placing it inside the carton before returning it to the pocket of her dress.

She turned and he counted fifteen steps. *Stay down, Donkey. Please!*

A door opened, then closed. With a soft sigh, Snake released the breath he was holding. He waited for Donkey to give the all-clear: the high-pitched creak of a mating frog. When it came, he lifted himself a little distance away from the trellis and looked left. The moon had just emerged from behind some cloud and threw a milky glow over the rear of the house. The concrete ledge shone whitely, giving him a perfect view of his target.

He unhooked his right plimsoll and moved it next to his left, which he now drew up to his stomach. Gripping with his right hand and supporting himself on the toes of his right foot, he readied himself to leap across to the window. *Never look down*. He'd given himself the same order countless times during his twenty-five years, from early days climbing trees to his teenage exploits investigating the rooftops and scaffolding of Hong Kong and on to his professional career as a thief, initially freelance, then as an employee of the Four-Point Star triad.

Breathe in all the way, out all the way, in all the way.

One, two, three, jump!

Snake sprang sideways, the treefrog taking flight.

Spread-eagled, he sailed out, fifteen feet above the crazy-paved patio. But he'd misjudged the trajectory. Was it the interruption? The moonlight? He was moving away from the wall as he reached the window ledge. Six inches, eight, ten, a foot, eighteen inches. As the ledge shot up in front of his wide eyes he stretched his arms out in a desperate attempt to arrest his fall.

His open palms banged against the top angle of the ledge and instinctively he curled his resined fingers into hooks. He was lithe, weighing just eight stone seven, but even so, the physics of falling objects dictated that when his arms reached their full extent, and his bodyweight slammed against his shoulder joints, it would hurt.

He heard a pair of pops and wondered for a split-second whether he had dislocated both shoulders. But no. It was just the synovial fluid inside the joints turning into gas as the pressure decreased. His knees swung inwards and banged painfully into the brickwork beneath the window. For one heart-stopping moment he felt the fingers of his left hand slide towards the edge. But he tensed every muscle in both hands and brought himself swinging to a stop.

Then it was just a simple gymnastics move to haul himself up and onto the ledge. Heart racing, he peered through the slit between the curtains. In the dim orange light radiating out from a hemispherical lamp plugged into a wall, he could see the baby, sleeping in her cot, the soft grey shadows of its bars lying across her face. Earlier, when he'd watched through the binoculars as the mother had opened the window, he'd offered a small prayer of thanks to the ancestors. He'd come fully prepared with his tools, but this was a good omen.

Crouching on the narrow ledge, he pushed his fingers under the sash. He gripped the smooth wood and lifted, using the muscles in his thighs and stomach to steady himself while his arms did the work. Without so much as a squeak, the sash slid upwards. He was so close to the wood he could hear the weights on their ropes knocking against the frame. He slid his left leg through the opening, ducked his head, edged his bottom over the sill and let his weight carry him into the room until his outstretched toes found the carpet. Crossing the room to the cot on silent feet he unwound a length of black cotton fabric from his midriff. He bent over the snuffling baby and slipped his cupped hands under its ribs, praying even harder to the ancestors to keep it from waking.

In one smooth, continuous motion, he lifted it up and began wrapping the cotton sling around it. He made twenty turns before pressing the immobile little bundle to his chest. He turned its face to one side so it could breathe, then retreated to the window.

On the ledge again, with the baby's body increasing his bulk just enough to alter his centre of gravity, he had to face outwards. He reached behind with one hand and closed the window. Then he glanced down, not wanting to break his rule, but needing to convince himself Donkey was in position. His partner's foreshortened body stood directly beneath him, arms spread wide.

Donkey nodded. The eyes in the slit between hood and mask were wide, encouraging.

Snake held the bundle out from the ledge. It reminded him, disturbingly, of a fly wrapped in silk in a corner of a spider's web. And then he dropped it. *Sleep, little gweilo!*

It diminished in size as it fell, apparently in slow motion, before Donkey caught it, swinging his cupped hands to the side in an exaggerated cradling movement before he brought it into his chest, just as Snake had done, muffling the beginnings of a whimpering cry.

A minute later and Snake was on the ground. The two men sprinted across the lawn. From the inside, it was a trivial matter to unbolt the tall gate in the fence. Donkey took the baby through. Snake closed and bolted the gate before scrambling up and over to join Donkey. Pressing themselves into the concealing evergreen foliage of the laurel hedge, they had to wait for two cars to pass before they could cross the road and enter the safety of the woods on the opposite side.

———

On the far side of the woods, hidden beneath a tarpaulin covered with dead leaves, lay a Honda 50 moped with a pizza delivery topbox mounted on the rear luggage carrier. Donkey drew the tarp aside and righted the moped. Snake unsnapped the lid of the topbox, in which he'd earlier drilled a set of sixteen half-inch diameter holes on the side facing the rider's back. Inside, a soft wool blanket, folded into eight, welcomed the sleeping baby. He'd placed a silicone pacifier – or what did the Brits call them, *dummies?* Snake had time to wonder – in the improvised bed and now Donkey lay the snuffling infant in the folds of the blanket before closing the lid. He donned a scuffed grey and red open-face helmet, mounted the moped and kicked it into life. Nodding once at Snake, he snicked the gear lever into first and, gently, pulled away, down the slope, across the pavement and onto the road, where he accelerated smoothly, heading for the house of a waiting triad family.

.   .   .

From that point, the plan ground remorselessly on. At eleven-thirty that evening, the official Jaguar crunched over the pea shingle and came to a stop outside the front door. The chauffeur got out and opened the rear door. Lin Wolfe went upstairs to check on her children and, finding Tara gone, raised the alarm. The police arrived fifteen minutes after that and began interviewing those staff who had been present during the Wolfes' absence.

The kidnappers' ransom demand showed they had grossly over-estimated the private wealth of the Wolfes. And if they were expecting the British Government to come to the financial aid of the panicking couple, they were unaware of HMG's unbending rule as it applied to Government employees and their families, and British citizens abroad. "We do not negotiate with terrorists, criminals or kidnappers." To do otherwise, it was correctly, if callously, argued in the corridors of Whitehall, would be to invite everyone from the IRA to Black September to start kidnapping British diplomats, engineers and security force personnel for profit.

The conversation with the Governor was brief to the point of being insulting.

"Jesus, old boy, I am so terribly sorry to hear that. But best leave it to the police. I'm sure they know what they're doing. Stiff upper lip, eh? If there's anything Judith and I can do to help, let me know."

Both men knew that the offer was a hollow one. No money would be forthcoming. Leave it to the police. Come round for a few stiff drinks if you need company. Don't make waves.

Eventually, in desperation, the Wolfes broke with protocol, risking Gerald's career, and approached Hong Kong's business community. Discreet enquiries were made and, finally, with three days to go before the kidnappers' deadline, a leading businessman agreed to provide the cash, after Gerald rashly promised him that he'd put in a good word for him when the New Year's Honours List came around. The police were kept well away from the plan, having already advised the Wolfes not to give in to the kidnappers, which would only lead to further, and greater, demands for money.

Following the instructions given in a ransom note, the Wolfes placed an ad in the *South China Morning Post*. They waited all day at their house for the kidnappers to make contact. By midnight, when no message had arrived, Lin Wolfe broke down. Screaming at her husband, she retreated to her dressing room with a bottle of gin.

4

HONG KONG | PRESENT DAY

Fang stopped speaking and looked over Gabriel's shoulder. His face split into a wide grin and he clapped his meaty palms together, a loud pop that all but the most brazen, or perhaps ignorant, diners around them managed to ignore.

"Ah! Here is our tuna! Now we will see whether your ham-fisted efforts caused the chef any difficulties."

The waitress placed their food before them. The gleaming plates were loaded with seared tuna steak, sliced on the diagonal and fanned out to reveal translucent, rose-pink flesh inside the black-crusted exterior. Slices of daikon radish and delicate coriander leaves floated in a fragrant amber broth, adding a flash of green and white to the palette of colours on the oversized plates before them.

Gabriel leaned over his food. Garlic, ginger and the smell of the sea itself rose into his nostrils, carried on curling wisps of steam. He felt saliva gather unbidden in his mouth, and picked up his cutlery.

The fish was firm, yet it yielded between his teeth, releasing a flood of flavour and aromas that made him smile. He chewed and swallowed, relishing the salt-sour taste of the broth.

Opposite him, Fang was sawing lustily at the thick slices of tuna, cutting each one into four and then transferring his fork to his right hand, in the American style, to spear the chunks and transfer them to his mouth.

"Very good!" he mumbled through a mouthful, catching a dribble of broth on his chin with his napkin. "Best in Hong Kong. Despite your knifework. But maybe you do better with bigger targets, eh?"

He laughed once more, revealing most of his mouthful of tuna and daikon, and flecks of coriander between his yellow teeth.

"I think I could get a job here with a little more practice," Gabriel answered, with a smile.

He was reflecting once again how far his life had turned away from the path – from Cambridge into the Diplomatic Service – envisaged by his father. Rather than entertaining visiting foreign dignitaries or minor royals on goodwill trips, here he was chowing down on thousand-dollar-a-kilo tuna with a triad boss. A triad boss, he now knew, who had ordered a series of hits on members of a Colombian drugs cartel. Fang had effectively wiped El Nuevo Medellín off the face of the earth, leaving only a handful of enforcers and minor-league dealers who would soon find employment elsewhere. Either as muscle and distribution for a rival outfit, or as nutritional supplements for marine life in the Pacific.

Fang chopped his way into another of the slices of tuna, then gestured with his fork, so that a drip of pale-pink juice flicked across the table towards Gabriel, who moved his arm back just in time to stop the drip hitting the sleeve of his pale-grey linen jacket.

"No. You keep the job you have. It's what you're good at. Just like Mei over there. Tomorrow morning I want you to come to the Golden Dragon. Eleven. I'll introduce you to my client and he can explain what he needs from us."

———

Back at the hillside house he'd inherited from his mentor, Zhao Xi, Gabriel poured himself a glass of white burgundy and took it through to the garden. He'd heard on the radio that the weather on the mainland was freakishly cold for early autumn, but here it was balmy. Maybe sixty-eight. Even the humidity had descended from the high nineties to something more manageable. With his bare feet digging into the soft, vivid-green moss that comprised the lawn, he stood and looked down at Victoria Harbour.

As the pleasure cruisers and sailing boats carved white swathes across the jade-green water he let his mind drift back to his last few days in England.

Eli had brought a couple of cases of clothes, toiletries and books with her from her Department-funded flat in Shoreditch to "have a holiday" at his place. She'd settled in as if the Suffolk coast was her natural home, taking long walks along the stony beach, chatting with the manager of the boatyard next door and even learning a few phrases in the Suffolk dialect.

Then Don had summoned her to MOD Rothford, the British Army base he used as his operational HQ, and deployed her to the Middle East. It was, he'd said, a natural mission for her as a recently recruited Department agent.

The Department, as the shadowy organisation Don led was known, had a simple remit. To despatch, without quarter, those enemies of Her Majesty that other state agencies were unwilling, unable or unready to take on. It drew many of its agents from the same talent pool as the Secret Intelligence Service, the Security Service, Special Forces and some of the army's more clandestine outfits, such as 14 Company, which had operated undercover in Northern Ireland for many years. But because its remit was purer, less riven by political concerns, and focused entirely on outcomes, Don and his recruiters were prepared to, as he put it, "have a poke around in some of the murkier parts of the pool".

In essence, this meant people who might, for example, have missed out on a place in the SAS by a few seconds on the infamous "Fan Dance", an up-and-over, there-and-back climb on Pen-y-Fan in the Brecon Beacons. Or those whose psychological preparedness to kill was at the point of tipping over into desire. Or, as in Eli's case, simply those without the requisite documentation to prove they were

British citizens. As an ex-Mossad operative, Eli and her Israeli nationality were welcome. So much so that Don had visited her former boss Uri Ziff in person to secure her services and made the necessary arrangements with the Home Office.

Gabriel had driven Eli to Heathrow in "Lucille", the Chevrolet Camaro he'd taken delivery of a few days earlier. The big black sports car had attracted plenty of attention on the A12 into London, with small boys in particular being attracted to its muscular, slab-sided looks, waving and pointing from the rear windows of their parents' chubby people carriers, duvet-filled estate cars or sleek executive saloons.

"Take care," he'd said, after a long kiss.

"I will."

As simple as that. No need for any more words between them. Department missions were dangerous, sometimes absurdly so, and its agents had learned that it was best to just get on with them – and life – as if they were doing nothing riskier than making a business trip.

He pulled out his phone and called her. It would go straight to voicemail. Department protocol. But he could leave a message for her, nonetheless. Her office-supplied mobile was strictly for her and her handlers.

"El, it's me." He hesitated, then ploughed on. "I just wanted to say thanks for being patient with me. And I love you. A lot. Bye. See you soon."

———

Gabriel woke the next day at 6.00 a.m. He dressed in a cotton kung fu suit, faded by much washing from black to a dark grey, and walked through the silent house in his bare feet. He reheated some pork dumplings and ate them for breakfast, washing them down with green tea. Then he descended a flight of stairs to the dojo.

He walked into the centre of the spacious martial arts practice area and knelt on the white canvas pad, toes tucked under so that they were bent back as he let his weight settle onto his heels. He placed his hands, palms together, on his breastbone, bent his head and closed his eyes.

I'm sorry, Master Zhao. You died here, on my account. Forgive me. Britta's dead, too. Perhaps you already knew that. I killed everyone connected with her death. In retribution. I don't know if it was a noble thing I did in Russia, but it was necessary. And I have been suspended. Don didn't put it in exactly those words, but his meaning was pretty clear. I think he considers me damaged goods. An operational risk. I hope I can prove him wrong.

Gabriel focused on his breathing, ignoring the growing discomfort from his folded-over toes, knowing that it would metamorphose into pain before he was fully able to take himself away from the present moment in time and space and find that quiet centre where he could just exist.

The trouble was, leaving a quiet space in his mind acted these days as a stage for a moustachioed fairground barker in candy-striped trousers, a gaily ribboned straw boater and a death's head mask, yelling through a red, white and blue megaphone:

"ROLL UP, ROLL UP!
COME ONE, COME ALL!
LADIES AND GENTLEMEN, BOYS AND GIRLS!
PREPARE TO ENTER THE TROUBLED SOUL
OF GABRIEL WOLFE!
GUNS! GIRLS!! FREAKS!!!
YOU WON'T BELIEVE YOUR EYES!!
THIS MAN HAS KILLED MORE PEOPLE
THAN YOU'VE HAD HOT DINNERS!
HE'S BEEN ABUSED! HE'S BEEN IMPRISONED!
HE'S BEEN SHOT, STABBED AND TORTURED!
AND STILL HE WALKS AMONG US!!!
ROLL UP, ROLL UP!"

Gabriel's stomach churned and he could feel his pulse zipping upwards, his fingertips tingled and pins and needles jabbed and sparkled in the skin of his feet.

"No!" he shouted, snapping his eyelids open and jumping to his feet.

He'd bought and installed a motorised sparring dummy. The six-foot wooden column had eight "arms" slotted home into sockets and would revolve on the push of a green button. He jabbed a thumb at the starter and while the "octopus" spun up, he donned a pair of gloves.

Keeping his weight on the balls of his feet he began a series of warm-up moves, launching coordinated hand and foot attacks, all the while dodging the slowly rotating wooden arms. They weren't travelling fast, but a mistimed blow would still hurt.

Once he could feel the sweat on his forehead, he flicked a switch to increase the rotational speed and began fighting in earnest, dancing in and out of range of his opponent, striking with blade hands, open palms and fists, executing flurries of kicks at knee, waist, chest and head-height.

Finally, the anxiety quietened and as the oxygen in his blood reached maximum saturation he felt his body become a machine in which he could sit, piloting it to faster and more devastating combinations of kicks and punches. A knock on the glass door leading to the garden caught his attention just for an instant. But it was enough. He mistimed a kick and got his upraised leg hooked over one of the turning wooden arms. It wrenched his leg sideways and he yelped with pain as he toppled backwards to avoid dislocating his knee.

From his supine position, he looked up at the visitor, now peering in through the plate glass.

5

Wei Mei's full, red lips were curved upwards in a smile. Gabriel had no trouble decoding it. Amusement. This *gweilo* might be OK with a gun in his hand, but proper fighting? No. Strictly an amateur.

He jumped to his feet, striving to pull off the move as gracefully as possible, and slid the glass door back, admitting a breeze scented with roses.

"We meet again. How was your trip back from Russia?"

"Fine. How was yours?"

"Fine, too. How are you?"

Mei dipped her head demurely, though he noticed the way she looked up at him from beneath her lowered eyelids.

"I'm well, thank you."

"I'm not due at the Golden Dragon till eleven. It's only, what, six forty-five?"

"It's almost seven. I came to talk to you."

"You'd better come in, then," Gabriel said, standing aside.

She stepped over the threshold and paused just inside the door while Gabriel closed it again. Her outfit, as always, was simple, yet striking. Skin-tight black jeans over black ankle boots, a t-shirt in kingfisher blue and a white leather biker jacket with diamond quilting over the shoulders.

"Nice dojo," she said, hands on hips, as she looked around the perfectly square room with its racks of practice weapons.

"Thanks. You should come over one day and spar. If you'd like, I mean."

"Yes. I'd like that. But I warn you, Mister Woody over there is a pussycat compared to me."

Gabriel smiled.

"I was doing fine until you distracted me."

"Which is perfect, since our enemies make sure we can fight them undistracted."

"OK, fair point. Have you eaten breakfast? Do you want some tea? Or coffee?"

She smiled, accentuating the delicate curve of her lips.

"Coffee would be great. Thank you."

"Come on, then. The kitchen's upstairs."

Gabriel tipped two generous scoops of coffee beans into an electric grinder and pushed down on the lid. Using the racket from the blades as cover for not speaking, he tried to formulate the question he'd been wanting to ask Mei since first setting eyes on her at Max Novgorodsky's dacha a week or two earlier. He released the pressure on the grinder's lid and the blades spun down.

"There's something I wanted to ask you."

"Ask, then."

"In the hallway of the dacha, I thought you were going to kill me. But you fired into the ceiling. Why?"

She shrugged, compressing her lips and frowning. But the move looked artificial to Gabriel.

"I don't know. Maybe because my master hadn't paid me to kill anyone except the Colombians."

"And do you only ever kill people Fang tells you to?"

"Why else would I kill someone?"

"I don't know. Maybe because they'd pissed you off?"

She placed her hand flat against her chest, fingers splayed.

"I am a peace-loving girl. I don't let people get to me."

"Not even inquisitive Englishmen who ask lots of questions?"

She laughed, revealing small white teeth.

"*Especially* not them."

"So we've not met before?"

She shook her head.

"No. Why?"

"I'm not sure. I thought when you were holding your Uzi on me, there was," he shrugged, suddenly unsure of his words, "I don't know, the way you hesitated. Like you'd been about to kill me and then something changed your mind. Did you feel it, too?"

Her large brown eyes narrowed, and she blinked slowly. Her lips parted, then he saw her clamp them shut and shake her head sharply. Left. Right. He knocked the ground coffee into a cafetière and switched the kettle on.

"I just decided you were there for the same reason as me so I could leave you alive. I don't believe in taking life unnecessarily."

"Nor do I. It's just sometimes these days I find I have more trouble deciding what's necessary and what isn't."

"It's very simple. Is he trying to kill you? Is he going to kill you by accident? Have you been commanded to kill him? Or paid to kill him? Are you exacting revenge for the death of a loved one at his hands? If the answer to any of those five questions is yes, then it is necessary to kill him."

Gabriel poured boiling water over the coffee grounds and set the lid in place. He carried the cafetière to the table and set out two moss-green cups.

"What if the answer to all those questions is no – he's innocent – but he stands between you and your intended target?"

Now it was her turn to shrug.

"I am not a philosopher. But if you are so close to someone who must be killed that you stand between him and his killer, maybe you are not so innocent after all."

"Maybe. Have you killed many people for Jian?"

Her lips tightened at Gabriel's use of her boss's first name. He saw disapproval mixed with something more subtle. What was it? Jealousy?

"What is *many*? I protect my master, that is all. I do not keep count. And you? Do you carve notches on your gun butt each time you slay a dragon for *your* master?"

He shook his head.

"Actually, my master is more of a mistress. But no, I stopped counting some time back." *When I had to run through a jungle compound so thick with white-clad corpses I had to tread on them.* "You said you wanted to talk to me?"

By way of answer, Mei shot out a hand and pushed down on the chrome button of the plunger. She poured out two cups.

Gabriel marveled at the Chinese woman's eerie combination of ruthlessness and domesticity. It seemed odd in one so young. Then he realised he had no clear idea of her age. Late twenties, he supposed. Although this was more of a wild guess than anything else.

"Yes. I did. Want to talk to you," she said.

"What about?"

She sipped her coffee, regarding him over the rim of the cup with those strangely round eyes.

"About the man who used to live here."

"Zhao Xi? What about him?"

"What was your connection to him?"

"He pretty much raised me. From the age of ten. I called him Master Zhao. Even when I came back as an adult, and he asked me to call him Xi, I couldn't. He was, will always be, Master Zhao to me. Why do you want to know about him?"

Mei sipped her coffee. She placed the cup in its saucer with a little *clink*.

"*My* master introduced us once. Master Zhao came to the Golden Dragon sometimes, to gamble or to drink. I liked him. He was always so courteous. Never rude to the waitresses or the croupiers. Not like some of them. Flashing their money around, acting like bigshots when they were pushing carts full of stinking fish round the market a few years earlier."

Gabriel smiled, remembering the old man's manners, and his fondness for mahjong and good Scotch. Perhaps wins at the Golden Dragon were how he'd found the money to acquire his precious collection of jade figurines.

"That sounds like Master Zhao." Then he frowned. "So, you came out here at seven in the morning just to reminisce about an old man you met a couple of times at Jian's casino?"

"I always rise early. At five. This is mid-morning for me. And I was passing. It looks like we might be working together for a while, so I thought I'd drop by and say hello properly. You know, without an Uzi aimed at your stomach."

She smiled, properly this time, with genuine good humour rather than amusement.

"It's a shame you don't have your kit with you, then. We could have sparred for a few rounds and really got to know each other."

"Next time I come round, I'll bring my stuff." She drained her coffee and stood up. "That was excellent coffee. Thank you. I'll see you at the Golden Dragon at eleven. Don't get up. I'll find my own way out."

Gabriel watched her retreating back as she headed for the stairs down to the dojo. *Drop by, my arse. You were here for more than that, Mei.*

6

At 10.00 a.m., Gabriel locked the front door behind him, walked up to the main road and climbed into the rear seat of the red and white taxi waiting for him.

For the meeting with Jian and his CPC client he'd opted for the soberest suit in his wardrobe, a single-breasted navy two-piece in lightweight wool. A white Oxford shirt, navy tie with white polka dots and a pair of highly polished black brogues completed the look. It was manifestly unsuitable for the weather, which had warmed up overnight, but he felt the need to go in suited and booted for the meeting with Fang's client.

"Where to, please, sir?" the driver asked, shooting Gabriel an appraising look in the rear-view mirror.

"Mody Road Garden, please."

The drive would only take twenty minutes or so at this time of the morning, and Gabriel planned to wander down to the harbour for a while before making his way to the casino.

The driver pulled away from the kerb with a lurch that sent Gabriel bouncing off the door panel. He wound the window down. As they descended to sea level, the smells of the city grew stronger, and those of the wooded hills receded.

The combined stink of traffic fumes, fast food of a hundred nations and the indefinable aroma of seven and a half million people going about their hurried business replaced the floral scents and the clean, green smell of the residential area he thought of as his home from home. Overlaying it all he could just detect the salty, diesely smell of the harbour itself.

"Fuck!" the driver shouted, slamming his brakes on and swerving, so that Gabriel was thrown hard against his seatbelt.

He caught a flash of black and white as a small dog darted under a gate and into the sanctuary of one of the houses that lined this part of the road.

"You all right, sir?" the driver enquired, glancing up again at his mirror.

"Yes, but if you could manage to get me to Mody Road without any more bruises I'd be grateful," Gabriel answered, trying and he thought possibly just failing to keep the irritation out of his voice.

"No worries!" the driver cheerfully exclaimed, resuming his hurtle down the steepest part of the hill.

Gabriel paid the driver and stepped out into the warm autumn air of Hong Kong's Victoria Harbour. Since learning the truth about his brother Michael's death in the water, Gabriel had had mixed feelings about this part of the city. Sadness that his little brother had drowned here mixed with relief that, after all, Gabriel had not caused him to jump in: it had been Michael's cocky, five-year-old personality that had led him to dive in after a mis-kicked rugby ball.

Gabriel stuck his hands in his pockets and wandered along by the water, staring down at the dark shapes of fishes that swam among the pilings, then across the harbour to the mainland. In front of him, a newly married couple who looked to be in their early twenties – he in a dinner suit, hired, to judge from the fit, she in a traditional red dress – posed for a photo. He stopped to watch.

He smiled back at the young woman clutching a fistful of cash-filled red gift envelopes as she looked his way and grinned, her face lit as much by some inner light as by the strong sun bouncing off the water. *Will I ever be that happy?* he wondered. He didn't have time to contemplate an answer.

With an angry roar from its overstressed little engine, a moped ridden by two black-clad figures with blacked-out helmet visors raced up to the photographer. The passenger leaned over and dealt him a blow from a cosh, grabbing the camera as he collapsed, clutching the back of his head.

As the family screamed and shouted, the passenger jumped off the bike, snatched the sheaf of red envelopes from the bride's unresisting hand, remounted and thumped the driver on the shoulder.

Gabriel looked around. A fisherman had left a pile of blue nylon nets by a steel bollard. He bent and grabbed the bird's nest of cords, weights, floats and rope. The moped was heading his way. He made as if to step out of its way. As the bike rode directly towards him, he spun in a full circle, letting the net unfurl from his right hand and released it as the moped drew level. The tangled mass flew out from his hand and wrapped itself around the rider's helmet. Blinded, he swerved right, scattering pedestrians and sending a couple of dozen gulls airborne, screaming their disapproval.

He might have escaped, finding just enough visibility through the netting to pilot the moped into the city streets. But then his luck ran out, in the shape of a ten-foot length of the sturdy bamboo scaffolding that was such a feature of Hong Kong's streets. Nothing more, really, than a grass stem, yet as strong as steel. One end of the pole connected with his head, snapping his helmet back into the passenger's visor. The other end was held by a young woman with her hair in a long plait, large, round eyes and a delicate mouth curved into a mischievous smile as she caught Gabriel's eye.

The bike wobbled furiously then the rider lost control and he, his passenger and the moped skidded and tumbled to a stop. Gabriel ran over and, as the two robbers got to their knees, dealt the passenger a stunning blow to the side of his neck that sent him crashing to the Tarmac. From his out-flung right hand, the sheaf of red envelopes scattered across the ground. The family of the newlyweds were hurrying over and an older woman, the mother of

ANDY MASLEN

the bride or her new mother-in-law, knelt to gather them into her hands. The photographer staggered over and grabbed his camera.

Beside Gabriel, Mei had the rider in a headlock. Her nimble fingers unstrapped his helmet and, none too gently, she pulled it free. Gabriel did the same to the passenger. Revealed beneath the fibreglass was a woman. She looked groggy. Her pupils were mismatched and she was mumbling about needing a doctor. The man was scowling at Mei and struggling in her grip until she pinched a place between his neck and collar bone and he emitted a high-pitched protest before lying perfectly still in her arms.

"Anyone call the cops?" Mei shouted.

"I did," the woman clutching the red envelopes said.

Gabriel looked across the short distance that separated him from Mei. *Do we leave before the cops arrive?* She shook her head. And he realised, at that moment, he *wanted* to be taken in for questioning. Don had instructed him to take time off from the Department's operations, and presumably its way of thinking. So rather than melting away into the crowd as he'd done after a recent excursion into assassination on the streets of Saint Petersburg, he sat tight.

7

Within a few minutes, during which time both Mei and Gabriel had improvised bindings for their captives from the fishing net, the cops arrived, screaming down Salisbury Road, sirens wailing, blue lights flashing. They shouted at everyone to stand back. Unnecessarily, in Gabriel's opinion, since the crowd had parted immediately to let two uniformed officers through. They burst into the small circle containing Gabriel, Mei and the would-be bandits.

One of the cops had sergeant's stripes on his sleeves. He appeared to be at least ten years older than his partner, a slightly-built young woman striving, it seemed to Gabriel, to settle her features into something half-fierce, half-bored.

"OK, what's going on here?" the sergeant asked in English. His voice was light, several tones higher than Gabriel was expecting, given the corpulent belly straining the buttons of his pale-blue uniform shirt.

The cop placed his hands on his hips, so that his right palm grazed the butt of his pistol.

"I was sightseeing, officer. I stopped to watch a wedding couple having their picture taken when these two," Gabriel nodded towards the bound man and woman, "raced up on a moped and grabbed the camera and the bride's gift envelopes. Then this lady arrived and helped me subdue them."

The cop turned to Mei, who was standing patiently, waiting for her turn to be questioned.

"That right, miss?" he asked. "You were just passing as well?"

The lady who'd collected the envelopes bustled forwards, elbowing her way to the front of the small crowd gathered around the robbers, rescuers and cops like a scene from a painting.

"Why are you asking them all these questions?" she asked, jabbing a pink-painted nail in the older cop's face. "They just saved my daughter from being robbed. Murdered, most likely! They're heroes!"

Then she stepped towards Gabriel and embraced him, kissing him on the cheek. As the crowd cheered and took videos, and a few of the younger men wolf-whistled, the cop looked flustered.

He stepped closer to Gabriel.

"Look, can you come down to Central Station with us? We need to take a statement from you and the young lady. Just a formality, OK?"

The pleading note in the cop's voice was more than enough to convince Gabriel, who'd been about to suggest the same course of action anyway. Gabriel subtly shifted the social register of his speech up a few notches, channelling his dead father's intonations and vocabulary.

"Of course, that won't be a problem. Would you prefer us to come now? It's just that I discern a distinct mismatch between your transportation and the needs we'll place upon it. One car, six people?"

He pointed at the robbers, now handcuffed by the female officer and sitting back to back under the baleful gaze of the wedding party.

"I'll get another car here, if you don't mind waiting, sir?"

Gabriel nodded graciously.

"Not at all."

. . .

Five minutes later, the second car arrived. The cops bundled the now thoroughly fed-up-looking robbers into the back seat of the first car. More cops politely ushered Gabriel and Mei into the second, whereupon the mini-convoy made its way to Hong Kong's Central Police Station at 2 Chung Kong Road.

While the thieves were being booked in, Gabriel and Mei were led by the sergeant and his partner to two separate interview rooms. It wasn't the first time Gabriel had been inside the police station. The last time he had been interviewed under caution as a witness and, he knew, potential suspect in the murder of Zhao Xi.

This time, he found himself in smarter, more comfortable accommodation. He assumed it was owing to his role in an act of public spirited crime-prevention. The sergeant gestured to a chair, simple, but with a padded seat and back facing another across a rectangular pine table.

"Please, have a seat. Can I get you a coffee?"

"Thank you. White, no sugar."

"A detective will be in to take your statement shortly. Sit tight, OK?"

Gabriel nodded and watched the cop as he left the room and turned left. A thought popped into Gabriel's head, the first time he'd had a moment to think since arriving at the police station. How was it that Mei had just happened to be passing? Was she under orders to keep an eye on him?

He wondered how Mei was being treated. Would the cops know her already? Working as a hitwoman for Fang Jian might have brought her to the attention of the Hong Kong cops before now, he supposed. But then, he could also think of a few different ways Jian might have lessened the risk of any overt police interest. Bribery was still a hugely effective tool. As were coercion, a fake ID and simply being so damn good at your job there was never any evidence connecting you to a body. She'd be fine, he decided.

A uniformed constable entered the small square room and placed a plastic cup of coffee in front of Gabriel with a murmured, "There you are," before turning on her heel and leaving. As Gabriel was taking a cautious sip of the coffee, the door opened again and a slightly-built man in a brown suit and yellow tie walked in.

"I'm Detective Constable Guo," he said in English, taking the chair opposite Gabriel and placing a yellow legal pad on the table in front of him.

"Gabriel Wolfe."

Guo was blushing and was having difficulty meeting Gabriel's eye.

"Ah, you were the gentleman who stopped the mugging down at Tsim Sha Tsui Promenade, yes?"

"That's right. The sergeant on the scene said I'd need to come down and give a statement."

"Yes, er, that is correct."

The detective rubbed his top lip as if feeling for stubble, though his face was immaculately clean-shaven. Gabriel could even smell a faint tang of aftershave.

"Is everything all right?" Gabriel asked.

"Yes... well, no, not really. Not exactly. The young woman you, hmmm, stopped, she has made an allegation of assault against you. She says you punched her. Is that right?"

Gabriel frowned, seeing in an instant where this was going.

"It's right that in the course of preventing a crime being committed, I used reasonable and proportionate force on one of two thieves attempting to steal a photographer's camera and wedding gifts from a newly-married bride, yes."

He could feel his pulse jolting in his neck and deliberately slowed his breathing in an attempt to restore equilibrium. The detective made a note on his pad. Then looked up at Gabriel.

"So that's a yes. You did hit her?"

"I had to!"

"Where was her partner at this point?"

"On the ground, I think."

"And the moped?"

"They crashed it. That's how they fell off."

"So the crime had already been stopped when you hit the young woman?"

"She was going to run, I could tell."

The detective made another note. Now he did make eye contact with Gabriel.

"Look. I know this must feel like we're picking on the wrong person here, but that's just the way it is. I don't think you did anything wrong, but once a complaint's been made, we're, er, duty bound to investigate."

Gabriel could feel his anger mounting.

"And what about the muggers? Are you investigating them? They rode up on a moped in blacked-out helmets, *assaulted*," heavy emphasis, "the photographer and stole an expensive camera, then snatched a bunch of cash-filled envelopes. Never mind their claims of assault, *they're* the bad guys here, not me."

The detective looked pained, as if his bowels were griping.

"Of course we're questioning them. I just have to get your statement."

"And then I'm free to go?"

Another squinched expression.

"Ah, I'm afraid not."

"What?"

"Until we can get some clarity around what happened I have to ask you to remain here."

"And if I refuse?"

"Then, um, and believe me, sir, this is not my own preference, but that of my superiors, I will have to arrest you."

Gabriel leaned back in his chair and folded his arms across his chest. *No way I'm fighting my way out of this one.* He glared at the clearly embarrassed detective, feeling devoid of pity.

"Fine. You'd better arrest me, then, Detective Constable Guo."

Reddening, the detective opened his mouth to speak.

"Gabriel Wolfe. I am, ah, arresting you on suspicion of assault. You are not obliged to say anything unless you wish to do so, but whatever you say, er, will be put into writing and may be given in evidence."

Gabriel remained still, eyes boring into the young detective's.

"Now what?"

"I have to ask you to come with me."

"Where to?"

"A cell."

"You're serious? You're putting me in a *cell*? I have to be at a meeting at eleven."

The detective rubbed at his top lip again.

"I'm sorry. There's nothing I can do about it."

"Do I get a call?"

The detective visibly brightened and his face, still pink, broke into a toothy smile. Perhaps he was just relieved he could agree to something, Gabriel thought.

"Oh, yes. For sure. Come with me, please."

Gabriel stood inside the Perspex hood surrounding one of three wall-mounted phones, his own phone having been confiscated by the custody sergeant in exchange for a handwritten receipt.

"Who is this?"

Jian sounded suspicious.

"It's Gabriel. You're not going to believe this. The cops have arrested me. Probably Mei, too."

"What did you do? You didn't shoot anyone, did you?"

Jian's laughter was loud down the crackly landline.

"No I bloody didn't. I stopped a mugging. Mei was there, too. Did you tell her to tail me?"

Jian grunted, the verbal equivalent of a shrug.

"No, but she is an independent woman. Maybe she thought it her duty to look out for you. You need a lawyer? I have several."

"Yes. But I have one of my own. Kenneth Lao, you know him? He's a partner at Ophelia Tsang & Partners."

"I know *of* him. Good lawyer. Leave it to me."

The line went dead. Gabriel clacked the receiver back onto its cradle. Keeping a respectful ten feet away, a uniformed cop was waiting to lead him to his new quarters.

8

Gabriel woke from a light sleep to find himself being addressed by a yet another uniformed cop.

"Your lawyer's here."

Gabriel got to his feet, rubbing at a sore place above his left kidney. Not the result of a beating, just the very thin padding on the bench in his cell. The cop unlocked the steel door and led Gabriel down a grey-painted corridor and into a conference room, from which he immediately withdrew.

Waiting for Gabriel was the solicitor he had first encountered on the day of Zhao Xi's death. Kenneth Lao. Lao rose and shook hands. His eyes, lined at the corners, were blazing. As always he was dressed in a bespoke suit, this one silver-grey sharkskin with his usual narrow lapels.

"Gabriel. I am so sorry. Those idiots have royally f—" He caught himself and exhaled sharply. "They have royally messed up. I'll have you out of here as soon as I can."

Gabriel sat down and ran a hand over his face.

"Did Jian tell you what had happened?"

"He did. And I have spoken both to the custody sergeant here and to the detectives in CID. I've persuaded them that as you own a property on the island, you are not a flight risk. I have guaranteed it. I'm arranging bail with the magistrates as we speak, though it might be a couple of hours before we can have you released."

"Thank you. What will happen then? They said the woman had accused me of assault."

Lao shook his head.

"Don't worry. It's a new wrinkle some of the lowlifes here have been trying out. I have absolutely no idea why the cops fell for it this time. Maybe they're new. But we have phone camera evidence from a couple of members of the bridal party. It's plainly a matter of a concerned citizen preventing a serious crime."

"*Two* concerned citizens."

"Yes, Miss Wei is apparently also facing similar charges."

"Can you get her out, too?"

Lao shook his head, though he smiled.

"No need. Jian has an even more expensive lawyer than you, dear boy. She's already gone. I expect there will be some fairly, what shall we say, incandescent phone calls between Jian and the station chief here."

"They're in his pocket?"

The elegant lawyer shook his head once more.

"Oh, no. Nothing so transactional. But regardless of which side of the law you sit, at the topmost levels of society in Hong Kong there are preferred ways of doing business. Let's just say Jian has his contacts, just as do you, I and everyone else."

"OK, I can wait a little longer, I suppose. But while you're here, Kenneth, there's something I want to ask you. I was going to call you later anyway, just not in such, er," he waved his hand around at the room's institutional furnishings and colour scheme, "pressing circumstances."

Lao took out a slim notebook covered in red leather, and a gold mechanical pencil, which he clicked twice.

"I'm all ears," he said.

"I want to look into my family background. You know my dad was a trade commissioner here?"

Lao nodded without looking up, making neat notes on the fresh page he'd turned to.

"Yes. And very highly regarded, too."

"I told you about my brother, Michael, didn't I?"

"Indeed. A sad story, though one, ultimately, with an ending, if not precisely happy, then at least comforting."

"There was a third child. Another sibling."

Now the lawyer did look up. He eyed Gabriel keenly.

"You are sure of this?"

"One hundred per cent. I have a memory of seeing a baby and thinking it was Michael, and my –" he hesitated, not embarrassed about the fact he saw a psychiatrist, or not exactly, "– colleague pointed out that the age difference meant it couldn't have been Michael. I need to find out who he was. Where he went. I have no memory of him after that."

"Well, in the first instance, once you have recovered your liberty, I mean to say, you should contact your father's solicitor. Do you know who he used?"

"All my papers are in England. I didn't have time to deal with it before I came out here." *Actually I was in such a rage at my boss I more or less jumped on the first plane out.* "A London firm handled the will, but they told me they were acting on behalf of his Hong Kong solicitors. As to his time here, I have no idea."

"I am sure I can track down the firm in question. Your father was an important figure here, after all."

"You were friends with Master Zhao. Did he ever mention a third Wolfe sibling?"

Lao shook his head, smiling.

"To be honest, Gabriel, we mainly played cards and talked politics. What would happen when the British would have to give the colony back to the Chinese and so forth."

"Sorry. Of course, the family life of foreign diplomats wouldn't have been the most riveting of subjects."

"Oh, no, not at all! Please don't think I meant any disrespect. Xi valued his friendship with your parents hugely, and he always felt it was a privilege that they had entrusted your upbringing to him."

A knock at the door forestalled any further conversation. The door opened. Standing in the opening was the uniformed cop who'd brought Gabriel to the cell.

"I'm sorry, Mr Lao. Time's up."

Lao stood. Gabriel followed his lead.

"Very well. But please ensure my client is treated with the utmost courtesy. He is no common criminal. I have arranged bail and in the fullness of time, once these ridiculous charges against him have been dropped, we shall be considering what action we will be talking against the Hong Kong Police Force and its officers," a pointed look at the bespectacled cop, who visibly paled, "for damages."

With this thinly veiled threat hanging in the air, Lao turned to Gabriel.

"Four hours, at the outside. Come and see me when you're released. You remember our address?"

"Forgive me, it's been a while." Gabriel frowned with the effort of remembering. "It's Chater Road, isn't it?"

Lao smiled and nodded.

"Yes it is. You'll find us between those two beacons of capitalistic excess: Louis Vuitton and Giorgio Armani. The nineteenth floor."

Back in his cell, Gabriel lay back on the narrow bench and stared at the ceiling, wondering how many people had occupied the tiny space before him, and what crimes they had committed. Or, he corrected himself, been accused of, since to his own mind, he'd committed no crime at all.

9

THE MISSILE BASE

Colonel Na appears before his remaining men in his full dress uniform. He is unaware, though they are not, that its dark-green fabric and gold braid, once pristine, are now stained and torn. On his chest, the row of medals that once glinted with polish are now dulled and pitted from neglect. He looks up. The sky is the colour of bullets. A cold wind from the mountains brings drizzle that coats every surface and worms its way into the skin.

These men are his own personal terracotta warriors, allocated him by the ancestors to serve as his protectors in this life and in the next. Thirty-three fanatically loyal fighters who, when his task is complete, will accompany him into the next world. *No*, he corrects himself, *not the next world. The new world. The world I shall have created. The three kingdoms united in one.*

He'd hand-picked them. Stupid country boys ready to believe whatever story he sold them, indoctrinated since birth, fed the myths of Mao along with their mothers' milk. "I am Mao!" he yelled at them for hour after hour. "He lives in me! Those bastards in Beijing sold out the Great Helmsman for Western, capitalist, imperialist baubles! Those who serve Mao, serve me! You are my chosen cadre. You are my warriors of the ancestral spirits."

They had been willing, eager to believe, especially as he increased their pay and fed them better, allowing them access to alcohol, drugs and women from the village in return for their unswerving loyalty. In his rational moments, which were becoming fewer, and further apart, he acknowledged to himself that he was running a cult. But then, hadn't Mao done the same thing? He'd taken them away from general duties, removed them from any influence but his own. And prepared them to slaughter their comrades.

To run a fully-functioning missile base takes a great many troops and political commissars. But when the missiles are rusting in their silos, their warheads decaying like flesh on bone buried beneath the earth, the numbers can safely be reduced. The ancestors told him what to do, and how. Which officers were influential. Which had to go first.

He remembers the night well. Standing on the roof of the command post, watching the muzzle flashes, listening to the screams, smelling the blood and the gunpowder, tasting it in the back of his throat. When the killing was over, he walked among them, a pat on the back here, an encouraging word there, a bullet in the back of the head for one he found crying beside a cook, gutted with his own knife and dismembered with his own cleaver.

The corpses he had ranged on the hillside to spell out a warning to any villagers thinking about escaping. But none did. Perhaps they didn't want to. He left them alone at first. But in that first, cruel winter, when the temperature plummeted to minus forty and the snows swept down from the mountains and blasted across the plain towards the base, and the fax from Regional Party Headquarters made it plain the colonel was on his own as far as supplies went, he took action.

Many villagers starved after he removed the produce they had set by from their meagre smallholdings. He sent their bodies up to the hillside on wooden carts drawn by oxen. Then he slaughtered the oxen.

In those early weeks and months, he had been nervous. What would happen if the Party discovered his transformation? But then he'd woken up to reality. The village, chosen for its very remoteness, had no cell towers. No landlines. These people were living a life practically indistinguishable from that of their ancestors in the Warring States Period. Ox-carts. Wood fires. Traditional medicine. The old ways.

The nearest human settlement was over a thousand kilometres away. From time to time someone would try to leave but one of his informants would always tell him and then the runaway could be fetched back to face their punishment.

It is one such punishment that he has decided upon today. The man is brought in chains to the square, writhing and struggling in his gaolers' grip. He was discovered by one of the patrolling ghost warriors a kilometre outside the sanctified realm, way beyond the fence line. His eyes are wild. He is strong, too. Well-muscled. *Where does he get the food to grow this big?* Na wonders. *He must be a thief.*

"This man steals from you!" he yells into the teeth of the biting wind that brings more sleet down from the grey mountains to the north. "What should be held in common, he takes for his private consumption. Look at him! He has grown fat and indolent, while you, my ghost warriors, serve me faithfully, working hard every day to help me in my mission."

He sweeps his gaze over the ghost warriors. Their eyes glitter with anticipation. Behind him, the ancestors huddle, shuffling closer to caress his red and gold shoulder boards. Whispering. Urging him to unite the three kingdoms.

He looks beyond the warriors. There, on the edge of the group, he sees what he fears the most. Those who dwell in the Kingdom of the Underworld. Demons!

Wolf-men, yellow drool hanging from their slavering jaws, licking their lips with long red tongues that flicker. Dragon-women, their bare breasts obscenely swollen, clawing at their private parts with taloned fingers as they grin at him. *Come to us, Na Keng. Fuck us! We'll never let you go.* Three-headed vultures, scraps of flesh swinging from their cruelly hooked beaks, hissing threats. *We'll tear you into pieces and consume every last morsel of your stinking flesh.*

He shakes his head. Looks down at the bound man in front of him. His head is that of a bull, horned and massive, a tousled forelock of coarse white hair draped over those rolling white eyes. He shouts.

"Kill it!"

The ancestors smile and nod, nod and smile. The demons fade. And Colonel Na feels the anxiety recede a little.

10

HONG KONG

Gabriel buckled on his watch, a rose-gold Bremont 1918 on a black alligator strap, and checked the time. He'd missed his appointment with Jian by four and a half hours. Frowning, he pocketed his wallet, phone and keys. He signed the property release form, passed it back to the impassive desk sergeant, and headed out of the station reception area into the sun.

He called Jian and rescheduled their appointment: 7.00 p.m., still at the Golden Dragon. Then he walked to the kerb and looked up and down the street for one of the city's ubiquitous Toyota Crown Comfort taxis.

"Excuse me? Gabriel Wolfe?"

Gabriel turned to see who had learned his name. Hurrying across from a coffee cart was a young woman dressed in a white shirt, primrose-yellow skirt and a pair of dazzlingly white sneakers. She wore her hair in a low, ruler-straight fringe and her eyes were magnified by thick-lensed glasses in lime-green frames, giving her the appearance of an over-eager college student. In her right hand she held a cardboard cup. In her left, a slim, metallic-pink laptop.

He waited for her to reach him.

"Who are you?" he asked.

She pushed her glasses up with the tip of a finger, which necessitated transferring the takeaway cup into her other hand first. Then she offered the now-empty hand.

"Oh, sorry. Of course. Sarah Chow. I'm a journalist. Harbour Daily? You know it?"

"Yes, I know it. News website. So what?"

"You were involved in the mugging on Tsim Sha Tsui Promenade this morning."

"Says who?"

The young woman grinned, revealing teeth fenced across with braces: thin silver wires and translucent pink fittings like gemstones.

"The custody sergeant," she answered, jerking her chin back towards the police station.

Already doubting the wisdom of his spur-of-the-moment decision to tackle the muggers, though not the final outcome, Gabriel tried for a smile.

"Yes. I am Gabriel Wolfe. And I was involved, as you put it, in the mugging."

"Which is totally fantastic by the way. I mean, you're a real hero. My readers are going to love you."

Gabriel held up his hands.

"Whoa! Slow down. First of all, your readers? What are you, eighteen, nineteen? Bit young to have a by-lined column, aren't you?"

She shook her head, frowning, so that the skin between her curved black eyebrows puckered, just a little.

"First of all, I'm twenty-five. Second of all, OK, maybe calling our visitors my readers was overreaching, but even so. We have one-point-three million unique visitors every week and they're not even all in Hong Kong. We have people in San Francisco, Paris..."

Fearing the intrepid reporter was about to list every city in the world where someone had once logged onto the site, Gabriel tried to take control of the conversation.

"I get it. It's a popular site. I look at it myself from time to time.

But I'm not saying anything. All this? It's off the record. You guys still believe in that phrase, don't you?"

"Yes, of course! They teach it on day one of journalism college along with 'protect your sources'. But this is already in the public domain."

"No it isn't. You picked up a juicy little titbit from a custody sergeant, so he was almost certainly breaking the law in talking to you."

"But you'll be famous! Think of your Twitter account. Instagram. Or –" she scrutinised his hairline, and he felt sure she was checking out the silver hairs among the black, "– Facebook. You'll probably get thousands of extra followers."

"Look. You need to calm down. I don't have any of those things. I don't want followers," he made air quotes around the word, "I don't want to be famous. And I don't want to speak to you. Now, are we done here?"

He turned and strode across the pavement, back to his search for a cab, all of which seemed simultaneously to have vanished from the streets of Hong Kong, just when he needed one most.

"Wait!" she called out, dumping her cup in a bin, then hurrying across to him, almost colliding with a management type hurrying along with his face clamped to his phone.

Breathless, she joined him.

"Fine. No interview. Although I think you're making a big mistake. But can you at least give me an anonymous quote? I swear I won't put your name next to it."

Taking pity on the journalist, whom he imagined was actually only a freelance looking for writing gigs, Gabriel relented.

"How about this? I saw the two muggers snatch a camera and the bride's gift envelopes and I just reacted. I guess the cops got their catch of the day."

Her face broke into a wide grin, exposing the jewel-like braces again.

"Thank you! That's perfect. Can I describe you as a handsome Englishman?"

Gabriel sighed.

"If you must. But no names, no pack drill, all right?"

"Sure, sure. I promised, didn't I?"

A thought occurred to Gabriel.

"Sarah, do you have a card?"

Her eyes widened and she pulled out her phone, which was encased in a worn, leaf-green leather folder. She extracted a business card and handed it over. Above the usual mobile number, email address and social media accounts, it bore the words:

Sarah Chow

Freelance Journalist, Content Creator, Blogger

"Words are my business!"

Gabriel slid it into his wallet.

"Thank you. Look, I appreciate your not going all-out on the investigative scoop of the year thing, so if I ever hear of a story, I'll let you know, OK?"

"Cool! Deal."

They shook hands again. Then Gabriel saw a red-and-white taxi dropping off a fare a few hundred yards up the road and held his hand out. The driver flashed his headlamps. A few moments later he was climbing inside. He gave Kenneth Lao's address then sat back and smiled at Sarah Chow, who was frowning with concentration as she typed with two thumbs into her phone.

Gabriel rolled his shoulders as the taxi's air conditioning chilled the sweat inside his shirt. He checked his phone, not really expecting any notifications. As he'd said to the journalist, and it wasn't a lie, he avoided social media. So few friends that the chances of an email arriving were slim to non-existent. But the text icon had a little white '1' in a red circle clipping its top-right corner. He tapped it. Eli had sent him a message. Smiling, he opened the text.

Hi. Got a burner. All OK?

He tapped out a quick reply, knowing he might have to wait days for a response and that, when and if it came, it would be

58

noncommittal to the point of being boring. But just to know everything was working out would be a help.

Yep. All good. U?

He stepped out of the taxi's chilled interior into the heat of the afternoon. Instantly, he broke out into a sweat. He shuddered at the contrast between the humidity and the cold moisture inside his shirt.

Inside Kenneth Lao's building, his skin's temperature receptors had to adjust again as the refrigerator-like air conditioning drove out the heat let in by the revolving doors. He introduced himself to the receptionist, who smiled and asked him to stare into a screen-mounted webcam. After she issued his visitor photo ID and directed him to the nineteenth floor, Gabriel made his way to the bank of stainless-steel-doored elevators.

On the nineteenth floor, he stepped out onto thick-pile carpet and made his way along the corridor to the offices of Ophelia Tsang & Partners. Inside, a calm, professional hush reigned. Beyond the reception desk were the open-plan offices for the junior lawyers and support staff and then the private offices of the partners. A huge grey-green ceramic vase mounted on a white cube dominated the space to the left of the reception desk. It held dozens of white chrysanthemums and some acid-green blooms Gabriel didn't recognise.

As he approached the desk, the receptionist looked up and smiled. Her hair was swept up and pinned to the back of her head in a shining twist like a coiled serpent.

"Yes, sir?"

"My name is Gabriel Wolfe. I'm here to see Kenneth," Gabriel said.

The young woman smiled more broadly.

"He's expecting you. Please take a seat and I'll let him know you're here."

Gabriel thanked her and wandered over to inspect an aerial photograph of Hong Kong. He had just identified the building in which he was standing when Kenneth's warm voice broke the silence.

"Gabriel! Come with me, please."

The two men shook hands and Gabriel followed Kenneth through the open-plan office to his private domain.

After pouring two generous measures of Japanese whisky into heavy-bottomed cut-glass tumblers, Kenneth motioned for Gabriel sit in a leather club chair. He took a second, plucking at the knee of his suit before crossing his legs. The gesture revealed silky-looking black socks embroidered with gold Chinese characters.

法

"Law," Gabriel said. "Is it treating you well, Kenneth?"

"Better than you, I'm ashamed to say. But don't worry. I am confident we can have this whole business cleared up in a few days. It may not even be necessary for you to appear before a magistrate. I am working very hard behind the scenes to have the charges against you dismissed."

Gabriel sipped the whisky, savouring the way Suntory's use of recycled sherry casks imparted a fruity note to the spirit.

"Thank you."

"You should stay in Hong Kong until we can clear this up. Even I," he held an open palm over his heart, "can only do so much to protect a man many in law enforcement would regard simply as an interfering Westerner."

Gabriel thought ahead to his rescheduled meeting with Jian. Hoped whatever it was he wanted him to do wouldn't take him outside the city.

"I'll do my best. Tell me, did you get anywhere finding my father's solicitor? I know it was only this morning, but —"

Kenneth shook his head.

"I've put my brightest intern on it. He'll have something by the end of the day, I am sure of it. I'll send you the details the moment he brings them to me. There is someone to whom I'd like to introduce you, if you have time?"

"As you know, I'm on enforced leave. My time is pretty much my own these days."

Kenneth smiled.

"Good. Excuse me."

He rose from the chair and crossed to his desk, where he bent closer to the intercom and clicked the button.

"Julie, would you ask Peter to join us, please?"

Gabriel didn't have long to wonder about the identity of this employee of Kenneth's. After a sharp double-knock, the door swung inwards. Filling the frame stood a man with the wide-shouldered build of a heavyweight boxer. A westerner, like Gabriel, though a little older, mid-forties maybe. Reddish-blond hair cropped short above eyes tucked away beneath a prominent brow-ridge. His lightweight black suit, while clearly well cut, did very little to disguise its inhabitant's impressive musculature.

11

Gabriel stood, and found himself looking up into the newcomer's eyes, which he now saw were an amazing, bright blue. They shook hands, Gabriel making sure to push firmly into the other man's paw to avoid having his knuckles crushed in some primitive display of strength.

"Gabriel Wolfe. Pleased to meet you."

"Peter Nesbitt," the man said in a broad accent Gabriel immediately identified as coming from Belfast.

He'd had army buddies who'd served in Northern Ireland who claimed they could tell within seconds of beginning a conversation whether someone was a Protestant or a Catholic. Although a talented linguist, Gabriel had never developed this skill. The name suggested the man might be a protestant, he thought.

"Peter, please take a seat," Kenneth said. "Whisky?"

"Never say no to a fine drop of Suntory." He turned to Gabriel and winked. "Though why you don't keep a bottle of Bushmills, I don't know."

"It saves having to worry about offending my clients' religious sensibilities. I know my whisky lore."

Nesbitt snorted.

"As I think you know, boss, that old 'Jameson is for Catholics, Bushmills for the Protestants' story holds about as much water as this tumbler," he said, raising his glass, which held precisely none. He turned to Gabriel. "Even if I *am* a Prod, that's not why I like it. Kenneth here is just a massive whisky snob, if you want my honest opinion."

His grin crinkled those shaded eyes and transformed his face from a Belfast bareknuckle fighter into something more akin to a friendly headmaster. Kenneth laughed aloud.

"Peter knows me far too well. He is our chief investigator. I would like to put him at your service. Without charge."

Something about the big Ulsterman's bearing and demeanour had led Gabriel to the conclusion he was ex-security forces. Maybe the Police Service of Northern Ireland. Maybe military intelligence. So the revelation of his job at the upscale law firm didn't come as a surprise. But Kenneth's offer did.

"That is extremely kind of you. But you must let me pay."

Kenneth shook his head.

"I won't hear of it. Let's just say it is something I feel I owe to Zhao Xi."

It was enough to settle the matter without any further discussion of the investigator's fees.

"In which case, thank you. And thank you, Peter. I'll try not to make too many demands on your time."

"Your call, mate. So long as Kenneth's happy, my time is yours. D'you want to tell me what you're looking into?"

Gabriel outlined his belief in a third Wolfe sibling. One who, in all likelihood, had been born in Hong Kong, then, apparently, disappeared. When he finished speaking, he looked at Nesbitt, waiting for a reaction.

There were many things he could say. *It's a bit thin, isn't it? One memory of a baby being breastfed? After all this time, with both your parents having passed, there's not a lot we can do. I'm an investigator, not a bloody miracle worker.*

He said none of these. In fact, for a longish while, he said nothing at all, though from the way his gaze travelled upwards to the ceiling, and his lips parted slightly, he was clearly preparing to say something. He looked back at Gabriel. Frowning.

Gabriel took a sip of his whisky. Waiting for Nesbitt to break his silence. Outside the window, a gull flew directly towards the glass. Gabriel flinched instinctively, waiting for the big greyish-white bird to break its neck against the pane, but it wheeled away at the last moment. Nesbitt spoke.

"Your dad's lawyer is the obvious place to start. But I don't think he'll be able to answer the question we're going to want to ask him."

"Which is?"

"How on Earth does the child – the infant child, at that – of a senior British diplomat simply vanish into thin air? I mean, kids go missing every day, we all know that. And a fair few of the poor wee things end up being trafficked. But not this child, surely?"

It was a good question. One Gabriel had asked himself a thousand times already. So having the big Ulsterman thinking along the same lines was encouraging at the very least.

"I was thinking the police were probably involved. So they may have records. Or even someone who was involved in the case, investigating the disappearance."

Nesbitt nodded.

"Yeah, that's good. I have a few contacts here and there I can tap up for info."

"And the papers from back then. Especially the *South China Morning Post*. In fact, I just met a freelance journalist this morning. Maybe she has a contact."

"OK, good, so we have at least three promising lines of enquiry: your dad's lawyer, the cops and the media. But there's a fourth angle we can try as well."

Gabriel frowned, trying to see what Nesbitt was driving at.

"Former diplomatic staff? People at the Foreign Office back in London? My parents' own staff?"

Nesbitt nodded and finished his whisky before speaking.

"OK, let's make it five. I was actually thinking about how, or more precisely, *why* kids disappear. Now, if they're from poor families, especially poor rural families on the mainland, say, there's a very high chance they just die of disease or malnutrition."

Gabriel's mind kicked into a higher gear under Nesbitt's gentle tutelage.

"Or if Mao's One-Child Policy was still in force, and it's a girl baby, maybe the parents leave her out to die."

Nesbitt nodded.

"Sadly, yes. Plenty of poor wee girls left out in the cold, or just smothered with a pillow, so the parents could try for a boy. Right up until 2016, if you can believe it."

"What else? They run away, but not babies, obviously. They get trafficked. They get murdered. Or they get kidnapped."

"Out of those possibilities, the one that strikes me is the last. Your daddy was a high-profile figure. A known face among the expats and the native Hong Kongers. Maybe someone fancied their chances extracting a ransom?"

Gabriel turned to Kenneth, who had been listening intently as he and Nesbitt kicked ideas back and forth.

"What do you think? Does that sound plausible?"

Kenneth frowned.

"I'm afraid that it does. There was a spate of kidnappings in the early eighties. Mostly the children or wives of businessmen. At the time it was believed to be the work of triads, although nobody was ever caught or prosecuted. The crimes stopped, presumably because whichever gang was perpetrating them moved onto other, less risky methods of extorting money from the island's wealthy."

A shadow passed over Kenneth's face. A blink-and-you'd-miss-it expression. But Gabriel was trained not to blink and not to miss such things. They could indicate a tribal elder's split-second decision to release a hostage, or a surrendering enemy fighter's change of mind about handing over his weapon.

"What is it, Kenneth?" he asked now.

"Nothing. Why?"

"You looked as though something had occurred to you. Something unpleasant. Please, if it's even slightly relevant, tell me. Tell us," he added, including Nesbitt in a gesture.

"Listen, Gabriel, I didn't know your parents. Not personally. So I have no right to be even saying this and please don't take what I am about to suggest as in any way casting aspersions on their decency. But—"

"But what?" Gabriel said, impatient to hear what the lawyer had to say.

"Sometimes, a mother or father may inadvertently, and I stress that word, Gabriel, injure or even kill their young child. In such tragic cases, there is an instinct to cover the events up. That is all. An extremely unlikely scenario, I grant you, but one I feel I must raise – even if only that you may dismiss it. I am sorry if I have injured your feelings."

The lawyer was blushing. Gabriel shook his head. The thought had already occurred to him.

"It's fine. Honestly, Kenneth. I don't blame you for raising it. It's an ugly thought but so is child trafficking, murder and all the others."

"If I may, gents," Nesbitt said. "What I was driving at was that our fifth line of enquiry is the underworld here in Hong Kong. Eighty-three was a long time ago in terms of the way this place has changed, but people have long memories. There are plenty of folks here who were around and up to no good in the eighties, and even the seventies. I know a good few of them. I can make some enquiries."

So, Gabriel realised, did he. His final suggestion was to add friends of his parents to the list of possible lines of enquiry.

After agreeing to meet Nesbitt at nine the next morning at a café near the law firm's offices, Gabriel headed back to his house. At 7.00 p.m. he had a meeting with one of the people in Hong Kong who had certainly been up to no good in the eighties. Someone who might be able to point him in the right direction before Nesbitt even got his wheels turning.

Suddenly hungry, Gabriel headed to the kitchen, where he washed his hands before tying on a blue-and-white, butcher-striped apron. From the fridge he selected a thumb-sized nub of ginger, lemongrass stems, a red chilli, bunch of fresh coriander and a bag of king prawns he'd bought at the fish market the day before. He set some rice to cook then turned his attention to the other ingredients. First reducing an onion to thin slivers and a clove of garlic likewise, he set them softening in some oil in a heavy-based frying pan. He added a little sea salt to stop them sticking.

The lemongrass he chopped into three-centimetre lengths with a deep-bellied cook's knife before bruising them with the heel of the handle so they gave up their distinctive citrus aroma. He peeled the ginger root and sliced it so finely he could see light through the pieces. Then he stripped the seeds and pith from the chilli and chopped the scarlet flesh into tiny cubes. Finally he chopped the coriander leaves roughly until he had a conical pile of emerald-green herb fragments.

Inhaling the smell of frying onions and garlic, and the aromatics, and relishing the way it made his mouth water, he poured himself a glass of Chablis from the fridge then went back to his work, peeling and deveining the prawns.

When the rice had a few minutes left, he scraped the chilli, lemongrass and ginger into the pan, stirred them for a few seconds, then tipped in the prawns. As they turned from blue to pink, he added a splash of rice wine and a few shakes of soy sauce. He topped up his glass while the prawns absorbed the flavours, taking another mouthful of the fruity, dry white wine before turning off the gas under both pans.

Rice first in a mound into which he pressed a serving spoon to make a well, then on went the garlicky, gingery chilli prawns and a final scatter of the chopped coriander. He grabbed chopsticks then transported the plate and his wine glass to the table, facing out onto the garden.

As he ate, he ran through the lines of enquiry he and Peter Nesbitt had identified. He didn't doubt Peter's prowess as an investigator. But with such limited resources he knew they'd have to prioritise or risk wasting their time and energy in a series of fruitless investigations.

He got up from the table, and returned with an A4 pad and a pencil. He wrote down the six lines of enquiry and, against each, the team member he thought best qualified to tackle them:

1 Wolfe lawyer – Gabriel
2 Diplomatic staff/house staff/(friends?) – Gabriel
3 Police – Peter
4 Media – Gabriel
5 Triads – Gabriel
6 Expats – Peter

He finished his meal and sat on, staring at the list and sipping the wine, which had warmed in the evening sunshine. In a clump of bamboo in a corner of the garden, two charcoal-and-yellow butterflies danced among the thick stems. Golden Birdwings, he thought, smiling.

At first angry at Don's decision to bench him for six weeks, Gabriel had, eventually, realised the sense of his boss's instructions. The Old Man had suggested he "Go fishing. Sail your boat. Learn a musical instrument". He'd done none of those things, hightailing it to his place in Hong Kong as soon as he was able.

But he had begun, tentatively at first, to take an interest in what was happening in his own back yard. Literally. The garden was alive with insects, amphibians, birds and the occasional reptile. Gabriel had tried to identify them all, eventually starting a log and consulting websites and reference books. The Birdwings were among his favourites, the forewings as sober as a banker's suit, the hindwings a vibrant lemon.

Like two separate butterflies, cut into halves and stuck together, he mused. Hearing a distant church bell striking six, he took his plate, glass and chopsticks into the kitchen, washed, dried and put them away, then went upstairs to shower and change.

12

Gabriel arrived at The Golden Dragon at 6.55 p.m., paid the driver, and climbed out into the humid, early-evening air. Though Fang kept the casino open virtually round the clock, at this time of day, custom was slow. The single doorman, hewn, seemingly, from teak, looked bored as he guarded the golden door against a non-existent queue of fervent gamblers. Behind him, two seven-foot-tall dragons reared up on their hind legs, fanged jaws clamped around illuminated glass globes.

Adjusting the cuffs of his suit, a lightweight two-piece in blue-and-white seersucker, Gabriel looked up at the backlit gold-painted sign advertising the casino in English and Cantonese. The capital 'G' flickered so that every few seconds it appeared to read

The olden Dragon

金龙

Looking up at the doorman, Gabriel experienced the peculiar feeling that he had been reduced to the stature of a child. Wordlessly, the giant unhooked the twisted rope from its golden pole, opened the door and waved him inside the casino.

Inside, the place felt subdued compared to his previous visit. That had been late at night, when the gambling had been in full swing. A few elderly women were playing games of mahjong at corner tables and a handful of westerners were leaning eagerly over one of the roulette tables, but that was it.

A single waitress looked after them all. Gabriel knew that any customer unwise enough to be lured into inappropriate action by the seductive slit up the side of her red cheongsam would find himself growled at. First by the scowling dragon embroidered around her torso. Then by the waitress herself. And, finally, by one of the discreet but ever-present security men. Depending on the level of inappropriateness, the growl might metamorphose into something a little more physical; up to and including immediate forcible ejection from the premises.

He walked across the central space in the red-and-gold palace and towards the private door that led to Fang Jian's office. From the shadows, a young Chinese woman emerged. She was dressed in a white leather jacket and trousers and was, as far as he could see, unarmed. Which counted for nothing. He'd seen what Fang's "unarmed" bodyguards were capable of.

"Sorry, staff only, sir," she said, in unaccented English, moving between him and the door while maintaining, just, a respectful distance.

Gabriel stopped and smiled down at her.

"It's OK. I have an appointment with Mister Fang."

"Name, please?"

"Gabriel Wolfe."

"Please wait at the bar."

Seeing no point in arguing, Gabriel wandered back to the bar and pulled up a stool. The barman, young like the white-clad girl, smiled and put down a martini glass he was polishing.

"Yes, sir. What can I get you?"

Gabriel looked down at the conical glass, sparkling on a red bar towel.

"How about filling that with a dry martini? Tanqueray Number Ten gin, not too dry, three olives."

"Very good, sir."

Gabriel watched as the barman built his cocktail, approving of the way he stirred the alcohol in a jug of ice rather than shaking it. He smiled. *I know it's what Bond asked for but it's colder this way.*

The drink was perfect. As the ice-cold spirit hit his stomach, he sighed with pleasure, enjoying the sensation of lightness as it crossed the blood-brain barrier. Maybe being on the subs bench for a while wasn't so bad after all. He swivelled round on the red leather cushion and surveyed the room.

A glamorous woman in a black sheath dress at a blackjack table looked up just as his eye roved over her corner of the room. Her full lips curved upwards in a half-smile as she met his gaze. She leaned towards the croupier and said something, slipped a chip into his palm, then left her cards for him to scoop up with his wooden palette and discard.

Not taking her eyes off Gabriel, she made her way across the floor to join him at the bar. Close enough to detect her perfume, something expensive-smelling, musky and spicy, he estimated her age at late forties. A tumble of blonde hair fell to her shoulders. Her skin lacked the smoothness of youth but also the over-tightened look of women who'd been under the knife. She extended a hand. He noticed the toned arm behind it.

"Valerie Duggan," she said, smiling broadly at him as they shook hands. "Were you just checking me out?"

Her accent was pure South London: street-wise, cocky and with just a hint of spikiness.

"Gabriel Wolfe. Not at all," he answered, taking a sip of his martini. "I'm just waiting for someone."

"Lucky girl."

"Not a girl. A man."

She pursed her lips in a moue of disappointment.

"Lucky man, then."

"Not that kind of man," he said, smiling.

"Oh, well, in that case, lucky me!"

"Would you like a drink?"

"Yeah, why not? Drown my sorrows. Lady Luck wasn't looking

after me over there," she said, jerking her chin in the direction of the blackjack table. "Moscow Mule," she said to the barman, who'd appeared behind them. "Make sure it knows how to kick."

"Are you on holiday or are you local?" Gabriel asked.

"Neither. Business trip. I've got a bit of free time before my next meeting. Cheers!" she added as the barman set her drink in front of her on a red and gold cocktail napkin.

"Cheers!"

"Mmm, that's good. Thank you," she called to the barman, tucking a five-dollar bill under the napkin.

"What line of business are you in?" Gabriel asked.

"Telecoms. You?"

"HR consulting."

"You're not gambling? Pretty expensive place to come just for a cocktail, isn't it?"

Gabriel smiled. He'd seen Fang emerge from the door at the far end of the room.

"That man I said I was meeting? He owns this place. That's him now."

She turned to look over her left shoulder. Then back to Gabriel.

"He a friend of yours, then?"

Gabriel shrugged. Wondering if she was just making conversation or actually gathering information. Something was telling him it was the latter. Maybe it was her body language. She was clearly aiming for a third-drink-of-the-evening, relaxed posture, but her back was too straight and her eyes hadn't stopped flicking around the room as they'd been talking.

"More of a client, actually. I'm helping him with recruitment."

She patted him on the arm and slid off her chair to stand closer.

"Well, enjoy your meeting, but a word of advice. Keep your wits about you."

Then she laughed loudly as if he'd told her the funniest joke in the world and sashayed back across the room to the blackjack table. Fang arrived and clapped a meaty hand on Gabriel's shoulder. He was wearing his trademark gold silk dinner jacket over black trousers.

13

"How are you, Wolfe Cub? Enjoying a drink, I see," Fang said. He beckoned the barman. "No charge for my friend here."

The barman nodded briskly, "Yes, Mr Fang," and returned to the other end of the bar.

"You made a friend," Fang said, nodding towards where Valerie Duggan was engrossed in her cards again.

"Businesswoman. Telecoms," Gabriel said.

"Ah, well, plenty of interest in that on the mainland. Now, come to my office. My client is very eager to meet you."

As they entered Fang's office, its occupant stood and turned to greet Gabriel. From his appearance, Gabriel could easily have assumed that, like Valerie Duggan, he was a corporate executive. A conservative blue suit, gold-rimmed rectangular glasses, hair cut short and parted on the left. Fiftyish, somewhat overweight. Only the direct, probing stare behind the glasses suggested anything of his true role.

Here was one of the new masters of the former colony. Maintaining, for now, the idea that Hong Kong's status as a special administrative region allowed it to operate as a freer, fairer version of the country across the waters of Kowloon Bay.

"Gabriel Wolfe, meet my good friend Liu Zhang," Fang said, standing back and beaming as the two men shook hands.

Once they were all seated, Liu spoke.

"Jian has told me a great deal about you, Gabriel. Recommended you. Your skillset, in particular. I think you will be a perfect fit for the job I have in mind for you to carry out."

"How did you hear about me in the first place? In order to ask Jian about me?"

"You are fond of travel?"

"Yes. I do a lot for my work."

"Ever been to Southeast Asia? Indochina?"

Gabriel sensed where Liu was headed. The Chinese had informants, tentacles, networks everywhere these days so why should he be surprised?

"From time to time, yes."

"Cambodia?"

"I think you know I have."

Liu nodded.

"Indeed I do know. I know that you took out an entire militia gang. On your own. Headed by an ex-Khmer Rouge commander. Not easy people to defeat militarily. Let alone singlehanded."

Gabriel shrugged. Happy that however good the Chinese intel was, their informant hadn't picked up that he was working alongside Eli, at least for the first part of the mission.

"Win Ya had grown careless," he said.

"Yes. And he paid with his life. And that of his men. All twenty-four of them."

"You're not telling me you're squeamish, are you?"

"Oh, no. They were terrible men. Every man – and boy – of them. Raping, torturing, looting, butchering, killing. Quite honestly you did the world a favour."

"So, you heard about that and thought, 'Yes, he's our man'?"

Liu spread his hands.

"More or less. There were one or two other candidates. A Syrian. A German. They fell by the wayside. And a Russian. But those bunglers are too close to home, and too cocky."

Gabriel decided to change tack. He was less concerned about the selection process and more about the operation.

"Forgive me, Mister Liu. Jian told me who you are, but nothing about the problem you face. Although he did say something about public relations."

The Party official laughed and passed a palm over his forehead.

"I suppose 'public relations' just about covers it. Let me explain. There is a PLA colonel. One Na Keng. Colonel Na commands one of our older defensive missile batteries in Xinjiang Province in Northwest China. It is a thousand kilometres from the nearest city, which is just as well given what is going on out there."

"Which is?"

"This is confidential, yes? Jian assured me I could count on your utter discretion."

Gabriel glanced at Fang.

"One hundred per cent."

"Colonel Na massacred the entire garrison about three months ago. All except for a single radio operator who had travelled to Urumqi for a minor operation. On his return journey, he got within twenty kilometres of the base before a cattle herder warned him off saying bad things had happened. The colonel is running the base and neighbouring village as a personal fiefdom. Which would be bad enough. But he has been –" Liu swallowed and wiped his forehead again before continuing, "– well, he is still killing people."

"And you want him dead."

"I do."

"Why not just send a PLA detachment up there to do it? Why shop around for a freelance?"

Liu lifted his chin and stretched his neck, giving him the appearance of a tortoise emerging from its shell.

"Along with several dozen other base commanders, Colonel Na is a Party commissar. That makes him my personal responsibility. So far I have managed to keep his, ah, transgressions out of the news. I value my job and the privileges that go with it." Liu glanced at Fang at this point and Gabriel wondered to what extent the two men were doing business together. "If this gets out, I will be forced to resign.

Or worse, given some menial role. Managing egg production in some shithole province out west or supervising steelwork production for a new bridge. No, on balance, I think it is best for an outsider to do it. I then have my plausible deniability, as the Americans call it."

"How am I supposed to get to him? Xinjiang's pretty much in the middle of nowhere."

"I have a trip to Russia in a couple of days. A summit in the Altai Republic on mutual defence and security. It is only two hundred and seventy kilometres from the border. You will board the plane with me as my interpreter. We will drop you over Xinjiang along with a vehicle. Once you have dealt with Na, you will call me and I will arrange for you to be picked up by helicopter and brought back to me. We fly back to Hong Kong and you resume your life here."

"What sort of defence force does he have there?"

"None to speak of. As I said, he massacred the garrison. Maybe a handful of loyal soldiers but, you must understand, he has terrorised the villagers and brainwashed them into believing he is some sort of spiritual being. They obey him without question."

"How will you explain away the death of a garrison commander?"

Liu tapped the side of his nose.

"Leave that side of things to me. That close to the Russian border, we have many options for throwing suspicion their way."

"I'll need equipment."

Liu nodded.

"Write down a list of the things you need and give it to Jian. They will be provided."

"Do you have maps? Plans of the base?"

Liu reached beneath the table and brought out a burgundy leather briefcase.

"Everything you need is in there. You will receive it when we board the plane. You understand, this is sensitive material. I cannot allow you to take possession."

"Especially since I am an agent of the British Government."

Liu smiled.

"Especially that."

"Yet you're comfortable requesting my help in the first place."

Liu placed his hands together as if in prayer and stared at Gabriel over the tips of his fingers.

"One of the reasons China has thrived while Russia has lurched from one crisis to the next is captured by the word 'flexibility'. As you probably know, Chinese Communism has always changed with the times. We have embraced the market. We engage with our opponents on the world stage. We seek to build bridges, not walls. This is one of those times.

"I know Jian has helped you. Now you are repaying that debt by helping us. You will not learn anything in Xinjiang that the Americans have not already learned from their spy satellites. The missiles we have out there are short-range, outmoded, non-nuclear. Half the technology is licensed from your country and the French in any case.

"Believe me, Gabriel, we may not follow the same political system, but surely you can see that this man's crimes transcend ideology? And know this. You will have a friend in China. Always. That can only be a good thing, surely?"

Gabriel nodded. It was a good speech. And very easy to believe. But for him, this operation was simply about repaying a debt of honour to Fang. He'd helped Gabriel track down the people who had betrayed his final mission in The Regiment and directly caused Smudge's death. Once this was done, Gabriel would return to Britain and his duties with The Department. And if the next target were to be Liu, he would carry out his orders without compunction.

"I'll let you have the list in the morning," he said.

———

Back home, Gabriel poured a generous measure of brandy into a snifter and took it out to the garden, where he sat and listened to the frogs and the crickets chirruping. His phone added its own chirp to the symphony: you have mail.

The email from Kenneth Lao was brief but packed with information.

Gabriel,

Your father's solicitor in HK was John Chang. He was a partner at Chang, Greaves, Luan and Whitney.

The firm is still in business: 23rd Floor, Suite #1218, Providence Building, Hennessy Road. Tel 3165 4492.

Kenneth

PS Charges dropped.

Resolving to call the law firm first thing in the morning, Gabriel sat on, sipping the brandy and listening to the mating calls of frogs.

———

A few miles to the north, Fang was speaking to a tall, thin man with a bald head and narrow, watchful eyes.

"She's been hanging round the Golden Dragon," Fang said, turning his phone round. The picture on the screen was grainy, taken in low light. It showed a glamorous woman in her late forties, blonde hair worn long, full lips. "I want to know everything about her. Who she is. When she got here. Where she's staying. What she's up to."

"Yes, boss. You want me to kill her?"

"No. Not yet. If I need to, I may do it differently. Make it look like a street robbery gone wrong."

"Can you send me the pic?"

Fang tapped his screen.

The bald man tapped his phone to upload the incoming photo, nodded once, and left the office without a backwards glance.

14

Nesbitt climbed the flight of concrete steps to the main doors of the Hong Kong Police Headquarters.

In the twenty-two years since he had left the Force, the complex of buildings at 1 Arsenal Street in Wan Chai had changed beyond all recognition. The old Arsenal House, where he had been based as a young CID officer in the late-nineties, was now at the foot of a forty-seven-storey skyscraper that towered above the neighbourhood.

But whenever he visited, as his work demanded, he was struck by all that hadn't changed. The smell of stale coffee in the open-plan incident rooms. The harassed look on the faces of detectives with too many cases and too few bodies to investigate them. Something else, too.

The buzz. That indefinable feeling all coppers, serving or former, got when entering the inner sanctum. The place where it all happened.

Being an investigator for a law firm was solid, well-paid work. Regular-hours work, which his wife appreciated, probably more than he did. But he missed the thrum of energy as a few thousand hard-working coppers investigated all the crimes human ingenuity could devise. Rape, murder and assault. Financial fraud and money laundering. Drug trafficking, prostitution rings. Kidnapping.

"Peter Nesbitt to see Detective Chief Inspector Chrissie Chu," he said to the civilian receptionist.

"Do you have an appointment, sir?"

"Mm-hmm." He checked his watch. "At ten. I'm a little early."

He was fifteen minutes early. Deliberately. Wanting to hang around in the building and absorb the atmosphere. Just for a quarter of an hour.

"Take a seat, please."

He did as he was told, crossing one long leg over the other, leaning back in the cloth-covered chair and watching the endless stream of people arriving, consulting, arguing, leaving. He smiled and interlaced his fingers behind his head.

At five to ten, the slightly-built detective inspector he'd come to see appeared before him. He stood and they shook hands.

"Chrissie, how do you do that?"

"Do what?" she asked, grinning.

"Creep up on a body like that?"

"I wasn't creeping, Peter. Maybe you're getting careless."

"Aye, maybe I am at that. Listen, thanks for seeing me at such short notice."

"It's fine. Come on. Let's get a coffee in the canteen and you can tell me what you need."

Seated in the canteen, which, like such institutions the world over, smelled of fried food and machine coffee, they faced each other across a pale-blue laminated table. Nesbitt looked at her. Ten years older than she'd been the first time they'd met, Chu had aged well. Her round cheeks were smooth and unlined and her eyes, hazel behind black-framed glasses, were as bright and enquiring now as then. *Like a bird's*, he thought, not for the first time.

"How's life treating you, Chrissie?"

She smiled again. She smiled a lot. He liked that. Never one to let the job get on top of her.

"Very well. We closed a big case last week. Anti-triad operation. Digital fraud. Big, big case. How is life treating you?"

He nodded. Wanting to tell her about the lump he'd recently discovered in his groin. About the suspicions he had that his wife was losing interest in him. About his grown-up daughter's drifting, purposeless lifestyle. What had Olivia said she was, the last time they'd spoken? "I'm a digital nomad, Dad. I have my phone and my laptop. Thanks to Wi-Fi, the world is my home." She'd been in Colorado at the time. Or was that the previous month?

"Oh, you know. Mustn't grumble. A few aches and pains, but at my age that goes with the territory."

Chu's eyes widened.

"At *your* age? You're a spring chicken, Peter!"

Wishing he could believe she was flirting and not bantering, Nesbitt turned to business.

"What would I do without you, Chrissie? So, look, this *chun ji* is looking at an old case. A baby who disappeared in the early eighties."

Chu nodded, her grin replaced by a serious expression.

"You know, lots of babies used to disappear in Hong Kong. And before the handover, you say? A lot of reorganisation in the HKPF since then."

"I know. But this wasn't any baby. The daughter of a senior British diplomat and his wife. Gentleman by the name of Gerald Wolfe, with an 'e'. Wife's name Lin. She was half-Chinese."

She'd pulled out a small black notebook and was jotting down words and phrases. At this, she looked up at him, fixing him with that enquiring gaze.

"And the baby disappeared?"

"Apparently. I'm looking into the case for a family member, that's all I can say. I was rather hoping you might be able to run a couple of searches on the databases, or maybe even put me in touch with a cop who worked the case back then."

"I can do both of those. But there's a good chance they'll be retired by now. Unless they were really young at the time. Leave it with me. I'll call you when I have something. It shouldn't take long."

"Thanks, Chrissie. Anything I can do for you while I'm here?"

She frowned. Looked up. Back at Nesbitt.

"Maybe there is. I picked up a bit of gossip. One of my informants said there was a British cop on the island looking into the triads. Have you heard of anyone asking questions? Poking their nose in?"

Nesbitt didn't answer at once. Closed his eyes and pinched the bridge of his nose. Ran through the last few months of informal conversations in bars, clubs, coffee shops, at the racetrack, among the expats he still liked to hang out with.

He opened his eyes.

"Honestly? Nothing. But I'll keep my ears open. I hear a whisper, you'll hear it next."

Chu smiled.

"Thank you, Peter. I'll call you, OK?"

After he left the police building, Nesbitt found a quiet spot and called Gabriel.

"Hi, Peter. What have you got?"

"I went to see a contact down at police HQ. She's going to have a wee squint at the databases and ask around. See if she can scare up a name from the original investigation. Soon as I hear from her, I'll let you know."

"Thanks. That sounds good. Anything you need, just let me know."

"Will do. Any joy your end?"

"I've got the details of my father's lawyer. I'm going to see him tomorrow."

After speaking to Gabriel, Nesbitt called an informant of his. A man who owned and ran a high-class fish restaurant.

15

After a late breakfast the next day, Gabriel texted his list to Fang, for forwarding to Liu.

Ram-air chute
Semi-automatic pistol + suppressor
Assault rifle + telescopic sight
Tactical knife
High-explosive grenades
Smoke grenades
Flash-bangs
Camouflage gear
Binoculars
Night-vision goggles
Wire-cutters
High-power torch
Battlefield first-aid kit
Survival kit
Food (fresh and battlefield rations) and water

"That should do it," he said to a sparrow hopping along the window sill.

With the morning sun warming his face as he drank a second mug of tea in the garden, Gabriel called Sarah Chow, turning her laminated business card this way and that as he waited for her to pick up.

"Sarah Chow, words are my business. How can I help you?"

"Sarah, it's Gabriel Wolfe. We met outside the police station yesterday."

"Oh, yes! Hi! How are you?"

"I'm fine, thanks. I may have a job for you. Not a story," he added hastily, "but a paid gig that will call for your journalistic skills."

"Okaay. What are we talking about here?"

"Could you come to my house? I'd rather discuss this face to face."

Chow said she could be at his place in an hour. While he waited for her, he called Kenneth Lao and asked if he could provide a simple legal document and email it over. Then he called the law firm that had employed his father's solicitor. After explaining who he was, first to the receptionist and then again to an executive assistant to one of the partners, he managed to fix an appointment for 11.45 that same morning.

Just under an hour later, the doorbell rang.

Chow looked more business-like than she had the day before. Black trousers and a crisp white shirt under a black jacket. But the green-framed glasses and the braces undercut the professional image even so. Gabriel wondered if he was doing the right thing involving such a young woman in his quest for information on his missing sibling. *Too late. She's here now.*

"Sarah, come in," he said, standing aside. "Would you like tea or coffee?"

She smiled.

"Tea please. Milk no sugar."

With her drink prepared, Gabriel led her into the garden. Her eyes widened as she took in the view down to the harbour.

"Oh, wow! This is such a cool place. You're really lucky to have it. Property prices up here have been going crazy for the last few years."

He bit back the sharp retort forming in his mouth. It wasn't her fault Zhao Xi was dead.

"I know," he said. "Have a seat."

"So, what's this job-not-story you have for me?" she said, once she'd arranged her mug of tea, her notebook and pen, her phone and a laptop on the mosaic-tile-topped table.

"I believe I have, or at least had, a brother or sister who was born here in 1983. When they were about six months to a year old, they disappeared. I'm trying to find out what happened and, in an ideal world, track them down. My father was a senior British diplomat so it's possible it would have made the papers. Or at least the expat gossip-machine. I need some help digging – I thought the *South China Morning Post* would be one avenue to explore."

While he spoke, Chow's hand moved feverishly across the page, taking notes in shorthand, a skill he'd imagined had been universally replaced with micro-recorders or phone apps.

"Old school," he added, pointing at the page of hieroglyphics.

She grinned.

"All my classmates at college thought so, too. But a pencil never runs out of charge halfway through an interview."

"What do you think?"

"Well, nobody else does it anymore so it's a pretty good way of keeping my notes private."

He smiled.

"About the job?"

"Oh, God, sorry," she said, rolling her eyes. "Yeah, I could do that. Are you sure I can't write it up, though? It would be such a great story."

Gabriel shook his head.

"It has to be totally confidential. In fact, if you do decide to take it on, I'll want you to sign a non-disclosure agreement."

The hopeful expression on her face dimmed for a moment, then returned.

"Fine! But I reserve the right to ask you again, OK?"

He smiled, unable to resist her infectious enthusiasm.

"OK. My lawyer is emailing the NDA over. I'll forward it to you as soon as I have it. Now. Are you interested?"

"Totally. Yes. One hundred per cent. When can I start?"

"Haven't you forgotten something?"

She looked up, frowned and tapped the end of her nose with her pencil. Then looked back at Gabriel.

"What's the deadline?"

He shook his head.

"The deadline's as soon as possible, but that wasn't it. Don't you want to give me your rate?"

Her eyes widened and then she actually smacked her palm against her forehead. The gesture would have looked theatrical performed by a worldlier journalist, but from her it seemed unaffected and natural.

"Duh! Words are my business but apparently business isn't," she said. "My rate is two hundred and fifty Hong Kong dollars an hour or fifteen hundred a day. I hope that's all right. I guess I could give you a discount as it's likely to be a few days' work."

Gabriel frowned. The equivalent of twenty-five pounds an hour or a hundred and fifty a day didn't seem like much for a skilled journalist. And she was negotiating with herself, cutting her prices before he'd said a word. He decided she needed some help in return.

"That's too cheap. For your time *and* for the work. And don't discount if the client isn't asking. And not even then unless they offer something else in return. How about I pay you your standard rate for your time and double the final bill if you discover a positive lead?"

"Really? You'd do that?"

"Call it compensation for not being able to write about it. Plus, you'll be more focused if you're not worrying whether you're losing out on a better-paid gig. Deal?"

She grinned, revealing her sparkling braces again.

"Thank you. Yes, it's a deal."

She stuck out her hand and, when he took it, pumped Gabriel's hand vigorously.

"What do you need from me?" he asked.

All business now, her grin vanished and she picked up her pad again.

"Parents' names and workplaces? Last known address?"

Gabriel gave her the information she needed and once she'd noted it down, she stood.

"Right. I'll start now. Do you want me to report in at the end of the day?"

"Please. And be discreet, OK? If anyone asks—"

"I'll say I'm working up background for a story, can't say any more, off the record, on the QT and very hush-hush. Don't worry. I'll keep it under my hat."

Amused by her quaintly old fashioned turn of phrase, and impressed by the *LA Confidential* quote, Gabriel smiled and showed her out. Alone in the house again, he changed into a kung fu outfit and went down to the dojo. He knelt in the centre of the matted floor and closed his eyes, bringing his hands palms-together in front of his breastbone. He breathed in deeply and let the air out in a sigh. He spoke to the empty room.

"I don't know where you are. I don't know if you're alive or dead. I don't know whether you were a boy or a girl. I don't know your name. I don't know what happened to you. But I will. I will know all these things. I will find you. I promise. One way or another, we will be reunited."

Then he opened his eyes and stood in a single, flowing movement. He crossed the dojo to a punch bag suspended from a wooden beam on a chain. Dropping into a fighting stance, and keeping his weight on the balls of his feet, he punched the shiny leather. And again, harder this time.

He danced back out of reach of its swinging bulk, then in again, jabbing short-armed punches into his imaginary opponent's midsection. He raised the speed of his moves, coordinating footwork and punches until his hands were a blur and his entire focus, his entire being, became a flow of controlled aggression directed at the person who had taken his sibling away from him.

He fought the punchbag and then the wooden sparring dummy for forty minutes. Physically exhausted, he sank onto his haunches and then bowed until his forehead touched the mat. And there he stayed, slowing his breathing until he could manage on just two inhalations per minute. Then he sat up and placed his hands in the prayer position over his heart once more.

"Thank you, Master Zhao, for all you did for me, all you taught me."

He went upstairs, showered and changed, pushed a couple of documents into an envelope and left for his appointment at his late father's solicitors.

16

Arriving at the offices of Chang, Greaves, Luan and Whitney with ten minutes to spare, Gabriel entered the air-conditioned lobby and took the lift to the twenty-third floor.

Pressed, he could have described the features that distinguished this law firm's reception area from any of the others he'd visited in his post-service career.

A red lacquer bowl of apples on the reception desk. A matching dish of wrapped squares of Swiss chocolate on the coffee table. A limited-edition art print on the wall depicting a traditional Chinese horse against a photographic background of graffitied apartment blocks. But the overall impression was much the same. "You can trust us," the decor said. "We have deep wells of integrity, skill and discretion."

He sat back in an oxblood leather armchair and reached for that day's *Financial Times* but had barely got past the headlines when an affable male voice made him look up. Its owner, striding across the thickly-carpeted floor, was in his late seventies, Gabriel estimated. Immaculately dressed in a brown three-piece suit, despite the outside temperature. Gold watch chain across his rounded stomach.

Thinning hair revealing a liver-spotted scalp. A deeply-lined face. He held out his right hand.

"I'm John Chang."

Gabriel stood. Ready to learn what had happened to the missing Wolfe sibling. He shook hands then allowed himself to be led to the lawyer's private office.

Chang sat behind a desk clear of everything bar a gold pen set in a stand, a desk-phone and a leather blotter, whose pale-blue paper was unmarked. He placed his palms on the polished wood.

"Forgive me, but do you have some form of identification?"

Gabriel had been expecting this, and withdrew the envelope containing his passport, birth certificate and driving licence from an inside jacket pocket and handed them to Chang. After scrutinising the three documents, Chang returned them. Now his faced broke into a wide smile. When he spoke, it was with a catch in his voice.

"Gabriel? It is really you. My goodness! The last time I saw you, you were a babe in arms. I wondered if this day would ever come. When my assistant told me who had just called, well, I confess I was shocked at first. Yes, shocked. After all this time. But here you are. As large as life."

"Forgive me, Mister Chang, but I—"

"John, please. I insist."

Gabriel nodded and smiled, warming to the lawyer's almost boyish enthusiasm.

"John, then. Why were you shocked?"

Chang frowned, and his smiled slipped. He smoothed the hair down at the back of his neck.

"Well, I suppose I had thought, given your family's tragic history, and your chosen profession, that you had not survived very far into adulthood."

Gabriel spread his hands wide.

"Yet here I am. Defying the odds. So you knew about Michael, then?"

Chang nodded.

"Such a sad story. Your mother was devastated. I tried to tell her it wasn't her fault. But she would not be convinced, by me or by your father. Or her doctor, for that matter."

"I'm sorry, but what do you mean? You know what happened, don't you? The rugby game I was playing with Michael? The ball I kicked into the harbour? Michael going in after it and –" Gabriel swallowed a lump that had formed in his throat "– drowning?"

Chang nodded rapidly.

"Of course."

"Then why do you say she thought it was her fault?"

Chang gave Gabriel a searching look, not speaking for a few seconds. Finally, he sighed and shook his head.

"I suppose you know of your mother's problems with alcohol." Gabriel nodded, waiting for Chang to get to the point and half-fearing what that point would reveal. "They began after the events of December 1983. By the time Michael was born, I regret to say that your mother's slide into alcoholism was complete. At the time of your brother's tragic death, she was not well. Not well at all. Once she had sent you boys off to play, she took a flask of gin from her handbag and passed out soon afterwards."

Gabriel passed a hand over his face, trying to recapture the pictures in his mind of those precious last moments with Michael. Hadn't his mother been there shouting encouragement, watching them kick and catch the ball? Yes, she had! He was sure of it. *Or do I just* want *to be sure of it?*

"How do you know all this? They didn't have CCTV in those days. How do you know she passed out?"

"Oh, Gabriel, I am sorry that you are hearing this from me, and for the first time by the sound of it?" Chang raised his eyebrows in a question, and Gabriel nodded mutely. "There were witnesses. Two nannies. English girls. When you screamed they raised the alarm, waking your mother. Your father was able, by virtue of his position, to intervene in the police investigation, steering them towards the narrative of a tragic and unavoidable accident."

Gabriel could feel tears pricking at the backs of his eyes. On top of everything else, all the loss, the doubt, the blame and the grief, the work he'd done with Fariyah, was he now to face the fact that

Michael's death might have been prevented, and by their mother herself, if only she hadn't been drunk at the time?

He was about to speak when a secretary arrived with coffee and biscuits. He held his tongue until the cups were filled and biscuits offered and declined. Then he did speak.

"You said 'after the events of December 1983'. You're talking about the baby."

"Yes. I had been working for your father for a little over three years when it happened."

"Tell, me, John. Was it another boy, or a girl?"

Chang smiled sadly and took a sip of his coffee, before replacing the delicate white cup on its saucer with agonising slowness.

"A girl. Tara. She was born on July the seventh."

Gabriel sat back in his chair, trying to fit the latest piece into the increasingly complex and sad puzzle of his family. *A sister. I had a sister. Or is she still alive? Do I have a sister?*

"Do you have any of my parents' papers? My dad's British solicitor handled the wills – I never thought to ask if they still retained a lawyer here when I heard they'd died."

"Indeed I do. Your father was a most precise and well-organised man. He told me a month or so before they left for England that he was transferring most of their legal business to a London firm. Understandable, of course, and I wished him well. But he was adamant that one set of documents should remain in Hong Kong. The papers relating to Tara."

Gabriel felt a squirt of adrenaline fizz into life in the pit of his stomach.

"And you still have them? In an archive or something?"

Chang shook his head.

"Better. They are here. In this office. I'll get them for you."

The lawyer stood and crossed the room to a row of polished wooden filing cabinets. He pulled one end of the watch chain from his waistcoat pocket and selected a key from a ring secured with a gold spring-clip. He unlocked the rightmost cabinet and crouched in front of the bottom drawer. Elegant fingers walked over the tops of the hanging file dividers, their owner humming.

"Here we are!" he said, selecting one. He reached towards the back of the drawer and withdrew a grey steel petty cash tin, then stood and turned to Gabriel.

Despite his excitement Gabriel had time to notice the ease with which the older man straightened from a bent-kneed position in a smooth movement. No cracking of joints, hand in the small of the back, old man's grunt of pain. *Yoga?* He wondered. *Tai chi?* Chang brought the folder and tin over to the desk and placed them reverently in front of Gabriel.

"Your father instructed me to hand these to you or Tara, should either one of you present yourselves here."

He unclipped a second, tiny key from his watch chain and unlocked the tin box before sliding it across to Gabriel, along with the folder.

Gabriel lifted the front cover, his gaze falling on an envelope. White, slim, marked in his father's neat handwriting for his – Gabriel's – attention. The room and its other occupant faded from his vision as he turned the envelope over and slit the flap with his thumbnail.

17

Just a few blocks to the east, in his office at Ophelia Tsang & Partners, Nesbitt leaned back in his chair and rolled his head from side to side. He did not enjoy the series of cracks emitted by the joints in his spine. He dug the tips of his fingers into the muscles each side of his neck and attempted to massage away some of the tension.

His employers were old fashioned and believed that people worked best when they had some peace, quiet and privacy. It seemed a rare outlook nowadays, judging by the stories his friends told of football-pitch-sized open-plan offices, humming with hundreds of conversations, ringing phones, clicking keyboards and the endless comings and goings when you put that many human beings together in one place.

The law firm's outlook, old fashioned, perhaps, meant he had his own office. Not as large as those enjoyed by the partners in the firm, but more than enough for his needs. In his line of work, he often needed to have the sorts of conversations best not overheard by junior lawyers, secretaries or people from the post room, or the firm responsible for keeping the indoor plants fed and watered.

In front of him lay a file of printed-out emails. In a code so simple a child could understand it, two executives from a local bank were discussing the bribing of an official within the Innovation and Technology Bureau. He sighed at their mixture of stupidity, corruption and greed. Then his phone rang.

He smiled.

"Hello, Chrissie. How are you?"

"Fine, Peter, thank you. And you?"

The lump is bigger, I'm sure of it.

"Oh, you know, fine. Overworked, but fine. So do you have something for me?"

"John Li. Retired detective sergeant with the RHKPF. Living in Kowloon. He worked on the case and he's happy to talk to you. It's his 'one that got away'."

She gave him the phone number and address of the retired cop, which he wrote down on one of the firm's branded notepads.

"Thank you, Chrissie. I owe you one. I've been asking around about this British cop, by the way. Nothing yet, but I'll keep on it."

He called Li's number. The ex-cop answered almost at once.

Nesbitt gave him a rehearsed speech.

"Mr Li. My name is Peter Nesbitt. I'm an investigator at Ophelia Tsang & Partners. One of our clients is looking into the disappearance of Tara Wolfe. I believe you worked the case. Could I come to see you? As soon as possible?"

"Give me your number please."

Nesbitt did as Li asked and ended the call. *Smart man.*

The reception desk called his phone a minute or so later.

"Peter, I have a John Li on the phone for you. He said you'd know what it's about."

"Thanks, Wen-wen. Put him through, please." The line clicked. "Mr Li. Thank you for calling back."

"I had to check you out first. Just to be sure. So, what did you want to see me about?"

"I'd prefer to tell you in person. Are you doing anything today?"

"It's my day off, as it happens. You can come round now, if you like."

Li gave his address in Kowloon and they agreed to meet in an hour's time.

———

Nesbitt arrived in Kowloon at 10.45 a.m. – fifteen minutes early for his meeting with Li. He left his Toyota in a car park on the junction of Heng Lam and Fung Mo Streets. The temperature had soared since he'd climbed inside his air-conditioned car and as soon as he reached the street, sweat broke out on his forehead. He took off his jacket and slung it over his shoulder.

The walk to Li's apartment would only take a couple of minutes, so Nesbitt climbed a flight of gleaming white stone steps to the football field opposite the car park and found a park bench in front of a tree smothered in white blossoms. He sat and watched as a rowdy group of schoolchildren raced around after a ball. *Like a swarm of bees*, he thought. *You need to spread out.*

Without warning, pain blossomed low in his abdomen and he gasped at its intensity, doubling over. He reached instinctively for his groin then stayed his hand, realising how such an innocent gesture might be mistaken this close to children.

"Excuse me, sir, are you all right?" someone asked him in Chinese-accented English.

The voice belonged to a young woman, dressed casually in jeans and a bright-yellow shirt. A silver whistle dangled from her neck on a royal-blue lanyard. *A teacher?* he wondered. She was bending over him, her brow creased with concern.

"I'm fine," he managed to grunt. "Indigestion. Too much to eat at breakfast."

"You don't look fine. You are very pale."

Then she surprised him by placing the back of her hand on his forehead.

"I'm fine, really," he said. *I'm absolutely not fine. I wish someone would take care of me.*

"OK. Well, if you're sure?"

The pain vanished as suddenly as it had arrived. Nesbitt straightened and managed a half-smile.

"Thanks. I'm OK. That'll teach me to eat too fast, won't it?"

Smiling and nodding, the young woman ran back to her charges, who were engaged in a noisy but apparently good-natured argument about a throw-in.

Nesbitt sighed, resolving to tell his wife of his worries that evening. He reviewed the questions he wanted to ask John Li. He'd done a little bit of cold-case work before leaving the Force and knew how tenuous the threads were connecting the past to the present. But on the other hand, DNA technology had advanced so far and so fast that victims and their killers could be identified from the tiniest traces of body fluids or skin cells on exhibits left to sit in evidence lockers for decades. And maybe Li would have held onto his files in the case of the kidnapping of Tara Wolfe. What had Chrissie said, "this was his 'one that got away'?" Time would tell.

He waited a few more minutes, then rose from the bench. He held himself taut, expecting a second burst of pain. It didn't arrive, and he reached the foot of the flight of steps feeling optimistic, about the case and about his health.

Li's apartment was on the fifteenth floor. Nesbitt pressed the button to call the lift. There had been a time when he would have taken the stairs, chosen them deliberately: a matter of personal discipline. He'd always been a fit man, turning out regularly for the Force's rugby team, and had strenuously avoided acquiring the look of so many of his former colleagues. Soft, round in the middle, a double chin, cheeks flushed from too much whisky: the trio of symptoms that said "overworked cop" the world over and which, sadly, led to so many of their owners waking up in emergency rooms after their overstressed hearts had decided they needed a timeout.

Emerging from the lift car, which smelled strongly of floral disinfectant, Nesbitt checked the signs on the opposite wall and turned left.

Li's front door was decorated with the Chinese character for

"Peace", rendered in flowing strokes of gold paint. He rang the bell. The man who opened the door was smiling. He was a head shorter than Nesbit, with plenty of silver mixed into the dark hair he wore in a Western cut, parted on the left.

"Peter?" he asked, extending a hand.

"John. Thanks for agreeing to meet me."

"Come in. You know it's no bother. Managing security for a local supermarket chain, well, it's not exactly testing. Coffee?"

"Please. Milk, two sugars."

With mugs of coffee in hand, the two men sat opposite each other in Li's spacious sitting room. The wall opposite the large picture window was lined with reddish-brown wooden shelves, and Nesbitt cast a professional eye over the knick-knacks and framed photos interspersed among the books. He pointed to one that showed Li with an attractive woman perhaps ten years his junior and two laughing children, a boy and a girl, somewhere in their mid-teens.

"Your family?"

Li looked at the picture.

"My wife, Margie, and our children. Leng is sixteen. She wants to be a cop like her daddy. Xan is fourteen. Apparently he's going to make his fortune as an e-gamer. You know what that is?"

Nesbitt shook his head.

"I'm guessing, something to do with computers?"

Li nodded.

"They play computer games, OK? In teams. And they're televised. Or livestreamed or whatever the kids do these days. There's sponsorship money, massive cash prizes, fan clubs. I tell you, Peter, it's a different world out there. I can barely keep up."

Nesbitt laughed, liking this retired cop instinctively. He took another sip of the excellent coffee. *Time to get serious.*

"Do you mind if we get straight to it? Chrissie told me you worked on the kidnapping of Tara Wolfe. I'm working for her brother, trying to find out what happened, see if she's still alive. You know, either closure if the poor wee thing's dead or a chance of happiness if she's alive."

Li put his mug down on the table between them. His face lost its good-humoured expression.

"That's right. The parents reported her missing on returning from a diplomatic drinks reception. About half-past eleven. They came home, and the mother, Mrs Wolfe, went upstairs to check on her children. She discovered the baby was gone and called the police. I got there about eleven forty-five. They were both worried but she was frantic. Kept screaming, 'You have to find her, you have to find my baby,' over and over again."

"What about the husband?"

"He had the training, you know? British reserve. Stiff upper lip. I think he thought he needed to stay calm so his wife didn't completely lose it."

As Li continued his narrative, Nesbitt recognised the symptoms. A cop unable to let go of the case that, for good or ill, had defined his career. Not necessarily by the official measure, but by his own lights. Whether a moral crusade or a psychological attachment to the victim or the perpetrator, cases like these never released a cop from their claws. Li's eyes drifted upwards. He wasn't remembering what happened – he was reliving it. Nesbitt pulled out a notebook and jotted down points as Li made them.

"By midnight, we had scene of crime staff inspecting every square inch of the house. The inside guys came up empty-handed. No fingerprints other than those belonging to the Wolfes, adult and child, and the staff. No hairs or skin cells."

Li explained that as the detective sergeant in charge of the initial investigation, he'd quickly determined that the method of entry used by the kidnappers was via the back fence and the trellis to the right of the nursery window. Once lights had been rigged up in the garden, a crime scene investigator discovered a minute scrap of black cotton fabric snagged on a sharp twig of the wisteria. DNA testing not existing in the colony at the time, the scrap was bagged, registered in the evidence locker and, eventually, forgotten.

"How about the ransom note?" Nesbitt asked.

Li nodded his head.

"It arrived in a most unorthodox fashion. They wrapped it

round the shaft of a crossbow bolt and shot it into the front door while I was talking to the Wolfes about who they thought might have a motive to kidnap their baby daughter. Whoever wrote it was taking no chances. The note was output from a dot-matrix printer. You know, that green-and-white lined computer printout paper that folds back on itself. We had it tested but, apart from the text, it was clean."

Nesbitt ran a hand over his jaw. Sighed, puffed out his cheeks. He knew the British Government had always had an unbending rule as regards ransom demands. *We don't negotiate with kidnappers.*

"What happened next? Did they raise the money?"

"To tell you the truth, I'm not exactly sure. We knew the British Government, Mr Wolfe's employer, would never pay up. We advised him to let us do our job. The island was a tight-knit community back then – no real interference from the Chinese. We were sure we'd hear something from one of our informants. Mr Wolfe more or less dismissed us out of hand.

"He said, and I remember his words so clearly, as if it was yesterday, 'John, they have my daughter. If I have to rob the Hongkong and Shanghai Banking Corporation to get the money, I'll do it.' I heard rumours that the Wolfes were trying to raise the money privately, against our advice, but he shut me out.

"The end of the story is very sad. They did get the money, though he never told me how. But the kidnappers never responded to his message. We searched and searched, kept trying new angles, but eventually the trail just went cold. Dead. I got transferred to the robbery squad and that was that. I kept copies of all the files. You know, copper's habit, couldn't let it go, but I never got so much as a sniff of what happened to Tara."

He spread his hands wide.

"That's all I have. You're welcome to look at the files. Borrow them, if you like."

"Thanks. I might just do that. Don't worry, I'll keep them under lock and key."

"Oh, it's probably best if I never see them again. Margie would be pleased. Says I'm obsessed with my 'Little English baby'."

"She not in today?"

"Playing tennis with her girlfriends. Ha! Can you believe that? Four women in their sixties and they call each other their girlfriends?"

Nesbitt grinned.

"Rosemary's just the same. Though with her it's swimming. Up and down they go, nattering away nineteen to the dozen. I tell her the only part of her that's getting any proper exercise is her lower jaw."

Li laughed.

"How does she take that?"

"Tells me to mind how I speak to the woman who cooks, cleans and irons for me. Says there's plenty of men who'd be grateful for the company of a woman in such good shape for her age."

Li shook his head, getting to his feet.

"Let me get those files for you."

He returned five minutes later with a large cardboard carton packed with folders.

"Take care of it. And please let me know if you discover anything. Oh," he added, as Nesbitt got up to leave, "one more thing. My partner at the time, Jack Yates. He retired and moved back to the UK. I'm afraid we lost touch so I don't have his address. He's in the files, though."

———

Back at his office, Nesbitt made himself a cup of coffee and opened the flaps of the carton. He lifted out the top folder and began to read. He stopped almost at once to text Gabriel with a brief outline of this new lead. A promising lead, in his opinion.

18

Ignoring a buzz from his phone, Gabriel pulled the folded sheets of notepaper clear and unfolded them. His heart was pounding as he flattened them on the desk, then picked up his father's letter and began to read.

Dear Gabriel,

I can only imagine how you must be feeling, reading this.

Your mother and I are both dead, and I'm sorry for the pain you must have felt losing us.

Although I can't be sure, I hope, and at the same time fear, that you have, by now, discovered what happened to Michael. If not directly, then from Zhao Xi. I want you to know that it was not your fault. It wasn't your mother's either. She was ill, please understand that. Which brings me to the matter at hand.

Your sister, Tara, was born on 7th July 1983 and taken from our house in Hong Kong on 16th December that same year. Kidnapped. We received a ransom demand, and I was eventually able to raise the funds. But we never heard from the kidnappers again. We had no way to make the exchange and get Tara back.

The police investigated but came up empty-handed. They said it might have been a triad but ultimately could prove nothing. When they told us they were scaling back their investigation, I'm afraid we each, in our own way, handled it badly. I retreated further into my work. Your mother suffered another of the nervous collapses that were to mark the rest of her life. Her battle with alcohol raged and I regret to say that I was unable to offer her the help and support I should have done. We both neglected you, and, later, Michael. Your troubles at school, I attribute directly to the cataclysm that tore our family apart.

Your poor mother. She drank to numb the resurgent pain she felt at the knowledge that her precious Tara, so far from being dead, might actually be alive. Alive, but far, far beyond reach, somewhere in that vast, impenetrable, unknowable landmass everyone called, simply, The Mainland.

We never spoke of Tara again, to each other or to you and Michael, burying our brief memories of her under mountains of paperwork and at the bottom of lakes of alcohol. You quickly forgot, as the very young do, that you had ever had a sister.

I handed all the official documents recording Tara's brief stay on earth to John Chang for safekeeping. My instructions to him were simple, and unequivocal. I remember what I said to him word for painful word:

"This stays out of sight, hidden and unmentioned unless or until one of our children comes asking for it. Then, and only then, you can release it into their custody on receipt of sufficient proof of their true identity."

Handling matters as quietly and as sympathetically as I could, including extremely generous settlement payments that went far beyond the customs of the island at the time, let alone its employment laws, I fired our household staff. As I handed them their severance packages in plain white envelopes, I asked them to respect our wishes by not talking, ever, of what had happened. In time, I replaced them with newcomers to the island who knew nothing of our family beyond the bare minimum necessary for them to carry out their duties.

We told anyone who asked after Tara that we'd sent her back to England to stay with her grandparents. She was sickly and we felt the British climate and British doctors would be better for her health. In time we intended to return home to reunite our family. Diplomats and army officers often sent their children to boarding schools in the UK, so our decision, on its face, was not beyond the realms of experience, even though Tara was just a baby.

Under the influence of this far-reaching conspiracy of silence, memories on the island of Tara's brief existence faded quickly, then winked out. Except for me *and your mother. As I believe you must know by now, if you are reading this letter, tragedy struck again a few years later. But by then your mother had descended fully into alcoholism, and I, I am sad to say, had become a remote father in the classic British mould, my emotions ossified and replaced by an unbending insistence on duty, obedience and self-discipline.*

I do not – cannot – know whether, as you read this, Tara is alive. I pray that she is, and that you will find her. John will offer you such help as he is able.

Gabriel, my son, we fought a great deal when you were growing up. I know your decision to join the Army was made, in part, to spite me. I deserved it. I was unable, or perhaps unwilling, to invest in you emotionally.

Please forgive me. I love you. I always did.

Your father,

Gerald Wolfe

His father's signature blurred. Gabriel struggled to focus and realised his eyes had misted with tears. He swiped a hand across them and stared at the paper in front of him. He looked up. Chang was making a great show of studying a document that had materialised in front of him while Gabriel had been reading. Swallowing in an attempt to dislodge the lump in his throat, Gabriel spoke, stumbling over the first few words and starting again.

"Can I keep this?"

Chang looked up. Laid his pen aside.

"It is yours, Gabriel. Of course you may keep it. As you may the rest of the file. Please, look."

Gabriel turned his attention to the other, scant, contents of the blue cardboard folder. A birth certificate. The results of a newborn heel prick test. A report from a health visitor stating that Tara was in excellent health, in the sixty-eighth percentile for weight and sixtieth for height, and was feeding well. The results of a hearing test, which showed Tara had excellent scores for both ears. And a sheet of computer printout, smoothed out but obviously tightly rolled at some point.

He opened it out and spread it out on the desk. As he read the opening paragraph, he could feel the anger banked up inside him threatening to burst free, as it had done on the night-time streets of Shoreditch. In the prison yard at Red Dog. And at Max Novgorodsky's dacha.

We have your daughter, Tara. She is safe, warm, well-fed and clean. And so she will remain. She has a birthmark on her left shoulder: pink, like a strawberry.

Grinding his jaw, he read on.

We require HK$1,000,000 for her safe return. You have two weeks to get the money.
When you are ready, place ad in South China Morning Post lonely hearts section. Text to read Queen Victoria looking for her Prince Albert.
Instructions for exchange will follow same day.
WARNING! Do not go to the media. One article, one line in the press, and she dies.

Gabriel laid it carefully to one side, battling an impulse to tear it to pieces with his teeth. The final item in the folder, enclosed in a clear acetate envelope, was a yellowing piece of newsprint about four inches by six. In the centre, among small ads for bicycles and fresh eggs, was the ad demanded by the kidnappers.

> Queen Victoria looking for her Prince Albert.

Shaking his head, he closed the folder, pulled the cash tin

towards him and turned the key. One by one he removed the items inside and laid them out on the desk in a straight-edged mosaic of his lost sister's early history.

Red envelopes decorated with gold Chinese characters for wealth, long life and happiness and containing bank notes. Christening cards. Two small, red-leather-covered boxes, one containing a silver horse on a fine chain, the other a solid silver rabbit, maybe an inch from nose to tail. And a photograph.

Gabriel picked it up. The photo was a professional studio shot, with a swirling cream background. A little boy, a toddler, really, dark-haired, wearing dark-blue corduroys and a white cricket jumper with a blue stripe round the V-neck, had his arms around a baby in a white babygro, a pink ribbon tied around her forelock, which was dark like her brother's hair. He stared at his sister's face. She had big, round, dark eyes and a little rosebud of a mouth. He replaced the contents of the tin box and locked it. Chang spoke.

"Your father asked me to offer you my help in finding your sister." He spread his hands wide. "He was a good friend as well as my client. You have only to ask. I will do anything and everything in my power."

"Thank you. I think I need some time to process all of this. It's a lot to take in."

"Of course, of course. Let me give you my card and I'll just –" Chang scribbled on the back of the stiff white business card, "– add my home number. Any time of the day or night, Gabriel, please call me if you need me."

———

Back on the street, Gabriel looked around as if Hong Kong were an alien planet, not the place where he had grown up. All the old certainties were falling away from him, leaving him feeling naked and exposed. Fang Jian had known Master Zhao. Maybe he had known his father and mother as well. Maybe he could shed some light on the location of the kidnappers, or if they were dead, their paymasters. This was a triad crime. Fang was a triad boss. His phone buzzed. He looked down. *Speak of the devil.*

Be outside Golden Dragon at 6.00 a.m. day after tomorrow. Transport ready. All kit ready.

He returned to the house and created a new document on his laptop.

Tara Wolfe
    Personal profile/history:
    Born 7th July 1983
    Kidnapped 16th December 1983
    Brown hair.
    Brown eyes.

Perpetrators???

Gabriel's fingers hovered over the keyboard. He desperately wanted to be able to add more information, but apart from the infant Tara's height, weight and hearing scores, he had nothing.

    Gabriel checked his messages. A text from Nesbitt.

Retired RHKP cop Jack Yates. Worked case. Now in UK. More when we meet.

He texted back.

Brilliant. Thx.

And an email from Chow. Her progress report. Knowing now

that she wouldn't have found anything in the back issues of any of the island's papers, he opened the email with a heavy heart.

Hi Gabriel,
I came up empty on the papers. Maybe they declared a news
blackout? I don't know. I could look into it if you want me to.
It's not all bad news, though. In fact, it's really good news. I found
an expat website with a forum. One of the posts linked to a
database of current and former diplomatic staff. From there, I
followed a link to a blog owned by this young Hong Konger, pen
name, Bobby.
He's been tracing his family tree, doing research, all that, and his
grandmother worked for your parents. Her name is Ying Ruo.
She's 80 now, but when she was 44, they hired her as a nanny.
I contacted Bobby, asking if I could meet his granny. I haven't
heard back yet but it's promising, right?
Shall I keep going?
Kind regards,
Sarah

Gabriel tapped out a quick reply.

Hi Sarah,
Amazing! Good work. Don't worry about the SCMP or other
papers. But yes, keep on with Mrs Ying. I have to leave HK for a
while. I'll call you when I get back.
Regards,
G

He tapped Send and, a minute or so later, the program pinged again.

Hi,
OK, cool. I'm on it. Are you OK with fees if I keep working on this?
KR,
S

Gabriel's fingers darted over the keys.

Yes. Money no problem.

He went inside to change. Time was against him, but he wanted to see Fang again before leaving for the mainland and his appointment with the murderous Colonel Na.

19

Sarah Chow climbed the stairs in a cheaply-made apartment building in Kowloon. The stairwell smelled of cat urine and boiled chicken. She wrinkled her nose, trying to breathe as shallowly as possible through her mouth, as she climbed to the eleventh floor.

Earlier, she'd taken a call from the young blogger, whose real name was Tan Bo. He'd told her his grandmother would be delighted to answer questions, especially if she took some cakes as the old lady had a very sweet tooth.

Arriving outside the front door, which was painted, like all the others, in an extremely thick coat of shiny red paint, Chow paused to catch her breath. She had to remove her glasses and wipe them clear of condensation where the heat from her forehead had misted up the lenses.

Before ringing the doorbell, she performed a sequence of exercises taught to her by her professor of journalism as a way to build confidence before interviewing a contact. She shook her head, squared her shoulders, straightened her back and huffed out a sharp little sigh.

"Hah!"

She rang the doorbell and waited. After a minute or so, she rang again, and knocked three times on the glossy painted door for good measure.

"Yes, yes, yes, I'm coming! These old legs don't work as well as they used to."

The voice was high-pitched and roughened by smoking. Chow knew it well, as a type rather than the individual owner. Elderly Hong Kongers who'd enjoyed smoking and drinking their entire lives and, if not felled by emphysema, lung cancer or heart disease, seemed to go on for decades after their peers had shuffled off the mortal coil.

The door swung inwards. Facing her was a brown-skinned old woman with grey hair scraped back into a bun, deep-set eyes twinkling from behind large circular glasses framed in red plastic. Her face was liver-spotted, with high cheekbones and a wrinkled mouth that even now was clamped around a half-smoked cigarette.

Chow held out the bag she'd bought from the bakery that morning.

"Hello, Mrs Ying. I'm Sarah Chow. I've brought you these."

Mrs Ying took the proffered bag of cakes and weighed it in her hand. Her expression broadened from a small social smile into a full-blown grin, revealing a few brown teeth and a great many gaps.

"Thank you, Sarah. Come in, come in."

Once the old lady had made tea and arranged the delicate little coconut buns on a plate, Chow took out her notebook.

"Hey, what are you doing?" Mrs Ying asked, pointing at the notebook.

Chow smiled and showed her the blank page, at the top of which she'd already written, *Interview with Mrs Ying Ruo*.

"Just so I can get your answers down correctly," she said.

"You won't show the authorities?"

Chow shook her head.

"Absolutely not. This is just for me."

Seemingly mollified, Mrs Ying took a bite out of one of the buns and washed it down with a slurp of tea.

"Mmm. Very good. Thank you, my dear. Now, what did you want to ask me about? Bo was a bit vague."

"I'm doing some research into a British family who lived here in the eighties. The Wolfes."

Mrs Ying's eyes widened, so that the crow's feet showed white as the wrinkles opened up in her tobacco-brown cheeks.

"Oh, yes! I was their nanny from, ooh, 1984 to 1986. He was such a lovely man, Mr Wolfe. Such beautiful manners." She sniffed. "She wasn't so nice, though. Treated us all like dirt. Drank, too. Lots of drink. Their poor little boy."

Chow made a note.

"Gabriel?"

Mrs Ying grinned.

"Oh, he was a terror, all right. A very cheeky little monkey. But sweet, too. He just wanted someone to play with."

Mrs Ying shared a couple of stories about Gabriel before Chow could steer her back towards the missing baby.

"Can you tell me about the time just after you started working for them?"

"They hired me in the January. All new servants – we started in the same week. Gabriel was four at the time. A real little handful. It was odd, though. I heard they had a baby as well. But they'd sent it back to England. For health reasons. But that's too young, don't you think? To send a baby away? I mean, I know the British are funny with children, but even so."

Chow shrugged. Made another note.

"He was a diplomat, is that right?"

Mrs Ying beamed and nodded.

"Oh yes. A very important man. Tall. Very handsome. Always beautifully dressed. Such lovely suits. Always a handkerchief in the top pocket. Polished shoes."

"Did you ever hear what was wrong with the baby? Why she had to go back to England?"

"Did I say she was a girl? Who told you that?"

Shit! She's sharper than she looks.

"Just a guess," Chow said, smiling and pushing the plate of coconut buns a little closer.

Mrs Ying took another cake and bit into it.

"Well, no they didn't. Tell me, I mean. But one thing I did hear from a friend. You see, her daughter used to work for the Wolfes in the kitchen. She told her mother, that's my friend, you follow me?" Sarah nodded. "She told her that the baby, Tara, her name was, well, she wasn't sent back to England at all. *They* took her."

"Who took her?"

Mrs Ying leaned closer.

"Triads," she hissed. "Very bad men. They kidnapped Tara to get a ransom. But even when the Wolfes got the money, they never gave the baby back."

Chow nodded, noting down in shorthand every word Mrs Ying said. Her heart was beating faster with each sentence.

"Did she say which triad was responsible?"

"Yes, she did. The Four-Point Star triad. Her nephew worked for them. An accountant. Such a clever boy."

"He didn't tell her their names, did he?"

"Whose names?"

"The kidnappers."

"No. He just worked in an office."

Chow asked a few more questions but Mrs Ying had nothing further to add.

20

Later that evening, Gabriel returned to the Golden Dragon. He had a question or two for Fang. The contrast between the interior of the Golden Dragon now, halfway through the evening, and Gabriel's earlier visit, couldn't have been starker.

The sepulchral silence had been replaced with a lively buzz from the full gambling tables, milling spectators and drinkers at the bar. There were plenty of westerners among the Chinese at the card, craps and roulette tables and, in his simply cut, shawl-collared dinner jacket, he felt better camouflaged than he'd done on many a lurk.

The same bartender was on duty and he smiled when he saw Gabriel.

"Your usual, sir?"

"Please."

With the cocktail in hand, Gabriel went in search of Fang. He was easy to spot. His gold dinner jacket blazed like a beacon and even a blind man would have been able to locate him, just by homing in on that bellowing laugh. As Gabriel watched, a tall, thin man, his bald head gleaming in the light from the many chandeliers, approached Fang. Their heads were inclined towards each other and the bald man's lips were moving.

Gabriel made his way towards the gangster and his companion, catching movement in his peripheral vision as he did so.

As before, his way was barred by one of the "lotus blossoms". He recognised Wei Mei at once.

"Was there something you wanted?"

"I need to speak to Jian. He's over there," he added, nodding in Fang's direction.

On an impulse he put his hand out to touch her arm as she turned to leave.

She spun round to face him. Quickly, he dropped his hand.

"What is it?" she asked.

"Can I ask you a question?"

"OK."

"Is it ever permissible to change your triad allegiance? Say, one day you're a member of the Four-Point Star and the next the White Koi?"

She lowered her voice.

"Once you are initiated, no. Then your life is given to your triad. If you tried to leave, you would be killed. But for 49ers or Blue Lanterns – they are uninitiated, just street thugs, really – yes. You could do business with a member of another triad, leave, or join another triad and nobody would really care. Why are you asking?"

"Just research. I'm thinking of writing a book."

"OK," she said.

Her scepticism was plain to see in every muscle of her face. She lowered her head in a half-bow, then left. Gabriel was within ten feet of Fang when he turned. Seeing Gabriel, Fang beamed at him and strode over.

"Wolfe Cub! Here to try your luck?"

"Not tonight. I want to save it all up for my trip. But I wanted to ask you something."

"Ask away, ask away!" the big man said, slinging a heavy arm across Gabriel's shoulders. He gestured at Gabriel's glass. "Drink?"

"Yes, please."

"Come, then. Let's get a bottle and find a nice quiet table."

Fang led Gabriel to a table at the back of the room on a screened-off dais. With champagne – more Louis Roederer Cristal – poured into flutes, Fang took a healthy swig, belched, as was his custom and folded his arms across his chest.

"So. What was it you wanted to ask me?"

Gabriel had decided to try an oblique angle, rather than hitting Fang for hard intel straight away.

"You remember when I came to see you here for the first time? With Master Zhao?"

"Of course! Such a loss when that bitch killed him."

"Yes. Though I paid her out for what she did. I'm looking for someone who may have worked for one of your rivals in the early eighties. I just wondered, if I had a name you might know how I could get hold of him."

Fang's eyes, already little more than slits in his fleshy face, narrowed further. He drank off his glass and took his time refilling it. Gabriel waited. *What are you playing at, Fang? Why the delaying tactics?*

"Maybe. But that was a long time ago. I don't keep a database of rival outfits and their underlings. Why do you want to know about this man? What is he to you?"

Gabriel paused before answering. Maybe the direct route would be better.

"He kidnapped my sister. She was never returned. I'm trying to find out what happened to her."

Fang shook his head and reached for his glass again, taking his time.

"Triad people come and go. I myself was not even in Hong Kong in the early eighties. I was living in San Francisco. And you will appreciate, I can hardly go and ask my business rivals for a quick look at their historic staff records."

Fang smiled as he delivered this line, but the expression didn't reach his eyes, and the laugh was noticeably absent.

Gabriel shrugged, and finished his own champagne.

"So you don't know anything about the kidnappers?"

Fang fixed Gabriel with a stare. When he spoke, it was in a low tone Gabriel hadn't heard him use before.

"You know, so far our relationship has been conducted on cordial terms. Zhao Xi introduced you as his ward, and as he was an old friend I accepted you as a new one. But you must not presume too far on my kindly nature. Men have met with untimely ends for questioning me as you just did."

Gabriel shrugged and smiled.

"Well, it was worth a try. Thanks for giving me your time. I'll let you get back to your customers."

Fang spread his hands wide in an expansive gesture and smiled.

"Any time, Wolfe Cub. Any time."

They stood and shook hands. Then Fang headed into the centre of the floor where a glamorous Chinese couple in their sixties were attracting a crowd of onlookers.

Gabriel made his way towards the doors when a familiar face brought him to a stop. Valerie Duggan was sitting at the bar stirring a green plastic cocktail stick in a martini. This evening she was wearing a narrow-lapelled black jacket over a white silk blouse and tailored trousers, a stylish riff on a man's dinner suit. Gabriel experienced a flashback. Sasha Beck. Dressed almost identically. There to kill him. On an impulse he changed course and went over to join her. She'd placed a handbag – black patent leather on a gold chain – on the neighbouring bar stool, but when she saw him threading his way through the crowd, she smiled and lifted it clear.

"Well, well," she said without preamble as he sat beside her. "If it isn't Fang Jian's little friend!"

"Hello, Valerie," he answered. "Not so much of the little, thanks."

She patted his forearm and winked.

"Oh, I'm sure you're big where it matters. How about a drink?"

"A quick one, yes. I have to be up early tomorrow."

"Client meeting?"

"Something like that."

She rolled her eyes.

"Ooh! Big secret! What, are you buying your way into this place, then?"

He shook his head, just as the barman arrived. Gabriel ordered a martini and a second for Valerie, who'd just polished off her own drink, tipping the glass up and letting the last few drops fall onto her tongue.

"I have some business on the mainland," he said as their drinks arrived. "Cheers."

She clinked rims with him.

"Bottoms up. So tell me. How did your meeting with our Mister Fang go yesterday?"

"Fine. And when you say 'our' Mister Fang ..."

"Oh, nothing. But you must know what they say about him. That he's a triad boss. Don't you find that exciting? Or do you like your excitement a little more, what shall I say, physical?"

Gabriel sipped his cocktail, buying time. Thinking. And what he mainly thought was, *You're fishing. You're too alert. You've been casing this place. You're not in telecoms, are you?*

"You're not in telecoms, are you?"

She drew her head back and frowned, fingering the pearls at her throat.

"Yeah, I am. I'm the sales director for a fibre optics and undersea cabling solutions provider called—"

"That's a great legend but I don't buy it."

She frowned.

"A, what did you say, a legend? What do you mean?"

"You're very good. But I'm afraid I'm better." On a whim he decided to lie. Just a little. "I had you checked out. Thoroughly. Immigration. Police databases. The works. So, who are you really, Valerie?"

She leaned towards him. He caught another whiff of her perfume.

"Tell me, what are the top three hot issues for HR consultants these days?"

He smiled and finished his drink.

"There's only ever one, isn't there? People."

"Smart boy. You're right. I have to go. See you around."

She uncrossed her legs with a hiss of nylon and made her way towards the exit. Gabriel watched her go, then noticed something. He wasn't the only one.

Three young men, late twenties he estimated, dressed in black suits, shirts and ties, had detached themselves from the group clustered round the swanky Chinese couple and were following Duggan to the door.

She seemed oblivious to the fact she'd picked up a tail. *Unsurprising if you're in telecoms. Odd if you're something else.* He slid forwards off his barstool, finished his drink and threaded his way after the last of the three black-clad men.

Once outside, Gabriel looked both ways along Wyndham Street, searching for Duggan. He hoped she'd jumped in a cab. He turned to the doorman.

"The western woman who just left, fortyish, glamorous, blonde. Which way did she go?"

Wordlessly, the doorman pointed. Gabriel set off at a run, and after a hundred yards saw the three men arrive at the back of a knot of American tourists, then barge their way through, to cries of indignation.

Gabriel ran into the road, skirting the group altogether, though earning himself a blast on the horn from an oncoming taxi.

On the far side of the tourists he caught his first glimpse of Duggan since leaving The Golden Dragon. Her pursuers were almost upon her and one, he could see, had drawn a knife. They were wearing black plimsolls, the rubber soles silent as they closed with their victim.

This end of the street was much quieter than the stretch outside the casino, and the men clearly felt this was their moment to strike. Gabriel was too far back to intervene so he took the only other course of action open to him while he sprinted on.

"Valerie! Look out!" he yelled.

She spun round at the sound of his voice, as did two of the men.

Not the knife-wielder though. He closed in on the unsuspecting telecoms executive.

In the slowed-down combat-time it took Gabriel to reach the small group, he watched as the knifeman went in for the kill.

The blade, glinting neon red and blue along its shining length, was travelling upwards, in a direct line that would take it under Duggan's lower ribs and up, into her heart.

It was a professional's strike, and would sever the thoracic aorta or carve a hole in one of the chambers of her heart. Either way, she was a dead woman.

21

The knife swung out wide to the right. Duggan's varnished nails were digging deep into the unprotected soft tissue of the man's inner wrist.

She held his arm out straight, then delivered a straight-fingered jab with her right hand directly into the vulnerable spot just below his Adam's apple.

Gabriel heard the hooting cough as the thug's airway collapsed. He reached the quartet a second later. Duggan stamped down on the fallen man's left thigh with her stiletto heel, drawing a high-pitched scream from his damaged throat.

Gabriel focused on the other two, who had turned to face him as he shouted his warning. Each had a knife in his right hand and were spreading out as they came for him, knees bent, weight on the balls of their feet: fighters' stances.

But it was two against two, better than evens as far as Gabriel was concerned. Especially given the vicious fighting technique he'd just seen from Duggan.

As the first blade came in he dodged to the right, grabbed the incoming wrist and jerked it down and across his body, pulling the man's face into line with his upthrusting knee, which caught him on the point of the chin and dropped him to the pavement.

In the corner of his eye he caught the flash of a second blade: more rainbow neon reflecting from the shop signs and electronic billboards above them.

He danced out of range, leaned back and shot his right foot out, catching the man's knife-arm and sending the weapon skittering into the road.

The man grinned as he advanced on Gabriel, hands hardened into blades.

Then his eyes bulged and his hands went to his throat, scrabbling at Valerie's arm, which she was tightening remorselessly around his airway. Gabriel lunged forwards and punched him in the solar plexus.

No fighter has the wind to survive a properly delivered blow to this nerve-rich anatomical feature. Valerie released her grip and the man crumpled, hands clutching his belly. Gabriel drew back his foot and kicked hard at the left temple.

He looked up. Duggan was breathing heavily as she turned to survey the remains of their attackers. Three comatose gangsters, limbs splayed like dropped puppets. She bent and picked up the two remaining knives and slipped them into her handbag.

"Come with me," she said. "Now."

It was the tone of command. And not the sorts of commands issued by telecoms executives, either. From start to finish, the fight had taken less than ten seconds. As time sped up again, Gabriel realised cops would be on their way. Even on a quiet street, someone would have seen something and made the call.

Together, they ran for a cross-street, the click of Duggan's heels sounding a trebly counterpoint to the deeper noise of Gabriel's handmade brogues. A taxi had just turned its For Hire light on. Duggan raised two fingers to her lips and whistled it down.

The piercing noise was loud enough to draw stares from a group of partygoers fifty yards away.

She yanked the door open and slid across the rear seat. Gabriel climbed in after her.

"Get going!" she ordered the driver as Gabriel slammed the door.

Her tone had the same effect on the cab driver as it had done on Gabriel. He peeled away from the kerb and only asked for a destination when they had travelled across the junction.

"Where to, ma'am?"

"The Sheraton."

"Nathan Road, yes, ma'am."

As his heartrate settled, Gabriel turned to take a closer look at the woman beside him. She was staring out of the side window, and he could see a vein pulsing in her neck causing the string of pearls at her throat to raise and lower by a hair's breadth with each beat of her heart.

The muscles in her arms weren't just toned, they were defined. By free weights, he could tell.

Her stomach was flat, even though she was sitting scrunched up in a car seat. And she had a physicality in the way she held herself that spoke of long hours in the gym and probably some sort of sports field or court. Or maybe on the back of a horse. Or at the helm of a yacht. Telecoms? No. Not in a million years.

She must have sensed him looking. She turned to face him. No friendliness, but no hostility either. Just a frank, appraising look, just as he had been scrutinising her a moment earlier. Then she did smile.

"Fancy a drink?"

Gabriel nodded.

The driver half-turned his head.

"Which crossing do you want, ma'am, Western Harbour Crossing or Cross Harbour Tunnel?"

"Cross Harbour, please."

They sat in silence for the rest of the short journey. Gabriel contented himself with spotting Rolls-Royces and reached six before the taxi pulled up outside the Sheraton.

Even though he'd stayed in some fairly upscale hotels, Gabriel's eyes widened at the sheer opulence of the lobby.

A sweeping Art Deco staircase with wrought-iron bannisters

dominated the double-height space. It looked the type down which a Hollywood actress from the 1930s might have sashayed in a floor-length evening gown. The floor was a mosaic of caramel and white marble diamonds. They reflected the creamy light from a huge chandelier.

Somewhere, a pianist was breezily playing a jazz tune and, everywhere, uniformed flunkies seemed ready to help with a bag, directions to the bar or a nightlife recommendation.

Duggan led Gabriel to the lifts, punched the button for her floor and, when they arrived, pointed left down a corridor. The soft chocolate-brown carpet muffled their tread completely.

"This is me," she said as they arrived outside 802.

Once she'd swiped her keycard over the black plastic pad, Duggan pushed the door open and stood aside.

"After you, Sir Galahad."

"I'm not sure you needed me."

"Maybe, maybe not. How about that drink?"

"Does your minibar run to a gin and tonic?"

"I think we can manage that. I'll join you. Be a love and get some ice. The machine's at the end of the corridor."

Saying this, she handed Gabriel a black-and-gold metallic ice bucket.

When he returned and knocked on the door, she opened it on the security chain, peering round the door before unlatching it and welcoming him.

"Stick a few cubes in them, then," she said, pointing to two half-full tumblers.

She took one of the drinks and sat in an armchair. Gabriel took the small sofa opposite her and raised his glass.

"To street-fighting skills."

"Cheers."

After a swig of the now cold gin and tonic, Gabriel put his glass down. Time to talk turkey. This woman was no telecoms executive. He'd narrowed her profession down to one of three. Spy, cop or killer. If three-sided coins were real he'd cheerfully flip one and not be able to bet which face would land uppermost. Maybe because the last woman he'd met in The Golden Dragon had belonged to the final category, he was minded to discount it, if only on the grounds of probability. Why not put the question to the lady herself, and let her solve the mystery?

"Did you learn to fight like that in the telecoms company's health club?"

She smiled and took another pull on her drink, regarding him over the rim, before answering.

"I suspect I probably learned in the same place you did, Mister HR."

"Are you a cop or a spy?"

"You first."

"Neither."

"Neither?"

"I'm what you might call a trouble-shooter."

"Freelance?"

"HMG."

She gave him a searching look, then ran a fingertip along the scar on his left cheekbone. Her eyebrows lifted.

"Oh God, you're not one of Don Webster's lot, are you?"

Gabriel frowned.

"Who?"

She leaned forwards and patted his knee.

"You think you can kid a kidder, do you? OK, fine. Since you ask, and since you helped pull my chestnuts out of the fire back there, I'm a cop. Not undercover, or not precisely, but it was a convenient story while I was hanging out at The Golden Dragon. Though obviously that part of the op's finished with now. Your turn."

"Yes, I work for Don. How on earth do you know about The Department?"

"Oh, baby, that's so sweet. You think you and all those misfits, mavericks and fuckups the old warhorse recruits are so far under the radar you could curl up in the prime minister's bed and he wouldn't notice, don't you?"

Gabriel let the dig go. Maybe she did know about The

Department but she didn't know how close he'd once been to doing exactly what she'd joked about.

"But how did you make the connection?"

"Honestly? A guess. Not a wild one. Here's a bloke, speaks Cantonese like a native, having cosy little chats on two of the nights I'm surveilling Fang Jian. Well, that could mean anything, couldn't it? But HR? Really? And he has a watchful look about him, fit, too. And when yours truly gets into a little bit of trouble with a trio of thugs, here's our boy, galloping to the rescue, puts two of them on the ground with some very slinky moves. And I'm thinking, well, he could be with our friends in MI6, but there's something about him that doesn't quite fit the mould. So, you want to tell me what you're doing hanging out with a triad boss?"

"Why don't you tell me why you're investigating him?"

"Why do you think?"

"I don't know. Is he wanted in the UK?"

"Can't say."

"So why did you ask?"

She shrugged.

"I don't know. Maybe I just enjoy crossing swords with you. How about you? He a friend of the family or something?"

"It's a long story."

"I'm a good listener."

So Gabriel told her the story of his relationship with Fang Jian, which meant telling her a longer story about his relationship with Zhao Xi. Which led to his childhood. Which led to his search for Tara. Which led to The Golden Dragon, a fight on Wyndham Street and her hotel room.

When he finished, she remained silent for a few seconds. Both their drinks were finished. She pointed at his glass.

"Refill?"

"I can't. I should go."

She pouted. Just a little. Fingered the gold hoop in her right earlobe.

"That's a pity. Just as we were getting to know each other. Seems like a shame to have to go scouting around for a taxi at this time of night. Why don't you stay the night here and we can carry on talking?"

Gabriel smiled. A year earlier and he would have accepted Duggan's invitation. He shook his head.

"I can't, Valerie. I'm sorry." He stood. "Tell me. Is that your real name?"

Coming close enough that he could smell the gin on her breath, she placed her lips against his left ear.

"If you'd stayed, I would have told you," she whispered. "Wait there."

She fetched her handbag from the desk and extracted a business card, which she tucked into his inside breast pocket.

"The details are fake. The number's real. Call me sometime."

Then she turned him by his shoulders and propelled him towards the door, her hand against the small of his back.

Before going to bed, Gabriel emailed Nesbitt and Chow, asking them to meet him at his house at 9.00 a.m. the following morning.

22

At 9.00 a.m. sharp, Gabriel convened the meeting of his intelligence team. A whiteboard stood facing a window onto the garden. Nesbitt arrived first, dressed in a silver-grey suit jacket over a pair of jeans with ironed creases. He caught Gabriel's glance and smiled wryly.

"It's Rosemary. She'd iron my underpants if I'd let her."

The doorbell rang just as Gabriel was pouring coffee.

"That'll be Sarah. Could you let her in, please?"

Nesbitt returned with Chow behind him. Gabriel stood to greet her. In contrast to Nesbitt, her outfit was decidedly funky. A bright-red T-shirt with a Snoopy motif, combats and shiny yellow Dr Martens. Once they were settled round the table, coffees in front of them, Gabriel cleared his throat.

"So, shall we start? Sarah, what have you got?"

Chow opened the lid of her laptop and after a two-second pause began reading – reciting, really.

"I went to see a Mrs Ling Ruo earlier today. She worked for your parents for two years, from 1984 to 1986. She was their nanny. I guess that means she was *your* nanny, really. Do you remember her?"

Gabriel looked up at the ceiling, noticed a spider hanging upside down from its web, searching his memories of his Hong Kong childhood. He returned his gaze to Chow's owlish stare.

"I was four in 1984. My brother was born a year later. He died when I was ten. My memories before then are pretty sketchy, I'm afraid."

She blushed and glanced at her laptop's screen. He'd noticed she had a habit of seeking solace in her various devices when she was troubled.

"I'm sorry. I didn't mean to intrude."

Gabriel smiled.

"It's OK. You weren't to know. But I'm afraid I can't remember Mrs Ling."

"She remembers you, though. She said you were, and these are her exact words by the way not mine, 'a very cheeky little monkey.' She told me she once caught you sneaking out of the kitchen with a handful of biscuits, ten minutes before supper. You asked her not to tell your mother and she agreed. She said she could never resist when you begged her."

"What did she say about our family? Did she know about Tara?"

"She said they'd sent her back to England for her health. Well, she said she'd been *told* that, but that makes it hearsay, technically."

"We're not in a court of law, though, are we?" Nesbitt interjected. "So we can probably take it as read."

"Ah, but that's just the point. We can't. Because *then* she said a friend of hers told her that Tara hadn't gone back to England at all. She'd been kidnapped and—"

"I know. I spoke to the lead detective on the case. John Li. I have his files," Nesbitt added, turning to Gabriel.

Chow clearly hadn't finished. She was shaking her head while Nesbitt was speaking, clearly anxious to finish.

"Did it say anywhere in Detective Li's files *who* had kidnapped her?"

She had a triumphant look on her face. Gabriel could see she was enjoying outfoxing the ex-copper.

"No. Only that they suspected triad involvement."

"They were right. And I know which one. The Four-Point Star."

She leaned back and folded her arms across her chest, partially obscuring the Snoopy motif. Her meaning was clear enough to Gabriel. *There! What do you think of that?*

"That's a brilliant lead. Thank you."

Nesbitt leaned forwards.

"Aye, so it is. And here's another. As I told Gabriel, I met the guy who ran the investigation into wee Tara's kidnapping. John Li, his name is. His partner at the time was a British cop named Jack Yates. Well, Yates retired back to the UK in 1997, but if he's still alive, Gabriel could probably trace him. He might have some information. Maybe he kept a copy of the files like Li did. Maybe even some originals. You never know."

"Was there anything else in the police files that might help us?" Gabriel asked.

"The forensics guys back in eighty-three found a single piece of physical evidence. A scrap of black fabric. No DNA testing out here in those days, so it was bagged and tagged and stuffed in the evidence locker."

"Oh, well. I guess we can't have everything."

"Hold on," Nesbitt said, patting the air like it was a horse. "I haven't finished. You see, I sweet-talked my friend at Police HQ into letting me borrow the fabric scrap. It's a cold case. Well, frozen'd be more accurate. She said she didn't see what harm it could do. Evidence gets misfiled all the time."

"You've got it?"

Nesbitt reached into his inner jacket pocket and withdrew a small plastic bag, sealed with red tape. Wordlessly, he handed it to Gabriel, who looked at the object in his palm, pondering the gulf in significance between its appearance and its meaning.

"This could have the kidnapper's DNA on it."

"That it could. You'd need to take it to a private lab. Back in the UK, I'd suggest. If they manage to give you a profile, you have a couple of options. You could ask a friendly copper, if you know one, to run it through UKDNAD. That's the national DNA database. If that comes up blank, you could see about asking Europol. Then INTERPOL."

Gabriel smiled as he tucked the evidence bag into his own pocket.

"Thank, John. I mean it. This could take me straight to the man who took my sister."

"Yes. And it could also be a bit of black cotton from your mum's gardening trousers, remember that."

"I do. I mean, I will. But can't you see, John? She's coming closer all the time."

Now it was Nesbitt's turn to smile.

"Of course, I see. And I hope you do find out what happened to her. Really I do. I just don't want you to get your hopes up, OK?"

"OK. Hope for the best, plan for the worst, yes?"

"Something like that, yes."

Gabriel jumped up, unable to stay seated with the adrenaline that was fizzing in his veins. He snatched up a fat black whiteboard marker and scrawled notes on the shiny white surface. Nesbitt pointed at the top-left corner of the board, where Gabriel had written 4-PT STAR TRIAD.

"I'm sure you're right, in principle. But you must know that you can't just call their HR department and ask for a list of employees from the early eighties?"

"Of course I do!" Gabriel snapped. Then regretted it instantly. "Sorry, Peter."

Nesbitt waved away the apology.

"Forget it. But unless you have a time machine and an invisibility cloak, I don't think that particular avenue is going to lead anywhere significant."

Maybe, maybe not. But you don't know that I have an acquaintance who runs one of the rival gangs.

The meeting wound down after that. There wasn't much else to discuss. Gabriel ascertained that Chow had spent three days on the project. He took her out to the front door, explaining he and Nesbitt had something else to discuss. On the way, Gabriel asked her to wait in the hall while he detoured into his office. He emerged with an envelope, its sides pushed outwards. He handed it over.

"There's fifteen thousand in there."

Chow's forehead creased.

"Wait. Three days at fifteen hundred a day is four thousand, five hundred. I brought you a solid lead, so doubling it makes nine. How did you get to fifteen?"

Gabriel smiled at her. Too young, and hopefully too untroubled by life's buffetings to have any idea what her work meant to him.

"You helped me take a step closer to my missing sister. I think that's worth a bonus, don't you?"

She smiled. Tucked the envelope into her laptop bag.

"I guess so. Thank you. It was really interesting work. And if you ever *do* hear of a story I can use, you know, something juicy, you'll let me know, won't you?"

"I promise."

———

Several miles away, in a fish-processing factory, Fang was standing in front of three chairs. Sitting on the chairs – tied to them – were the three young men who had attacked and then been repulsed by Valerie Duggan, with help from Gabriel.

The men's faces were sheened with sweat. They gleamed in the harsh white light of the lamps dangling on chains from the corrugated iron roof. Behind them stood three more men, built to a different plan: heavier, more muscular, designed for power rather than speed. Their shaved skulls revealed white scars here and there, but no tattoos. Those were all covered by their identical white shirts and black, tight-fitting suits.

Fang stood completely still, five feet from the centre chair. His arms dangled at his sides. A spectator, had one been allowed inside, might have regarded the scene as benign, maybe some sort of disciplinary hearing. Fang's face was a mask. No lines grooved his forehead. No tension drew the skin tight around his eyes. No anger, or none that was obvious, caused clenching jaw muscles.

Then he spoke, at which point the mythical spectator's view of the proceedings would have taken an abrupt turn.

"I am going to kill you myself. To set an example. How could you be so careless? So useless? So shit! A woman, for fuck's sake. A middle-aged British woman cop. And you let her beat you like little kids in a playground fight."

"But, boss," the man in the middle chair whined. "She had this guy with her. I saw him here. Drinking with her at the bar. You know him."

"Who was this man?"

The man to the first speaker's left answered.

"He's the one you had with you in your office with the Communist guy."

Fang's eyes widened.

"Wolfe? You're talking about Wolfe?"

"Yeah, yeah! If that's his name, I mean."

This was the centre man again, smiling now, relieved that they'd diluted the blame for their failure to carry out his orders.

Fang sniffed in a breath.

"I'll deal with him another time." He rolled his shoulders. "Master Lo!" he yelled.

The old man who'd taught Gabriel how to behead a tuna appeared from behind some slatted plastic blinds. In his bony right hand he held a cleaver. In his left a thick wooden chopping board.

"You are ready, Jian?"

"Yes."

Lo walked past the chairs and handed the blade to Fang, who hefted it in his right hand, grunting his approval. Then the old man laid the chopping board on the ground behind the centre chair.

Without saying another word, Fang strode forwards, lifted his right leg, placed the sole of his shoe on the man's breastbone and pushed. It was a demonstration of balance lost on the recipient, who screamed as his chair toppled over and the back of his skull smacked against the chopping board.

Fang knelt by the man's right shoulder and placed his palm over his forehead, pushing down hard.

"Hold still. You don't want me to strike more than once, believe me."

Eyes wide, breath coming in hyperventilating gasps, the man complied.

Fang lifted the cleaver high above his head, paused for a second while he focused on the spot he wanted to hit, and brought the blade down, fast, in an arc that ended an inch below the back of the man's neck.

He got to his feet as the failing heart pumped jet after jet of bright-red blood out of the neck and across the concrete floor towards a drain fifteen feet away. The corpse's legs spasmed twice then stilled.

Five minutes later, three headless corpses lay on the floor, side by side, joined by their severed necks to a lake of blood that one of the three goons was now washing down the drain with a high-powered hose.

Fang finished taking photos of the heads and turned to the fishmonger.

"No wasted meat on those, is there, Master Lo?"

The old man cackled.

"You can come and work for me any time, Jian."

23

With the house to himself once more, Gabriel pulled out Valerie Duggan's business card. He called the number she'd assured him was genuine, half-expecting it to ring out or be disconnected. *But then why give it to me? Unless she was—*

"Valerie Duggan."

Neutral. Non-confrontational. Not giving anything away, neither surprise nor suspicion.

"Valerie, it's Gabriel."

"Couldn't stay away from the older woman, eh? I don't blame you."

There it was again. That teasing, sexually suggestive tone he had no way of countering. Momentarily discomforted, he ploughed on.

"I was hoping you could help me with something. Do you have some time today?"

"What is it?"

"I'd prefer not to talk about it on the phone."

"Ooh, big secret. OK then. Do you like boat trips?"

"What?"

"Boat trips! You know, a trip. On a boat. I love them. Always have, ever since I was a little girl. Let's take a trip round the harbour, find a quiet spot on the top deck and you can tell me all about your little problem."

"When?"

"No time like the present. Meet me at the ticket booth for the *Kowloon Queen* at," she paused, evidently checking the time, "12.30 p.m. Thereabouts, anyway. Ciao!"

The line went dead, leaving Gabriel feeling outgunned and outclassed.

———

For his boat trip with Duggan, Gabriel selected a navy linen jacket over an open-necked, sky-blue cotton shirt, faded Levis and a pair of blue deck shoes. He stuck a pair of Ray-ban aviators in his top pocket, patted his wallet reflexively, and went downstairs. He arrived at the harbour at 11.55 a.m., wandered down to the *Kowloon Queen* ticket booth and bought a ticket.

"Next sailing in half an hour, sir," the sales clerk said as he turned away to serve the woman behind Gabriel in the line.

Feeling fresher than he had for at least a week, Gabriel leaned on a railing and watched the boats criss-crossing the harbour. He filled his lungs with the heady smells of fish, diesel and fast-food that locals never noticed but which seemed overpowering to tourists and those recently returned to the island.

He turned at a sudden outburst of laughter. A group of Australians in their early twenties were cackling at some shared joke. Backpackers, he assumed, from their colourful printed cotton trousers, strappy vests and faded T-shirts. They looked carefree, their tanned faces open, unlined and split by wide, white smiles.

One of the boys caught his eye.

"Hey, mate! Take a picture, would ya?" he called over.

Gabriel removed his sunglasses and stepped forward to take the camera the boy was holding out. It was a high-end model, a digital SLR with a long lens.

"It's on Auto, yes?" Gabriel asked him.

"Yeah. Just squeeze the shutter button to focus and then press.

Hold for a burst." He turned to his friends. "Come on, guys. Get into position!"

After some good-natured jostling they were ready, the girls either draping their arms around each other or striking Charlie's Angels poses holding up imaginary pistols, the boys flexing their biceps or making "rabbits' ears" behind each other's heads.

"OK, three, two, one, smile!" Gabriel shouted.

He held the button down and the camera fired off a rapid sequence of pictures. As he handed the camera back, someone tapped him on the shoulder.

He turned to find himself face to face with Valerie Duggan, resplendent in oversized sunglasses, a fitted leopard-print top, and tight white jeans that were cropped at mid-calf. Like him, she'd opted for boat shoes, but where his were worn and curled up at the toes, hers looked brand new and matched her top. Her lips sparkled with a glossy pink lipstick and she'd arranged her hair in a complicated-looking twist, through which tortoiseshell chopsticks were poked.

"Wow! You look amazing," Gabriel said, meaning it.

She smiled.

"Thank you, Sir Galahad," she said, leaning in to kiss him on both cheeks.

"You have a little bit of lipstick on your tooth," he said.

"And you have some on your cheek," she replied, rubbing her thumb against his jaw before running the tip of her tongue behind her top lip. She bared her teeth. "Better?"

"Gleaming."

"Got your ticket? The boat's coming in, look."

She pointed, and Gabriel turned to see the *Kowloon Queen*, a wide-hulled pleasure boat with all-round windows on the lower deck and a top deck open to the sky, cruising up to the pontoon behind the ticket booth. The boat's top deck was crowded with sightseers, pointing phones and cameras in all directions, though principally at their owners' grinning faces.

· · ·

Once the boat had disgorged its incoming complement of passengers, the crew member on the pontoon unhooked the rope holding the queue back and waved them through. Gabriel and Valerie headed up a narrow stairway and found a spot on the port rail between two stacks of orange lifejackets just big enough for the two of them.

"Coffee?" Gabriel asked.

"Go on then. White, no sugar, please."

He made his way down the steps to the lower deck and bought two coffees.

"So," Valerie said once he'd returned with the drinks. "What's the big secret you wanted to talk about? Or should I say, ask my help with?"

"I need to track down an ex-cop. He was RHKP. That's—"

"Royal Hong Kong Police. No need for mansplaining, thank you, I'm a serving cop in case you'd forgotten."

She softened the rebuke with a smile, but Gabriel felt suitably chastened. He reminded himself that behind the glamour was a woman smart enough to be assigned to an undercover anti-triad job. One tough enough to take on Fang's thugs, albeit with a little help, when her cover was blown.

"Sorry. Bad habit." He took a sip of his coffee. "His name's Jack Yates. I believe he moved back to the UK at the time of the handover. I have a favour to ask you."

"And that would be?"

"How long are you going to be out here?"

"After that little business the other night I've been keeping to my hotel room, most of the time. I'm flying home tomorrow. Why?"

"I'm going to try to find Yates and I wondered... "

"Whether I'd be able to help, you mean?"

"Well, I did save you from those thugs."

"You what? Saved me? Let's say you helped me deal with them and leave it at that, eh?"

"OK, fair enough."

"Have you checked the RHKPA? You know what that is, I'm assuming?"

Gabriel smiled.

"Would it be the Royal Hong Kong Police Association, by any chance?"

"Smart boy. Now I won't have to womansplain it to you."

Gabriel licked the tip of his index finger and chalked up a point to her in the air between them.

"No, I haven't. I guess they might have a membership list."

"They might. But it'll probably be a members-only thing. You could give them a call, anyway. Probably best to wait until you're back in the UK, since that's where this Yates guy is."

"I'll do that, but if they blank me, *could* you help me? If I needed, say, some info about where Jack Yates might be living?"

Valerie stared out across the harbour for a few moments. Then she turned back to face Gabriel.

"No promises, OK? But, in principle, yes. For services rendered." A beat. "Such as they were."

24

At the end of his long working day, once the takings had been added up on his old abacus, and the bills similarly calculated and then subtracted from the first figure, Lo nodded with satisfaction. Then he made a call.

"Mr Nesbitt?" he asked, in English.

"Who else would be answering my phone?"

"Can't be too careful."

"Agreed. It's late, Mr Lo. Why are you calling me?"

"The other day, you ask me about British cop."

"You've heard something, have you?"

"No. Not heard. Seen. Fang Jian just execute three of his own men for failing to kill British police officer. A woman."

"D'ye get her name, by any chance?"

"No. No name. He said she middle-age. And she know this man call Wolfe, who is friend of Fang's. They meet a Communist man. That is all I overhear."

At the mention of Gabriel's name, Nesbit's mind performed a complicated piece of mental gymnastics. As he thanked the elderly restaurateur and promised him the usual payment for information, he was running the angles.

What's going on, Gabriel? Ye've been hanging around with a triad boss and getting friendly with a middle-aged British cop. Who sounds like a detective.

He pulled his notepad towards him and jotted down a list of questions.

Why is G friends with a triad boss?

Why is Fang talking to a "Communist man" (Party official?) with G?

Why is G friends with British cop?

Why is British cop in HK?

He sighed.

"Leave it, Peter. You're not a cop anymore," he said to his empty home office. "But you know one, and you can repay her favour with this."

He called Chrissie Chu and relayed the information passed to him by Lo.

"This is very interesting, Peter. Thank you. I'll check in the morning, but I haven't heard of any joint operation with a British force."

Satisfied he'd rebalanced the scales with Chrissie, Nesbitt joined his wife in the sitting room. She was watching a soap opera and glanced up as he sat beside her.

"Everything all right, love?"

"Yes. Just a work thing."

"OK. Only you've been different this last two weeks. Tetchy. Is it Olivia?"

Nesbitt sighed deeply.

"No, it's not Olivia. It's just… "

"What?" she asked, turning to face him and taking his hands in hers.

"It's probably nothing."

Rosemary rolled her eyes.

"*What's* probably nothing?"

"Goddammit, woman, I found a lump!" he shouted, unable to contain the surge of emotions – anxiety mainly, and dread – that were festering inside him.

"Where, love? Where did you find a lump?"

Now he'd said it, the rest seemed to follow so much easier. It was a relief to talk.

"In my groin. You know, on one of my balls."

Her face softened. She was frowning, but with concern now, rather than puzzlement. He realised he'd been unfair, keeping it a secret from her.

"Let me guess. You haven't seen the doctor about it. You're a man, and men don't, do they? They just wait until it's raging bloody cancer and then it's too late! Well, not you, Mister Peter Albert George Nesbitt. First thing tomorrow, you call Dr Yuan and make an appointment. An urgent appointment."

"OK. I'm sorry, love."

She smiled.

"It's fine. You silly wee thing. It'll probably turn out to be nothing. A cyst or something. Now come on. Give me a cuddle and let's watch a little TV together."

Rosemary Nesbitt snuggled into her husband's side and he put his arm around her, drawing her close and feeling as if someone had removed a tight steel band from his chest. And trying not to think about why an obviously wealthy expat who was friends with his boss was also chums with a gangster, a member of the Communist Party and apparently the Scotland Yard copper – *because it's bound to be the Met, you know that, Peter* – who was operating on the island under the radar of the local plod.

25

At 6.00 a.m. the next day, Gabriel was standing outside The Golden Dragon, dressed in a T-shirt, fleece, chinos and work boots. In a daysack, he'd packed some basics for the trip, relying on Liu for the hardware. Dried fruit, nuts and bottled water. A camouflage ripstop nylon groundsheet. Spare T-shirt and underwear. Wash and shaving kit. Ten minutes from sunrise, the sky was charcoal-grey, fading to a washed-out pale-blue at the horizon, streaked with orange. The morning was cool and the lack of humidity made a welcome change from the stifling heat of the last few days.

He looked around. No tourists. Too early for office workers. But the streets were far from empty. He watched an elderly man pushing a handcart full of glistening silver fish along the pavement. Coming the other way, a grey-haired woman in her sixties strode along beneath a wooden yoke across her shoulders, from which swung two rush baskets of chickens, plucked except for their lolling heads.

A couple of young men dressed in chef's whites were smoking on a street corner, laughing loudly at some shared joke. The road itself was quiet, but not deserted. Red-and-white cabs were still plying their trade and he watched, amused, as an entire family –

mother, father, two toddlers, a baby and a scruffy tan-and-white dog – buzzed past on a Honda step-through scooter.

Drawing on a career's worth of training and self-discipline, he'd parked all his thoughts about Tara to focus on the next few days. He began running through the likely shape of the operation he'd agreed to undertake for Liu, and which would wipe his slate clean with Fang. Since his late-night conversation with Valerie Duggan he realised he'd started thinking of the triad boss as Fang again, not Jian. *Interesting. Not so friendly anymore.*

The enemy appeared to be a psychotic PLA officer and political commissar. Something had sent him over the edge and turned a presumably fiercely loyal Party animal into a mass killer. He'd have weapons, up to and including medium-range ballistic missiles, though they'd be no problem for a lone operator. In fact, on recent performance, Gabriel reckoned he was more of a threat to the missiles. So, the usual small arms plus heavier weapons mounted on trucks or observation posts and guard towers. And what about men? Liu had said "a handful". But could he be trusted?

His thoughts were interrupted by a loud blast from a car horn. He looked left to see the wide chrome mouth of a top-end Mercedes, a S-class, grinning at him from the side of the road. The car's gleaming black paintwork reflected the rising sun, an orange ball fractured across sharp creases in the body panels. He walked across to the passenger side and waited. The blacked-out window dropped soundlessly. Liu looked out at him, a cigarette between his lips.

"Good morning, Mr Wolfe," he said around the cigarette. "Are you ready?"

"Yes."

"Get in then."

Gabriel climbed in and sank back against the thickly-padded leather upholstery. The German-engineered climate control system was battling valiantly to dispel Liu's cigarette smoke, but losing, just. The smell was not unpleasant, however. Gabriel looked to his right. A black leather document case lay, almost perfectly camouflaged, on the seat beside him.

"Is that the briefing?" he asked.

"Everything you need to know about Colonel Na is in there. Please, feel free to acquaint yourself with the man you must kill."

As the car silently wafted them towards the airport, Gabriel undid the catches on the document case. He lifted out a transparent plastic document wallet, pulled out the topmost sheet and started reading. He learned that the People's Liberation Army Missile Battery Command #371 lay at the heart of a largely featureless plain extending for thousands of miles in all directions. North towards Russia's Altai Republic, east towards Mongolia, south towards inland China – mostly mountains and a vast sandy desert – and west towards Kazakhstan. A printout of a satellite photo showed the base alongside a schematic drawing with the various buildings and access roads labelled in Cantonese and English.

Next was a dossier on Colonel Na Keng, the battery commander. To the officials who had overseen his upbringing, induction and advancement through the ranks of the PLA and the Communist Party, no doubt it would have brought forth nods of approval. It drove a cold spike of revulsion deep into Gabriel's soul.

After his parents, fishmeal factory workers, aborted two female foetuses and left a third girl outside to die the previous winter, Na was born on 16 October 1964. The date was auspicious: China detonated its first atomic bomb in Xinjiang Autonomous Region. Someone had noted this confluence on the file in red pen. Mao Zedong ruled the vast country with a rigid belief in his own Godlike ability to know what one billion people needed in order to prosper.

Gabriel read on, the already whisper-quiet interior of the limousine fading entirely until he inhabited a silent world comprising him and the document he held in his fingers. In 1966, Mao ordered The Cultural Revolution. As revolutionary fervour swept the country, teenagers and young adults formed themselves into brigades of Red Guards, Mao's shock troops. Pouncing on anyone thought an enemy of Mao Thought, they beat, tortured, raped and murdered hundreds of thousands, millions, of their fellow citizens. Children denounced their parents; wives, their husbands; brothers, their sisters: all frantically pointing the finger before it could be pointed at them.

Too young to take part in the Revolution itself, young Na Keng was imbued with its values. His childhood was awash in blood. Steeped in the stuff. After his nine compulsory years of education, he travelled south to Beijing and enrolled in a state military high school. On graduation, he moved seamlessly into the People's Liberation Army.

Once in uniform, and in possession of a Chinese-made copy of a Kalashnikov AK-47 assault rifle, he rose steadily through the ranks, initially via a series of acts of "loyalty and class-appropriate courage" – in one such, he shot dead twenty university lecturers who had published an anthology of ancient Chinese poetry and then gathered to read extracts at a public library.

Throughout his military career, Na attended meetings of his local Communist Party branch, moving from being a passive consumer of the lectures and writings to an active speaker, organiser and whipper-in of slackers and dabblers. His enthusiasm was noted approvingly by the local Party ruling committee, who put him forward as a trainee political commissar for his PLA company.

From that moment on, his political and military activities became inextricably intertwined, growing through his nervous system like two vines, each vital to the wellbeing of the other. If any of his annual army medicals picked up anything untoward going on in his mind, the doctors did not record it.

The last few pages of the dossier referred to the recent events at Missile Battery Command #371, 114th Division, Xinjiang Province, Eastern Theatre. The official record added nothing to what Liu had already told him. Gabriel closed the file and looked out of the window.

The sun was clearing the rooflines of the shorter buildings. Gulls wheeled in the sky over the harbour. The darkened glass gave the view a depressing grey cast, as though someone had turned a knob and leached the colour from the scene outside.

He faced forward again.

"Did you get my list?" he asked.

"Everything is in the trunk. Best quality. All-Chinese equipment."

Gabriel bit back a remark that would only antagonise his temporary client. He reflected ruefully that at least the man he was going up against would only have access to the same level of quality.

At the airport, Liu led Gabriel through the departures hall to a small, white-walled booth in a corner, well away from the rows of airline check-in desks. Here, two smartly dressed staff, a man and a woman, smiled and bowed as they approached. Liu placed two glossy red ticket folders, a document with an official-looking crest and his passport down on the desk.

"Comrade Liu Zhang. Flying to Altai Republic via Urumqi." He turned to Gabriel. "You have your passport?"

Gabriel offered his passport to the young woman. She took it with a smile and opened it to the photo page, before looking back at Gabriel. Seemingly satisfied, she handed it back.

"Come with me," Liu said.

The two men walked through a grey-painted door into a corridor that led, after five minutes steady walking, to a sumptuously furnished executive lounge, access to which was controlled by another young official, also female, but this time dressed in a fuchsia-pink trouser suit. Checking Liu's documentation again, she smiled and gestured for him and his guest to find themselves a seat.

Gabriel took in the occupants at a glance. All were Chinese. All men. All dressed alike, in dark grey or blue suits, white or pale-blue shirts and dark, plain ties. *Looks like an IBM conference from 1970*, he thought.

The young receptionist approached their seats.

"May I fetch you a drink from the bar, gentlemen?" she asked.

"Bring me a Hennessy XO," Liu said, unsmiling. "Large. And some nuts. You?" he asked Gabriel.

Irritated by Liu's brusqueness, Gabriel went out of his way to provide a contrast, and spoke in a courteous, formal register as he ordered his drink.

"Thank you, I'd like a gin and tonic, please, with ice. If you have lime rather than lemon, that would be my preference."

He smiled as he spoke and was gratified to see a flicker of an answering expression at the corner of her deep-red lips.

Once she had brought them their drinks, and a small porcelain bowl of nuts for Liu, Gabriel spoke.

"What aren't you telling me, Mister Liu?"

He didn't know for sure that the man was holding anything back. It was more of a fishing expedition, just to see what he might say. Liu's reaction was eloquent. He turned sharply to his right to face Gabriel directly, eyes narrowed, mouth a straight line, as if by clamping his lips together he could prevent himself from blurting out an uncomfortable truth. His answer was brief.

"You have all the facts in the dossier. Why do you ask?"

Gabriel shrugged.

"In my experience, clients often prefer to tell me a simple story. They believe it will engender a greater level of loyalty to their project, or cause. Black and white, rather than shades of grey."

"Not in this case, I assure you," he said, scratching his nose before taking a slug of the expensive cognac. "Everything about Colonel Na is black and white. He is insane. He has murdered his own soldiers. He has abandoned correct thought for some perverted imperial fantasy of his own twisted creation."

"No thought of re-educating him?"

Gabriel chose his reference deliberately. The time-honoured Communist Chinese practice of sending intellectuals, dissenters – even people following the wrong religion – to prison camps for what the authorities delicately called "re-education". That the teachers, poets, journalists, Muslims and "wrong-thinking" Party officials usually ended up on the wrong end of a rifle-butt or a pair of crocodile clips was a truth never admitted by those with their fingers on the triggers or the battery switches.

Liu smiled.

"I am afraid no amount of education will pull ex-Comrade Na from the abyss into which he has so gleefully jumped. I take it you are no fan of our country, Mr Wolfe?"

Gabriel drank some more gin. Then he shook his head.

"On the contrary. I think it's a fine country. A rich history, artists and writers who are only now beginning to be appreciated outside China, fantastic cooking, wild, unspoilt landscapes, and some of the friendliest people on God's green earth."

Liu frowned at Gabriel's invocation of the Supreme Being.

"We do not believe your God had anything to do with the creation of the earth, let alone the modern miracle that is China. And I notice you omit the huge strides in technology and wealth that the Party has made possible. A provocation, I assume."

"No, not really. I just prefer my technological progress not to come at the expense of millions of lives."

"Then living in Great Britain must make you deeply uncomfortable. Your colonial history is as blood-soaked a tale as any you will find in the works of Shi Naian."

"I am a fighting man, not a politician, and certainly not as skilful a debater as you, Mister Liu, but even you must admit that there is a world of difference between the Victorian era and twenty-first century China. Britain abandoned its empire and granted independence to all those countries. Helped them with foreign aid, sent volunteers from universities and charities. We have done our best to right any wrongs."

"Perhaps you have. But you see, China lags behind Great Britain and its allies in the West. We have been playing catch-up for many decades. Just as you have forgiven yourselves your own imperial mistakes, you must, surely, grant China the same privilege."

"Imprisoning people for their religious beliefs, or punishing them for expressing ideas the Communist Party doesn't like, is hardly a privilege."

Liu rolled his eyes and uttered a short coughing sound that Gabriel realised, with a start, was supposed to be a laugh.

"Please, Mr Wolfe. Stop there. I fear you will start to mention human rights in a moment, or the situation with the rebels in Taiwan or Tibet. No," Liu said, slapping his right thigh. "I will take no lecture from a Westerner on the subject of China's internal governance. We are a sovereign nation. We do with our people as we see fit. This discussion is over."

Liu drank his cognac, clicked his fingers at the receptionist and indicated that she should bring him a refill, then pulled out his phone and began tapping and swiping.

26

When Gabriel saw the plane in which he and Liu would be travelling, he understood why the Party official had made so free with the cognac and other creature comforts of the lounge. He'd even taken a shower, returning after twenty minutes with damp hair and a smell of pine about him.

Waiting for them on the concrete apron, well away from the sleek commercial airliners was a wide-bodied military transport, painted a uniform matte grey except for red stars on the tail fin and rear fuselage.

Noticing his curious stare, Liu spoke.

"The Xi'an Y-20. Also known as the Kunpeng. You know why?"

Gabriel shook his head.

"Sorry, no."

"The Kunpeng was a mythical bird that could fly a thousand miles. Our aviators nicknamed it 'Chubby Girl'. A disloyal but perhaps understandable lapse of protocol."

Uniformed airport workers wheeled a set of steps up to the rear passenger door just ahead of the tailplanes. Gabriel followed Liu to the steps and took a last look back at the terminal building before climbing. The door at the top was pulled back and they entered the dark interior in single file.

Inside, the plane was a simple metal tube, with webbing, elasticated nets and crude welded metal benches hung around its walls. Occupying the centre of the cargo space and mounted on a wooden sled atop polished steel rails sat a sand-painted military 4x4. It resembled the Hummers Gabriel had travelled in on joint ops with US Special Forces, and the Israeli-designed Caracal Gabriel had used with Eli on a previous mission. Gabriel did a walk-around, running his palm along its angular armoured flanks, and noting the heavy machine gun mounted on the roof. Metal grilles protected the split windscreen and the headlamps. At the rear of the vehicle, he saw three big, cuboid parachute packs tethered to massive eyebolts on the roof.

"This is a VN-4 multi-role, light-armoured personnel carrier," Liu intoned as if he were a salesman at an arms fair. "Nickname, Rhinoceros. On the roof you have a 7.62mm heavy machine gun and smoke grenade launcher. The armour will protect against small arms fire and shell splinters. It is air-conditioned and you have GPS, night-vision and video surveillance."

"All of which will be perfect if it doesn't break up on landing," Gabriel observed drily.

"The pilot is an expert. A senior officer with the People's Liberation Army Airforce. He has made many, many such drops. The Rhinoceros is tough like its namesake. It will not break up. It is you who should worry about arriving in one piece."

Gabriel placed his right hand over his heart.

"Ex-Parachute Regiment. I'm not worried. What about the other items on my list?"

"Come this way," Liu said, walking further into the cargo bay.

A rack mounted on the inside of the fuselage held a parachute, a large rucksack and an array of firearms, long and short. Liu picked up the larger of the two longs. Consulted his mental database of infantry weapons.

"QBZ-95?" Gabriel asked.

"Just so. What you Westerners call a bullpup design with the magazine behind the trigger. Excellent ergonomics, range and accuracy. Box magazine carrying thirty 5.8mm x 42mm rounds. We've also provided a submachine gun. Try it."

Liu gestured at the second long, another bullpup design but more akin to an extended pistol and fitted with a suppressor.

Gabriel picked it up. It fitted his hand nicely.

"QCW-05, yes?"

"Exactly. Chambered for fifty subsonic, armour-piercing 5.8mm x 21mm pistol rounds. Effective out to fifty metres. We thought you might welcome the additional weapon, especially as it shares ammunition with your pistol. I ordered several spare magazines."

The final firearm Gabriel picked up from the rack was a generic semi-automatic pistol. All-black, hammer-fired, manual safety. He dropped out the magazine and slotted it back into the grip with a satisfyingly firm click.

"Everything else you asked for is in the rucksack," Liu said.

"You don't mind if I check it over, do you?"

"Don't you trust me?"

"Old habit."

Liu spread his hands wide.

"Be my guest."

Gabriel pulled the straps holding the bag closed through the buckles and opened the top flap. He removed each item and placed them on the floor, mentally checking off each bit of kit against his checklist. All present and correct, just as he had asked, from the grenades to the survival kit. The latter was every bit as impressive as anything he'd been issued with at Hereford. A length of fishing line complete with barbed hooks. Candle and damp-proof matches. Striker. Compass. The works. The first-aid kit was exemplary. It contained everything a soldier might need to treat everyday injuries, from cuts and broken bones to bullet wounds. Two syringes pre-loaded with morphine were sealed in plastic pouches.

The amplified voice of the pilot boomed through the cargo space telling them to take their seats for take-off.

"Come with me," Liu said. "We're riding up front."

Having prepared himself to make the eight-hour-plus flight to

Urumqi old school, sitting on a hard metal bench, Gabriel was relieved to follow Liu forward and into the plusher surroundings of the passenger cabin. Though by no means as comfortable as the planes he usually flew in between Hong Kong and London, it was several steps up from the cargo bay. The faint smell of aviation fuel was comforting rather than alarming.

The engines spun up and Gabriel settled back into his seat and closed his eyes..

27

Gabriel woke from a doze when Liu tapped him on the shoulder.

"What is it?" he asked, instantly alert.

"The pilot just told me we're two hours to drop zone. He thought you might want to check your equipment."

Without saying anything, Gabriel unclipped his seat belt and went aft. Beyond the soundproofed passenger cabin, the Chubby Girl was as noisy and uncomfortable as any of the many transport planes he'd flown in. Mainly the Lockheed C-130 Hercules and its variants, but also Airbus A400M Atlases, Boeing C-17 Globemaster IIIs and even, on one memorable occasion, an ageing, Soviet-era Ilyushin Il-76, *Candid*, which, if it wasn't actually held together with string and sealing wax, felt like it was.

It was cold. That was the first thing to hit him. High above the Chinese hinterland, the cargo hold was barely above zero. He could see his breath condensing in the air in front of his face. The noise from the four engines was a steady, deafening roar that began as something he experienced in his ears but gradually infiltrated his whole body until he seemed to be built of vibrations. Ignoring all these distracting and unpleasant sensations, he walked back down the centre of the fuselage to the Rhinoceros and, beside it, the racks of gear for the operation.

What concerned him most was the parachute itself. An initial visual inspection told him that the gear was if not new then, at least, unused. Every piece of webbing was smooth-edged, without a single fray, scuff or tear. The olive-drab nylon pack was clean and unwrinkled, undamaged even by careless handling. The parachute cord ties were smooth and tight – no fraying or loose threads to be seen. The red ripcord handle was seated securely and the inch or so of exposed wire was shiny and smelled of light oil.

He turned his attention to the reserve chute, repeating his meticulous inspection of the parts in the same sequence as his main chute. Again, a clean bill of health. He stood and looked behind him. In the dim glow from the bulkhead lights he could see that the cargo floor was clean and more or less dust-free. No sharp edges or jagged protuberances.

"Better safe than sorry," he said to the empty steel tube, before flipping the main chute onto its back and beginning to unpack it.

With the long rectangle of green silk laid out along the length of the cargo area floor, Gabriel began a fingertip inspection. If, for amateur parachutists, having properly packed and checked gear was a routine safety procedure, for members of the world's elite airborne force, the Parachute Regiment, it was a matter of professional pride, personal morality and, frankly, religious faith.

When he'd been a paratrooper, Gabriel and his mates had neither the skills nor the specialist compression equipment to pack their Irvin PX4 round chutes. But take a Para and badge him into the SAS and the idea of using a piece of kit without having first dismantled it, figured out how it worked and how you could repair it, and then put it back together again would get you thrown off a cliff by your mates. At the end of a rope they'd checked, of course. So when it came to their smaller ram-air chutes, they didn't rely on packers, preferring to take a course and learn how to do it themselves.

Satisfied that the Chinese chute was fit for purpose, he repacked it and stowed it on the gear rack before repeating the process with the reserve. It, too, passed muster. That took him to the weapons, two longs and a short. He retrieved a tarpaulin rolled into a fat green sausage underneath the racking and laid it out on the smooth steel floor.

Rifle first, he thought, sitting cross-legged with the QBZ-95 bullpup assault rifle across his lap, muzzle to the right. He started field-stripping the rifle. As his hands caressed the cold metal, a rapidfire sequence of thoughts, sparked by the word 'rifle', flew through his mind. Basic training – "your rifle is your best friend, your mistress and your saviour, all rolled into one," the instructors, often battle-hardened sergeants, told the new recruits. Endless drills, marksmanship training, war games and deployments. Especially deployments.

While his fingers released catches and depressed switches, removing the working parts and the magazine, Gabriel's mind wandered back through time.

It was early 2002, three years after he had been accepted by the Parachute Regiment. As a member of 16 Air Assault Brigade, the young Lieutenant Wolfe found himself assigned to the International Assistance Security Force. Their job was to help the new Afghan Interim Authority create and maintain stability and security in Kabul. One of his comrades had been a fan of Rudyard Kipling, and was fond of quoting lines from the great man's work. One, in particular, had struck Gabriel and never left him. He could hear Will Thacker's thick West Country accent even now.

"'When you're wounded and left on Afghanistan's plains, and the women come out to cut up what remains, jest roll to your rifle and blow out your brains, an' go to your Gawd like a soldier.'"

One scorching Wednesday, Gabriel and his patrol had seen just how sound Kipling's advice had been when he wrote *The Young British Soldier* all those years ago in 1890. Walking down a dusty street in a poor neighbourhood on the southern outskirts of Kabul, they heard a woman wailing. The sound, high-pitched and clearly cracked with grief, had sent the hairs of Gabriel's neck erect.

"This way," Gabriel shouted, signalling for the others to split into two smaller groups.

Rounding a corner, rifle at the ready lest the whole thing was an ambush, Gabriel came face to face with a scene that would haunt him for the rest of his life.

On her knees, a young Afghan woman dressed in desert camo fatigues and wearing an American-issue helmet was kneeling by what remained of a US marine. His hands and feet were missing. His ears, eyes, nose and lips were gone, leaving blackened craters, swarming with flies. His groin was a blackened patch of dried blood and when Gabriel saw what had been stuffed into his mouth, he turned and vomited onto the sun-baked earth.

His training kicked in. Gabriel held his right hand out.

"Step back, miss, please. Step back! Now!"

Staring up at him with reddened eyes, she stood shakily and staggered back. He caught her before she could fall and dragged her away, his left arm around her waist before turning to his sergeant.

"Get her away. Get Tom to radio for support. We need the bomb squad out here pronto."

While his sergeant led the woman to safety and began relaying orders to the other members of the patrol, Gabriel took one look at the mutilated Marine, whispered, "I'm sorry," and left, too, his rifle ready, eyes anxiously scanning the street.

The woman told him she was a translator, embedded with the Marines. As she spoke, in halting but fluent English, punctuated by sobs, the story came out. The dead Marine was a Sergeant Henry Jackson. He'd been captured a week earlier by the Taliban after a firefight.

She'd been called by a contact who'd told her about the body dumped in the street. Without thinking about the possibility that the corpse was boobytrapped, she'd driven straight to the road junction.

When a team from the Royal Logistic Corps' Explosive Ordnance Disposal Regiment turned up an hour later, Gabriel's patrol had made the area safe and a team of US Marines had also arrived, anxious to recover the body of their fallen sergeant.

Sure enough, beneath the body, the lead bomb disposal expert, a female captain, found an IED. If the translator had raised the torso by just a couple of inches, a simple spring-loaded release would have detonated the device. When she'd finished disabling the device, the EODR captain explained what she'd found. The IED was a five-pound, flat sheet of ANFO explosive – ammonium nitrate/fuel oil – packed around with three-inch nails and wrapped in kitchen foil. The explosion would have killed the translator outright and killed or seriously wounded anyone within ten to twenty feet of the body. Outside that blast radius, the injuries from flying glass and the pressure wave would still have been horrific.

The roar of an incoming Chinook drew all eyes skywards. Its twin rotors chopped at the air, raising a swirling cloud of tawny dust and preventing further speech. As its fat rubber tyres kissed the ground the roar built to almost unbearable levels...

...and merged with the roar inside the cargo hold. Gabriel looked down. The rifle lay across his lap, reassembled. He shook his head, clearing his inner eye of the hellish vision of the dead Marine's lacerated body. He replaced the rifle and went to work on the submachine gun.

28

With all three firearms stripped, checked and reassembled, Gabriel grabbed a torch from his daysack and went to the rear of the Rhinoceros. The heavy door swung open on well-oiled hinges. He lifted his right boot to step inside just as the plane hit a patch of turbulence, throwing him sideways and cracking his cheekbone against the door.

He stretched for a grab-handle and clung on as the ungainly transport plane juddered and lurched in the pockets of empty air around it. Finally, the plane settled. Gabriel had sensed the pilot gaining altitude in search of quieter air and was thankful for the man's training. He folded the door back on itself and climbed inside, switching on the torch. He smelled gun-oil, diesel, stale sweat and dust. *Not quite box-fresh.*

Here was another example of the generic armoured personnel carrier. Behind the crew compartment, rudimentary seating for troops – not floating, he noticed, so anyone caught inside if it hit an IED or a mine would most likely suffer terrible spinal injuries. On the floor lay a black canvas holdall. He unzipped it: boxes of ammunition, camouflage gear, a combat helmet, field rations, a zipped nylon sausage containing a one-man tent and bottled water. He nodded with satisfaction.

The crew compartment was better equipped. Padded seats for the driver and navigator and a space behind for the machine gunner. Gabriel pushed the hatch open and stood, his head, shoulders and upper torso poking through the thick armour. In front of him, the grips and trigger for the machine gun. He raised the lid of the ammunition box and lifted out the end of a fresh belt, which he fed into the receiver before latching it closed again.

He left via the driver's door, slamming it behind him: a harsh metallic sound in the stripped-back interior of the fuselage. He nodded with satisfaction. Whatever else he was up to, at least Liu had equipped Gabriel properly for the operation.

Thirty minutes later, the pilot spoke, in brief, clipped sentences.

"Twenty minutes to drop zone, sir. Conditions are perfect. Ten-knot headwind. No cloud. Horizon visibility."

"Good." Liu turned to Gabriel. "Begin your preparations. When you have completed your assignment, use this to contact me. My number is programmed in." He handed Gabriel a chunky black satellite phone.

Gabriel took the phone and pressed the home button. The screen lit up at once. A single press of the menu button brought up a single word. Liu. He checked the charge indicator. Five vertical bars out of five.

"Charger?"

"You shouldn't need one. You only need to make one call. Keep it turned off until then."

"Yes, but I'd like one all the same."

Liu smiled.

"And you will find one in the back of the Rhino. There's an eighteen-volt power supply connected to the battery."

"Good. I like to have a Plan B."

"You have studied the maps?"

"Yes. Once I'm down, it shouldn't be more than two or three hours' driving to reach the base."

"The cab is equipped with GPS. There is your Plan B."

Gabriel couldn't resist a quick jab at what he felt was the Chinese official's complacent attitude.

"And you're happy relying on American technology?"

Liu turned round fully to face him, eyes narrowed.

"For now. But the US Airforce will be losing a customer soon. BeiDou will be online by 2020 and then we will no longer be reliant on GPS."

Having experienced at first hand the glacial pace of military development in the West, Gabriel had his doubts "Big Dipper" would be ready anywhere close to the target year, but he held his tongue. No need to antagonise the man who he'd be calling in a few days to pull him out.

"OK. I have to go. Be ready for my call. I don't want to hang around."

"I will have my phone on me round the clock." Then Liu offered his hand. "Good luck."

"Thank you. I hope I don't need it."

Gabriel left the warmth of the cabin through the bulkhead door and returned to the cold, noise and vibration of the cargo compartment. He made his way along the juddering steel runway to the Rhino, and changed into the camo gear and helmet. He knelt by his parachute rig. After a final visual check and a tug on each strap and buckle, he wriggled his way into the harness and tightened the webbing until he felt that familiar, comforting embrace. Main chute on his back, reserve high on his chest. Rucksack next, below the reserve chute, a thirty-foot coil of nylon rope hooked onto two D-rings. The submachine gun and assault rifle went into a canvas weapons bag that he strapped to his left side. The pistol into a holster strapped high on his chest to the left of the reserve chute.

Ready for the jump, he staggered to the side of the Rhino and grabbed a loop of webbing. Nothing left to do now but wait. He cleared his mind, focusing first on the jump and then on reuniting with the Rhino. The mission goal could wait for now, his priority was getting down without breaking a bone. Do that and the op would fail before it had even started. No CASEVAC. No support. No Forward Operating Base to return to. Just hundreds of thousands of square miles of Chinese wilderness.

Feeling his adrenaline levels rising and enjoying the sense of anticipation, he looked back down the plane to the black rectangle of the loadbay door.

A loud clank. The door dropped by a few inches, admitting a piercingly bright shaft of sunlight. Beyond it, once his eyes had adjusted, a sliver of pale-blue sky.

The door began its slow progress downwards, transforming as it reached its lowest point into a ramp, though one was not needed on this particular operation. Four metallic clonks echoed through the cargo area as the thick steel studs immobilising the skid holding the Rhino slammed down into their housing.

The cargo door was fully open now. The pilot tilted the Chubby Girl's nose up. The commotion, even through his helmet, was immense. Wind roar. Engine noise. And the shriek of steel grinding over steel as the skid began sliding towards the bright square. Gabriel took a firmer grip on his webbing strap as the pilot tilted the plane's nose upwards.

Slowly at first, than faster, the Rhino slid along the rails, the screech cutting through the deafening sounds of wind and engines, before falling away, dragging its parachutes behind it before they too raced over the edge of the ramp and disappeared. The folded strap that would open the chute zigzagged in a blur of canvas before it reached its full extent. With a crack like a gunshot, it tautened to a quivering straight line, then went slack as the chutes below deployed and detached.

Gabriel staggered towards the ramp, struggling to stay upright under the weight of the cumbersome combat load he was carrying. Finally, he was there, four feet from the lip. His blood was saturated with adrenaline, his thoughts with the bright-white light of excitement.

He strode forwards and fell out into the void.

And was calm. Just like on every jump he'd made from basic training onwards.

He yanked the ripcord, felt the vibration and jerk as the canopy deployed and caught the air, bellying upwards before stiffening into its wing-like form. He relaxed, as he always had done. One second you were immersed in noise, shouting, shoving, engines roaring, the potent cocktail of fear, anticipation and excitement, the next...

...immediate and utter silence. A trancelike calm, as if God had removed everything you had ever worried about, strove for or fought over and replaced them all with a singular sensation of just being present. The sky, something most people – and you, most of the time – perceived to be *up there* was now *here*. Yes, the ground, and hostile forces, might be waiting for you, but just for now there was nothing but you and the silent silk above your head.

He looked down. Hundreds of feet below him he could see the Rhino, swaying beneath three huge brown chutes like mushroom caps. Barring a catastrophe, that meant he would have transport. The terrain looked as it had in the satviews he pulled up on his laptop. Empty, in other words.

Scrubby, undifferentiated vegetation in shades of grey-green, brown and a washed-out, acidic yellow. No regularity of field strips. No settlements. No roads. Mostly scabbed desert like lichen on an ancient gravestone. Way over to the east, a river, almost dried out to judge from the pale-sand colour, wound sinuously across the plain. He released the rucksack from the D-rings, feeling the separation as a welcome relief as it fell to the end of its thirty-foot tether.

Steering with the chute's two handles, he followed the Rhino down, matching its trajectory.

The ground was approaching fast. He readied himself.

To the west, judging by the sun's position, he saw the Rhino make landfall, raising a dustcloud like a stone hitting the bottom of a muddy pond.

He pulled on both handles simultaneously to slow his descent. And then he was down, running forwards for a few paces as the canopy collapsed to his right, a deflating jellyfish undulating in the light breeze.

He extracted himself from the parachute harness and gathered up the silk into an ungainly ball. He anchored it beneath a rock. Once behind the wheel of the Rhino, he'd return to stow it in the back, along with the reserve. His own Countryside Code: kill nothing but the enemy, take nothing but care, leave nothing but the faint tang of gun smoke.

From the top of the rucksack he took out a pair of binoculars and scanned the land to the west, searching out the Rhino. He located it about a mile and a half away, looking like an angular, ugly beetle, its slightly squinty eyes pointing directly at him.

He shouldered the rucksack, adjusted the weapons bag and began walking. A lone figure in a vast expanse of emptiness.

29

XINJIANG PROVINCE, NORTHEASTERN CHINA

High above him, a large bird of prey wheeled on the warm upcurrents of a thermal. Over the years, he'd come to regard raptors as his spirit animals. He wasn't sure why. They seemed pure, somehow. Perfect flying machines capable of carving out a living in most countries of the world, or most of the ones he'd visited, at any rate. Never killing for fun, or for sport. Just to eat. To feed themselves and their chicks and ensure the survival of their family. On ops, he'd make a point of searching one out, identifying it, and hoping that, at some level, he was following their simple way of life.

As he looked up, Gabriel experienced a brief but unsettling flashback to the mission Liu had referred to as a part of his selection process. A clearing in a humid forest in Northern Cambodia. Bugs whining about his ears. Sweat dripping inside his shirt. His position behind a tripod-mounted M60 general-purpose machine gun, right hand clamped around the pistol-grip. Bodies falling, ripped to pieces by the 7.62 mm rounds that sped from its smoking muzzle. Screams.

Then silence. The M60's barrel red-hot. The smell of hot brass and burnt gunpowder acrid in the heavy air. And, below that, the rank stench of blood, and shit spilled from still-warm intestines. A dead warlord and twenty or more of his men.

Men? Some of them couldn't have been older than fifteen.

He shook his head, fighting down a wave of nausea that had risen in his gorge. Win Yah had got what he deserved. The men under him knew what they were doing. No more Khmer Rouge to force them to join him. No Pol Pot pulling the strings like a demon clutching a copy of Chairman Mao's Little Red Book.

"It was their choice!" he screamed up at the raptor.

He clawed at the flap securing his pistol and pulled it free of the holster. Aiming at the horizon, he emptied the magazine, still shrieking his defiance. The bird peeled away to the south, gaining height.

As the last brass cartridge plinked onto the stony ground, he dropped the pistol and fell to his knees, panting. He knelt that way for five more minutes, staring into the distance. Finally, he spoke.

"I thought I'd fixed things, Britta. I thought by avenging you, I'd put the universe back on its axis again. I want to be a good person. I'm not a murderer. I had to kill those men in Cambodia. I had to!"

Britta's voice sounded in his head.

And in Russia, too?

"Yes! Especially there. They had you murdered."

Then be at peace with yourself, Gabriel. Do what you have to do and stop torturing yourself.

"I'm trying. Believe me, I'm trying."

After half an hour's tabbing under a burning hot sun, Gabriel reached the Rhino. He unshouldered his rucksack and weapons bag and did a walkaround inspection, mopping his forehead with his sleeve.

The chutes had done their job, landing their payload not only in one piece but in the same condition as when it had left the Chubby Girl's cargo bay. One by one, he loosened the webbing straps lashing the wheels to the skid then unfastened them completely. He opened the rear door and lugged his gear inside.

Before driving anywhere near the missile battery, he had one important task left. He unbuckled the strap closing the weapons bag and pulled the two long guns free. Leaving them on the floor of the cargo space, he walked away from the Rhino for a hundred paces, where he looked around for something that would make a decent target. An environmentalist looking over Gabriel's shoulder would have been delighted. This far from civilisation, not a bottle, a beer can or a cigarette packet marred the sparse greenery or the sandy ground. Settling on a football-sized rock, he balanced it on a tree stump before returning to the Rhino and the long guns.

He picked up the assault rifle and pulled back the charging lever, letting it go with a crack. He brought it up to his shoulder and looked through the telescopic sight. A minute adjustment to the focusing ring brought the rock into pin-sharp clarity. Centring the cross hairs on the rock, he inhaled, let the breath out slowly, waited for a beat of his heart, squeezed the trigger to first position, waited for another beat, and fired.

The recoil was mild, some sort of clever damping in the stock, he suspected. But the rock remained undamaged. Another fractional adjustment to the sight. Another shot. This time he hit it dead-centre, knocking it off its perch.

No point trying out the submachine gun for accuracy. That wasn't really the point. More of a spray-and-pray kind of weapon. So he contented himself with a quick yank on the charging lever and firing a couple of bursts at the tree stump. It worked. And that was enough. With the gunfire ringing in his ears, he stowed the weapons and slammed the door behind them.

Inside the crew cab, he flicked on the ignition switch, a stubby steel toggle with a black plastic cover. Then he pushed the engine start button, offering a small prayer as his thumbnail faded from pink to white under the pressure. With a gruff roar, the engine turned over and caught, emitting a gout of dark-grey smoke from the rear that drifted forwards, briefly enveloping the cabin before dispersing in the air.

"OK, ladies and gents! Next stop, Missile Battery Command Number five-seven-eleven," he shouted before slamming the truck's transmission into first gear and pulling away with a squeal of rubber against steel, before the four-tonne vehicle left the skid and hit the sandy soil of Xinjiang province's desert terrain.

———

Colonel Na stood perfectly still. His breath came in gasps and his hands were shaking. The body before him was beginning to smell. The ancestors were so demanding, so angry, that he had found the only way to appease them was to create some sort of distance between himself and his victims. Otherwise he couldn't go through with the necessary rituals. The mutilations were both calming and a way to reduce the sacrifices to cuts of meat: all the ancestors wanted, after all.

He had dragged out the intestines and wound them round the waist and neck, glistening purplish-grey coils that bulged here and there and, unless he watched them closely, wriggled and squirmed as if they were filled with snakes. The head, removed with a ceremonial sword sat a few feet away, the eyes punched in with the end of his pistol and the tongue cut out and laid on the altar.

Now he had to begin the process of uniting the three kingdoms. He took down a heavy axe from the wall and gripped it in both hands, eyeing the spot at the hip joint where he intended to make the first cut.

The sound – a wet smack – made him flinch. When he opened his eyes, it was to discover that the axe head was embedded in the pelvis. He had to stand on the body and lever the blade forwards and backwards before it came free. He swung again, trying to keep his eyes open, while behind him the accusing whispers grew into murmurs and then, as the blade fell, this time partially cutting through the joint, shouts.

"Stupid little boy!"

"Why can you not do anything right?"

"You are so disrespectful!"

"Do it now or we will cut *you* into pieces!"

Gritting his teeth, Na swung a third time, as hard as he could manage. With a crunch, the axe sliced through flesh, cartilage, sinew and bone before embedding itself in the earth floor of the hut.

He bent to lift the leg, which was heavy, and carried it to the door. Outside, the firepit was blazing merrily. It would be an hour or two before the charcoal had turned white and ashy.

The work was hard, and he was not as young as he used to be. By the time he had reduced the body to its constituent parts, he was sweating freely, and shaking. He sat down in the centre of the pool of blood, letting the liquid cool his burning skin.

He swivelled himself round, to face the altar. The tongue he had so recently removed from its natural home twitched. Then the tip curled upwards.

"Colonel Na," a voice said.

Na turned slowly towards the source of the voice.

The head with the smashed-in eye sockets was speaking to him.

"What is it?"

"My tongue. I need it."

Na got to his feet and fetched the tongue, stuffing it any old how into the open mouth. He sat cross-legged before the head. Waiting.

"Thank you. I have a message for you. From them. They say you need to work harder. The kingdoms are sliding apart just as fast as you bring them closer together."

"The villagers grow wary. I have to be so careful. It is not easy."

"Use the Ghost Warriors."

"But they protect me. I can't kill them."

"The ancestors protect you. Nobody else."

"It's a bad idea."

"It's a good idea. It's the *only* idea. Fail in this and the ancestors tell me you will suffer in ways you cannot even begin to imagine. Compared to the tortures that lie ahead for you, Na Keng, what Mao inflicted during your infanthood will seem as the cuddles of an adoring father."

"No!" Na shrieked, jumping to his feet and kicking out at the head, which rolled over and over, spilling the severed tongue onto the dirt.

He ran outside, where the fire had died down a little. Over the mountains to the north, dark-purple and grey thunderheads boiled up. The sun was setting, lighting their undersides an infernal orange. He turned towards the barracks hut occupied by the Ghost Warriors. Laughter and good-natured jeering came from inside. He stumbled towards the hut, mumbling to himself. Nearing the door, he checked his pistol. Thumbed off the safety. Stuck it back in the holster then pushed open the door.

Inside, the men were drinking beer and eating from a wok filled with delicious-smelling noodles in a rich brown gravy. A case of Tsing Tao lay open on the floor. Another, empty, had been thrown, or kicked, into a corner. At the sight of their commander, the men jumped to their feet and saluted. But many of them were drunk and the salutes were off-kilter. A can fell from its perch on the edge of a bunk and sprayed foamy lager across the floor.

Na pointed to the man closest to him.

"You. Come with me. I have an important task for you. The rest of you, go back to your recreation."

The Ghost Warrior joined Colonel Na.

"What is it that you want me to do, sir?"

"Liaison work."

Outside the hut, the last rays of the sun were streaking the sky pink. Colonel Na sniffed the air. The wood smoke masked the stench from the altar hut, although, sniffing harder, he fancied he could smell the putrefaction.

"Are you getting a cold, sir?" the Ghost Warrior asked.

"No. I am immune to human diseases now. They promised me."

"They, sir?"

"Never mind."

"Who will I be liaising with, sir? Is it the villagers? Headquarters?"

Na drew his pistol.

"No. It's them. All who went before. All who are yet to be."

Then he brought up the pistol and shot the Ghost Warrior through the throat. The man collapsed sideways, a terrible gargling issuing from his wide-open mouth, blood spraying from the rent in the soft tissue below his jawbone.

Kicking away the hands scrabbling at his ankles, Na waited for the man to die. Once he was still, and the blood had ceased to flow, he picked up the ankles and dragged the corpse back towards the altar hut.

30

A moraine of pinkish-grey rocks, ranging from footballs to fridge-sized cuboids, made driving difficult as Gabriel powered northeast towards the missile base. The Rhino, like all its breed, had been built to withstand external threats but not particularly to cosset its inhabitants. The specially sprung "floating" driver's seat absorbed the worst of the primitive suspension's jolts and jounces, but the noise and the stink of diesel were enough to make him wish he was closer.

Before leaving, he'd rigged up a sling for the weapons in the back, using cargo netting and webbing to lash them to the ceiling and floor. The last thing he needed was for one or both of them to be damaged.

Every few seconds he had to adjust course to avoid one of the larger rocks, and even the smaller ones set the whole vehicle clanging as they shot up under the chassis or fractured beneath the wheels. He checked the route on the map spread out on the passenger seat and the compass he'd attached to the windscreen on a sucker. They gave the same answer as the Rhino's onboard navigation software. Fifteen kilometres to go to the small village that lay to the south of the base itself.

As he drove on, cursing the lively steering wheel, which bucked and writhed under his hands, the sky darkened to a sickly yellowish-grey. On the horizon storm clouds were massing, their charcoal and purple flanks fading to orange on their undersides where the sun hit them aslant. Five minutes later the first spots of rain spattered the split windscreen. He flicked on the windscreen wipers and burst out laughing.

The single blade flopped half-heartedly from side to side, smearing the water and accumulated dust into a thin film of yellowish mud.

"Oh, Jesus, you have to be kidding! We've got GPS, night-vision, central tyre inflation system, and wipers off a 1970s Ford Escort."

Suddenly the Rhino's left side lifted clear of the ground as a much louder bang from underneath stopped his laughter in his throat. When it landed, the steering felt heavy and unresponsive. He brought the vehicle to a halt, fearing the worst. As he climbed out, the rain intensified and the air lost its warmth as if a heating element had been switched off.

Shivering as bullets of ice-cold water hit his exposed skin, Gabriel crouched at the front of the Rhino then got into a press-up position to look under the armoured front-end. A lump of rock the size of a grapefruit had lodged in the suspension and was preventing the wheel from turning freely. He crawled under until he could get his hands on it and gave it an experimental shove. It didn't move by so much as a millimetre. Up close he could see where one of its sharper edges had scored a bright silver trough in the greasy metal of the control bar. Spinning round on his back, he tried kicking it free, but only succeeded in hurting his foot.

He shook his head, wriggled out again and got to his feet. He needed something to loosen the rock and knock it or pry it free. He opened the rear door. His improvised weapons sling had done a good job of keeping the firearms safe: they were hanging peacefully like sailors sleeping in their hammocks. He climbed in and walked to the front of the troop compartment. What he wanted was a lever of some kind. An entrenching tool or a pickaxe would be perfect. But though Party Member Liu had equipped him with plenty of materiel for the operation, his thoughtfulness hadn't extended to rock-clearing equipment.

Returning to the front, he looked down and saw the winch.

"Fool. Use that!" he said over the growing wail of the wind, which had picked up and was now blowing the rain directly into his face.

He unlatched the steel hook, let off the brake and walked back for twenty metres, tugging free the braided steel hawser. He looped it around the waist of one of the larger boulders and brought it back to the Rhino. Crawling underneath, he threaded it over then under the chunk of rock obstructing the steering and tightened the hook against the wire.

Standing by the winch again, he depressed the button marked IN. With a whine the electric motor spun up and began taking up the slack in the hawser. Gabriel let it run freely until the wire was suspended, vibrating, a foot above the ground.

"OK," he said, blinking as another sudden squall drove icy water into his eyes, "let's do this."

He pressed the control button again and squinted at the cable as it tightened against the rock. The pitch of the motor increased. Gabriel held his breath. Suddenly the wire loosened with a pop audible above the rain, which was now hammering on the Rhino's slab sides.

"Shit!"

He took hold of the cable and pulled, expecting it to have snapped or pulled the hook free, but it was still connected to the rock. He crouched down and looked underneath at the suspension. All that had happened was the cable had slipped over to one side of the rock. He crawled under and reseated it, keeping tension on the cable until he could wind it in again.

This time, when the cable tautened, nothing slipped. The motor whined, the cable sang and then, with a crack like a gunshot, the cable flew out from under the Rhino trailing a half-pound steel hook like a medieval mace. The lump of metal hissed past Gabriel's right temple and stopped when it clinked against the boulder he was using as a fulcrum. Not wanting to think what the hook would have done to his skull if it had connected, Gabriel simply wound it back in.

He took a third and final look under the Rhino. The rock was clear, lying beneath the offside wheel. He inspected the suspension components, but apart from the gouge in the control arm could detect nothing out of the ordinary.

Since he'd stopped to repair the damage, the sky had darkened further and was now a deep maroon-grey. The rain had thickened to a pale-grey curtain that obscured everything out from about twenty metres. He pulled open the door then cursed as the wind caught it and tried to yank it out of his hand, wrenching his shoulder.

Inside he dragged the door closed against the wind and leaned back in his seat, panting heavily. He started the engine, cranked up the heating and then stopped, hand midway to the transmission lever. His plan had always been to approach the base under cover of darkness. It was 9.00 p.m. now and he was cold and soaking wet. He climbed out again and ran round to the back. Safely inside the cargo area, he clambered out of his wet clothes. Liu had provided a sleeping bag so Gabriel climbed inside and lay down, setting an alarm on his phone for 11.00 p.m.

"You! Private Wolfe! What the bloody hell do you think you're doing? Pick up your rifle and fix bayonet. You heard what Captain Liu said. We're going over the top in five minutes. When that whistle blows, all I want to see is your arse disappearing over the lip of this trench."

Gabriel looked down. He'd been calculating his chances of surviving the first day of the Battle of the Somme on his abacus. It didn't look good.

"Yes, sergeant," he said, placing the abacus in the mud and picking up his short Lee-Enfield by its wooden fore-end and slotting home the foot-long bayonet.

Overhead, shells were whistling towards the German lines from the Royal Artillery battery five miles to the rear. The crumps from the two-hundred pounders shook the earth and sent vibrations running up his shins and into his belly. Machine guns chattered from the eastern end of the redoubt and men's screams cut through the mechanical noises like the very demons of hell in their torments.

He looked left and right. At his mates. The young lads he'd joined up with from Suffolk. Dusty Rhodes. Daisy Cheaney. Smudge Smith, the only black man in their whole regiment. And Britta Falskog and Eli Schochat, faces smeared with mud, lips set in straight lines of grim determination, rifles gripped in white-knuckled hands. Odd that they allowed lasses to fight, rather than keeping them well back behind the lines as nurses or auxiliaries. Still, needs must.

Suddenly, all along the line, whistles starting blowing, their shrill calls to arms sending everyone clambering up the ladders and over the top.

"Come on, you Suffolks! Let's give them a taste of British steel!"

This was Sar'nt Major Webster, striding along the duckboards, firing up his troops. They loved "The Boss," as they called him. The officers were wet-behind-the-ears public schoolboys but The Boss had seen real action. In Afghanistan and South Africa. They trusted him.

Gabriel clutched his rifle in his right hand and mounted the ladder. Seconds later, heart racing faster than a runaway horse, he broached the lip of the trench and was rushing headlong into the smoke and the fire, weaving left and right, working the Lee-Enfield's bolt back and forth and firing at the distant spot he hoped was the enemy.

The mud was the devil's own work to traverse. Thick and sticky, like brown glue, punctuated with body parts, here a lower leg, its khaki puttee unwinding like a filthy bandage, there a bodyless head, its eyes staring upwards.

He heard a scream to his left. He turned, only to see Smudge falling, his lower jaw shot away. He pressed on, crouching to reload his rifle. But the bullets were the wrong calibre. Stupid little snub-nosed pistol rounds when he needed the long .303 rifle cartridges.

Another screech of agony. Dusty toppled backwards, a knife sticking out of his neck. The logo on the hilt – Beck – suggested to him it was of German manufacture.

Gabriel charged forward, yelling defiance at the enemy, squinting through the smoke in his frantic attempt to keep on track, running towards their position. The toe of his right boot caught on something and he fell headlong into a bomb crater half-full of water, dropping his rifle. He splashed about in the waist-deep water, trying to find it, and screamed as his fingers closed on something slimy. The hand closed on his and as he pulled back, Daisy appeared from beneath the stinking surface, his face burnt beyond recognition.

He scrabbled backwards, finding the muddy side of the crater and scuttled out. Then the guns fell silent. In the next second, the smoke cleared and he found himself on the beach, in Aldeburgh. Britta, Eli and he were strolling along in the sunshine, demobbed, their uniforms gone, replaced with simple olive-green cotton trousers and matching jackets, the breasts adorned with red stars.

A scrunch behind them made him whirl round.

He was standing there.

Aiming his pistol.

Kristersson the assassin.

Only this time, Gabriel was ready. He had enough time to save Britta.

He pushed her away from him, so that she stumbled on the rounded pebbles and fell to the ground.

Kristersson aimed, looking straight down the barrel at Gabriel.

Gabriel watched as his finger tightened on the trigger and as he fired, Gabriel yelled out his defiance.

"No!"

The report of the pistol was enormous. A huge, shattering bang. Gabriel felt no pain. He looked down. No bloody crater in his chest.

"You missed!" he shouted at Kristersson's retreating back. "You missed, you bastard!"

"No he didn't," Eli said beside him.

Gabriel turned. Eli smiled, sadly, then fell backwards, blood fountaining from a hole in her forehead to lie beside Britta.

She hit the ground with a second, huge bang.

"No!" Gabriel screamed. "Eli! No——"

31

"No!" he groaned, flailing his arms free of the sleeping bag and banging his left wrist against the steel side of the troop compartment.

He sat up and swiped his hand across his forehead, which was slick with sweat. From outside, a sound like cannon-fire boomed. He crawled to the door and, holding the handle tightly lest it be pulled free of his grasp, opened it a crack. A ferocious storm battered the landscape with rain so thick the air had turned white.

Thunder crashed and pink streaks of fork lightning crackled so close he could smell the ozone as the massive charges ionised the air. He checked the time: 10.53 p.m. Rubbing his face with both palms, he readied himself for a dash round to the cabin and was behind the wheel five seconds later, slamming the door against the howling elements.

He started the engine, switched on the headlights and pulled away, checking the compass and GPS before adjusting course slightly.

Even with the night-vision system switched on, filling the cabin with its eerie green light, he could manage no more than five miles per hour, unless he wanted to drive straight into one of the huge rocks that still littered the ground. The lightning flashes illuminated a landscape so alien it might have been another planet. Bare of trees and vegetation of any kind, the flat plain stretched on and on until the pelting rain obliterated the view.

After an hour during which he doubted he had been able to hold the wheel still for more than a few seconds at a time, the storm ceased abruptly, a final boom of thunder signalling the end of hostilities.

The gibbous moon emerged from behind a cloudbank, casting a silvery light over the land ahead. Mercifully, the moraine petered out, too, losing first the larger blocks, then the football-sized pieces until all that was left was a scree of gravel, until that, too, disappeared, replaced by hard-packed earth.

He turned off the night-vision system and accelerated. Visibility had increased from maybe ten yards to infinity. In the distance he could see pinpricks of light. The village. And beyond that, the base.

32

Half an hour later, the village was close enough to make out individual huts and a few larger buildings.

This was no modern Chinese settlement, all gleaming glass and neon billboards. It was as far from the Westernized cities of modern China as it was possible to imagine.

This was the old China. The China that had existed before Mao. The China that would always exist. Ordinary people, working on the land, tending livestock, plying the basic trades of simple communities the world over: blacksmiths, basket-weavers, seamstresses, schoolteachers, farmworkers.

Gabriel turned the wheel and began tracking northeast, keeping a couple of miles between him and the nearest buildings. He circled the village, at one point easing the Rhino down into a semi-dry riverbed, its centre marked by a meandering stream that glittered in the moonlight.

On the far side of the settlement the missile base came into view. Tall floodlights cast a yellowish pall over a collection of low buildings. Razor-wire coils glinted at the top of high chain-link fences.

Switching off the headlights, Gabriel re-engaged the night-vision driving system and drove closer on the lowest revs he could manage without stalling. In the bright light of the moon, the green screen was more or less redundant, but he kept it on anyway. Half a mile distant, he killed the engine and climbed out.

After the wild fluctuations of the earlier storm, the air was now a more seasonal temperature. Warm, not hot, and thankfully not too humid.

He retrieved the binoculars from the rucksack and his long guns, placing them on the lip of the cargo floor. Next came the grenades. Liu had provided a dozen, which was overkill. Gabriel took out two of the high-explosive grenades and hooked them onto his webbing. He added a single smoke grenade and a flash-bang. The knife, wire-cutters and torch went into his patrol pack along with the first-aid kit.

He looked down at the rifle and submachine gun, lying loaded and ready to serve him. He'd asked for both just to be on the safe side, but only wanted to take one with him. But which one?

For stopping power, and range, the assault rifle was the easy choice, though it was heavier and noisier. In an urban environment, where close-quarters fighting was likely the order of the day, the lighter submachine gun would be the better choice. Its shorter barrel made it more manoeuvrable. And its magazine offered a twenty-round advantage over the rifle's.

In the end, the decision was simple. Range was unlikely to be the defining issue within the confines of the base. But having twenty extra rounds per magazine might be. He picked up the submachine gun and stuffed three extra ten-round stripper clips into his pack.

His loadout ready, he slung the submachine gun over his back, locked the rear door and set off towards the base. Finding a patch of lichen-scabbed earth, he stooped to scrape up a handful and smeared the mixture across his forehead, cheeks and chin, then the backs of his hands.

As he walked towards the base, and his appointment with Colonel Na, he thought back to the dream he'd had in the Rhino. Its meaning wasn't hard to decode.

He'd lost too many friends. He was frightened of losing Eli, as he had lost Britta. But Eli was different.

Not reckless, not by any stretch of the imagination. You didn't survive on the frontline of Israel's war with its enemies without maintaining the highest levels of preparedness and discipline. But her personal philosophy seemed rooted in a combination of living for the moment and trusting to God to keep her safe until it was her time to go. It let her live free of worries about what the future might hold and, as far as he could tell, regrets about what the past had delivered.

He sighed. *Maybe I can learn from you, Eli. Maybe there's a way for me to live in the present as well.* He checked the time: 2.17 a.m. That gave him forty three minutes until his attack.

This was the most exposed he'd ever been in an approach on a target. In desert warfare there had been dunes to use as cover. Jungles were *all* cover. Most theatres of war offered something you could use to get close to the enemy unseen. But this Chinese plain was a cover-free zone. Way over in the distance, a range of mountains, silver-grey against the night sky, was the only geographical feature you couldn't roll a billiard ball over.

With less than a quarter of a mile to go, he stopped short as bright-yellow flashes from inside the base perimeter sparkled and died. Moments later, the crackle of small arms fire followed.

He dropped to his belly and pulled out the binoculars to get a better look. Nobody and nothing was moving. No attacking force, though God knew what anyone would be doing this far into the hinterland – *apart from you, Wolfe.* No obvious signs of defenders, either. In fact, inside the wire, the place looked deserted. He swung the binos left to right, searching out the source of the gunfire, which was continuing in sporadic bursts.

Just as a hut slid out of view, yellow light flashed from one of the windows. Gabriel moved the binoculars back and watched. There it was again. A short burst of automatic fire. Then, silence. He waited for five minutes. The shooter inside the hut had stopped firing.

"Have you run out of ammunition, or victims?" Gabriel

murmured, thinking of American school shooters and their pauses to reload before continuing on their murderous sprees.

Another five minutes passed and still no more shooting. He was about to get to his feet when the door at the side of the hut opened and a figured stumbled out into the moonlight.

A Chinese man carrying a semi-automatic rifle similar if not identical to the one strapped across Gabriel's back. Heavyset, with thick, oddly long black hair tied back from his face into a ponytail.

In the pin-sharp image offered by the binoculars, Gabriel could see that the man had a long wispy moustache and beard. But what made him wonder who this character was had nothing to do with his weirdly styled hair and everything to do with his clothes.

Instead of the uniform of a private soldier or officer in the PLA, some sort of camo or olive-green battledress or fatigues, he was clad in a long robe of white fabric that glistened like a pearl in the moonlight. A wide dark sash encircled his waist.

He looked up at the moon, then turned his head towards Gabriel's position. His mouth moved as if he was talking to someone, though he was alone in the space beside the hut. He gestured wildly with his left hand, shaking the rifle in his right.

Gabriel frowned as he watched the spectacle playing out in front of him. Was this Colonel Na? Impossible. Why would a high-ranking PLA officer, a missile battery commander at that, be dressed up like a priest out of a Confucian fable and arguing with an invisible companion?

The door behind him opened and a uniformed man staggered out, arms held wide in supplication. His face was bloody, the streaks and spatters rendered black by the moonlight.

The priest spun round, brought the rifle up one-handed and shot the man in the head, painting his brains against the wooden side of the hut in a black splatter.

Gabriel considered what the action he'd just watched through his binos meant. Despite a prolonged firefight inside a hut on the base, nobody had come running. No klaxon had sounded, no dogs were barking, no floodlights had blasted the ground with their searing white light. Nobody had returned fire: Gabriel was sure he'd only heard the sound of a single weapon being fired. The conclusion was inescapable. The priest was the last man alive on the base.

That brought things to a simple question. If he wasn't Na, whom Gabriel was there to kill, then who was he? In Gabriel's experience, which spanned multiple continents, cultures and communities, genuine men of God didn't wield automatic weapons.

So the oddly garbed shooter was only borrowing the raiment of a priest. The odds of a second assassin having travelled this far into the Chinese interior to massacre a base full of soldiers were not even vanishingly slim. They were zero. And even if there existed, through some statistical fluke in the universe, the infinitesimally small chance that the shooter *was* a hitman, why would he have chosen to dress in so distinctive and visible a style?

No, the figure still gesticulating and arguing with the empty air in front of him was neither a priest nor a hitman. It seemed unlikely he'd be an ancillary worker such as a cook or storeman. Guys like that, if they did lose their shit, tended to go AWOL and return to base days later stinking of cheap alcohol and tarts' perfume. That left only one option.

The man's easy way with the long gun – only an experienced fighter could wield an assault rifle one-handed like that – told Gabriel he was a combat solider.

33

From a pocket Gabriel withdrew the photo of Na that Liu had included in his dossier. It showed the colonel in full dress uniform, a peaked cap ruler-straight on his head. Obviously he was clean-shaven.

Using a small torch and shielding the beam inside a cupped hand, he scrutinised the face before him and compared it to the visage of the priest. They could be the same person, but the ponytail and facial hair made a positive ID impossible. He stowed the photo and picked up the binoculars again.

As he watched, the man strode across the front of the hut towards a small building on the extreme edge of the compound. He threw open the door and disappeared inside, closing the door behind him.

Gabriel thought back to Liu's speech in the Golden Dragon. He said Na had massacred the garrison. No, wait. He *had* said that, but then, in a throwaway remark, mentioned that Na may have gathered a few loyal soldiers around him. So, either one of these ultras had truly lost the plot or the shooter was Na.

Gabriel would find out soon enough. He stood, packed the binos away in his rucksack and walked on, towards the base. The lack of action after the firefight inside the hut meant the only man left alive on the base was the shooter, who he'd dubbed the priest.

He unscrewed the suppressor from the submachine gun's muzzle and stuck it in the rucksack. That immediately lopped almost eight inches off the gun's length, and about ten ounces off its weight.

He arrived at the fence at 3:01 a.m. He'd chosen a spot on the eastern side of the perimeter between two watch towers, well away from the scene of the earlier firefight. The towers were dark, silent, unmanned. This close he could see the perforated barrels of heavy machine guns, drooping over the edge of the wooden walls.

Working quickly, he clipped a slit in the chain-link fence with wire-cutters, pulled the two sides of the cut towards him and away from each other and slid through.

The sharp ends of the cut wires made getting in a delicate operation, but in the event of his needing a rapid exit, he'd be able to literally dive through without snagging his clothes or equipment. The voice of Don Webster came floating to him across the gulf that separated them: "By such small things are lives saved, Old Sport".

Inside the wire, he pulled on the night-vision goggles, leaving the lenses flipped up against the front of his helmet. If the clouds rolled in again, he'd need them, but not until.

Staying in the lee of the various buildings, Gabriel made his way towards the building where he'd last seen the priest. After tabbing in to the base in full combat gear, he was sweating. But he was loose, too. Ready. Breathing easily, pulse high but not racing uncontrollably. Adrenaline levels sharpening his senses and reaction times.

He rounded a corner, and came face to face with three missile trucks, parked haphazardly in front of some fuel pumps.

The six-wheeled vehicles, painted in broad camouflage bands, loomed above him as he came closer. Mounted on each were a pair of dark-tipped white missiles, angled upwards at forty five degrees. *Short-range ballistic. Probably non-nuclear.* But something was wrong.

The sides of the warheads were streaked with what appeared to be rust. The centre truck listed to its left. When Gabriel went closer he saw the cause. All three tyres on the left-hand side were flat as pancakes. *Someone's been neglecting basic maintenance. And for a long time.*

He continued his recce, peering around the front of the final truck before continuing on his way. The base appeared to be deserted. The door on the next building he came to was hanging off its hinges. Gabriel went inside. Gasped. Then immediately wished he hadn't, as the smell hit him.

Bodies lay everywhere, in various states of putrefaction. Some were intact, but most were missing heads or limbs. The floor was a sticky black lake of blood, and he could see spatters extending up the walls and onto the white-painted ceiling. Gagging at the stench of decay, he retreated into the fresh air.

Was this the scene of Na's massacre? It was impossible to tell. The next building, a two-storey brick-built blockhouse, was missing all its windows. Shot out, he assumed, from the sharp-edged triangles clinging to the frames. His boots crunched over a carpet of glass fragments. He shifted his grip on the submachine gun, tucking it more tightly into his body, and checked that the fire mode selector switch was set to full auto.

He moved on, looking all around as he neared the scene of the firefight he'd watched through the binoculars. As he approached the door, he saw more dark patches of blood staining the earth and occasional squares of weed-strewn concrete.

Something bad had happened here: Gabriel could feel the hairs on the back of his neck rising. Not just a massacre, though that was bad enough. This was something else. Because... where were the rest of the bodies?

Massacres happen in war. They shouldn't. But they do. And the evidence is usually plain to see. Bodies. Everywhere. Old men, women, children. Sometimes even babies. Domestic pets. Livestock. All fall under the bullets, the clubbing rifle butts, the grenades and bayonets.

Here, though, there was only blood. A great deal of blood.

As he approached the hut, Gabriel saw more and more of the stuff. Old, dark stains on the ground, little more than discoloured dirt. But also sticky patches and even fresh slicks and drag marks, all leading towards the door.

Sprawled in front of the door was the soldier Gabriel had seen the priest shoot point-blank in the head. His arms and legs were riddled with bullet holes. His head had burst open and was little more than an empty bone shell. Gabriel stepped over him and went inside.

The windows were all shuttered. Not wanting to turn on the lights and risk the priest seeing the glow, however limited, Gabriel flipped down his night-vision goggles and turned them on.

With a rising whine, the electronics woke up and after a second or two, Gabriel's field of view turned an acid green. He saw what he was expecting to see, but even so, he clenched his jaw.

Around thirty young men lay dead. On the floor, lying across bunks, piled on top of each other. None were armed. Most were shoeless. A large wok had been overturned. The smell of the food it had contained mixed queasily with the stench of death.

The place was a charnel-house, made all the more disquieting for being rendered only in shades of green. The blood spatters were black, as were the cavernous wounds inflicted on unprotected flesh by the rounds from the priest's assault rifle. Shaking his head, Gabriel turned and left the hut, closing the door carefully behind him.

Readying himself mentally and physically for what was to come, he turned away from the hut and made his way across fifty yards of open ground to the building into which he had seen the man he was now sure was Colonel Na disappear.

The hut measured roughly thirty-feet square. Shuttered windows to each side of the door, a shallow-pitched roof. Oddly old fashioned clapboard construction, completely out of place on a modern missile base. Even one as strange and apparently neglected as this one.

He looked past the hut. The sky there was just beginning to lighten, a pale-blue wash appearing on the horizon fading through cobalt and indigo to a soulless, unforgiving black. According to Liu, who'd briefed him on the flight out, sunrise would happen at 4.58 a.m. He had ninety minutes of darkness left.

Heart bumping against his ribs, he crept closer to the door. Had the windows not been shuttered, he would have thrown in a flash-bang, waited for the detonation of the grenade to disorientate the priest, then burst in and opened fire. As it was, that option wasn't open to him. He could try unlatching the shutters, but there was no guarantee there wouldn't be internal blinds as well. The noise would almost certainly give him away to the occupant.

Standing on the hinge side of the door, he backed up against the wall and considered his next move. On the inside was a man – a madman – armed with an assault rifle and, for all Gabriel knew, further weapons. *Test his defences, then. If he is in there, he's not going anywhere unless you let him out.*

He backed up ten yards, lay down in the dirt, aimed up at the door and fired a short burst from his submachine gun. Then he then rolled, fast, to his left before scrambling to his feet and running for cover behind a larger blockhouse.

The priest returned fire, an extended burst that tore holes in the door and wall, blowing lethal splinters towards Gabriel's previous position along with the deformed rounds. From the duration of the burst Gabriel knew Na had burned through the magazine. *Now or never!*

He rushed the door, shooting at the lock as he came within a couple of yards, and burst through, ready to kill whoever was inside. And he stopped dead.

Of the priest, there was no sign. But what faced Gabriel in the lamplit space was so horrific, so utterly alien to every standard of military behaviour, every standard of *civilised* behaviour, he had ever witnessed, that he was momentarily frozen.

34

Bones. Limbs. Heads. Internal organs. Lengths of – *Oh my God!*
strung together into a hellish... *What is that?* Struggling to process the
scene before him Gabriel groped for the right word. Na had
fashioned a grotesque altar – *Yes, altar. That's what it is* – from his
victims. Most disturbing of all were the tiny skulls placed left and
right of the main tower of human body parts, their sightless eyes
looking straight at Gabriel.

The place reeked of incense, which issued from hundreds of lit
sticks glowing redly in holders placed around the periphery of the
hut. But the sickly sweet smell was failing utterly to mask the stink
from the altar. Trying to breathe shallowly through his mouth, and
avoiding thinking of the implications for his lungs, Gabriel swept the
barrel of his submachine gun left and right, finger curled round the
trigger and itching to squeeze it, to obliterate the monster who had
created this obscene travesty of a place of worship.

Not expecting an answer, Gabriel shouted into the blackness.

"Colonel Na! Come out. It's over."

He heard a noise from the rear of the hut, behind a rough
wooden partition. A man's voice, singing. Gabriel dropped to one

knee, aiming at a spot roughly head-height where the screen ended, halfway across the space. He shouted again.

"Na! Get out here!"

His heart was racing. Whatever he had been expecting inside the wire perimeter fence of a Chinese missile battery it hadn't been this. A male voice called out.

"Grandfather! Come and see! I am uniting the three kingdoms. Have I succeeded? Is my work over?"

Gabriel got to his feet. He backed away from the partition, took one final look at the grotesque assemblage of body parts then silently opened the door and left. He ran round to the rear of the building, where he found a second door.

With the submachine gun in his right hand, he placed his left on the door handle and pushed down. Something inside the mechanism grated as it reached the halfway point. He increased the pressure and the handle overcame the internal obstacle and reached the end of its travel. He threw it wide and strode in, gun lowered.

"Oh Jesus!"

Facing the door, Na was kneeling before a crude wooden table, just six inches off the floor. To Na's left lay a male corpse, before him, an arm, the bicep muscles removed from the bone. He held the bloody chunk of flesh in both hands and was gnawing at it. The lower half of his face was covered in blood, his beard and moustache matted. He looked up at Gabriel.

"Is that you, Grandfather? Is it over? Have I succeeded?" he asked in a light, high-pitched voice, almost that of a child.

Despite his horror, Gabriel was fascinated by the man's appearance and oddly distracted manner. Even though he was facing an armed intruder in full combat gear, Na seemed not to be seeing Gabriel at all. He looked oddly calm. Forehead smooth, eyes relaxed, though swinging from side to side in their sockets, mouth in a slack smile.

"What do you mean, 'Grandfather'?"

"Then you are *Great*-Grandfather? I am so sorry. I am not sleeping well these days. You all become so mixed up in my mind. But I am done, yes? You are pleased with my work?"

Na half-turned and pointed at the altar, which was half-visible beyond the partition.

"No, I'm not pleased. What have you done? Who are those people?"

Na smiled.

"Those? The villagers. Mostly, I mean. Towards the end, I had to start using some of the Ghost Warriors. They died willingly." He held up the dripping piece of meat. "I am uniting the three kingdoms, Great-Grandfather, just like you told me. Like you all told me."

He waved his hand in a vague semi-circle, flicking drops of blood around, and smiled at the empty hut. Then he threw the bloody lump up at Gabriel. Gabriel squeezed his trigger, firing a short burst at Na. But the man was quick. As Gabriel ducked away, Na pulled a small pistol from his sash and rolled sideways. He screamed as a round hit him in the thigh, then fired back. His aim was wild and the pistol round struck the partition, yards from Gabriel.

Gabriel fired again, and this time he didn't miss. His second burst took Na in the torso. Na crumpled, blood fountaining from the wounds in his stomach and chest and foaming from his wide-open mouth.

Gabriel bent to pick up the pistol Na had dropped. The base commander looked up at him and, in a gurgle, spoke one final time.

"I have united them all. Heaven, Earth and—"

"No. You haven't. You're insane."

"– and the Underworld. You do understand that, Great-Grandfather, don't you? You have to understand. Otherwise what was the point?"

Gabriel levelled the submachine gun.

"There was no point."

Waiting for a dawning comprehension in Na's eyes, and seeing none, Gabriel pulled the trigger a third time and sent Colonel Na to meet his ancestors for good.

Gabriel shouldered the submachine gun and took a few photos of Na's bullet-riddled body on his phone. He debated whether to return to the scene of carnage beyond the partition and photograph that, too, but decided against it. If Liu wanted pictorial evidence of Na's descent into madness he could come and take them himself.

Outside, he filled his lungs with clean, cool air, taking several huge breaths and roaring them out again in an attempt to cleanse himself of what he had witnessed. The sky had lightened further and the first glimmer of the sun showed pale orange on the eastern horizon.

Keeping the submachine gun level at his hip, he wandered out from the hut where he had killed Colonel Na. Some twenty yards distant he saw a large wooden-sided vat, standing on a square of concrete. Its circular lid lay on the ground beside it. Fearing what he would see if he leaned over the rim, yet unable to resist the pull of his own curiosity, he approached the vat. As he drew closer a sharp chemical stink reached his nostrils. He recognised it. Acid. Holding his breath, he closed the gap with the vat and leaned over the side, his eyes smarting from the fumes.

As he peered into the dark liquid, a bubble the size of an orange wobbled its way to the surface, followed by several more, all diminishing in size. He watched, horrified, as a whitish shape turned lazily in the depths of the vat. Two dark circles appeared, a smaller black space beneath them, and then, causing him to rear back, a grinning double-row of teeth.

Gabriel turned and walked away. Took one final tour of the now-deserted missile base, checking every one of the buildings for signs of life, but finding none. The place was silent.

Shouldering his weapon, he found the slit in the fence and pushed through, standing up on the exterior side of the chain-link and striding off, back towards the Rhino.

As he marched, he kept seeing the grotesque altar that Na had built from human remains. The man had been clearly insane. He had murdered men, women and children. He deserved to die. Deserved to be put down like a diseased animal, without compunction, without pity. And yet, Gabriel did feel pity. The man had clearly been suffering from a delusion that his ancestors were ordering him to commit his heinous acts. Gabriel had done him a favour. It was no way to live.

Then he thought of his own motivation. His own reason for travelling deep into the interior of mainland China, doing the combined bidding of a Triad boss and a high-ranking Communist Party official. An official who, if he was consorting with Fang, was almost certainly corrupt.

Is this what your life has come to, then? he asked himself. *A hired killer. Wandering the world snuffing out the candles of people's lives on the whims and orders of other people. Not for queen and country. Not even for money. Just to pay back a favour?*

He found the notion unsettling and shoved it down somewhere where he couldn't see it anymore. As the sun rose he was able to see the terrain through which he was walking for the first time. A barren place, nothing in the way of vegetation beyond scrappy grass and patches of yellow lichen. He realised he was hungry and decided to eat as soon as he reached the safety of his vehicle.

After a further forty minutes walking, he reached the Rhino. He unlatched the rear door and stowed his gear, then fetched out a pack of C-rations and broke the seal. Inside was pretty much what he had been expecting; a brown goop that smelled vaguely of meat. He spooned it down, grateful for the calories if not the flavour, then drank a bottle of water.

In the crew cab he pulled out the satellite phone and called Liu, who answered immediately.

"Is he dead?" was Liu's opening question.

"Yes. He was mad, did you know that? He had some fucked-up temple with an altar made of human body parts. And he was a cannibal. I found him chowing down on a man's arm."

"My intelligence was... " Liu paused before continuing, "... not clear on that point. But anyway, I thank you on behalf of the People's Republic of China. Remain in position and leave the satellite phone on. I will send a team to extract you in a helicopter. They can home in on your GPS signal. It will take them about four hours to reach you. Oh, and one last thing. It would be best, safest I mean, for you to leave the Rhino and your weapons at the base and

ANDY MASLEN

change back into your own clothing. Then get a few miles away. Fewer awkward questions to answer if local police should come across you."

Liu ended the call. Gabriel leaned back against the headrest and closed his eyes. What on earth was Liu talking about? He was in the middle of nowhere, thousands of miles from the nearest police station. The only forces of the Chinese state were lying dead and dismembered within the perimeter fence of the missile base. He decided to ignore the instruction. Instead, he drove five miles away from the base, on a bearing that would take him towards the village from which Na had taken so many of his victims.

He stopped at a meander in the dry river bed, took the binoculars and climbed onto the roof. Through the lenses of the binos he could see clearly the roofs of the village houses. Little more than huts, most of them, maybe a mile and a half distant. *Might as well go and have a look.*

He climbed down and stripped to the waist before splashing another bottle of water over his torso and cleaning off the grime and blood spatter. Dressed again, he wandered away from the Rhino, armed with just the pistol, leaving the satphone on the driver's seat, its green ON light glowing weakly. The sun was higher in the sky and it warmed Gabriel's back as he walked. In the distance, away to his right, he saw movement. At least one human figure and what might have been animals of some kind. He checked through the binoculars and frowned.

He was looking at a peasant in traditional brightly woven clothes that looked more Central Asian than Chinese. He was driving a small herd of bony-looking cows with a long stick. But smaller, dog-like animals seemed to be attacking the little group. The peasant was waving his stick above his head and bringing it down. It looked as though he was trying to hit the dogs.

Gabriel ran towards the group. As he closed the gap between them he could hear the peasant's voice, high-pitched, screaming – *maybe a woman, then, not a man at all.* The wild dogs, for now he could see their tawny pelts, were darting forwards to bite the peasant woman and her cows. He picked up speed and when he reached the

208

fifty-yard point, started yelling. A couple of the pack of dogs turned at this new sound, baring their teeth at Gabriel.

He sprinted on, drawing his pistol and firing a shot above their heads. At this, much louder, noise, which maybe they'd heard before, the whole pack broke off their attack and turned as one to face the intruder. Up close, Gabriel could see there were around ten of the beasts.

"Get lost! Fuck off!" he screamed at them as he got within twenty feet and brought himself to a stop.

The animal nearest to him growled and advanced a few steps on stiff legs. Its hackles had erected in a ruff that doubled the size of its neck. Its yellow fangs were long, bared right down to the roots.

Without hesitating, Gabriel extended his right arm and shot the beast through the head. It spun sideways with a drawn-out scream before dying. Their leader down, the remaining dogs turned tail and ran off, yipping and crying to each other.

Gabriel ran over to the woman, who had collapsed on her side and was breathing heavily. The dogs had inflicted a few nasty-looking bites on her lower legs.

35

Liu stared at the mobile phone in his hand for a few seconds after the British assassin had ended the call. Then he smiled with satisfaction. Na was dead. Liu, his job and his privileges were all safe. He dialled a number from memory. A PLA airforce captain whose new summer residence on the shores of a picturesque lake Liu had paid for. He spoke briefly.

"Comrade Xin, it is time. Go and get the Englishman."

"Yes, Comrade Liu. You told him to keep his satphone on?"

"Of course!" Liu snapped.

With this final detail taken care of, Liu left the office building. Suddenly hungry, he headed for a nearby restaurant, smiling as he thought how easy it was to manipulate people. The story about the summit was a pretence. No need to let the Englishman know how important this was to him. He'd laid on the flight specifically to get the assassin to the base. After dropping him and the Rhino, they'd flown south again.

36

The woman looked to be in her late seventies, tanned to a deep nut-brown, with her iron-grey hair scraped back into a bun beneath a wide-brimmed straw hat. Her lips were drawn back from her teeth and she was hissing in pain.

Gabriel knelt beside her. He stared into her eyes.

"Don't worry, Mother," he said in a calming voice. "I'll help you. I have medicine in here."

He pointed over his shoulder, then shucked off his backpack and brought it slowly round in front of him. Her eyes followed his hands, as if fearful of whatever he might bring forth.

After undoing the plastic clips, he slowly opened out the top and reached in to retrieve a bottle of water and the first aid kit. He cracked the seal on the water bottle and washed the bites. Most were superficial, grazes more than puncture wounds, but one dog had clearly fastened its canine teeth into the woman's calf. Blood was flowing freely from four holes. She moaned as the water washed into the wounds, carrying away more blood that streamed down her calf and into her boot.

"I'm sorry, Mother," Gabriel said. "I will be as quick as I can."

He puffed white sulphonamide powder over the whole area then squirted blobs of antiseptic cream onto each of the puncture wounds. He added more to the centre of a square sterile field dressing, which he placed over the bite. Gently taking her right hand, he pushed it against the dressing.

"Hold it there, as hard as you can."

She nodded, then pressed her palm flat against the padded white square. Gabriel picked at the end of a roll of micropore tape and, once he'd freed it, fixed the dressing in place. He treated her other wounds with more antiseptic cream, relieved to find that none were bleeding.

The cows had scattered during the wild dogs' attack but were now wandering around, nibbling at scraps of grass and lichen. Gabriel stood and picked up the long stick the woman had been carrying. For some reason he couldn't fathom, a song his mother used to sing to him when he was a small boy unable to sleep popped into his head. He crooned it now as he approached the cows, arms wide, the tip of the stick dragging in the dirt.

The beasts were obviously expecting to be collected: they reformed themselves into a loose knot under Gabriel's gentle prompting. He worked his way behind them and, still singing, ushered them back towards their owner.

By the time he reached her, the old woman had got to her feet. She smiled as he arrived and handed her stick back to her. She reached out and stroked the forelock of the nearest cow. It lowed with pleasure and came closer until its slabby head was nudging her side. She wrapped an arm over the cow's neck and leaned on it.

"Thank you, Son. You are a very kind man to help an old woman like that. You had no need."

Gabriel offered her a small bow.

"I had every need, Mother," he said. "I couldn't stand by and let the dogs hurt you and your animals."

She nodded and smiled.

"Are you from the base, then? You don't look like you're from round here."

"No, not from the base."

"Then you are a long way from home. Where do you come from? Beijing?"

Gabriel laughed. Perhaps she mistook his unfamiliar, Western looks for those of a city dweller. They were fifteen hundred miles from Beijing after all, and her closest town of any size was Urumqi.

"No, Mother. I am from England."

Her eyes opened wide, revealing irises of a startlingly bright blue.

"England? I have seen England on the TV. We have satellite, you know," she said with obvious pride. "What are you doing all the way out here? And how come you speak our language so well?"

He opted for a version of the truth.

"My mum was half-Chinese. She taught me. And I am travelling. I have always wanted to see this part of China."

She shook her head, displaying on her features a mixture of amazement and acceptance. She spread her hands.

"Are you hungry? Thirsty? I am on my way home. You should come to see our village."

Gabriel was about to decline when he realised he had enough time. He wanted to spend some time with other human beings – other human beings who weren't so far off their rockers they were coming round to meet themselves on the other side.

"Thank you. I would like that very much. Can you walk?"

She grinned, revealing brown teeth.

"It will take more than a dog bite to stop me from getting where I want to. But I will take your arm, if that's OK. Here, have this."

She handed him the stick, then threaded her arm through his. As they set off he looked behind him, worried that the cows might wander off again. But the stick was clearly more for show or from force of habit than any genuine need. The cows were contentedly walking along behind them as they headed towards the village.

"Is your leg all right?" he asked her.

"It's fine. Just a bit sore, that's all. You are a fine doctor!"

He laughed.

"How is life in your village?"

She frowned. He wondered whether she had lost family members to Colonel Na's temple.

"We have suffered in recent years. You see, the colonel, he—" She broke off, looking back towards the missile base. "Can you hear that?"

"What?"

"Shh!"

She looked over her shoulder. Then she pointed upwards.

"Over there. One of their helicopters is coming."

He listened and heard it: the distinctive sound of a helicopter approaching at full speed, the hard-edged clatter of its rotor blades travelling through the wide-open airspace.

Gabriel suddenly felt torn. He picked out the chopper, a black shape in the sky to the north, growing larger. It was his ride home. But he also wanted, for reasons he couldn't fathom, to continue helping the old woman, and to return her safely to her village.

He checked his watch and frowned. *They're way too early. Liu said it would be four hours.* A flicker of apprehension ignited in his gut. He recognised it for what it was. A message. Not from his subconscious. Not from Master Zhao. From his army training. And the message was simple to decode. *If it feels off, it is off. Find cover. Wait. Watch. Prepare.*

He didn't want to alarm the old woman. He turned to her.

"That will be for me. They are sending one to collect me."

"Who?"

Gabriel hesitated.

"The British Government. We can call a special phone number if we get too far from home."

Her eyes widened.

"That is amazing! I don't think our government would be so caring. Do you want to go back? I will be fine."

"It's OK. Let's just watch them land. I can get back there in ten minutes if I run. They won't leave without me."

She pointed at his pistol, which he'd stuck in his belt.

"You could always fire your gun. They'd be bound to hear it."

"That's a good idea. But let's just see what happens."

She leant against him as they stood side by side, for all the world like two spectators at an air show. Albeit one attended only by two humans and a handful of bony cows, who seemed more interested in scraping a few mouthfuls of lichen up than the latest Chinese military hardware.

A few minutes later, the chopper landed to the left of the Rhino. Gabriel brought out his binoculars and held them to his eyes. What he saw half a mile away confirmed that his training-backed intuition had been on the money.

37

Four soldiers jumped down from the black square of the chopper's side door. They wore camouflage and helmets, which might have been justifiable. But what made Gabriel pat the woman's shoulder with his left hand to get her to crouch alongside him wasn't their clothing. It was their equipment.

All four men carried assault rifles. To protect their charge from the remnants of Colonel Na's forces? Tenuous at best. But while two of them held their rifles ready to fire, two had theirs strapped across their backs. They wanted to free their hands for their other weapons: rocket-propelled grenades. That settled it. He'd been right to hang back. Without taking his eyes off the soldiers he spoke.

"Mother, please may I borrow your hat? Could you put it on my head for me?"

She complied wordlessly, settling the wide-brimmed straw hat over his forehead so that it touched the top of the binoculars.

"And could you drape your cloak over my shoulders?"

Again, without speaking, she slipped her brightly-coloured woven cloak off her own shoulders and draped it around Gabriel's.

"Now you look like one of us," she whispered, showing a fine grasp of military tactics even from so brief an exposure to them.

The soldiers spread out into a line about a hundred yards from the Rhino. Gabriel watched, with a mixture of anger and incredulity, as the two carrying the RPGs shouldered their weapons and aimed at the truck. They fired in unison, and Gabriel followed the white smoke trails as the rockets streaked towards their target. Him.

The rockets only took a few seconds to reach the Rhino. One flew straight through the side window of the cab, the other exploded against its thinly armoured sides, igniting a fireball that rolled upwards, surrounded by a writhing web of oily black smoke that twined and shifted on a column of flame. The noise of the detonations reached them moments later, a deep-bellied double-thump overlaid with a tenor crackle as Gabriel's remaining ammunition, and that for the roof-mounted heavy machine gun, began exploding.

Behind him, Gabriel could hear the cows lowing with apprehension, their hooves scuffling on the dry ground. The old woman got to her feet.

"I have to calm them or they will run away."

Gabriel listened to her caressing voice as she settled the cows and tapped her long stick on the ground to bring them back into a tight group. While she mumbled little nonsense phrases to the agitated animals, he watched the endgame playing out in front of him.

The four soldiers were approaching the burning Rhino, rifles at the ready. They stopped about thirty metres away from the burning wreck and began firing on full auto at its side. Once they'd burned through the first magazines, they stopped to reload, moved fore and aft and repeated the assault. At that point the petrol tank exploded with a dull crump and another yellow-orange explosion, driving them back.

Finally, apparently satisfied they'd killed the British hitman, they about-turned and ran back to the chopper and were airborne seconds later. The pilot wheeled the bird away to the north, overflying the missile base on his way to report, presumably to Comrade Liu, that the clean-up had been completed.

Adding Liu to a list of personal enemies that never seemed to drop below five, Gabriel got to his feet, stowing the binoculars in his backpack and sliding his arms through the straps again. *Shit! That was my ride. Now what? I'm stuck in the arse-end of nowhere with a pistol and a first-aid kit. But I've been in tighter scrapes. And I have a friend.* He turned to look at the old woman, who was regarding him through narrowed eyes, her left hand resting on the thin neck of a cinnamon-coloured cow.

"I don't think your government likes you very much, Son," she said. "To do that to your car. You're sure you're just a traveller?"

Gabriel made a split-second decision and took a deep breath.

"I'm sorry, Mother. I lied to you. I wasn't sure how much it was safe to tell you. I'm not a traveller, I'm a soldier. I came out here to kill Colonel Na. I *did* kill Colonel Na. He was murdering people. Did you know that? Is that what you were about to tell me?"

She nodded and her face creased with pain he felt sure had nothing to do with her recent wounds.

"He sent his soldiers to our village. They came with guns and took people. Youngsters, mostly, even children. Even babies. Nobody ever came back. Four of our elders went to the base to complain. They didn't return either. After that, we tried to keep our children hidden when the soldiers came. They called themselves Ghost Warriors. We could do nothing. The colonel was a very powerful man. The Party, you know. He told us he was our God. We pretended to believe him. We thought it would make him go away and leave us in peace. We were wrong."

She winced then, and stumbled, squeezing Gabriel's arm harder to prevent herself falling.

"Hey," Gabriel said. "You need to rest. Can you ride on one of your cows? Will they let you?"

She nodded.

"Charming Flower will let me."

She pointed at a cow at the back, its hide a mixture of white and brown splotches. Gabriel helped her mount the docile beast, which stood still until the old woman was astride its bony back. Gabriel walked alongside, but the cow seemed used to bearing human cargo, and in this way, the unlikely group covered the remaining few miles to the village without further incident.

She introduced herself as Zhan Yan, though Gabriel knew better than to use her name and persisted in using the respectful 'Mother' whenever he spoke to her. Her attempts to pronounce his own name made both of them laugh. In the end she threw up her hands in despair.

"I will give you a new name. One I can say. How about Jié Bai-Luo? That means Brave He-Who-Shines. It fits well, yes?"

"Done. For you I will be Jié Bai-Luo."

"So, Jié Bai-Luo. Now we have introduced ourselves, and I am comfortable, it is time for you to tell me what that man was doing with our youngsters."

"It is not easy to tell, Mother. And it won't be easy to hear."

Over the next few minutes, speaking in plain language, without hiding anything, but avoiding painting too graphic a picture, Gabriel told her what he had seen. Throughout his telling, she said nothing, nodding from time to time and covering her mouth at one point. When he had finished, she remained silent for a while. Finally, she spoke.

"If you killed that evil man, I am glad. We will do what we can to help you make your way home."

The village turned out to be a sizeable collection of huts and small white-painted houses, built, seemingly from local stone, and roofed with corrugated iron, wooden shingles or even a rudimentary thatch made of long reed stems, though Gabriel couldn't see where they would have found them.

A main street hosted a couple of small shops, little more than wooden shacks with merchandise displayed on tables outside or hanging from racks. A café occupied a prime spot in the centre of the village. Old people were playing cards at battered aluminium-and-plastic tables and chairs arranged outside.

Chickens strutted and pecked between the tables, bullying sparrows out of the way, and everywhere he looked, stray cats and the odd, yellow-coated dog prowled, sniffed, scratched or slept in the sun.

Their arrival was greeted at first with curiosity about Gabriel and then with concern as Mrs Zhan explained what had happened. Two burly men in middle-age lifted her down from the cow's back and carried her into a house in the centre of the dirt road running north-south through the village.

Before she let them carry her there, Mrs Zhan told the villagers to look after their guest, who had saved her life, and that of her cattle, and who would explain about Colonel Na.

The villagers, from old men and women to toddlers with runny noses and podgy little bellies, crowded round Gabriel, asking questions, trying to touch his face, smiling, grinning, laughing each time he spoke Chinese in his "fancy" accent.

He allowed himself to be led to a building larger than the neighbouring houses. This appeared to be the village hall. Inside, most of the space was given over to a large, rectangular meeting room, with bright tapestries hanging on the walls, and, somewhat incongruously, an upright piano in one corner.

Strong tea, sweetened with dark-brown sugar, was brought, along with delicious buns flavoured with honey. Suddenly aware he was ravenously hungry, Gabriel smiled and nodded, offering his formal thanks as he munched on the sweet pastries and drank the tea. As soon as he emptied his cup, a slender woman with pale-blue eyes and long dark hair came forward to refill it, smiling at him.

"Yan is my grandmother," she said, shyly, looking at him as she poured more tea. "We keep telling her she should let one of the younger ones take the cows to the pasture, but she won't listen."

Wondering where on the baked landscape he had seen there could be pastureland sufficient for cows, Gabriel smiled.

"She seems like a very strong-willed lady."

At that moment the strong-willed lady entered the room to cries of delight and a flurry of questions.

"What happened, Grandmother?"

"Are you all right?"

"Who is the stranger?"

"How can he speak our language so well?"

"What is a *gweilo* doing all the way out here?"

At the use of the slang term for a Westerner, Mrs Zhan's blue eyes flashed with anger.

"Who called my friend that?"

The room fell silent. She continued.

"This man just saved my life. You should bow down before him for what he has done for us."

She turned to Gabriel.

"Tell them about Colonel Na, Jié Bai-Luo."

Gabriel stood and watched as the villagers, perhaps a hundred in all, angled their chairs to face him, as if he were giving a mission briefing. At the back, some of the younger children had wandered off and were playing a clapping game in the far corner of the room, but every other pair of eyes, most the same shade of bright-blue as Mrs Zhan's, never left him.

"Colonel Na, as you know, was an evil man. I was sent here to stop him or his Ghost Warriors murdering anybody else. When I arrived at the missile base I discovered he had shot all of his men. I found him in some sort of temple. I killed him there."

One of the two men who had lifted Mrs Zhan down from the cow stood and addressed Gabriel, though from the way his eyes swept the room it was clear to Gabriel he was the village headman.

"Thank you, Jié Bai-Luo. That man was a monster. He deserved to die for what he did to us. In the morning, I will take some of the men over there. We need to find the bodies of our loved ones."

Gabriel desperately wanted to warn the man of what he would find at the base, but was fearful of the crowd's reaction if he did it in open forum. He caught Mrs Zhan's eye. She shook her head once, a barely visible movement that communicated plenty. *Not now. Later. We need to bury our dead, whatever is left of them.*

"I will help you, if you'll let me."

The headman nodded.

"Thank you. But what can we do for you? You have done us a great service. We are in your debt."

"I don't feel you owe me anything. But my vehicle was destroyed. I need to get away from here, if you can help."

"Where is your home?"

"He comes from England," Mrs Zhan said.

This simple sentence caused a collective gasp.

"It's true," Gabriel hastily interrupted, assuming that these villagers, whether or not they had satellite TV, would be overcome with the magnitude of the task of returning a visitor to the other side of the planet. "But I am heading to Hong Kong."

"Ah. That will be a little easier, but you know, that is still many thousands of miles away."

A hand went up in the third row of seats pulled into a shallow semicircle in front of Gabriel.

"I am driving my truck over to Kazakhstan the day after tomorrow. Ayagoz first, then south to Taskesken, then Urzhar, then back home. A week-long trip. I have a load of textiles to trade. You can come with me, if you like. Maybe pick up a ride from one of the long-distance boys heading down the A-350 to Almaty. Big city, Almaty is. They've got an airport. You could probably fly all the way home to Hong Kong from there. Maybe even to England."

Gabriel smiled at the man. It was a pretty good plan.

"Thank you. I'll take you up on your kind offer."

The man smiled and placed his hand on his chest, over his heart.

"Name's Chan. But everybody calls me Little Dog, on account of I used to chase cats when I was a baby."

The man's use of his own nickname caused laughter from the others. Gabriel hoped they would find time to laugh like this once they learned the gruesome fate that had befallen so many of their children.

Later, once the meeting had broken up, the headman came to stand in front of Gabriel. He knew what was coming. Readied himself to deliver the awful truth. The headman's question was as short and as simple as it could be.

"What happened to them?"

Gabriel sighed. No. This was not the moment to use euphemisms or to dress up the truth in delicate language.

"Colonel Na killed them. He ate parts of them and used other parts to build an altar. I think he believed he was doing the bidding of his ancestors. There was – is – a vat of acid. He was using it to clean the bones. I am sorry."

The man's eyes closed for a couple of seconds, and his lips tightened, drawing vertical lines through his top lip.

"You have nothing to say sorry for. Thank you for telling me the truth."

Gabriel nodded. The man's stoicism in the face of such terrible news was impressive. He wondered how harsh life would have to be before you could marshal your emotions in the face of the news that your friends and family had been murdered and eaten.

38

After a meal of roasted chicken and rice, cooked by the village women and served in the hall, Gabriel sat patiently, answering questions. To prevent his thinking they weren't up to the task of entertaining a stranger, the villagers had clearly decided that beer was the answer.

Two teenaged girls, pretty in their traditional woven outfits, brought him a fresh can as soon as he finished its predecessor. They seemed slightly overwhelmed by their role as waitresses to this strange-looking foreigner, and blushed each time they approached him. Smiling at them only made it worse, eliciting embarrassed giggles. Although they seemed unmoved by the news, Gabriel noticed that the older people's faces were drawn, their mouths downturned.

Much later – his watch said 1.45 a.m. – he found himself alone in a hut in the centre of the village. The owner, Little Dog, had vacated the property for him, assuring Gabriel that he had changed the bedding and would collect him in the morning to enjoy breakfast together.

Sipping from a cup of green tea his host had made for him before departing, and trying to ignore the dizziness threatening to send the room spinning, he spread out his kit on the single bed. He had the pistol, a box of fifty rounds of spare ammunition, the binoculars, the first-aid kit, and his wallet and phone.

On an impulse, he picked up the phone and called Eli.

"If it's voicemail," he slurred, "I'm going to be really—"

"Hello. How are you? *Where* are you?"

Eli's voice was so clear she could have been standing behind him. She sounded happy. The sound of her voice made Gabriel smile. He sat heavily on the bed.

"Me? Er, I'm in this village. In Northern China. Habahe County, Altay Perfec–, no, Prefecture, Xinjiang Autonomous Region. It's called Ulungur. The village is, not the region, that's called—"

Eli laughed.

"Wolfe, are you drunk?"

"I might be. The people are very hospital. Hos-pit-able, I mean. I've had about ten beers and then we had this local firewater. They call it Dragon's Tears. Tastes of plums. Very strong. I called to tell you I love you."

She laughed again.

"I love you, too. Are you OK?"

"Yeah, I'm fine. Tippy-top. Colonel Na isn't though. I killed him. Bastard was eating people, El, can you believe that? A fucking cannibal. I mean, literally an insane, cannibalistic, fucking communist nutcase."

"Whoa! Slow down. We haven't spoken since you dropped me at Heathrow, remember?"

"Oh yeah. Right. Long story, short. Fang Jian is a triad boss. I owed him. He owed this Communist Party guy. The Communist Party guy wanted a rogue PLA colonel dead. I deaded him. Now I'm in a village in the boondocks."

"How are you getting out? What's the plan?"

"Ah, ever the practical one. Well, there's been a bit of a hitch. I had a Rhinoceros. Not a real one. Like a Humvee or what was it we had in Kazakhstan that time? That one we used to blow that factory all to shit."

"A Caracal."

"Yeah. Exactly! A Crackerel. So, *we* had a wildcat and *I've* got a rhino. Only now I haven't because bloody Liu blew it up with RPGs."

"Who's – oh, never mind. So how are you going to get away? Presumably there'll be PLA troops after you now if you just killed a base commander."

"Nope. They're the ones who hired me. But I'm thinking they want to clean up after themselves. Outsourced the wet work, now they airbrush me out of the picture. Only I got away disguised as a peasant with this old lady called Mrs Zhan. To answer your question, I'm going to work the day after tomorrow as a driver's mate with this bloke called Little Dog. Over the border to Kazakhstan then I'm gonna hitch down to Almaty and catch a plane back to Hong Kong."

"Don't they have border controls?"

"Yeah, but Little Dog says his cousin's on the gate and anyway, even if he isn't, you just bung them a few notes and it's 'on you go, sunshine,' which is funny because his first name is Sun. Not like Sun in our language, but in Cantonese. You know, like Sun Tzu. He wrote *The Art of War*."

"Yes, Gabriel, I do know that. Now, listen. Drinks lots of water, take some painkillers and get your head down, OK? I want you back here safe and sound ASAP. You hear me, soldier?"

"Yes, ma'am! Night night."

"Night night, you drunken bum."

———

Seven hours later, Gabriel woke up. He opened one eye and saw the empty glass jug beside the bed. Two cardboard packets lay beside it, both open. He remembered following Eli's orders, popping out two paracetamol and two ibuprofen and chasing them down with the contents of the jug. He lifted his head off the pillow, waiting for a sudden jolt of pain. None came. *Excellent! Must be the local air.*

He was washed and dressed and waiting outside in the sunshine when Little Dog came to collect him. Breakfast was a simple meal. Rice and vegetables at the café, washed down with green tea.

As his host was settling up with the owner, having absolutely refused Gabriel's sincere attempt to pay, the village headman arrived outside in a gleaming white pickup. Gabriel went out to meet him.

Four men sat facing each other in the truck bed and another two sat forwards in the crew cab. They smiled, but these were just social expressions, completely different from the happier faces that had greeted Gabriel the night before. They were dressed for work, too. Dark cotton tops and black trousers or jeans over work boots.

The rear passenger door of the four-man crew cab opened, pushed by a muscular arm.

"Get in," the arm's owner said, not unfriendly, but clearly tense at the thought of what he was about to do.

Gabriel climbed in and slammed the door behind him.

"Good morning," he said.

The men mumbled greetings, all betraying their feelings through tight faces and downcast eyes. Gabriel could feel their pain: it leaked out of them in waves, making the cramped cabin feel as sombre as a funeral parlour.

They had good reason. They knew they were only there to collect human remains, of loved ones, of friends, of mothers, fathers, sons and daughters. The headman rounded the front of the truck and climbed in. He started the engine and pumped the accelerator a couple of times, making the motor roar. He turned in his seat and looked at Gabriel.

"You're sure they're all dead? The soldiers, I mean."

"Yes. I checked every building. Some were quite recent, but there's no doubt in my mind. You'll be safe."

"I'm not sure my people will ever feel safe again, but thank you. OK, let's go," he finished, pushing the gear lever into first and letting off the handbrake.

Half an hour later, they arrived at the front gate. On a huge white-painted sign, block-printed type announced that they had arrived at:

People's Liberation Army
114th Division
XINJIANG PROVINCE, EASTERN THEATRE

A red-and-white banded barrier blocked the entrance, the long, cantilevered pole resting in a steel cradle to the right of the gate. The cinder-block gatehouse was empty. Beyond the barrier, the base looked deserted. *All it needs is a tumbleweed*, Gabriel thought.

"I'll get the gate," he said, climbing out and stretching before walking over to the barrier and pushing down on the weighted end.

The headman rolled to a stop, and wound his window down.

"Which way?"

Gabriel pointed in the direction of the hut where he'd found Colonel Na.

"Over there. It's the last building on the access road. I'll meet you there."

The headman nodded and put the truck in gear. Gabriel crossed an open expanse of concrete, heading for the main building. Inside, the stench of decay was nauseating. Breathing as shallowly as possible, Gabriel got out his phone and began taking pictures and video. Once he'd captured all the details he felt might have military value, he left. He repeated the process in a couple of the other buildings, especially those housing communications equipment.

Finally, he entered the barracks hut where Na had slaughtered the last of his men. Ignoring the carnage as much as he was able, Gabriel stooped to retrieve an assault rifle. He dropped out the magazine, found it full, and slotted it back into its receiving slot. *No harm in having a little extra firepower, even if the enemy has destroyed its own forces.*

Outside again, he filled his lungs with clean, warm air and walked towards the altar hut. A heavy weight settled over his heart as he thought of how the village men must be feeling.

He pushed the door open and stepped inside. He could hear the murmurs of the men beyond the wooden partition. Low, sad voices, but purposeful, too.

He crossed the room and joined the men beyond the partition, leaning the rifle against the wall. Tear-streaked faces were bent over the altar as they dismantled the unholy assembly of bones and body parts. They'd brought plastic sacks with them and were placing the remains inside. Two of the men had the unenviable task of dismantling the wall behind the altar. Reverently, they carried the bleached skulls over to the pile of bags and wrapped them individually before placing them in a row against the wall.

"Where is Na?" Gabriel asked.

One of the men jerked his thumb over his shoulder at the open door.

"We chucked the bastard out there."

The smell – a mixture of stale incense and rot – was thick and clinging, coating Gabriel's throat as he joined them in their grisly task.

Every ten minutes or so, they took a break, leaving the cloying atmosphere inside to breathe some fresh air. Na's corpse lay, facedown, a few feet to the right of the door.

A couple of the men pulled out cigarettes, and one offered his pack to Gabriel, who shook his head.

"No thanks."

"It's not for the nicotine. It helps with the smell. Go on," the man said, pushing the pack at Gabriel a second time.

"OK, thanks."

Gabriel took a cigarette and bent his head towards the match cupped in the other man's weathered hand. He sucked down some smoke, coughed and choked it out again, eliciting a brief burst of jagged laughter from the others. Shaking their heads, they finished their own cigarettes, ground out the butts beneath their heels and went back inside.

The work took another two hours. The altar had disappeared, a dark brownish-red stain on the wooden floor the only remaining sign of Colonel Na's insane tribute to his ancestors' demands. In its stead, an array of twenty or so black plastic bags, lumpy and misshapen from their sad contents.

Gabriel helped the village men carry the bags outside and load them into the truck.

"This is only some parts of our people," the headman said, lifting the last bag onboard then closing the rear door of the pickup. "Where's all the rest? That madman can't have eaten everything."

Gabriel thought of the acid bath.

"I don't know. He might have buried them, but my guess is he didn't bother. I'm sorry, but he probably left them out for scavengers."

The headman grunted his acknowledgement.

"You're probably right. There are plenty of wolves out here, the red dogs, too, like the ones you rescued Mrs Zhan from. Plus eagles, vultures, all kinds of creatures who feast on the dead."

Gabriel opened his mouth to answer but the sound died on his lips, replaced by a gunshot.

39

The headman grimaced and clutched his left arm, blood flowing between his fingers, before falling sideways. Gabriel whirled round. A hundred yards away, a soldier was staggering towards them, his rifle waving wildly from side to side. His face was a mask of red and a loop of intestines was dangling from a wound in his side. Gabriel ran into the hut and snatched up the rifle he'd taken from the dead Ghost Warrior.

"Get down!" he yelled at the men still inside, whose faces betrayed their fear.

"You said they were all dead," one complained, as he lay face down in the dirt.

"I thought they were. This one's badly wounded. Stay here."

Gabriel ran to the front door of the hut and peered around the door jamb. The soldier was only fifty yards away now, firing single shots into the side of the hut. He was heading for the headman's position, not looking at Gabriel's end of the hut. Gabriel switched the rifle's fire selector to semi auto then slipped out of the doorway and got down on one knee.

He sighted on the man centre-mass and shot him twice. At this range he reckoned even a rookie marksman would have put his target down. And Gabriel, even if he had never been as good a shot as Britta Falskog, was no rookie.

The man collapsed with a scream, blood spraying out from his upper torso where Gabriel's bullets had created massive wound cavities. His right hand was still tight on the rifle's pistol grip and in his death throes he clamped his index finger down over the trigger.

Bullets whined overhead as he twisted and rolled on the ground. Gabriel waited him out. After a couple of seconds the magazine emptied and the rifle emitted a final dry click as the striker hit an empty breech.

He climbed to his feet and walked over to the soldier, kicked the empty rifle away, and shot him once in the head. The last Ghost Warrior was dead.

Back at the far end of the hut, the headman was leaning against the wall, his face taut with pain. One of the others was tying a strip of torn cloth around his arm, just below the shoulder. His shirt was soaked in blood, the wet fabric glistening in the sun.

"I need to look at that," Gabriel said.

The man stood back. Gabriel rested his rifle against the wall. He drew his pocket knife and opened the scissors to cut the sleeve away from the wounded man's shirt. He sighed with relief at what he saw.

Although messy, the wound was superficial. The Ghost Warrior's bullet had merely scored a bloody trough across the outside of the upper arm. An inch to the right and it would have smashed the humerus and possibly ripped a fatal hole in the brachial artery. Gabriel ran to fetch his daysack from the pickup.

Minutes later he was dusting the wound with sulphonamide powder before applying a field dressing, just as he had the previous day with Mrs Zhan. He secured the dressing with tape and tied on an improvised sling made from a triangular bandage. He injected morphine into the man's deltoid muscle.

"That'll kick in in a minute or less. You won't feel any pain for a while. Do you have a doctor at your village?" he asked.

The headman, white-faced but breathing easier now, shook his head.

"We have to go to Urumqi. Or else there's Grandmother Pin-Xi. She's our healer. But I don't think she has anything strong enough for this." He gestured angrily at his elevated arm.

"OK. We need to get you some more morphine, or some stronger painkillers at least. And we need to get that stitched."

"She can do that. She delivers all the babies in our village."

"Good. Are you finished here? I know it's hard but we should go and get that seen to."

The man nodded. Colour had returned to his cheeks as the morphine did its work on his central nervous system. He smiled lazily.

"Yes, we are finished. We must take the bones away and give them a proper burial. I wish we could erase this evil place from the face of the earth. Can't you fire their missiles back at the base?"

"I don't think we can do that. Even if I knew how to handle the targeting software and the launch controls, it would just bring more trouble onto your village. It would be an act of war on my part. My boss in England would want my head on a plate."

Suddenly horrified by his inadvertent slip, Gabriel turned away. The headman laid his good hand on Gabriel's shoulder.

"It's OK. You have done so much to help us. Please, don't worry. I know what you meant."

Gabriel cleared his head and looked the man in the eye.

"We can't fire the missiles, but we could at least burn this hut down."

The man nodded.

"That would be fitting. But leave Na out here. I want him to suffer the same fate as our people. Let the dogs and the vultures have him."

Gabriel helped the headman into the passenger seat. He called the others out from the hut and they, too, climbed into the pickup.

"Wait here," Gabriel said.

Shouldering the rifle, he trotted back towards an open-sided hangar-like building containing a number of trucks and jeeps, plus fuel pumps, mechanics' tool benches and a couple of four-post ramps. Clearly, the base motor-pool.

Along one wall, olive-green steel jerrycans had been stacked. Gabriel lifted one marked PETROL. It was full, sloshing deeply as he swung it down. He took it back to the hut and flipped off the metal closure cap.

Starting at one end, and walking backwards, he swung it left and right, splashing the wooden floor and walls with the inflammable spirit. Reaching the door beyond the altar, he poured the last few litres of petrol over the threshold and in a trail back towards the pickup. Back at the truck he asked one of the smokers for a match.

"I'll take one of their jeeps," he said. "Head off now. I'll see you back at the village."

As the pickup took off with a spurt of grit from the tyres, Gabriel turned to take one last look at the body of Colonel Na. Then he struck the match with a rasp against the side of the box and dropped it into the petrol.

He ran back from the door before circling the hut, heading for the motor pool.

The tinder-dry wooden walls and floor ignited with a soft *whoomp*.

Gabriel spun to watch as the flames raced through the hut from the back section to the front.

He reached the motor pool and walked along the row of vehicles looking for something relatively lightweight. This far into China's interior, security standards had clearly slipped. Or maybe it was Colonel Na's brutality that had sent base standards into a death spiral. Either way, none of the vehicles were padlocked or secured in any other way. He selected a camo-painted 4x4 and climbed inside, sticking his rifle in the passenger footwell.

He flicked on the ignition and the engine caught straightaway. OK, so maybe standards hadn't slipped that far. He drove away, looking to his right as he emerged from the hangar to see that the altar hut was ablaze, flames racing upwards, smoke drifting away towards the perimeter fence.

Heading into the central compound, he flicked his gaze left and right, looking for the base medical centre. Eventually he found it, a low blockhouse behind what appeared to be living quarters. He parked the 4x4 and went inside to find the pharmacy.

Inside, the first sight to greet him was a pile of corpses. All male, some wearing white coats. They had putrefied badly and the stench had Gabriel gagging as he ran past. He kicked open one door after another, finding sick bays, and larger, ward-type rooms filled with empty beds separated by fabric screens on rails.

Finally, he found what he was looking for. The sign screwed to the door told the visitor he had reached the pharmacy. Gabriel tried the handle but the door was locked. He kicked out at the flimsy mechanism and the door burst inwards, splintering at the jamb with a loud crack.

Facing him was a counter and beyond it, racks of shelving laden with white boxes labelled in plain black type. There were hundreds of sections. Gabriel's heart sank. He lifted the hatch in the counter and leaving the rectangle of wood propped up against the wall, went through to begin searching. Realising the villagers might find a use for more than just morphine, he grabbed an empty cardboard carton and resolved to fill it with anything and everything that might conceivably prove valuable.

In went ibuprofen, paracetamol, sleeping pills, anti-diarrhoea tablets, anti-malarial drugs, boxes of pre-filled syringes for tetanus shots. He found a section packed with first aid supplies and added stacks of bandages, plasters, antiseptic creams, sulphonamide powder, splints and vinyl pouches containing tweezers and small pairs of medical scissors.

Finally, he rounded a corner and found the mother lode. A single shelf, stretching from one wall to the other, laden with the heavy-duty pharmaceuticals he'd been expecting to find.

Reading the labels, he discovered stimulants, mainly Benzedrine, anti-anxiety medication, including a Chinese version of Valium, antidepressants and, occupying a whole shelf to themselves, ampoules of morphine and syringes, packed in sterile pouches.

He grabbed a couple of handfuls of the last two and laid them on top of the rest of his hurriedly gathered supplies. He closed the flaps and carried the carton back out to the 4x4, holding his breath and running past the semi-liquid corpses littering the corridor.

Driving away, he wondered what Liu would make of the destruction when he inevitably came to check on what remained of his underling's murderous reign. Surely it wasn't enough to be considered an act of war. In any case, hadn't Liu himself been operating outside the PLA command hierarchy? Gabriel was fairly sure securing the services of foreign mercenaries to assassinate wayward PLA officers would not be considered true to the teachings of the Great Leader.

But then another thought intruded. *You wanted me dead, you bastard. And you failed. Like all the others before you. And one day soon we are going to meet up again.*

40

Gabriel arrived back at the village to find a crowd gathered round the pickup. Women were keening, children crying or, in the case of the younger ones, looking on, wide-eyed, sucking thumbs or holding raggedy soft toys by their floppy limbs.

Most of the bags had been unloaded from the back and the men were laying them out in a long row along the dirt road running through the centre of the settlement. One by one, they slit the knotted black plastic shrouds and spread the tattered flaps apart to reveal their contents. A woman in her twenties fell to her knees before one of the grisly exhibits and began banging her forehead against the ground. In front of her lay a long, narrow bone with a bracelet of black and white beads encircling its lower end.

Gabriel looked on helplessly. Then he felt a hand on his arm. He started. He'd been joined by Mrs Zhan.

"Her daughter," she said. "That's her bracelet. They took her at the beginning of the summer."

"What will you do with the remains? I don't suppose there'll be many you can identify."

"We were talking about that while you were collecting them.

Our traditions are not sufficient to cope with this evil man's work. So we will bury them together. In one grave. All the families who lost someone will know where to come to see their loved ones. The village will mourn together. I hope, in time, our wounds will heal. Myself, I will be dead long before that happens."

"I am sorry I couldn't have got there sooner, Mother. Maybe I could have stopped him from killing just one."

She smiled up at him, shaking her head.

"You did plenty. Don't punish yourself for not doing more."

Unable to help, and feeling that his presence was harder to deal with than his absence, Gabriel retreated to the outskirts of the village. He found a stunted tree that offered a little shade and sat with his back to the gnarled trunk.

He stared at the horizon, asking himself how any human being could so completely lose their mind as to commit the acts that Na had. Almost immediately, he realised the answer.

Very easily.

He'd seen plenty of sights that still haunted his dreams. Not committed by monsters, but by men, and occasionally women. And what drove them to it? Not madness. Not usually. Instead, ideology. Greed. Stupidity. Rage. Hatred. Cruelty. Bloodlust. Plenty of good old everyday human emotions crawling around people's brains and bloodstreams to justify the most shocking acts.

Footsteps behind him arrested his train of thought. Grateful for it, he turned to look over his shoulder. Little Dog was ambling over, hands hanging by his sides, a small smile on his open face. Gabriel wondered if he was lacking something on the inside, to be apparently unaware or untroubled by what was happening just a few hundred yards away in the centre of the village.

"Hello, Jié Bai-Luo," Little Dog said, sitting next to Gabriel, legs crossed like a school child. "Are you feeling OK?"

"Yeah, I'm fine. I just felt I was in the way back there. I hope you didn't lose anyone."

Little Dog grinned, revealing large, even teeth.

"Me? No. I'm lucky, I guess. Only child and my mum and dad both died ages ago. But some of the others are in a pretty bad way."

Gabriel nodded.

"People may come, from the government in Beijing or the local prefecture. If they ask questions, don't say anything about me. Tell the others, too. Just play dumb."

Little Dog thumped the side of his head with an open palm, and rolled his eyes.

"That won't be too hard. You know my other nickname?"

"No."

"Ox. Know why I got it?"

"Is it because you're strong?"

"Yeah, maybe. But mainly on account of I'm a bit slow, you know?" He knocked the side of his skull. "They say my mum dropped me on my head when I was a little baby. Knocked the sense out of me."

"But you've got a good job, haven't you? Long-distance driving? Trading textiles? That has to take some smarts?"

Little Dog frowned and scratched his head. Maybe he'd never thought of himself except as the butt of others' jokes.

"I do get good deals with the Kazakhs, it's true. Hey!" His face lit up. "Maybe you're right. Maybe Ox is a Fox?"

Delighted with his joke, Little Dog laughed loudly, throwing his head back.

Gabriel smiled. Here was someone uncomplicated. No baggage, or none so obvious it transformed him into a vengeful killer. Seemingly happy out here in the boonies so far from Beijing that the capitals of three neighbouring countries were closer.

Even as his neighbours and friends were sorting through the bones of their relatives, he was content to sit, cross-legged, chatting with a stranger – a *gweilo* at that – as if the cares of the world heading his way had turned off at a sign marked, DETOUR.

His possessions amounted to a truck, a two-room hut and its meagre contents and that was all. No house on the English coast, no hillside residence overlooking Hong Kong's Victoria Harbour, no boat, no American sports car, no art and antiquities collection, no US bearer bonds in a Swiss bank. And yet, and yet... which of them was the happier, the more content?

Gabriel was afraid he knew the answer. And the knowledge didn't please him. He wondered if Little Dog had a girlfriend. Eli's tanned face appeared before him. Grey-green eyes rimmed with kohl crinkled as she smiled at him.

"Hey, what're you thinking? You went away somewhere."

Gabriel smiled at his neighbour.

"I was thinking about a friend of mine. My girlfriend, I mean."

"Oh, yeah? What's her name?"

"Eli."

"Eli. OK, I like that. She pretty?"

"Mm-hmm. Very."

"Pretty how?"

"Well, she has really nice eyes. They're the colour of —"

"Of what?"

"Like, when you see pinewoods on a mountainside, you know, but it's misty. That sort of green."

Little Dog closed his eyes for a few seconds. Then he opened them, smiling.

"OK, I see them. What else?"

Gabriel smiled. Enjoying the mild but insistent interrogation.

"When she smiles, she gets little crinkles on the bridge of her nose, here." He touched the spot on his own nose. "And she smells really nice. Lemony. Sandalwood. You know those smells?"

"Sure I do! I do a bit of trading with this guy in Taskesken. He sells soaps and creams and stuff like that. The girls love it. Hey, you have a photo of her?"

Gabriel frowned, realising that he didn't. Not printed out and tucked into his wallet. Not on his phone, either. *Why haven't I? Fariyah would have a field day with that one.*

"They're all at home."

"What, you don't even have one on your phone?"

"It's a new one. I haven't transferred then over yet. So how about you? You have someone special?"

At the question, Little Dog's face creased into a smile. He reached into his inside pockct and brought forth a creased colour photo, which he handed to Gabriel.

"Her name's Inzhu. She lives in Ayagoz. Our first stop tomorrow. We're saving up for a place together. Hey! Maybe you could meet her? You'll love her. She's so smart. And pretty, like Eli. You see?"

Gabriel looked at the photo.

The colours had faded but the woman smiling out of the frame was undoubtedly attractive. Thick dark hair arranged loosely around her cheeks, which were as red and round as apples. A full mouth and a generously rounded figure. He could see why Little Dog was smitten.

"She's beautiful," he said. "You're a lucky guy."

"I know," Little Dog said, tucking the photo away again. "That what I say to Inzhu, but she says I'm being daft. She says it's not luck, it's love."

Gabriel felt an even stronger pang of envy. Could he be happy doing a job like Little Dog's? Trucking hundreds of miles to trade cloth for scented soaps, with a beautiful girlfriend in a completely different country?

He realised, with a shiver, that he had absolutely no idea. Recently, happiness hadn't been high on his list of priorities. Life seemed to consist of one op after another, either in pursuit of private demons or those identified by his Government paymasters.

Maybe Don was right after all. Maybe he *did* need to take a break. A proper break. Not one that degenerated within weeks into an unpaid hit job for a Communist Party official who was in thick with a triad boss to whom Gabriel owed a favour.

He'd tie things up in Hong Kong, including Comrade Liu, and then he'd fly back to England. Eli could work while he continued his research into his family, and tried to trace Tara. That, at least, seemed to make sense to him.

Tomorrow he'd start drawing the line under the business with Colonel Na, heading west with Little Dog. Which led to another thought.

"Hey. Can you help me with something? We need to return the 4x4 I took from the base."

"Sure. You want me to follow you? I have a pickup like the boss's. Great Wall, 2.8 litre turbodiesel. Very reliable."

"That would work."

"OK. I can do that."

They got to their feet and walked back to the village, avoiding the main street, where the mourning was in full cry. Gabriel took the box full of medical supplies out of the 4x4 and, following Little Dog's instructions, left them outside the headman's house.

Their two-vehicle convoy – Gabriel's stolen camo 4x4 and Little Dog's snazzy, flame-painted pickup – crept out of the eastern end of the village then picked up speed as they headed back to the base.

———

A thin grey column of smoke rose over the camp, feathering in the breeze blowing west to east. Gabriel drove in through the front gate and headed straight to the motor pool. He re-parked the 4x4 in its spot and wiped down the steering wheel and all the controls. The lie of his absence wouldn't survive a full forensic examination, but he wasn't expecting the Chinese to go that far.

He retrieved the rifle from the footwell and used the butt to close the driver's door. Little Dog was waiting for him outside, engine running. Gabriel climbed inside.

"We go, yes?" Little Dog asked.

"Yes. Step on it."

Little Dog nodded, shoved the gear stick into first and hit the throttle hard, arms straight on the steering wheel, back pressed into his seat. He didn't ease up until the base was a tiny collection of shapes in the mirror, pointed to by the smoke plume.

———

Little Dog turned up at 7.00 a.m. the following morning, knocking on the front door as if he intended to break it down.

"We're having a farewell breakfast for you in the café. Feed you up for the trip," he said when Gabriel blearily opened the door.

Gabriel dressed hurriedly, grabbed his daysack and the rifle, which he'd brought in from the pickup, and met Little Dog outside.

Arriving at the café, it seemed to Gabriel as though the whole village had turned out for the communal breakfast to see him and Little Dog off. After pork dumplings and rice, plus more green tea and a couple of glasses of water, Gabriel thanked the headman, who was sitting to his left, and Mrs Zhan to his right. She handed over a woven basket covered with a white cloth.

"For your trip," she said with a smile, patting his forearm.

Gabriel lifted a corner of the cloth and smiled. The old woman had packed the basket with foil-wrapped parcels, bottles of water and cans of beer.

"It smells heavenly, Mother. Thank you."

She smiled.

"It isn't much compared to what you did for us. But I want you to know I will be asking my ancestors to keep watch over you as you make your way back home."

Little Dog stood up. He'd been sitting at the table behind Gabriel's.

"Ready to go? It's a long drive."

Gabriel nodded, and followed him out of the café towards a large truck painted in gaudy hues of pink, blue, green and a startling buttercup yellow. Anything not painted was chromed: the hubcaps, bumpers, exhaust pipe sticking up behind the cab, and decorative trim strips along the sides. Mounted on the roof was a gold-painted crown.

Before he could climb up into the cab, Mrs Zhan enveloped Gabriel in a hug. She kissed him on both cheeks. The headman came next, also offering a hug, though without the kiss. Children were waving little paper flags and singing, more or less in key. He stowed his gear and climbed in.

As they pulled out of the village he watched the waving people in the wing-mirror, and hoped that Comrade Liu wouldn't decide to go looking for him in Ulungur. He'd impressed on the headman the need for one hundred per cent denial among the remaining villagers that Gabriel had ever been there.

As far as Liu, the PLA or the Party were concerned, Gabriel had been blown to atoms by the hit squad's RPGs. As for the burnt-out hut at the missile base, that could easily have been part of the final confrontation between Colonel Na and his Ghost Warriors.

41

They reached the border crossing – a blockhouse and red-and-white swing-up barrier – later that day. A white pickup was parked to the left of the blockhouse. Gabriel climbed down from the cab, grateful for the chance to ease the muscles in his lower back, which were protesting at the battering they'd taken on the rough road. He reflected ruefully that if Little Dog had spent half as much on his suspension as he had on his decoration, the long-distance runs he had to make would be far less of an ordeal.

A warm breeze blew towards them from the Kazakh side of the border. Standing between them and trade, in Little Dog's case, and escape, in Gabriel's, was a single border guard armed with an ageing Chinese copy of an AK-47. Was he the cousin? Gabriel watched as Little Dog sauntered over.

The two men embraced, laughing and exchanging thumps on the back. Little Dog pulled out a crumpled pack of cigarettes from his pocket and offered one to the guard.

"Hey," he called over to Gabriel. "Come and meet my cousin."

Gabriel walked over and shook hands with the guard. The man regarded him with a frown, looking him up and down and ending his visual inspection by staring into Gabriel's eyes.

"We don't see many like you out here," he said, finally, with a small smile.

Gabriel shrugged.

"I'm travelling. Seeing the world."

"Yeah?" the man said, pulling his head back as if to say, *and you think this part of it is worth seeing?*

Gabriel looked around. It was true, this part of Northeast China didn't have a lot going for it in the scenery department. Yet more rocky plain and scrubland. He wondered what the cousin had done to land such a posting.

"Do you get much traffic coming through?" Gabriel asked, genuinely curious.

"Not really. Mostly it's just local stuff. A few trucks like Little Dog's, trading with our neighbours over there." He waved his arm vaguely in the direction of Ayagoz. "We do one week on, one week off. It's OK, really. I read a lot."

Gabriel nodded, finding it extremely easy to believe. He said goodbye and left the two cousins to finish their cigarettes. When he saw Little Dog wave, he re-joined him in the truck.

With the barrier raised and Little Dog's cousin knocking off a flamboyant salute, earning a farewell blast on the horn, they rumbled out of China and into Kazakhstan. Gabriel sighed out a breath he hadn't realised he'd been holding.

"You OK?" Little Dog asked.

"Yeah, fine. Just glad to be putting some miles between me and the missile base."

"Ah, I don't blame you. It's a bad place. I prayed for our dead last night. It's gonna be a long time before they're able to rest, I think."

———

They stayed overnight at a rudimentary truck stop, little more than a gas station with a couple of wooden cabins behind it. Little Dog clearly knew the owner, greeting him with much the same level of affection as he'd shown towards his cousin. The man's wife brought them plates of hot food – boiled chicken and rice in a thick onion gravy – and a couple of hours later at 9.00 p.m., with no electric light in the cabin, the only option was sleep. Gabriel tried his phone, but had no signal.

Rising at 5.00 a.m., aware of a high-pitched sound like radio interference from outside, Gabriel walked out of the cabin into the chill dawn air. He looked up.

"Bloody hell!"

Directly overhead, a flock of birds, seemingly millions-strong, swirled and undulated, here coalescing into darker blobs, there thinning out until they looked like grey dust against the pale-blue sky. The sound, he now realised was their calls to each other, an endless, hypnotic screech that drowned out his thoughts. Head hanging back on his neck, he watched for five more minutes as the cloud of swarming birds pulsed like a single, living organism. Eventually, perhaps dictated by the sun's rising, or some unfathomable signal of their own, the birds streaked out at the western edge of the blob, forming an arrowhead that drew their fellows off towards the next stop on their migration.

Little Dog appeared at Gabriel's elbow, yawning and scratching the back of his head.

"You saw the starlings, did you?"

"Yes. They're amazing. Have you seen them before?"

"At this time of year it's quite common. Some folk say they're sent by the ancestors to keep an eye on the living."

"Is that what you believe?"

"Me?" Little Dog grinned, "No. I think they're just birds."

Breakfast, again provided by the lady of the gas station, consisted of chewy wheat noodles, dry-fried and seasoned with lots of pepper and shredded ginger.

Little Dog was twisting the key in the ignition at 6.15 a.m., joking through the open window with the garage man as he pulled away, the rising sun casting the truck's shadow along the road ahead of them.

"Next stop Ayagoz, eh? Then you can meet Inzhu."

"I'm looking forward to it," Gabriel said with feeling.

Meeting the girlfriend would be fine, but what he was really looking forward to was a hot bath and a good night's sleep.

42

KAZAKHSTAN

Gabriel woke with a start. Little Dog was shaking his shoulder.

"Wake up! We've got trouble."

Gabriel straightened in his seat and looked ahead. A hundred yards away a red pickup truck sat across both lanes of the narrow road. The driver was looking straight at them, but what really concerned him was the man in the truck bed. Dressed in jeans and what looked like an army surplus combat jacket, he held an AK-47 in his right hand.

"Who are they?" Gabriel asked, sliding his arm over the back of his seat to collect his own rifle.

Little Dog sneered.

"They call themselves the Highway Patrol. They're just bandits, though. I've been lucky. They haven't stopped me before, but some of the guys I know have been caught. They're just after money."

"Yeah? Do you feel like paying?"

Little Dog turned to Gabriel and grinned.

"I never feel like paying."

"OK. Let me do the talking. Drive closer, do whatever you normally do."

When they were twenty feet from the bandits' pickup, Little Dog stopped the truck and killed the engine, yanking on the handbrake with a loud squawk.

"Do you go to them or do they come to you?" Gabriel asked.

"They come to me."

As Little Dog answered, the man in the truck bed clambered out, swinging his legs over the side, and swaggered over to the truck, grinning to reveal stained brown teeth. Heading for Little Dog's side of the cab, he had the AK resting on his right hip.

He arrived, looked up at Little Dog and tapped the AK's muzzle on the window. Little Dog wound the window down. The first eight inches of the barrel intruded into the cab.

"Haven't seen you around here before," the bandit said, speaking a rough version of the Cantonese dialect they used in Ulungur.

"We're new on this route," Gabriel said.

The bandit took a step back, the better to see Little Dog's new driver's mate.

"Who the fuck are you?"

"I'm his assistant."

"Oh, yeah? Business must be good then, if he can afford an *assistant*. Maybe we should double the toll just for you, eh?"

"That's cool," Gabriel said, speaking past Little Dog's chest. I've got your money right here."

The man pulled his gun back and rounded the front of the cab. Gabriel turned and followed his progress, swivelling on the smooth vinyl seat. When the bandit reached the corner of the front end, and had the least visibility into the cab, Gabriel unlatched the door and pulled his knees up to his chest. He placed the soles of his boots flat against the inside of the door. And waited.

One step, two, three. The bandit arrived on Gabriel's side of the cab. Up came the AK's barrel. Gabriel shot his legs out with all the force and speed he could muster, slamming the door into the bandit and sending the rifle back to smash into his face. Gabriel followed the door, jumping down and kicking the man hard in the groin. The bandit dropped his AK and grabbed his crotch, yelling in pain as he fell backwards into the dust.

Bandit Number Two was slow to react. Gabriel fired a warning shot over the man's head. The man froze, hand halfway to a holster at his hip.

"I'll put the next one between your eyes!" he shouted. "Drop the gun. Finger and thumb only. Now!"

Not taking his eyes off Gabriel, the man pinched the butt of his revolver and slowly drew it clear of the holster before dropping it.

"Kick it over here."

He complied, sending the revolver spinning towards Gabriel, raising a swirl of dust, then, perhaps feeling a greater show of obedience was needed, raised his hands. Gabriel stooped to grab the gun – an ancient Nagant – and stuck it in the waistband of his trousers.

From behind him, Gabriel heard the injured bandit wheezing and getting to his feet. He stepped sideways and back, until he could see the man.

"Join your friend," he said.

Still clutching his injured private parts, and walking in a pained crouch, he stumbled over to join his partner in crime. They made a sorry pair.

"What are you going to do to us?" the second man asked, brown eyes locked on to the muzzle of Gabriel's rifle, which was pointing straight at his heart.

Gabriel glared at him, saying nothing, knowing that silence is often more unnerving than shouting, especially when the silence is accompanied by an automatic weapon.

"We took some money earlier," the first man said, a note of pleading in his voice. "Take it! Take it all. Just don't kill us."

Gabriel acted as if Little Dog had said something. He turned his head towards the cab.

"What's that, boss? OK, hold on." He turned back to the bandits. "If you move, you die," he growled.

Then he strode round the front of the truck to Little Dog's window.

"I didn't say anything," Little Dog hissed.

"Well, I say we kill them both and chop them up for the wild dogs," Gabriel shouted back. He paused. Cocked his head as he leaned into the cab. "What's your favourite food?" he whispered.

Frowning, Little Dog answered.

"Chicken dumplings and wheat noodles in gravy, why?"

Gabriel winked, then stepped back.

"OK, fine," he said, loudly. "You're the boss. But I think you're making a big mistake."

He marched over to the two men.

"He says I should let you go. That you don't deserve to die."

"Yeah, yeah, he's right, your boss," the first man said, grinning wildly. "It was a mistake, OK? We shouldn't ever have asked him for money."

Gabriel closed the gap between them to the length of the AK's barrel, which he pushed into the man's belly.

"I'd die for that man. He saved my life. Three PLA men were about to beat me up and he stopped them. No guns: he didn't need them. Near enough ripped one guy's arm out of its socket. So if the boss says you live, you live. But –" he added as the two men smiled more broadly, adding nods to their relieved expressions, "– if I hear you've been stopping him again, I'll come and find you. And I'll kill you. But not before I've had some fun with you. Understand?"

"Yes," they chorused.

"Good. Now get back in your truck, move it off the road and wait for twenty minutes before you leave."

They turned and ran back to the pickup, the man with the injured groin adopting a hobbling trot in an attempt to keep up with his partner in crime. The engine started and the pickup lurched off the road with a spurt of dust from all four tyres.

Gabriel climbed back into the cab next to Little Dog.

"Let's go, boss. And when we get to Ayagoz, I'll buy you some chicken dumplings, OK?"

Little Dog grinned.

"OK."

As they rumbled past the pickup, under the watchful gaze of the two bandits, Gabriel looked sideways and caught the eye of the man in the driver's seat. He mimed pointing a pistol at the man's head.

43

Once the pickup had disappeared behind them, Little Dog turned his head to Gabriel.

"Thank you."

"You're welcome. I hope they took my warning seriously."

"I don't think they'll give me any trouble. They're cowards, really. Without the guns, they're nobody."

Gabriel leaned forward and put the Nagant into the glovebox.

"Why don't you keep it?" he said. "Maybe they won't give you any more trouble, but there might be others who will."

Little Dog shook his head.

"I will keep it, but I don't think I'll need it. Word gets around and they'll just look for easier pickings. What about that?" he asked, gesturing at the AK, which Gabriel had between his knees.

"Any rivers between here and Ayagoz?"

"Yeah. A big one about ten kilometres out. We cross it on a bridge. Beautiful sight to see, it is."

"OK. We'll dump it there."

. . .

It took another long day's driving before they reached Ayagoz, driving through a vast plain, on which nothing above knee-height grew. Brownish-green scrub covered the landscape, except for grey scars where rock broke through the soil. As Little Dog had promised, they reached a deep gorge crossed by a rusting steel latticework bridge.

Gabriel asked Little Dog to stop halfway across. With a few practised movements, Gabriel field-stripped the rifle. He climbed down from the cab and dropped the separated components, and finally the rifle itself, into the green waters.

Ayagoz's main street looked in many ways like any big town in the west. Tall, elegantly curved streetlights, cars and trucks parked more or less parallel to the kerb, shops, restaurants bars and hotels, plus low-rise office buildings.

Gabriel noticed a couple of bikers on expensive BMWs trundling towards them at virtually walking speed, leaning their heads in towards each other so they could talk. Both wore open-face helmets and sported silver beards and wraparound sunglasses. Little Dog beeped his horn and waved at the bikers, who gave him a thumbs-up in return.

Women strolled on the pavements carrying baskets of produce over their arms, whether to sell or take home, Gabriel couldn't tell. Little Dog bumped the heel of his hand against the steering wheel boss to toot at them and they all smiled broadly, waving back.

"You're a popular man in Ayagoz," Gabriel said, smiling.

"Yep. I reckon pretty much everyone in town knows me. It's on account of Inzhu. She's a schoolteacher." He looked at his watch. "It's nearly three. The kids'll be coming out soon and we can go and meet her. You're going to love her. She's so smart and so beautiful."

Little Dog turned right off the main street and made a couple of further turns before parking on a narrow, grit-surfaced road lined with single-storey houses built out of wood and painted in blues, reds and browns with bright-white woodwork around the windows and doors. Gabriel saw mesh satellite dishes on most of the roofs and reflected on how the whole world could probably get the same TV shows these days.

"The school's just down here on the left," Little Dog said. "Come on."

Together they walked the fifty yards from the truck to the school gates, which were painted in rainbow colours. Women were clustered on the playground in pairs, or small groups, checking phones or chatting and laughing as they waited for their children. A few looked round as Little Dog and Gabriel arrived and smiled or waved. They threw a few curious glances Gabriel's way but, clearly, being with Little Dog was his passport to acceptance in Ayagoz.

A bell rang from somewhere inside the building, a low-built, steel and concrete block. Instantly the air was full of high-pitched laughs and screams as from three separate doors, first one or two then a handful then twenty or more and finally a hundred or so children aged, Gabriel estimated, between five and thirteen, burst out into the sunshine.

Mothers collected the younger children or stood open-armed and smiling as they ran to show them clay models or paintings. The older ones strolled away from the school building, chatting to their friends as they headed home through the wide-open gates.

Five minutes later, the playground was empty. Gabriel followed Little Dog across painted snakes, numbered boxes and spirals to the centre door in the building.

"Inzhu's classroom is that one," Little Dog said, pointing to windows to the left of the door.

Sun reflecting off the glass made it hard to see in, but Gabriel caught a glimpse of a figure moving around inside. He looked to his right. Little Dog was smoothing his hair down with his palm. His open, honest face was split by a ridiculously wide smile.

He pulled open the door and led Gabriel inside and then to their left, where he pushed through a blond wood-and-glass door into the classroom. The woman Gabriel had seen turned at the sound and her face, far more attractive than it had appeared in the photograph, lit up.

"Bunny!" she said in Russian.

Then she saw her fiancé was not alone and she blushed furiously, her throat and cheeks a deep pink.

Little Dog grinned sheepishly.

"Inzhu, I want you to meet my good friend, Jié Bai-Luo. No, wait. That's not your real name, is it? Just what Mrs Zhan called you." He spoke in Kazakh-accented Russian, surprising Gabriel once more.

Gabriel shook his head. As Inzhu wore no headscarf, he assumed she wasn't a Muslim, and offered his hand. She took it in her own, which was cool to the touch and shook briefly.

"Gabriel," he said, enunciating each syllable clearly for her benefit.

"Like the angel. You are from the UK?" she asked him in English, smiling.

"Yes. You speak very good English."

"Thank you. Also Russian and a little Cantonese."

"She's a genius," Little Dog said proudly. "All the kids love her."

Inzhu smiled once more.

"He makes me embarrassed? Is that the word?"

"Yes. But you don't need to be."

"I have some work to do here. But I would be honoured if you would eat with us tonight. At my mother and father's house. You should stay, too. They have plenty of room."

"Thank you. I'd love that."

Gabriel had long ago ditched his original British reserve about accepting hospitality from people he'd only just met.

He'd learned that in most places in the world, from rural Africa to the jungles of South America, when people said, "eat with us, share our home", they meant it and would be puzzled, if not downright offended, if you refused out of some misguided idea of politeness. They might have almost nothing, and live on or only just above the poverty line, but they would gladly share what little they had with a stranger.

"Good. Come at six. Chan knows the way."

They left Inzhu to her after-school work and headed back to the truck.

"Well?" Little Dog asked as they climbed into the cab, eyes alight with excitement.

"Well, what?" Gabriel replied, unable to resist teasing him.

"Inzhu, of course! What do you think, now you've met her? Isn't she beautiful? And so clever, right? Speaks English as good as you do. Russian, too. Teaches all those subjects. I'm the luckiest man alive, I tell you."

"You're right. Beautiful and clever. And she clearly loves you. My advice? Settle down with her as soon as you can. Marry her, have lots of kids, whatever'll make you both happy."

Little Dog nodded.

"That's exactly what I'm going to do. I'm just waiting for a cousin in the Prefecture Government to sort out my emigration papers. Maybe you should do the same with Eli, eh?"

"Maybe."

Even though Inzhu had offered Gabriel her parents' hospitality, Little Dog had been adamant that, as the husband-to-be, it would be inappropriate for him to sleep under the same roof.

"I always stay in a guesthouse," he said as they drove away from the school. "The landlady knows me. She always gives me her best room. We should get showered and cleaned up. Have you got any other clothes?"

Gabriel shook his head.

"Only what I'm standing up in. I had some other stuff but the PLA blew it all up."

"Oh yeah, I forgot. Sorry. Well, a shower anyway. I can lend you some of my aftershave."

Gabriel smiled, amused at the big man's obvious desire to impress his future parents-in-law.

44

Gabriel showered and shaved in the guest house's tiny bathroom. Emerging in the midst of a cloud of steam, he started as Little Dog's palms clapped aftershave against his cheeks. The stuff was strong, no doubt about it, and he felt the newly bare skin of his cheeks smarting from the alcohol. The smell hit him next, a woody, spicy mixture so potent his eyes started watering.

"What is that?" he asked, thinking back to his days in the Paras, when Brut 33 had been the go-to pulling fragrance for half the lads in his platoon.

"You like it? I got it in Urumqi. I'll show you."

Little Dog turned and opened the door to his room, returning moments later clutching a bright-green cylindrical bottle with a silver cap. He held it up for Gabriel, who stifled a laugh.

The name, picked out in a silver typeface almost a match for the original, read "BURT 33".

Little Dog frowned.

"What is it? You don't like it?"

"It's great, honestly. Come on. Let's get ready."

———

Gabriel walked beside Little Dog down Aktamberdy Avenue, a tree-lined boulevard of white houses with roofs the blue-green of weathered copper. The cars passing them were mostly Chinese-made, although the occasional Japanese or Korean model drove by. *Plenty of mopeds, though*, Gabriel thought, recalling the Honda-choked thoroughfares of Phnom Penh.

Arriving at number 345, Little Dog adjusted his tie, a lurid brown-and-yellow striped number, marched up the path and pressed the doorbell. Inzhu opened the door, beamed at them both, kissed Little Dog quickly on the cheek and then led them inside. She'd changed into a long-sleeved electric-blue dress with ornate red-and-white stitching around the cuffs and neckline. Gabriel noticed the way her nose twitched as she embraced her fiancé. He grinned. *Burt!*

Inzhu's parents were waiting for them in the garden, a complex arrangement of raised beds, large terracotta pots, glazed troughs and metal containers, among which wove cobbled paths edged with white stones. The flowers the couple had grown, with obvious care, drenched the garden in scents and fought with each other for visual dominance. In a corner where five wicker chairs had been arranged around a mosaic-topped table, giant red poppies competed for attention with flame-orange canna lilies swaying above dark purple leaves as wide as a man's hand.

Gabriel allowed himself to be introduced by Little Dog, learning that way that his hosts were Mr and Mrs Yuldashev. Both appeared to be in their early sixties, the husband a shade under six foot, his wife much shorter. Shaking his hand gently with both of hers, Mrs Yuldashev spoke first, in Russian.

"Welcome to our home, Gabriel."

"Thank you for allowing me to stay with you. It is a great honour."

Next came Mr Yuldashev. He repeated his wife's two-handed greeting, though with much firmer pressure. His blue eyes were sharp behind silver-rimmed glasses. He spoke in English.

"Ours is the honour. You are what we call a *kudaiy konak*, which means a guest sent by God."

"Thank you again. You speak English as well as your daughter."

Explaining that as a businessman, he had to be able to converse with his clients and contractors in English and Russian, as well as Kazakh, Mr Yuldashev gestured towards the chairs.

"Please, sit. Inzhu, bring drinks, please."

"Yes, Papa."

She returned with a tray bearing a bottle of vodka, five shot glasses, a bowl of cashew nuts and another of black olives.

"Gabriel, would you like to pour the drinks?" Mr Yuldashev asked.

"Of course."

Gabriel filled the five shot glasses and followed Mr Yuldashev's lead, raising his glass.

"*Konak keldi, irisyn ala keldi*. It means 'The guest comes and brings happiness to the home'."

"I hope I do."

The five clinked glasses and emptied their glasses.

Over more vodka and the delicious olives and nuts, the Yuldashevs explained, taking it in turns, that they were what they called 'Kazakh Muslims'. Praying, and believing in the central tenets of that faith, but not obeying the dietary laws or the prohibition on alcohol, nor the over-proscriptive rules about contact between the sexes. Gabriel thought back to his earlier assumption based on Inzhu's lack of a headscarf. *Never assume anything, Old Sport*, Don's silent voice cautioned.

After another round of drinks, Mr Yuldashev looked at his watch and smiled.

"Dinner time."

He led Gabriel into a simply furnished dining room and Gabriel gasped. The table, which occupied virtually the whole space, groaned with dishes filled with meat, salads, a rich stew garnished with chopped parsley, rice, puffy fried breads and vegetable side dishes. The plates set at each place shone, their red and gold glaze bright under the chandelier-style light in the centre of the ceiling.

Inzhu, who took the seat to his left, leaned closer.

"It is a Kazakh tradition. Guests are very important. To leave a guest hungry is to commit a great offence."

Gabriel needed little prompting from Mrs Yuldashev to help himself to the bewildering array of foods before him. As the group relaxed and gelled, the conversation flowed in a shifting mixture of languages. When someone's vocabulary proved insufficient, sign language came into play as, amid laughter, they attempted to make their meaning clear.

Wiping his lips on a starched white napkin, Mr Yuldashev leaned across the table.

"Chan said he was bringing an Englishman to dinner. But he didn't say what an Englishman is doing all the way out here."

Gabriel looked at Chan, who returned his gaze with a smile as if to say, *Your call how much you tell him*.

"I'm travelling. I live in Hong Kong part of the time and I decided to see some of mainland China. I met Chan at his village and when he said he was driving into Kazakhstan, I asked if I could join him."

"A traveller. I like that. You know, our surname means 'son of the traveller'. Where are you going next?"

"Back to Hong Kong. Chan said I might be able to get a ride down to Almaty with a long-distance lorry driver and fly home from there."

"Did he indeed? Well, you *could* do that, of course. But why not fly there?"

"I'm sorry, I didn't realise Ayagoz had an airport. I had no internet on the way over here."

"Yes, we have an airport! I travel to Almaty a lot myself. In the morning, I will drive you there and we can sort out a ticket for you."

Gabriel's heart lifted at this welcome bit of information. The prospect of trying to hitch a lift with a lorry driver for the almost four-hundred-mile journey from Ayagoz to Almaty had been preying on his mind since they'd crossed the border into Kazakhstan. Now it fluttered away like one of the acid-yellow butterflies he'd spotted in the Yuldashev's back garden.

. . .

After eating half a dozen *baursak*, fried balls of sweet dough dusted with sugar, Gabriel placed his knife and fork together on his cleared plate and thanked Mrs Yuldashev for the feast – what he had learned to call the *dastarkhan*. She beamed at him and nodded to Inzhu, who rose from her chair and began clearing the plates with her mother. Little Dog jumped to his feet to help them, leaving Gabriel with Mr Yuldashev.

The conversation during the meal had been restricted to the easy social subjects everybody could grasp and take part in. Where did Gabriel live in England? What was life like there? Did Inzhu enjoy teaching? Now, as Yuldashev poured them both another shot of vodka, Gabriel asked his host about his business.

"Engineering. We manufacture tool parts for the oil and gas industry. It is not a huge business, but it is profitable. It enables me to support my family. I put Inzhu through the best schools, and university, so she could achieve her dream of becoming a schoolteacher."

"You didn't want her to join you in the business?"

"In fact, I did. But her heart was set on education. What can a father do but support his child in her ambitions? Tell me, what line of work do you follow that allows you to travel so widely? Kazakhstan and Western China are, how do you say, off the beaten track?"

Once again, Gabriel felt bad about having to lie to someone who had done nothing but offer hospitality and kindness to a stranger. Maybe half a lie would be enough.

"I'm a security consultant. Government work, mostly."

Yuldashev's eyes widened and he nodded.

"Ever do any work in Kazakhstan?"

Gabriel thought back to an encounter with another Kazakh businessman. Also involved in manufacturing, though of more lethal articles than machine tools. Now dead. He shook his head.

"No."

"Pity. There are plenty of people here who could use help from a man like you."

"What sort of help?"

Yuldashev sipped his vodka.

"In Kazakhstan, we are behind Russia and China in moving to a free economic system. But we are catching up fast. That means lots of opportunity. For criminals as well as legitimate businessmen like me."

"Extortion?"

"Yes, but also corruption. Sometimes, a bribe is the only way to get a contract agreed."

"Is that something you have had problems with yourself?"

Yuldashev laughed.

"Of course! Everyone does."

"I wish there was something I could do to help."

"Maybe there is. Our new regional governor has announced a new anti-corruption drive. He wants to be known as the man who cleaned up East Kazakhstan. I have made a dossier, that is the correct word?" Gabriel nodded. "So, a dossier on the Mayor of Ayagoz. A very greedy man. On all businesses wishing to operate here, he levies what he calls 'business taxes'." Yuldashev's lip curled as he uttered this phrase. "He works with a gang that controls most of the trade between here and Almaty. If you could get my dossier into the governor's hands, maybe he could start here. Ayagoz is a small town, but big enough that a victory against corruption would be in the governor's interests."

Gabriel nodded, understanding without needing to have it explained to him, why only a hand-to-hand transfer would do.

"I can do that for you. It would be my pleasure."

"I will give it to you when I take you to the airport in the morning."

Mrs Yuldashev appeared in the doorway. She spoke to her husband in Kazakh. He smiled and turned to Gabriel, who had recognised two of her words.

"She says, we should move to the sitting room and perhaps our *kudaiy konak* would sing for us. It is a Kazakh tradition. The guest repays his hosts with a song."

Heart suddenly racing despite the vodka, Gabriel nodded

automatically as he struggled to think of a single song to which he knew even some of the lyrics.

By the time he and Yuldashev had met the others in a more sumptuously furnished room than the dining room, replete with soft, squashy sofas and a huge flat-screen TV, he had landed on the only song he thought he could manage with this much vodka swilling around his system.

Mrs and Mrs Yuldashev sat beside each other on one of the sofas, beaming at him. Inzhu and Little Dog were nestled together on a second. Gabriel stood before them, his back to the TV. Their faces were alive with anticipation. Feeling unaccountably nervous, Gabriel cleared his throat.

"Er, I used to be in the army. In my regiment, we had a song we used to march to. It's called 'Lili Marlene'. I hope you like it."

He looked upwards, so as to avoid making eye contact with his audience, and began to sing, uncertainly at first, then with growing confidence as he found the tune.

"Underneath the lantern, by the barrack gate. Darling, I remember the way you used to wait…"

45

As the opening few lines left his lips, his eyes misted over and the tears pricked. Not from the words, which he'd always thought sentimental, but at the memories they evoked. He sang on, trying to keep the tune, seeing the faces of the men he'd fought alongside, with whom he'd joked around, trained with and shared the hardest of hardships; men who had experienced the supreme emotion of victory and the crushing sense of failure when an operation went sideways.

He thought of the men who'd returned in one piece, and those the survivors had brought home in their "sleeping bags".

He thought of Smudge, shot dead and crucified in a Mozambican forest. Of Damon and Daisy, murdered by Sasha Beck on the orders of Lizzie Maitland.

And of others, wounded not in the body, but the mind, like Gabriel himself had been. Unmanned or unhinged by the horrors of war and the sheer, unmitigated evil of what men could do to other men, and women and children, when pushed hard enough, or just freed from the normal rules of civilised behaviour.

With the tears running freely over his cheeks, he kept singing.

Singing and remembering, finally, Britta Falskog. He finished the song:

"'Twas there that you whispered tenderly that you loved me, you'd always be, my Lili of the lamplight, my own Lili Marlene."

The room was utterly silent. He blinked, and looked at the four people gathered in front of him. They, too, had wet cheeks, and the two women were unselfconsciously weeping. The room lights formed stars in his vision as he blinked to clear his eyes.

Then they started clapping. Mrs Yuldashev got to her feet and embraced him.

"I'm sorry," he said. "I don't know why that happened."

"You sing so beautifully," she said. "Now, sit. It is my turn."

Much later, after everyone had either sung or recited a poem, Little Dog rose unsteadily to his feet and announced that he was going home but would return in the morning to see Gabriel off. The party broke up and Gabriel made his way upstairs to the bedroom Mrs Yuldashev had prepared for him.

———

The next morning dawned bright. Gabriel climbed out of bed, ignoring the thumping in his temples, drew the curtains and opened the casement window. The street was quiet. He leaned on the windowsill and watched a yellowish mutt trotting down the centre of the road then, yelping in its excitement, sprinting after a tortoiseshell cat that had appeared from a garden gate.

He smiled and shook his head, then wished he hadn't. He fished his first-aid kit out of the daysack and palmed a couple of paracetamol, swallowing them with water from the glass flask on the bedside table.

As he stood there, a long, low black Mercedes cruised past the house. The side windows were blacked out. A small Kazakh flag fluttered from a chromed mast on the leading edge of the roof and

Gabriel wondered whether this was the mayor he had agreed to help take down.

After a breakfast of fried eggs, served with onions and fried green peppers, followed by sourdough toast with tartly sweet plum jam, and washed down with fragrant, but lethally strong coffee, it was time to leave for the airport. Gabriel waited on the street with Inzhu and her mother while Mr Yuldashev brought his car round from a garage down an unpaved track to the side of the house. A shout made them all turn round.

Dressed in a red plaid work shirt, grey jogging bottoms and scuffed white trainers, Little Dog was running down the road towards them, waving. In his left hand he carried a blue-and-yellow plastic bag that swung and flapped wildly, apparently empty.

"I overslept!" he panted, as he arrived to join the trio. He thrust the carrier bag at Gabriel. "Here. I got you something to remember me by."

Gabriel took the bag. When he saw what was inside, he smiled. He lifted the object out and held it up so the others could see it. It was a wooden dog, sitting back on its haunches. Perhaps four inches from nose to tail, which was so well executed it seemed to be wagging.

"Did you carve this?" he asked.

Little Dog nodded.

"I thought you would like it. You know, so you think of Little Dog when you go back to England."

Gabriel swallowed down the lump that had formed in his throat.

"Thank you. Thank you all," he added, turning to Inzhu and her mother.

They exchanged hugs, in Little Dog's case fierce enough to leave Gabriel struggling for breath, then the purr of Yuldashev's Audi announced it was time to leave.

After a final round of goodbyes, Gabriel stepped into the car's air-conditioned embrace and stowed his daysack between his feet.

The drive out to Ayagoz Airport took them west, through neighbourhoods that grew shabbier as they neared the outskirts of the town. On the final approach to the airport road, the dwellings were little more than tin shacks, outside which children's bikes in bright shades of pink, green and blue lay on their sides, or leaning against walls, tattered streamers fluttering from their handlebars.

Compared to the desirable middle-class street on which the Yuldashevs lived, this felt more like a third-world country. More of the scruffy yellow mutts nosed among the rubbish that lay between the shacks and Gabriel wondered whether they ever posed a danger to the children whose bikes he'd seen.

"Here we are," Yuldashev said, interrupting Gabriel's thoughts.

He took the Audi along the front of the terminal building and parked in an open lot, the bays demarcated by faded white lines that looked as if they had been laid during the Soviet era. His was not the only European model there. Gabriel saw a few Peugeots and a single, banana-yellow Saab. But most were anonymous Russian or Chinese models, mostly in shades of grey, silver or white.

Inside, the terminal building's design revealed that oddly universal civic pride that turns even a provincial airport into a statement destination.

Grey-and-black granite floor tiles sparkled in the sunlight angling in through floor-to-ceiling plate-glass windows. A long row of check-in desks stood unstaffed, the electric-blue screens above them displaying a trio of scrolling messages in Russian and Kazakh:

> *Almaty: Your True Destination*
> *Live, Love, Laugh: Fly Air Astana*
> *Dream BIG: Dream Kazakhstan!*

Gabriel felt they had been penned more in hope than expectation, but were none the worse for their sincere if clunky patriotism. Yuldashev opened his briefcase and took out a buff cardboard folder. Wordlessly, he passed it to Gabriel before leading him to a ticket desk at which a young woman in a crisp white blouse and a blue-and-yellow striped neck scarf was staring at a monitor and frowning.

When they arrived she looked up and smiled, revealing a

dazzling set of teeth and eyes set off by the longest lashes Gabriel had even seen.

Yuldashev spoke with an air of authority that Gabriel imagined he'd honed during a long and obviously successful career in the engineering business. The ticket sales girl nodded enthusiastically and replied in rapidfire Kazakh, her glossy red fingernails tapping the keys on her PC. Yuldashev turned to Gabriel.

"There is a single flight every day at 10.20 a.m. No business class, unfortunately. I have booked you a seat by the emergency exit. More legroom."

"Thanks. How much is it?" Gabriel asked, reaching for his wallet.

Yuldashev laid his hand on Gabriel's.

"No. I have put the ticket on my corporate account."

"But I really can't accept that. Your hospitality has already embarrassed me. Please let me pay."

"Just see that my dossier makes its way into the right hands. That will be a more than generous act on your part."

———

Almaty had full international ticketing. Gabriel bought a ticket to Hong Kong. The flight had a ten-hour layover, at Seoul's Incheon Airport, where he intended to get some sleep.

At 11.20 a.m. the following day, after a bumpy three-hour-forty-five-minute flight from South Korea over the Yellow Sea and the Chinese provinces of Jiangsu, Anhui, Jiangxi and Guangdong, Gabriel looked out of the window to his left. He saw the blue-green waters where the South China Sea merged into Tung Way Bay. Pleasure craft left white trails in the water as they sailed amongst the large rectangular barges lying stationary in the water. Five minutes after that, with a comforting rumble, the Air Astana Airbus A330-300 touched down.

Gabriel looked out of the window as the plane taxied towards the terminal building. *Home again, home again, jiggety-jig. Now I have to find Comrade Liu. Tell him I did what he asked. Then send him to meet his ancestors. And there's the small matter of my missing sister.*

46

Back at his house, and refreshed after a shower and change of clothes, Gabriel made a call to a number he had memorised. To recall it, he pictured a plain white business card bearing the letters SBZ, which stood for Saul Ben Zacchai. And the number itself: 07700 900134. It needed the international dialling code 972. Israel.

He listened to the burr of the phone ringing at the other end, somewhere in Jerusalem he imagined, though Ben Zacchai could be anywhere in the world. For all Gabriel knew, he might be visiting the Israeli Consulate down the road from his own house on the hill.

"This is Saul." The tone neutral. Maybe a hint of wariness.

"Saul, it's Gabriel Wolfe."

Instantly, the voice at the other end warmed up.

"Gabriel! How are you?"

"I'm fine, thank you. All good. How are you?"

"Oh, you know, under siege from enemies within and without, as always. But that's the job. Now, what can I do for you?"

"I hope you won't think this is trivial, but I was in Kazakhstan recently, and I promised someone I would put a dossier on corrupt officials into the hands of the Regional Governor of East

Kazakhstan. If there's any way someone could get me in to see him... "

Saul laughed.

"Is that all? You don't want me to arrange a drone strike on someone, or introduce you to the president of the US?"

"Just the meeting would be good."

"Leave it with me. I'll have a word with my Minister of Foreign Affairs. She'll have someone send you the details. Now, tell me, how is that girlfriend of yours? Young Eli Schochat?"

"She's well. On active duty at the moment."

"Where she belongs. That woman was born to it, Gabriel. Tell her I asked after her."

"I will. And thank you."

"Listen, I have to go. Call me anytime, for any reason. The debt we owe you can never be repaid."

Next, Gabriel went online and booked a flight to Heathrow for the following day. Normally he'd fly non-stop on either British Airways or Cathay Pacific. But this trip involved a brief stopover in Oskemen, the regional capital of East Kazakhstan.

Gabriel called Nesbitt, inviting him to the house for a debrief. Nesbitt said he was finishing up a report for Kenneth Lao and could be over in a couple of hours. Gabriel was too impatient to wait.

"Can I come to you? Just give me ten minutes."

Nesbitt laughed.

"Fine. Come over whenever then. You know where to find me."

———

Nesbitt looked up as Gabriel knocked and entered his office.

"Nice tan you have there, chief. How was your wee jaunt to China? Get everything done?"

Gabriel paused before answering. He ran his fingers across his scalp and scratched the back of his neck.

"Yeah, more or less. I took the opportunity to do some sightseeing while I was there, too. Kazakhstan. Ever been?"

Nesbitt frowned, shaking his head.

"Sightseeing?"

A one-word question packed with several more.

"I can rely on your discretion?"

Nesbitt mimed zipping his lips and throwing away the key. Gabriel continued.

"I owed a favour to a local triad boss. He owed one to a Communist Party official. Comrade Liu had a little local difficulty with a missile battery commander up in Xinjiang Province. Long story short, he was killing and eating people. Totally mad, of course. I flew up there and stopped his clock. Liu was supposed to bring me out but instead he sent a chopper full of troops to clean up after himself. They blew up my wheels with an RPG. I found a friend in the village this Colonel Na had been using as his private larder. I hitched a ride into Kazakhstan with a trucker, then flew from there back to here."

Nesbitt blew out his cheeks.

"I thought *my* job had its shades of grey, but that's a rare wee life you lead, Gabriel, if you don't mind my saying so."

Gabriel grinned.

"That would just about cover it. Speaking of which, I'm going to have another chat with my triad friend." He made air quotes round the final word. "I asked him before about the triads back in the eighties. He said he was in San Francisco. But now Sarah's given us the specific triad, I'm going to ask him again."

"You think he was involved somehow?"

Gabriel shook his head.

"No. He's White Koi, they were Four-Point Star. I'm assuming triads don't work together unless it's something like a global threat to their existence. You know, a Government-level crackdown."

"Aye, well, you're probably right on that score. It'd be like the IRA and the UDF pulling bank jobs together."

"I need to go back to the UK and find Jack Yates. Get him to talk to me."

Nesbitt snorted.

"If he's anything like John Li, or the hundreds of other ex-cops nursing cases they can't let go, your problem won't be getting your man to open up. It'll be getting him to pipe down."

47

Something about Fang's swift denial that he had been in Hong Kong at the time of Tara's kidnapping had rung false to Gabriel. He wanted to talk to Fang again, but with the added element of surprise.

No more wandering in through the front door, negotiating first with the doorman then again with the lotus blossoms. He wanted to go in tooled up, for a start. That in itself would pose problems for the average citizen. Hong Kong's gun laws being on a par with the UK's, owning and keeping a handgun at home was barely possible, and keeping ammunition with it was a definitive no-no.

Gabriel had circumvented the law by the simple expedient of joining the Hong Kong Gun Club. He'd bought a Sig Sauer P226 with a barrel threaded to take a suppressor, and a couple of boxes of Federal Hi-Shok 9mm jacketed hollow-points, then simply entered the club's armoury late one night and taken them.

The Sig, along with a custom-made suppressor Gabriel had commissioned from a little engineering business in Kowloon, now lived in a box at the back of his wardrobe, always with a full magazine.

Fang had once told Gabriel that although he preferred to

conduct his business affairs from the Golden Dragon, he might just as easily be found at another of his retail premises or warehouses – *every day except Friday*. Friday was the day he liked to unwind at the casino with a bottle or two of Louis Roederer Cristal and "some pleasant female company". Today was a Friday.

At 10.00 p.m., he packed for his flight, then changed out of his jeans and T-shirt and into a black kung fu uniform, faded by much washing to a charcoal grey.

He slipped a pair of black plimsolls on, and stuffed a hood and facemask made of black silk into a jacket pocket, and a small torch into another. This was to be a covert operation from start to finish.

He had no idea whether Fang would accede to his request, hence the pistol, which he'd secreted in a concealed-carry holster clipped to the waistband of his trousers.

Keeping to the shadows, and crossing darkened city parks rather than staying on the well-lit paths, Gabriel took forty-five minutes to traverse the neon-lit city from his house to the rear of the Golden Dragon. The front entrance, with its brass poles and twisted red ropes, its oversized, wall-mounted gold dragons snarling down at passersby and queuing punters, its flashy neon window displays, was on a prosperous street thronged by wealthy Hong Kongers, expats and tourists. But just two right turns away from Wyndham Street, the landscape changed markedly.

No more BMWs, Mercs and Porsches. In their place a broken-down rickshaw, a couple of beat-up Nissan hatchbacks and, bizarrely, a baby-pink Cadillac, of so ancient a provenance that rust had eaten away gaping holes in all four wings, and rats or other vermin had taken up residence in the fat, comfortably upholstered seats.

The smell of rotting food permeated the block, drifting on the warm autumn air from the backs of several restaurants. Overfilled blue commercial dumpsters leaked their contents onto the ground: more food for the urban scavengers and their multiplying offspring. The pavement crunched with broken glass, and Gabriel could see used syringes littering the vacant lots.

The rear of the building occupied by the Golden Dragon was a plain expanse of red brick. No windows, unless you counted bricked-up apertures complete with ledges.

The double doors were painted in a greasy-looking black paint, over which clearly fearless graffiti artists had sprayed their artwork and tags. They were held closed by a thick chain and padlock. Clearly the idea of providing an escape route for his patrons in the event of a fire had not found favour with Fang.

Gabriel squatted on the other side of the street, observing the building, picking his way in. The most likely route appeared to be via the fire escape that zig-zagged up the outside of the four-storey building. He looked around, then behind him.

The coast was clear. He sprinted across the road on noiseless soles, took a check-step then leaped for the lower rungs of the fire escape. Swinging himself up onto the ladder, he righted himself and then ran up the eight flights of steps.

On the fifth flight, his heart leaped into his mouth as the whole precarious arrangement of iron railings, steps and wall-mounting brackets squawked in protest and seemed to give under his weight. He swore and held on tight, but it was a minor tremor rather than a full-blown earthquake, and after the initial creak from the metalwork, settled down again. He ran on, reaching the roof in another fifteen seconds or so.

From the roof, turning in a slow circle, he could see most of downtown Hong Kong stretched out before him in a rainbow-hued lightshow. Among the glittering skyscrapers a few stood out. Central Plaza, its needle-pointed spike appearing to puncture a low cloud lit pinkly by the lights underneath it. The Bank of China Tower with its triangular glass sections. And the International Commerce Centre, a looming rectangular monolith.

The overall effect was of standing in the glowing, flickering centre of a video game. Animated digital advertising displays enticed the viewer to drink more whisky, eat more pineapples, watch more TV, buy more clothes, join more social networks, date more people, consume, consume, consume. On the far side of the bay, the lights of Kowloon twinkled, throwing splintered reflections off the water. The air was deliciously cool, and carried a flinty edge, the faintest promise of winter to come.

Gabriel settled the hood and face mask over his features, then walked across the roof space towards a pair of workmen's hutches faced with steel doors. One was locked, the other opened with a creak when he applied gentle pressure. He closed the door behind him and waited for his eyes to adjust to the darkness.

Often a little patience was all that was required for a seemingly pitch-black interior to yield enough light to steer by. Sure enough, as his pupils expanded and his brain made better use of the minimal signals bouncing off his retinas, Gabriel started to be able to distinguish lines, and surfaces. Below his feet, a short staircase descended to a half landing and another door.

He made his way carefully, placing his feet on the outermost edges of the eight wooden treads, where there would be the least chance of his weight drawing forth a squeak from the aging timber.

In this way, step by step, he reached the half-landing. He drew the Sig from his waistband and, holding it up beside his face, pushed his left ear against the door. Through the wood he could just make out the bass from the casino's sound system, which Fang never had turned up very loud anyway.

He reached down and took the doorknob in his left hand, tightened his grip, and twisted. The door opened outwards, which he preferred.

As he inched it wider, thankful that someone had seen fit to oil the hinges in the not-too-distant past, he readied himself for a scrap or a firefight should there be one of Fang's men – or one of the lotus blossoms – on the other side.

48

Nobody shouted or burst through, lunging at him with a knife or a sword. No beefy fist cleaved the air on its way to his temple. He found himself in a long, narrow corridor, lit by the green glimmer of an LED mounted in a smoke alarm on the ceiling.

His heart running at a steady eighty in his chest, he walked down the corridor, his rubber-soled plimsolls silent on the worn-smooth lino flooring. He was hot inside the hood, but preferred to maintain his anonymity rather than get comfortable. The corridor doglegged right then left about three-quarters of the way along, and he came to a wider, carpeted passageway that he recognised from his previous trips to the Golden Dragon.

It housed the private offices. One for the casino duty manager, from where he could watch what was happening in the main room and the side parlours for private games, and one was Fang's own office: the effective headquarters of the White Koi triad. Without looking down, Gabriel racked the Glock's slide, muffling the metallic snap between his torso and the wall. Sliding along the wall, his back pressed against the paintwork, he reached the door to Fang's office and grasped the handle.

Here we go then, Wolfie, nice and quick, pistol pointing at the big man in his chair. Three, two, one, go!

He pressed down on the handle, pushed the door open and stepped inside in a single, flowing movement that ended with his back to the now-closed door and gun arm levelled at the space where Fang's head would be if he was working at his desk.

Gabriel sighted along the Sig's barrel at the space behind the large mahogany desk. The empty space. He spun round, pistol still aloft, but the room's owner was elsewhere in the building. Gabriel strode across the thick Chinese carpet and installed himself behind the desk, luxuriating in the soft embrace of the padded leather chair. He laid the gun on the desk with a quiet clonk and pulled the hood and face mask off, rolling them into a fat sausage and stowing them in his jacket pocket.

With the pistol in his hand again, he settled in to wait for Fang. How long had it been since he had sat here with Fang and Comrade Liu? It was only a few days but it felt like longer. And all the time, Liu knew he had no intention of pulling Gabriel out of the wilds of Northwest China. He'd intended that Xinjiang Province should be Gabriel's final resting place. Blown to smithereens by RPGs, and if not dead, finished off by small arms fire.

Then another thought occurred to him. How much did Fang know about Liu's plan? Were they in it together? It seemed unlikely. After all, hadn't Fang helped him out with access to Wūshī? But then, what had that cost him? Not a great deal. Gabriel had repaid him handsomely by fingering Sasha Beck as the person who'd killed his doormen. And if Fang couldn't keep her under lock and key long enough to kill her, that was down to him not Gabriel.

Be logical. Fang knew Master Zhao. The favour was to him, not me. Then he called it in to help butter up Liu. He's a triad boss in cahoots with a Communist Party official based in Hong Kong and up to God knows what nefarious business.

A noise from the other side of the door broke into Gabriel's thoughts. He heard Fang's booming laugh and a high-pitched giggle in response.

"Get back on the floor," Fang said. "I'll see you later."

"Yes, boss," the giggler replied.

Gabriel picked up the Sig and rested the butt on the desktop, so that the suppressed muzzle was pointing directly at the door, angled up so that Fang would be looking straight down the barrel. He watched the gold-coloured metal handle move down and then back up again, as Fang entered his office. He was still talking and had his head turned away.

"Make sure the Wongs get free drinks all night, OK?"

"Yes, boss. On it."

Then he turned.

And his expression told Gabriel all he needed to know.

The eyebrows shot up, almost disappearing into the hairline. The eyes, normally slits in Fang's puffy cheeks, opened wide. The cheeks drained of colour, becoming deathly pale. And, almost comically, the fleshy red lips gaped like a landed fish.

You thought I was dead.

In the half-second or so that Fang was immobile, Gabriel was able to pursue his line of thinking from initial hypothesis to final, irresistible conclusion.

I think you knew all along. You look like you've seen a ghost because in your mind that's exactly what I am. You introduced me to Liu as a tame assassin who owed you and, by extension, your cronies a favour. And you served me up to him on a platter. Use him. Then kill him. Clear the decks. Erase your tracks. Leave no witnesses. Give nobody any leverage, any power over you. Yes, you bastard, you knew!

Fang finally managed to rearrange his features into a semblance of a smile.

"Wolfe Cub!" he said, walking towards Gabriel and stopping a few feet short of the desk. "What's with the gun? You know you can ask me for anything. There's no need to point that thing at me."

Gabriel found it amusing, watching Fang acting as if coming face to face with a dead man pointing a gun at his corpulent belly was nothing more than a silly misunderstanding. Fang might be smiling, but Gabriel could see a vein pulsing on his right temple. His

Adam's apple was bobbing up and down in his throat as he swallowed repeatedly. Gabriel let the Sig's barrel drop a little.

"Sit down."

Slowly, never letting his gaze stray from the Sig's muzzle, Fang advanced a few more steps and slid into the far less generously appointed chair on the visitor side of the desk.

"H-how did you get in? I didn't see you downstairs."

"I came in the back way. I didn't want to make a fuss, or bother the lotus blossoms. Plus, I wanted to bring this with me," he added, tapping the end of the suppressor on the polished mahogany.

"But why? Like I said, Wolfe Cub—"

"Don't call me that!" Gabriel barked, loudly enough to make Fang flinch. "Master Zhao called me that and he was a thousand times the man you are."

Fang spread his hands wide. He essayed another smile, pulling it off more convincingly this time.

"You are right. Xi was a great man. A teacher. I am a mere gangster. Still just little Ricky Fang on the inside, struggling to make a living in Hong Kong under the noses of the Chinese."

"Is that why you're so tight with Liu?"

"You know what they're like. They say, 'one country, two systems' but that's just a smokescreen, a nice slogan we're all supposed to repeat until we don't even notice that they're absorbing us like rice taking up soy sauce."

"So helping him get rid of Colonel Na?"

"The first favour is a favour, the second an obligation, as the proverb has it. I had already helped him once. Now he is in my debt. You like proverbs, Gabriel? Here is another. When the winds of change blow –"

"– some people build walls and others build windmills. Master Zhao taught me many. So Liu is helping you build windmills."

Fang beamed.

"Exactly! Although," he winked, "the finished product will be white heroin not flour, but the principle is the same. Maybe I could cut you in."

"Why did you conspire with Liu to have me killed after I took out Colonel Na?"

Gabriel's sudden change of tack wrongfooted Fang, whose relaxed posture and easy smile told Gabriel he was growing more confident, despite the Sig. He reared back in the chair, making its chromed metal frame creak.

49

"What? No, you are wrong. I arranged for you to help him. Why, is that what happened?" Fang laughed, but it was forced and it died in his throat. "No, of course not! You are here and very much alive."

"He sent a squad of men to kill me. And you knew all about it."

"No, no, I swear I did not," Fang said, an air of pleading entering his voice, his hands outstretched towards Gabriel.

"I saw it on your face the moment you walked in here. Keep lying if you want. I don't really care whether you admit it or not."

Fang kept his hands out for a moment longer, then his expression changed and he let his hands fall with a double-smack onto his muscular thighs.

"Let us be men about this. Yes, I did know Liu wanted to have you killed. I tried to talk him out of it. But he was immovable. Like a rock. He wouldn't budge however much I tried to persuade him you were no threat. Are you going to kill me?"

"No. Bring Liu to me and your betrayal is wiped away."

"You swear?"

"Bring him here. Tonight."

Fang's eyebrows headed northwards again.

"Tonight? He won't just drop everything and come here. He is a very important man."

Gabriel extended his right arm so that the tip of the suppressor was only a couple of feet from Fang's nose. He aimed off a little, and squeezed the trigger. The bullet splintered a lacquer cocktail cabinet with a satisfying smash of glass from the bottles and glasses inside. Fang had flinched away, twisting in his chair as he tried to make himself as small a target as possible. Now he turned back to Gabriel, his knuckles white as he gripped the leather-covered armrests.

"Right now, I am the important man in your life," Gabriel said in a low, threatening voice. "What's left of it. Call him, now. Make up a reason he can't ignore."

White-faced, Fang fumbled in the inside pocket of his gold dinner jacket and pulled out a gold-coloured phone. He looked down at the screen and tapped a few times, then brought the phone to his ear, not taking his eyes off Gabriel's.

Gabriel watched him closely, alive to any signs that Fang might be sending a signal to Liu.

"You lie, you die," he said.

Fang nodded, grim-faced. Then he looked up at the ceiling.

"Comrade Liu. We have a problem."

...

"Serious. I can't tell you more on the phone. You need to get over here."

...

"Well, cancel it! Unless you want to spend the rest of your life in a re-education camp. Or worse."

...

"As soon as possible. Before it gets out of control. Hurry. Come straight to my office."

...

"OK."

Fang ended the call but kept hold of the phone.

"He'll be here within the hour. I need to tell the doorman to let him through. And the lotus blossoms."

He raised the phone, index finger poised over the screen.

"Who's on duty tonight?" Gabriel asked. "The lotus blossoms, I mean. Which ones?"

"Wei Mei and Jenny Yuan."

"Get Mei in here. We'll sit over there in the armchairs. The gun will be out of sight. If you try to signal to her, the same rule applies as with Liu."

While Fang called Mei and asked her to come to his office, Gabriel rose from the chair, rounded the desk and took the armchair facing the door. By letting his arm hang down between the chair and the wall, he could keep the Sig ready but out of sight.

After making the call, Fang joined Gabriel at the arrangement of armchairs and the coffee table where they had sat a few years earlier, drinking champagne with Zhao Xi. He smoothed the black trousers down over his thighs and straightened the lapels of his gold dinner jacket. He went to cross his right ankle over his left knee, twitching at his trousers, then changed his mind, returning his hovering foot to the ground.

"Stop fidgeting," Gabriel said. "Liu will die anyway. But if Mei thinks something's up and tries anything, you both die, too."

Someone knocked at the door.

50

Fang glanced at Gabriel, raising his eyebrows. Gabriel nodded. Fang twisted round in his chair. "Come!" he shouted.

Mei entered in her working dress of white leather trousers and biker jacket. She glanced at Gabriel, clearly surprised to find him there and especially in such unorthodox evening wear.

"Hello, Mei," he said.

"Hello. Nice outfit."

"I came straight from a kung fu lesson."

"Ha. OK." She turned to Fang. "Master?"

Fang's mouth was tight. He looked angry. Maybe because his lotus blossom had spoken to Gabriel first.

"Comrade Liu is coming here this evening. Let him through and tell the boys on the door to bring him straight in, OK?"

"Yes, master. Was there anything else?"

Gabriel tightened his grip on the Sig's grip. Watching. Waiting.

"No. That's all."

She spun on her heel and left without a backwards glance. Gabriel was glad, for once, that Fang had instilled such rigid codes of obedience in his people.

Once the door had clicked shut behind Mei, Fang turned back to face Gabriel.

"You want a drink?"

"No. I'm good."

"Mind if I have one? You're making me nervous with that pistol."

"Knock yourself out."

Fang levered himself out of the armchair and crossed the room to a mahogany cupboard with brass fittings.

"Fang!" Gabriel barked.

Fang halted mid-stride, rotated his head slowly.

"If there's a gun in there, my advice is focus on the drinks instead."

Fang reached the cabinet and opened the doors to reveal a second collection of bottles and glasses. Even from halfway across the room, Gabriel could see these were significantly more expensive brands than those he had shot to pieces in the cocktail cabinet. He levelled the Sig and aimed at the centre of Fang's broad back.

Fang poured himself a generous measure of what Gabriel took to be cognac from an ornate, flask-shaped bottle. He turned to Gabriel with the snifter in his hand.

"Remy Martin Louis XII cognac. Twenty-eight thousand dollars a bottle. You sure I can't tempt you?"

What, and swill it down with a powdered roofie? No thanks.

Gabriel contented himself with a brief shake of the head, watching Fang closely as he returned to his chair, warming the cognac in the palm of his hand. He gulped half of the caramel-coloured spirit down, five and a half grand's worth by Gabriel's rough estimate, and grimaced.

"Ah, that's good stuff. Those French know how to make a decent drop of brandy, you know?"

"Whereabouts in San Francisco did you live?"

"What?"

"When you lived there? What street?"

Fang's eyes shifted upwards and to the right.

"It was a long time ago. I can't remember."

"You remember the neighbourhood though?"

"Yes, of course."

"Where was it then, Bayview? That's a pretty upscale neighbourhood."

It was a simple trap. Gabriel had been online and researched the poorest and most rundown neighbourhoods in 1980s San Francisco. Bayview, despite its chi-chi name, was among the worst in terms of unemployment, poverty, gang violence and environmental pollution from toxic waste. Nobody with any money, legally acquired or not, would have chosen to live in Bayview back then, especially not a Hong Kong triad operator.

Fang walked straight into it. Up went the eyes again.

"Yes, Bayview. I had an apartment looking out over the water. Just like home."

And fell onto the sharpened sticks lining the bottom.

"That's odd. Because Bayview isn't on the shoreline. You'd need to be in India Basin or Hunter's Point."

Fang didn't miss a beat.

"I moved to Hunter's Point straightaway. That's what I meant."

You mean you moved from the first to the second-worst neighbourhood in San Francisco?

"Have you always been a White Koi?"

"Why all these questions? Can't we just wait for Liu to get here?"

Beads of sweat had broken out on Fang's forehead. He took another pull on his drink.

"Have you?"

"Yes. Always. Since I was little Ricky Fang, a White Koi 49er. You know that."

Gabriel brought the Sig up and laid it across his lap.

"I know nothing of the sort. I asked you before if you knew anything about my sister's kidnapping and you denied it. You're sure about that?"

"Yes! Like I told you."

"And you were never working for the Four-Point Star."

"No! How many more times. It doesn't work like that."

Gabriel looked at his watch. It was time to put the next part of his plan into action. He didn't like the odds of having Liu and Fang to deal with, even with the pistol. There were still plenty of armed casino staff in the building, any one of which could come in to the office and spoil things. He pointed the pistol at Fang, who jerked back in his chair as if stung.

"Get undressed."

"What?"

"Down to your underwear. Do it!"

Scowling, Fang got to his feet and took off the gold dinner jacket, which he laid across the back of the chair. He shrugged his elasticated braces off his shoulders then removed his white dress shirt, revealing a sleeveless white cotton singlet. Still glaring at Gabriel, he took off his black trousers, which he picked up, folded and laid over the shirt.

"Shoes, too," Gabriel said.

Fang complied, lining up the black patent moccasins with as much care as a soldier facing a kit inspection. He stood facing Gabriel, hands held out from his sides.

"You satisfied now? Want me to take off the rest, do a strip show for you?"

Gabriel shook his head.

"Turn around. Face the wall. Hands locked behind your head. Try anything and I'll shoot you in the spine."

Fang turned slowly, interlacing his fingers and cupping the back of his head.

Holding the pistol at all times, Gabriel extricated himself from his kung fu jacket. Underneath he wore a white T-shirt, which he left in place. He tossed Fang's trousers to one side and picked up the shirt. It was easy to slip on as Fang was a couple of sizes larger than Gabriel.

Swapping the Sig between his hands, he managed to button it up. The jacket went on next. It hung on Gabriel but by tugging it at the back and squaring his shoulders, he had it sitting more or less correctly.

Fang was standing perfectly still. Presumably he'd decided he wouldn't stand a chance if he tried a surprise attack. The action of bringing his arms up and over his head had caused the singlet to slide inwards towards his neck, leaving an extra inch or two of his shoulder blades visible.

Now Gabriel looked more closely, he saw something on Fang's skin he hadn't noticed before. Peeping out from beneath the singlet's puckered right armhole was a narrow, triangular tattoo. Or, rather, a triangular portion of a larger piece of skin art obscured by the rest of the undergarment. Its top half was inked in red, its lower, blue.

"Take off your vest," he ordered.

Fang's arms remained in position. Gabriel watched as the biceps flexed. Fang adjusted his stance, distributing his weight differently, so more was on his right foot. Gabriel took a couple of steps back. Levelled the pistol, aiming at the back of Fang's head.

"Last chance, Ricky," he said. "Take it off. Slowly."

Fang unlaced his fingers. He brought his hands lower down on his back, gripped the white fabric and drew the singlet up and over his head. As the rest of the tattoo appeared, Gabriel realised Fang's secret. He leaned closer to read the Chinese characters inked in underneath the four-pointed star.

51

Fang whirled round, flinging the singlet into Gabriel's face. Gabriel clawed at the sweaty scrap of material that had wrapped itself around his head. He fired blind, a double-tap, but clearly missed, as the next second Fang was on him, his brawny torso barrelling into Gabriel and knocking him to the floor.

The singlet fell away just as Fang clamped his hands around Gabriel's wrists, pinning him to the floor. Kneeling astride Gabriel, his weight crushing his chest, Fang leaned down and spat in Gabriel's face. It was an expensive insult. As Fang's lips puckered, Gabriel jerked his head up and butted Fang on the nose, breaking it with an audible snap.

Rearing back and howling, Fang let go of Gabriel's wrists in a reflex action as he clamped his palms to his nose. Bright-red blood flowed from between his curled fingers.

It was all the opportunity Gabriel needed. Maybe in his younger days Fang would have been able to stay in the game. But his nose was gushing blood like a tap, and decades of high living had dulled his reflexes, and diminished his ability to withstand shocks and pain. He was finished.

Gabriel brought the gun round in a fast arc and clouted Fang on the left temple. Fang's eyes rolled up in their sockets and he topped sideways, hitting the carpet with a thump,

Gabriel wriggled out from under the deadweight of the gangster and got to his feet. He took the black display handkerchief from the pocket of the golden dinner jacket, mopped his face then folded it carefully and pushed it down into his trouser pocket.

Fang had installed a huge gold-framed mirror on the wall facing his desk. Gabriel checked his appearance. His face was spattered with blood, which he wiped off with a tissue dipped in the remains of Fang's cognac.

Breathing heavily, he bound Fang with the cable ties, gagged him with a strip torn from the kung fu jacket, then dragged him into the far corner of the office, concealing him behind a gold velvet-covered sofa.

He crossed to the window looking out over Wyndham Street and drew the heavy gold velvet curtains. He turned on the Anglepoise desk lamp and pulled it down until it was just a few inches from the polished mahogany surface, then switched off all the other lights in the room.

Now the office was so dim, it was hard to see from one side to the other. He sat in Fang's chair behind the desk. What Gabriel could see in the mirror on the far wall was the lower half of his own torso, and his hands. Everything from his third shirt button upwards was in darkness.

He laid the Sig to one side, out of the pool of light cast by the Anglepoise, rested his right hand on it, and waited.

52

Ten minutes later, there was a knock at the door, which swung inwards. Gabriel's eyes had adjusted thoroughly and he could see Liu clearly as the target, dressed in a dark suit and white shirt, crossing the threshold, blinking and looking towards the desk.

"What's so important you drag me out of a meeting with the local Party Committee?" he said irritably, as he walked over to the desk and sat facing Gabriel.

Using his left hand, Gabriel pushed slowly on the underside of the desk lamp's metal shade, lifting it. As the circle of light expanded, its leading edge crept over the Sig, with Gabriel's right hand curled around it.

Liu lurched backwards, his eyes wide, his mouth dropping open.

"What the fuck? What are you doing?"

Now Gabriel spoke.

"Fang is fond of proverbs."

At the sound of Gabriel's voice, the expression of shock on Liu's face turned to one of horror. It deepened as Gabriel brought the Sig up and aimed at a spot between Liu's eyes.

"But you're——"

"Dead? Your boys were careless. They didn't check the Rhino after they blew it to shit or they'd have seen there was no body."

Liu started to tremble violently, as if someone had applied an electric current to his spine.

"Let me go. I can pay you handsomely. I have money."

"I don't need it, I have my own. You know, I'm not surprised Na went mad. Living under your fucked-up ideology would send any sane person crazy. And compared to the tens of millions you lot have murdered or starved to death, Na's crimes pale into insignificance, don't you think?"

"Progress is never bought cheaply."

"Where did you get that? Inside a fortune cookie? I said Fang is fond of proverbs. We were swapping them before you arrived. But I didn't get to share one of my personal favourites. It's Confucius. 'Do not impose on others what you yourself do not desire.'"

Liu shook his head.

"Pl—"

The suppressor did a decent job of quietening the crack from the pistol. A heavy book slammed on a desk rather than a firework in a dustbin. The bullet entered Liu's forehead an inch above the bridge of his nose.

His skull exploded outwards, sending blood and brain matter spraying in a cone behind him. Gabriel leaned back in his chair to avoid the back-spatter as the pressure of the hollow-point round blew the front of Liu's head out.

Liu's chair fell over backwards, jets of blood shooting up towards the ceiling as the pressure from the cranial arteries drove it out through the massive wound.

Gabriel rose, tucked the gun back into his holster and walked over to the sofa where he'd stashed Fang. Grabbing him by his ankles, he dragged him out and over to the desk. He yanked down the improvised gag and slapped Fang a couple of times to wake him up.

Eyes rolling like a stunned calf, Fang looked to his right and gasped as he saw Liu's body, the head now at the centre of a rapidly expanding lake of blood that soaked into the carpet, turning it from gold to bronze.

Gabriel leaned back and sat on the edge of the desk. He pulled out the Sig.

"You used to be in the Four-Point Star, didn't you?"

"No."

"I saw the tattoo, Fang. I read the text. Try again. Tell me the truth or I'll shoot you through your left kneecap."

To emphasise his intentions to follow through on the threat, he lowered the Sig and aimed at Fang's exposed left leg.

"Yes," Fang muttered.

"Speak up, man, I can't hear you."

"Yes, I said."

"Good. That's better. We're establishing some trust. Next question. What do you know about my sister's kidnapping? It was a Four-Point Star operation, so think very carefully before you tell me any more lies."

"Fuck you."

The pistol jerked in Gabriel's hand. Fang's left knee blew out, spraying more of his blood into the air. The prostrate man screamed.

"I'll do the other one next. Then your elbows."

"I don't know anything about it," Fang hissed out. "There were hundreds of us low-level guys back then. We operated independently. It could have been any one of a dozen separate little gangs. As long as we paid our tax up the chain, nobody minded what we did."

"You're lying," Gabriel said, aiming at Fang's other knee.

"No! I'm not."

Fang's eyes flicked away from Gabriel's to look at a wall-mounted clock. He grimaced with pain, although Gabriel thought he saw a flicker of amusement on the gangster's twisted features.

"What is it?"

"Staff meeting in two minutes. All indoor security come in for a midnight briefing for the rest of the session. If you're still here they'll kill you. You won't get out of here alive."

307

"You're lying."

"Fine," Fang grunted. "Stay. Shoot me through the other knee. I'll learn to walk again. You never will."

"I could just kill you right now."

"Yes, you could. But what if I *did* know something about the kidnapping? You'd never find out."

Gabriel extended his arm, pointing the pistol directly at Fang's face. But this time he didn't flinch. Instead, he stared right down the barrel. Gabriel tightened his finger on the trigger. Every fibre of his being was straining in the same direction. *Tighten it again until the hammer hits the firing pin. Kill the fucker.*

Fang lay back and closed his eyes, his forehead creased with pain, but his posture as serene as a stone knight atop a tomb.

"If I see you in Hong Kong again, *Wolfe Cub*, I will have you killed. No." He raised an index finger. "I will do it myself for your disrespect."

Gabriel ran for the door. Fang would have to wait. Outside, the corridor was quiet, but then he heard voices from the direction of the stairs leading down to the gambling floor. He turned and ran the other way, rounding the dogleg – right-left-right – reaching the flight of steps. He took them two at a time and in four fast strides reached the door leading to the roof.

He pictured the scene ten or more feet beneath his feet. The casino manager, lotus blossoms, floor-walkers and security staff arriving in their boss's office. Discovering his bloodied, cable-tied form by the desk, and next to him the remains of a top-ranking local Party official with his brains blown out.

He took the fire escape at a run, slithering and stuttering on the grid-like steps, absorbing the sudden lurch on the fifth landing, then jumping from the lowest level to the ground. He sprinted across the road and kept going, down a long, narrow side-street, taking random turns but always course-correcting towards home.

Arriving back at the house at 1.05 a.m., he locked the Sig in his office safe, called a taxi, then changed into jeans, T-shirt and a lightweight jacket. He was paying the driver and pulling his bags out of the boot at the airport at 1.59 a.m.

He didn't doubt that Fang would have set people to discovering his address in Hong Kong. If they did, they might trash the place, but he had a feeling he wouldn't be returning anyway. All his valuables were in a bank vault or the safe at Kenneth Lao's law firm. All apart from a trio of jade figurines – a monk, a fisherman and a dragon – which he'd taken from his desk and wrapped in a pocket handkerchief before placing them in an inside pocket of his jacket.

53

The day after Gabriel boarded the Air Astana flight from Hong Kong to Oskemen, Ahmet Ismailov, East Kazakhstan's recently elected regional governor, arrived for work, as usual, at 8.15 a.m. His bodyguard opened the limo's door for him and accompanied him into the Regional Legislature building.

A hangover from the old Soviet days, the best thing that could be said for the building was that, in winter, the radiators were ferocious in pursuit of their duty to cook the inhabitants.

On the way up the steps, he glanced to his left. Once a statue of Lenin pointing to the mythical glories of a future workers' paradise had stood there on a red granite plinth. Weeks after the collapse of the Soviet Union in 1991, persons unknown had raided the building at night and pulled the statue down. Now, in its place, stood a new statue, to Janybek Khan, one of the two founders of Kazakhstan.

They took the lift to the third floor, where Ismailov dismissed his bodyguard. He entered his outer office and greeted his PA, Irina, a stern-looking brunette in her late forties who had been with him for most of his political career. She was five years older than him and he saw her as more of a big sister than a secretary.

"Morning, Rina. Is he here?"
She nodded to a door set off to one side of the outer office.
"He's in the waiting room."
"Did you offer him a coffee?"
She smiled.
"Of course? Do you think I don't know how to treat guests? Especially when they come so highly recommended?"
"Sorry. I'm a little…" He paused. *Yes, Ahmet, what exactly is the right word to describe your feelings when the Foreign Minister of Israel calls you at home at night and asks for a "favour"?* "Distracted. As you can imagine."
She smiled again.
"You're playing in the big leagues now."
Ismailov squared his shoulders and opened the door to the waiting room. Its sole occupant, a fit-looking man in his late thirties, short black hair flecked with silver, scar on his left cheek, stood and smiled. His right hand was extended. In his left he carried a brown padded envelope.
"Thank you for seeing me, governor," he said in Russian. "I've come to help you with your anti-corruption drive."
He handed over a cardboard folder.
Ismailov took it and glanced inside. Documents. Nothing more than he had expected.
"What is this?" he asked the stranger.
"It is proof that the Mayor of Ayagoz is corrupt."
He closed the folder and rested his hands on top of its smooth cardboard cover. Something in his gut told him that the folder's contents were genuine. His route to the next level of power in Kazakhstan gleamed before him. But there were some questions he wanted answering first.
"Who are you? I mean, really? Who are you, that Israel's Foreign Minister calls me at my home, at night, and she *suggests* that as a favour to the Government of Israel, I meet you?"
The man facing him smiled.
"Isn't it enough that she did, governor?"

Ismailov thought for a moment. He realised the stranger was right.

He nodded.

Things were about to change in Eastern Kazakhstan.

54

LONDON

After his unorthodox courier mission in Oskemen, Gabriel continued on his long journey to the UK. With Eli still away, he didn't bother going home. He booked into a hotel in Central London, half a mile northwest of Trafalgar Square. The Ham Yard Hotel was tucked away in a pedestrian precinct amidst the theatres, restaurants and souvenir shops clustered on the south side of Soho.

He had taken to staying there because it was close enough to Whitehall that if Don wanted to see him, he could walk. But then, the boss wouldn't want to see him at the moment, would he? What with Gabriel being put on unofficial "gardening leave". *Would you approve of how I've been spending my holiday time, boss?* Somehow, he doubted it.

Sitting in the hotel's busy cocktail bar later that afternoon, nursing a Martini, Gabriel pulled up a contact he hadn't spoken to for a while. He listened to the phone ringing. It was answered mid-ring.

"Gabriel Wolfe! Long time, no speak. And how is the world of off-books, state-sponsored assassinations these days?"

Stella sounded out of breath.

"I'm guessing you're somewhere private?"

"Now what made you think that? Actually, yes, I'm in the middle of Regent's Park. Got a break and thought I'd fill it with a run. What's up?"

"I just need a little bit of information."

"What? Where to get an untraceable pistol? I could help you with that, you know."

Gabriel laughed.

"No. As a matter of fact I can do that myself. I was actually wondering if you knew of a good forensic science lab. I have a couple of things I need to get checked out."

"Oh. OK, well that's not too difficult. We use MHD Forensics in Richmond."

"Can a private citizen use them as well as the police?"

"As long as that private citizen has the money, they'll work for anyone. The benefits of privatisation. Out of interest, what are these things you need checking out?"

"One's a thirty-six-year-old fabric sample that looks as though it might be bloodstained. The other's a more recent sample: saliva and more blood."

"Thirty-six. That'd be, what, 1983? Getting into cold-case reviews, are you?"

"I'm investigating my sister's kidnapping. She was taken when she was a baby."

He heard her inhale sharply at the word "baby".

"Was she ever returned?"

"No. I hope she's still alive, though."

"Do you think it might be her blood?"

"No. It's from the kidnapper."

"You'll be able to get your samples tested. That's not the problem. But unless you have a police operation name and a reference number, you can't get them to check against NDNAD, sorry, the National DNA Database."

"Meaning, unless I'm a cop, all I'll end up with is two very expensive DNA profiles and nothing to identify who they came from."

"Yes, although even if you *were* a cop, you wouldn't get an ID if they hadn't been swabbed, tested and entered onto the database in the course of an investigation."

"So, what you're saying is, I'm buggered, basically."

"If it was someone else, yes I would. But seeing as it's you, and seeing as it was you who helped clean up after my…"

"One-woman vigilante justice campaign?"

"Something like that. I guess what I'm trying to say is, I owe you."

"You helped us catch Tim Frye."

"I did. But he was a common enemy. This is personal. Look, get your results from MHD and bring them to me. I'll have them run against the database, and share the findings. OK? It might be nothing, but it might be something, and at least you'll know one way or another."

"Thanks, Stella. I will. As soon as I have them."

Back in his room, Gabriel made a coffee then took it to the desk. He launched a browser on his laptop and typed in a search query:

Royal Hong Kong Police Association

The Association's website came out top of the search results and he clicked through. There, just to the left of the Login button, was the link he'd hoped to find. He clicked Members, scrolled down to Member List and clicked again.

Member List
This content is for members only.

. . .

Next he tried the Contact Us page, but this only offered a form to fill in to apply for membership. Gabriel sighed, then noticed text instructing prospective members to download and fill in a form. He clicked the link, not expecting to find anything useful, but there, at the top of the page, was the name, address and phone number of the honorary secretary. Glancing at his watch and making a swift calculation of the time in the UK, he called the number.

"Barry Johnson."

"Mr Johnson, my name is Gabriel Wolfe. I'm doing some research for a book and I wondered if you could help me?"

"Go on."

"I'm trying to trace a particular officer from the RHKP. He retired in 1997. If I gave you his name would you be able to tell me where I could find him?"

The man answered without a pause.

"I'm afraid not. GDPR means we have to guard our members' personal data very carefully, but to be honest, even before that, it's not something I'd have done. If you give me your details, I'll get in touch with him and then if he wants to contact you, that's up to him."

Gabriel thought fast. He didn't want to warn the guy he was looking for him. He wasn't sure why.

"That's OK. I'll leave it for now. Thanks." He ended the call. "Shit!" he said to the empty room.

Come on, mate. You didn't think it was going to be that easy, did you? On to Plan B. Looks like you'll be asking Valerie for another favour after all. Give her a call.

"Hello, stranger," she said, her voice containing just a hint of mockery.

"Hi, Valerie. How are you?"

"Oh, you know. Bored shitless sitting at my desk, writing reports. And there's something else you should know, especially if you're about to ask me for help."

"What's that?"

"My name. It's not Valerie Duggan. I'm Penny Farrell. Detective Inspector Penny Farrell, to be one hundred per cent accurate."

"In which case, hello, Penny. I wondered whether you could help me out after all. I tried the RHKPA, but they don't give out members' contact details to any random stranger who just calls out of the blue. Can't think why."

"Huh. Some people, eh? What's this ex-cop's name again?"

"Jack Yates."

"Leave it with me. I'll do a bit of digging. If he moved to the UK in ninety-seven it shouldn't be hard to track him down, one way or another. You checked Facebook, I suppose?"

"Yes."

After the call ended, Gabriel rose from the armchair and crossed the room to the window. He pulled back the net curtain and stared across the rooftops towards the London Eye, the top half of which he could see clearly through the mist. He texted Eli.

Back in UK. All OK with u?

He stared at the screen for a few seconds, knowing it was foolish to expect an instant reply. But still he stared. In the end, he pocketed the phone. *Be safe, El. That's all. Be safe.*

Suddenly the room felt claustrophobic. A wave of anxiety washed through him. He hated being at a loose end, having no operation, no mission, no purpose. But this was definitely one of those times. He changed into running gear and headed out.

Dodging pedestrians, and jinking into the road to avoid knots of tourists, he ran down Haymarket and turned right onto Pall Mall, then left into Waterloo Place, passing the Athenaeum Club with its gold statue and frieze of classical figures on a royal blue background. *What happened to you, Tara?* He jogged past the Duke Of York Column, wondering how the dead nobleman would have felt, had he known that ten years later his memorial would be surpassed in height, design and location by that raised to his near-contemporary Admiral Lord Nelson.

He took the centre flight of steps, swerving to avoid a pair of elderly Japanese who stopped suddenly to take a selfie with the column in the background.

Where did they take you?

Across the Mall, glancing right to the London home of his ultimate employer, before entering St James' Park. The path forked around a statue, which Gabriel stopped to admire. This was the Royal Artillery Boer War Memorial, and he walked closer to read the inscription. In plain English, it stated that the bronze and Portland stone monument had been "erected by the officers and men of the Royal Artillery in memory of their honoured dead in South Africa 1899–1902". Plain, but all the more affecting for that.

Are you still alive?

He checked on his phone. The bronze plaques contained 1,083 names of the fallen. He closed his eyes for a moment and offered a soldier's prayer for the dead men, a few lines he had memorised from Psalm 91.

He will cover you with his feathers.
Under his wings you will take refuge.
His faithfulness is your shield and rampart.
You shall not be afraid of the terror by night,
nor of the arrow that flies by day.

He ran on, into the park. Settling into a steady pace that carried him clockwise around the lake then across the Mall just in front of Buckingham Palace and into Green Park. More memorials to war dead. From Canada and then Bomber Command, before leaving the second park and entering Hyde Park.

Please, God, give me one living relative.

Heading north, he passed the Holocaust Memorial Garden on his left and then, with a twinge of irony, the Royal Humane Society. He wondered whether its staff ever paused on their walk to work and asked themselves how it was that a species could inflict so much suffering on its own members and then give out prizes for those who saved lives.

Circuiting Hyde Park, he tried to arrange the pieces of the puzzle around his sister's disappearance into some sort of coherent pattern. Kidnapped aged five months. A ransom note sent. The ransom raised, no doubt against the advice as well as the policy, of HMG. The response demanded by the kidnappers made. And then, nothing.

Why go to all that trouble? Take all those risks? Because Tara wasn't some street kid, to be snatched from the gutter in a poor neighbourhood before being trafficked God knew where. She was the daughter of a diplomat. A British diplomat, at that. The living, breathing heart of the Establishment. *What about me, Gabriel? Don't forget about me!* His mother's voice, as faint as a wisp of bonfire smoke in the October air. *She was my child, too.*

And now, finally, he understood. Why his mother had been powerless to arrest her slide into alcoholism. The slide that ended with her husband's death from a stroke, on board the yacht he'd named after her, while she was passed out below decks. His death and her suicide. It had all begun with Tara. He ground his teeth together until his jaw muscles cramped. Triad greed for money had destroyed his family as surely as if they'd shot them all in their sleep. Except that would have been a quick and painless end. He ran on.

He arrived back at the hotel hot and sweaty, but free of the squirming knot of apprehension that had propelled him out of the lobby an hour and a half earlier. Somewhere on the run his phone had died, and he plugged it into the charger before going for a shower.

When he emerged from the steam-filled bathroom fifteen

minutes later, the first sound to greet him in the bedroom was the ping that alerted him to a text. He snatched up the phone.

Done. All good. Extract tomoz. x

55

Penny Farrell called Gabriel at 9.10 the following morning.

"I've found him for you."

"Penny, that's fantastic! Where is he?"

"I'd prefer not to do this over the phone. Or by email, before you ask. Have you got time for a coffee today?"

"How about I buy you lunch instead? I think it's the least I can do."

He heard the pleasure in her voice as she answered.

"Lunch! Now there's a word you don't hear round here every day. OK, that would be nice. Where and when?"

"Say, 1.30? Do you know Brasserie Zédel on Sherwood Street?"

"No, but if you're picking, I'm sure it'll be lovely."

Smiling, he put the phone down and got dressed then called the restaurant to book a table. It was short notice, but he'd eaten there many times and the manager recognised him.

"We have a table or two we like to keep free for regulars, Mr Wolfe. We will see you at one."

. . .

The sun shone in through his bedroom window. With a few hours to kill, he decided to go out. Heading this time for Regent's Park, he walked northwest through Soho, crossed Oxford Street, continued up Great Portland Street and entered the park. He made his way to the boating lake and strolled around the perimeter path, watching as parents held their children close enough to the water to toss bits of bread for the ducks.

His phone rang. It was Eli.

"Hi!" he said, smiling, his system flooding with a sudden surge of happiness. "Did it go OK? Are you all right? Where are you?"

Eli laughed and he felt his heart lift.

"Too many questions! OK, one, yes. Two, I'm fine. Three, Rothford. Don wants a full debrief. I think it'll be this evening before I'm free. Where are you?"

"I'm in London. Do you want to meet me? I'm staying at a very nice hotel."

"Would you mind if I came down tomorrow? I'm shattered."

"Of course. I mean, of course I wouldn't."

Gabriel spent another hour in the park, meandering amongst the tourists, trippers, joggers and office workers out for a sneaky coffee or cigarette. He returned by way of the boating lake.

A group of mums were chatting beside pushchairs and buggies, some with oversized bicycle-style spoked wheels. Toddlers were running in circles a few feet away, screaming at the pigeons trying to snaffle up the bread they'd inexpertly thrown for the ducks. He smiled indulgently. Then, feeling an inexplicable tug of regret in the pit of his stomach, turned away.

———

At five to one, he left the hotel for the second time and walked down Denman Street to the junction with Sherwood Street. He turned left, leaving the bunched one-way traffic for the relative freedom of a pedestrianised stretch that led down to the entrance to Piccadilly Circus underground station on Glasshouse Street.

On his right sat Brasserie Zédel, looking as if someone had lifted the entire building bodily from Paris in the 1930s, and placed it down amongst the red-velvet-and-brass steakhouses and the gaudy theatres of the West End.

Outside the double-fronted building, the warmth of early October had led a dozen or so people to opt for the cream-and-red bistro chairs at circular white tables. Gabriel wanted something different. The surprise that awaited first-timers and still delighted regulars like him.

He pushed the polished brass handle on the narrow front door and walked into a tiny bar area with a corner counter selling coffees, continental bottled beers and wine, plus authentic-looking baguettes filled with ham, cheese and salad. Nodding to the barman, he threaded his way through the tables and left the bar for the stairs.

It was as if the designer of the building had set out, quite deliberately, to disguise the true reason most patrons came to Zédel. The staircase, bordered by geometric gold-painted banisters, widened out and descended to the mezzanine level and the basement in a graceful, curving sweep that took Gabriel past a curtained-off nightclub. "Crazy Coqs": it never failed to make him grin. It didn't now.

At the front desk, a young woman in the brasserie's simple uniform of black trousers and waistcoat over a white shirt smiled when she saw Gabriel. She had a freshly scrubbed look: blonde hair tied back and minimal makeup over a clear complexion.

"*Bonjour, Monsieur Wolfe. Pour quelque personnes?*" How many people?

"*Bonjour, Florence. Pour deux.*" Two.

"*Oui. Votre amie, n'est pas encore là.*" Your friend isn't here yet.

She signalled to a waiter, who took Gabriel to a table for two in the corner of the vast square dining room. He took the chair with its back to the wall, the better to see Penny when she arrived. Not knowing whether she would be drinking, or whether the whole "not while I'm on duty, sir" thing was a myth, he ordered a bottle of sparkling water.

He leaned back and took in the extraordinary surroundings. The basement of Zédel seemed to have been stuck in a 1930s timewarp. Everywhere he looked, he saw Art Deco flourishes, from geometric tiles to gold paint and black-and-white chequerboard designs.

The buzz of hundreds of conversations was ameliorated by the high ceilings and the absence of canned music. Everywhere, black-aproned waiters bustled among the tables, carrying trays of delicious-smelling food and rounds of drinks. The aromas of grilled meat and garlic prevailed. He looked upwards, at the rectangular light fittings that bounced their soft, creamy light off the gilded tops of the columns, painted to look like marble.

A movement in the corner of his eye brought his attention back to ground-level.

Following the line of Florence's extended right arm, a woman, blonde crop, dark glasses, slash of red lipstick, was making her way towards him, a black leather messenger bag over her right shoulder. Gabriel stood, unsure whether it would be a hug or a handshake, now that she was no longer playing the role of a high-rolling cougar at the Golden Dragon.

Arriving at the table, she solved the problem for him, holding out her right hand. Penny's outfit was as business-like as her greeting. A black trouser suit over a blue shirt, with low black heels. She'd pulled her hair back into a bun and, like Florence on the front desk, wore very little makeup.

"Well," she said, taking a look around as they sat down, "I'm glad to see someone in public service is making a decent living. I couldn't afford this place on a DI's salary."

"Nor could I on what The Department pays me. I'm basically a freelance."

She pouted and put a finger to her pooched-out lower lip.

"Aw, poor baby on zero hours, is he?"

"More or less. I get a small retainer and a daily rate on

operations. Don has a few people on the payroll but I didn't want to be tied in like that."

"And Old Dobbin's OK with that, is he?"

Gabriel frowned.

"Does *everyone* know his nickname?"

She grinned.

"Not everyone. Just some people."

"People who make it their business to know?"

"Something like that, yes? So is he?"

"Is he what?"

"OK with you earning your corn elsewhere?"

"As long as it doesn't conflict with my official duties, yes he is."

"I need to push you on that a bit. But before that, what does a girl have to do to get a drink around here? I assume they have a wine list?"

"A very good one. I wasn't sure if you'd be drinking."

"Ah." She adopted a stiff copper-in-court voice. "Not while I'm on duty, sir."

"I did wonder."

She shook her head, loosening a strand of hair, which she tucked behind her ear.

"Just one won't hurt. It's more when you're over the limit doing ninety past a school that the powers-that-be tend to get exercised."

Gabriel signalled a passing waiter.

"Could we have the wine list, please?"

"Certainly, sir. I will bring some bread, also."

He returned with a basket of sourdough and the wine list. About to hand it to Gabriel, he was stopped in his tracks by Penny's outstretched hand.

"I'll take that, thank you," she said with a disarming smile. "Don't go away."

"Of course, madame."

Gabriel watched her as she scanned the list. She ran a fingertip down the whites, then the reds, before returning to the first column. She looked up at the waiter.

"I'll have a medium glass of the Sancerre, please."

"Very good, madame. And for you, sir?"

"The same, please."

The waiter gone, Penny fixed Gabriel with a stare.

"Twelve quid for a glass of wine? Your non-government earnings must be in decent shape if you can afford to bring people here."

"We could always change it to a bottle. It would be much more economical."

He meant it as a joke, but she appeared to take him seriously. She looked at her watch and frowned.

"Yeah, why not?" she said. "All I've got this afternoon is paperwork. We'll call this developing a confidential informant. After all, you are friendly with Mr Fang, aren't you?"

"Hold on," Gabriel said.

He rose from the table and pursued their waiter, catching up with him at the bar and changing the order. Back at the table, he shook out his napkin and settled it across the knees of his suit trousers.

"You look nice," he said. "Not quite so Valerie as before."

She laughed, a full-throated sound that had diners at neighbouring tables turning their heads and smiling.

"What, you think I'm going to turn up for lunch in my knock-off Louboutins and a leopard-print cocktail frock, do you?"

"I don't know. I thought you carried it off pretty well."

She rolled her eyes.

"*Now* he flirts with me!"

"Now it's safe," he replied.

The wine arrived. The waiter poured a little into Penny's glass. She took a sip and pronounced herself satisfied, whereupon he topped up her glass and filled Gabriel's.

He raised his glass.

"Cheers!"

"Cheers!"

The wine was excellent. Cool, dry and fruity without being overpowering. Penny put her glass down and leaned across the table.

"You said Don lets you work for other people as long as there's no conflict of interest, right?"

"Right."

"And you decide when that would happen, yes?"

"Right again, officer."

"How do you know?"

"What, whether there's a conflict of interest?"

"Yes. I mean, suppose some, I don't know, Arab gentleman in a dishdash and a diamond-studded Rolex says, 'Oh, me and my mates are getting aggro from some terrorists at one of our oilfields, can you go and sort them out?' would you go?"

Gabriel sipped his wine. Penny was sharp. Pugnacious. Fiercely intelligent. Good street-fighting skills. Maybe she'd like a job working for "Old Dobbin". Stranger things had happened.

"Not just because he asked, no. I'd do my due diligence. Find out a bit more about him. Look at his business. Try to get a handle on who these so-called terrorists actually were. They might be Greenpeace activists, for example, or local tribespeople forced off their land. I don't just go in all guns blazing for the highest bidder, if that's what you're asking."

Then why is my pulse racing? Why do I feel defensive? Am I really that squeaky clean?

She patted the air in a calming gesture.

"It's fine. I'm sorry, I shouldn't have pushed you like that. I'm sure you know what you're doing and it was out of order for me to question your ethics."

"It's OK. And you're right. It can be murky at times. To be honest, I genuinely believe I've always been fighting for the good guys. The closest I've come to the dark side is doing personal protection for the odd banker here and there. But even if you think they're somewhere below pond-slime in evolutionary terms, it's not against the law."

"Like I said, it's none of my business. Bad habit of mine, treating new acquaintances like they're suspects."

Her face fell, just for the briefest of moments, but Gabriel caught it. The mouth turned down, the gaze slid away from his, the space between the eyebrows narrowed. Then her face was clear again, like a pond after the ripples from a stone tossed into it have flattened out.

"Did someone hurt you, once?"

Her eyes flashed and she jerked back as if stung.

"What?"

"Sorry. My turn to apologise. Stupid thing to ask."

"No. You've been open with me. And we certainly shared a near-death experience in Hong Kong. I guess I owe you a little candour."

She took a sip of her wine and cleared her throat.

56

"Someone did hurt me. A guy, as you've probably guessed. He proposed to me in the middle of a restaurant. Not one as nice as this, mind you. Down on one knee, ring in a box, the whole nine yards. Everything went fine, right up to the first day of our honeymoon. I remember it like it was yesterday. I came in from the balcony and he was sitting on the edge of the bed on his phone. He had this look on his face, like his dog had died."

An image flashed, unwanted, into Gabriel's mind. Seamus, his beloved greyhound. Dead under the wheels of a car. He pushed it away.

"What was it?"

"He said he'd lost all his money. I asked him what he meant, you know, was it a business deal gone wrong? He was in finance, like your banker clients. Only Harry's business was advising rich people on what to do with their spare millions. Turned out he'd been using his clients' funds to speculate in the US sub-prime mortgage market. You know about that, right, the financial crisis?"

"Banks bundling up mortgages taken out by people who couldn't afford to repay them and selling them on to investors."

She nodded and took a healthy slug of her wine.

"It's a bit more complicated than that but, basically, yes. We got married in August 2007, you see. The whole house of cards came down while we were unpacking our suitcases in Mauritius. Harry was broke. Wiped out. And what was worse, he'd lost all his clients' money along with his own."

"Shit! What happened?"

"I asked him if he was serious. I mean, I couldn't believe it. He'd never given me any reason to doubt he wasn't what he said he was, a successful wealth adviser with a portfolio of satisfied clients. I mean, he bought me these diamond earrings the size of bloody duck eggs. So, he puts his phone down and stands up and crosses the room to where I'm standing in a sarong and a bikini top, holding a champagne cocktail and—" Her voice cracked, and she paused, clearing her throat again.

Gabriel had a horrible intuition he knew what was coming next.

"Penny, please. You don't have to tell me this if you don't want to. It's really not necessary."

"No. It's fine. Bastard doesn't deserve it. He hit me. A proper punch. In the stomach, which made me think he'd done it before. No bruises, you know?"

"Christ! I'm so sorry. What did you do?"

"Do?" she answered, her voice rising, before she made a visible effort to bring it down to conversational volume again. "I fucking decked him, didn't I? Then I left. Got a cab to the airport, flew home, hired a solicitor. Oh and I sent a text to a mate in Financial Crime."

After that, she fell silent. Gabriel took the opportunity to reach for the bottle of wine in its table-side cooler and refill their glasses. A waitress appeared and asked if they were ready to order. Gabriel asked for a little more time and, smiling, she withdrew.

Penny sipped her wine and bit into a piece of the bread.

"Sorry about that. Don't know where all that came from," she said.

"It's fine. Better out than in. And I know this is a shit link," Gabriel continued, "but maybe we should talk about other kinds of crime."

She sighed, shook her head vigorously and ran her hands over her hair.

"Good idea. I've got something for you."

She reached down to her bag and unsnapped the catches, bringing out a single sheet of paper, which she handed to Gabriel.

He glanced at the typed information.

John "Jack" Yates.
RHKP 1981–1997

51 Rochester Road
Carshalton, SM5 1QQ

01632 962857/07700 915001

Below the phone numbers, a passport-style photo had been copy-and-pasted. It showed a man in his late fifties or early sixties, balding with wings of dark hair at either temple, thick black eyebrows above dark eyes, lips raised in an approximation of a smile. His shirt collar, open, was just visible at the bottom of the picture.

Gabriel looked at Penny.

"Thank you."

She shrugged.

"Least I could do. Although as we seem to be in the process of trading favours, maybe you could give me a little bit of help with Mr Fang."

"Let's order first, then, yes, of course. Hungry?"

"Very. I'm going to have the sea bream for my main course but as you seem to be the maître d's best friend, what do you recommend for a starter, then?"

"It depends on how adventurous you're feeling."

Penny rolled her eyes.

"Aaand there he goes again with the flirting!"

"Not at all. I was only going to say, if you like trying new things, the frogs' legs are great."

"And what makes you think I haven't had *cuisses de grenouilles* before? It wouldn't be my accent, now would it?" she added, roughening her South London rasp so that the French phrase came out as "quayce duh grunwheels".

Gabriel felt a blush heating his face. He'd been caught, not for the first time, making assumptions about the woman sitting opposite him and who, he reminded himself, was a senior officer at Scotland Yard.

"Sorry. They are nice, though," he added.

"I wouldn't know. Never 'ad 'em."

After the waiter had taken their order, looking mildly puzzled at the grins flashing between his two patrons as "madame" ordered the frogs' legs in a passable French accent, Gabriel raised his glass and took a sip.

"What do you want to know about Fang?"

"Whatever you can tell me."

"Aside from the fact he runs the White Koi, there's not a lot I *can* tell you. He told me a story about how he murdered the leader of the Coral Snakes some time ago."

Penny shook her head.

"We need current stuff. We have a witness who's implicated him in a human trafficking operation, but it's thin gruel at the moment. What we need is a way in to his organisation. A weak link. Someone we can influence."

Gabriel saw a small, scruffy apartment in Hong Kong. A room stuffed with high-end computer gear and comic book memorabilia.

"He has an IT guy. Goes by the name of *Wūshī*. It means 'Wizard'. He helped me out a couple of times. Knows his way around the dark web, all that. I'd imagine you might be able to lean on him."

Penny nodded and pulled a notebook from her messenger bag.

"Sounds perfect. And where might one be able to find this Wizard character? Has he got a castle somewhere in China?"

"No. But he has got a flat in Hong Kong. Ko Shing Street. Hold on."

Gabriel searched his phone for *Wūshī*'s contact details and held the screen towards Penny.

She jotted them down in her notebook, nodded and favoured Gabriel with a wide smile.

"Thank you. I think that calls for a toast."

She raised her glass.

"What are we drinking to?"

"How about to justice?"

"To justice."

They clinked rims and drank.

———

Later, using the same cover story he'd employed with Barry Johnson, Gabriel called Jack Yates. He introduced himself as Terry Fox, not wanting to reveal his connection to Yates's last unsolved case until they were face to face. Yates told him he was about to leave for a short break in Portugal.

"It's a lads' golfing trip, you know. A few of us go every year. Play a few rounds, have a few bottles of the local vino collapso, do a bit of sightseeing, chat up the expat totty. How about when I get back?"

They agreed to meet at 11.00 a.m. in six days' time. Then Yates said he had to go as his taxi was waiting outside.

Next, Gabriel pulled up the number for the forensics lab. He fixed an appointment with the deputy director for 4.30 p.m., the day he was due to meet Yates. With almost a week before anything could happen in his search for Tara, Gabriel decided to return home and meet Eli there. He called her to explain his change of plan.

57

ALDEBURGH

Not for the first time, Gabriel had left for a trip encumbered with luggage – gear, materiel, kit, whatever – and arrived back with just the clothes he stood up in. He'd bought new clothes in London and was wearing them now as he climbed out of the minicab parked by the front gate of his house in Aldeburgh. Boat shoes, jeans, a white shirt and another blue linen jacket.

England was enjoying an unseasonably warm October, which the cab driver was all over as he accepted the fare from the station.

"I tell you, boy, this is that global warming they're all on about, innit?"

Climate change or just a fairly common occurrence in this part of the world, Gabriel was thankful for the warmth of the sun on his back as he walked over to the gate and let himself into the garden. Eli had her back to him. She was sitting on a teak lounger reading a book, white wires from earbuds snaking down over her chest to her iPhone.

He bent down and kissed the top of her head. She turned and

smiled, pulled him into an awkward embrace and kissed him back, hard and long, on the lips.

When she released him, he sat beside her.

"I missed you, El."

"I missed you, too."

"What are you reading?"

"It's called *How to Cure a Fanatic* by Amos Oz. He's talking about how extremism flourishes and how you can counter it. I think you'd like it."

"Maybe I'll read it after you, then."

"You smell nice," she said.

"Do I? I don't feel it. I've been travelling for bloody hours."

"Why don't you come inside and have a shower, then? Maybe I'll join you."

Later, as the afternoon turned into evening and the light outside began to dim, Gabriel awoke to find Eli curled up inside his left arm. He lay there listening to her breathing, enjoying this brief interlude in a life that seemed at the moment to be on permanent high-alert. After making love, they'd had the promised shower, then debriefed each other, as far as they were able, on their respective operations.

"Hello," she murmured. "That was nice."

"Hello. It was, and now I'm hungry. Do you want to go out and get something to eat?"

"That would be nice. There's a new fish place opened. We could go there. I doubt we'll need to book on a Tuesday."

"Tuesday, huh. I lost track of what day it was."

Gabriel shaved while Eli applied a little makeup and fixed her long auburn hair into a bun, from which a few stray tendrils coiled against the side of her neck.

They dressed for dinner, he in a pair of stone cotton chinos and a fresh indigo shirt beneath an old, scuffed leather jacket, she in a coral dress that just swept the ground as she walked, a cream cardigan knotted around her shoulders.

From her earlobes dangled silver and coral earrings Gabriel had bought from a local jeweller. The Rolex he'd bought her on the way back from Britta's funeral glittered on her left wrist.

The Steel Scallop on Crabbe Street lay about five hundred yards from the sculpture on the stony beach from which it had taken its name. Though Maggi Hambling's monumental work had proved controversial among the local community, the new fish restaurant seemed to be meeting with approval. A waitress smiled at them as they pushed through the front door revealing braces much like those Sarah Chow had sported.

"I'll be right with you," she said, before jinking round a waiter coming in the opposite direction with a tray of golden fish and chips borne aloft on tented fingers.

Despite Eli's assertion, there was a single table available, but it was in a quiet corner with a view out over the sea front. They ordered picked crab on sourdough toast to start then a fish stew for Gabriel and the battered fish and chips for Eli. With a bottle of chilled Chablis sitting in a cooler between them, Gabriel raised his glass.

"*L'chaim!*"

"Cheers!"

The wine was dry and fruity, and as his first sip slid down his throat, Gabriel smiled.

"What are you looking so happy about?"

"This," he answered. "All this. Just you and me having dinner together in a restaurant. I could get used to it."

"Me too. On which subject."

"Yes?"

"My place in Shoreditch. The Department lease is up on it and facilities want to know if they should be finding me a new place."

"What have you told them?"

"I haven't told them anything yet."

Gabriel took another sip of the wine. Eli did the same, eyeing him over the rim of her glass.

"You know, you could always—" he began.

"Yes, please. I'd love it!"

Gabriel laughed loudly, causing a few diners at nearby tables to turn round, smiling, to see what was so funny.

"Smart, sexy, brave and apparently telepathic. You'll have me down on one knee if you're not careful."

As the words left his lips, he realised he wasn't joking. Then he experienced a wave of nervousness. *What if she thinks it's all too soon? That I'm not properly over Britta. Which I am. I was before Kristersson gunned her down.*

Eli wasn't smiling anymore. She put her glass down and reached across the tablecloth to take his hand in hers, squeezing ever so gently.

"I think we should probably get the rest of my stuff moved in first. That's enough to think about for a while, don't you think?"

"Yeah, yeah. Of course. I didn't mean we, you know, I wasn't thinking, I'm just happy with you, that's all."

Now she did smile. His heart unclenched.

"There's nobody I'd rather be with than you," she said. "Not now, not ever."

To Gabriel's relief, their starters arrived. Gabriel took a slice of the sourdough and liberally spread it with crab before squeezing lemon over it. It was delicious, tasting of the sea. As they ate, the conversation took an unexpected turn.

"Remember Bev Watchett?" Eli asked.

"Yes. What about her?"

"I met her in the High Street yesterday. We went for a drink in the Cross Keys. She still wants to paint your portrait, you know? Like she said that time in her garden. Seems dead set on it, as a matter of fact."

"What did you say?"

"I said I was sure you'd be delighted. Especially after all the help she gave us tracking down Kristersson. Not that I mentioned him by name, of course. In fact, I promised her you'd do it."

Gabriel felt he was being played, skilfully. The twinkle in Eli's eye and the twitch at the corners of her mouth reinforced the impression. He swallowed his last mouthful of crab, biting down on a fragment of cracked black pepper. Took another sip of the wine – and another – and decided.

"Oh well, I might have been able to disappoint you. But Bev? No way. Especially as you gave her your word."

58

Two days later, Gabriel Wolfe, MC, veteran of two of the world's most elite fighting forces and numerous high-risk, covert paramilitary operations since, found himself facing a challenge that had his insides fizzing with nerves.

As he waited in Bev's paint-spattered, canvas-strewn studio, arms folded across his chest, he reflected that he'd rather be jumping across a six-foot gap from the Outer Hebridean island of North Uist to a column of basalt called Old Tom. Far less scary. Bev had switched on a space heater but even with the air artificially warmed he felt goose bumps all over his skin.

Sitting on a bar stool in a corner, sipping a mug of coffee, Eli, fully-clothed, winked at him.

"Looking good," she said.

"You're enjoying this, aren't you?"

She grinned.

"I don't seem to remember you had any complaints about nudity when it was the lovely Tanis flashing her tits at you in the garden." Eli put on a girly voice. "Ooh, Gabriel, the tree bark is hurting my posh little bottom. Could you put your big, strong arms round me and lift me down?"

"OK, fine. Where's Bev, anyway? The sooner we get this started, the sooner we can finish."

"And you can put your clothes back on."

"Er, nobody's putting their clothes back on. Not until I've made my preliminary sketch," Bev said as she re-entered the studio, now clad in a long white smock decorated with multicoloured stains from washed-out paint.

"Where do you want me?" Gabriel asked, ignoring Eli's snort.

Bev stared at him, appraising him as he imagined people buying horses might do. She looked at him frankly, up and down. Taking her time, pausing at the various scars on his body.

"You've been in the wars, haven't you, my love?" she said, finally, breaking the silence. "I think you have a classical look about you. Now, how about something to help you get into character? Here, I've got just the thing."

She bustled off to a corner of the studio and opened a door that led, evidently, to a props cupboard. She disappeared inside and Gabriel listened as she muttered and cursed before emerging clasping a short sword in her right hand and a round shield in her left. Both appeared to be the genuine article, but when she handed them to him he realised they were made of wood, painted skilfully so that they resembled battle-worn bronze and steel.

"Did you make these?" he asked.

"Oh, no. I'm hopeless with anything 3-D. No, these were made by a friend of mine. He works at the National Theatre."

Gabriel hefted the weapons, adopting a martial pose, sword aloft, shield held in front of him.

"Like this?"

Bev shook her head.

"Too obvious. There's a vulnerability about you, Gabriel, that I think we should bring out. Do you know the Fallen Warrior from the Temple of Aphaia on Aegina?"

"Not really my specialist subject, I'm afraid."

"It's a famous Greek statue. Ancient Greek, that is. Aegina is an island in the Saronic Gulf. About twenty miles southwest of Athens. The warrior is in the Glyptothek in Munich now. It's a public museum devoted to antiquities. You should go some time. Yes. I think this will be your pose. Let me help you. Can you lie down on your left side?"

After a few minutes during which Bev arranged Gabriel's limbs and torso how she wanted them, she pronounced herself satisfied. He was propped up on his left hip and the edge of the shield, his left arm threaded through the two leather straps. His right arm was curled across his stomach, his fist on the ground, gripping the sword, which lay under his left armpit.

"Now, just look down at a point between your right hand and where your shield touches the ground. You've been fighting all day. The Trojan Wars. You're wounded, badly. You're dying. You're resigned to it but you're not frightened."

As Bev issued her instructions, Gabriel found he was able to go inside himself, finding a place not too far off from the scenario she was inventing for him to inhabit. Her voice faded.

He was lying on a battlefield. His lifeblood was leaking from his wounds into the foreign soil. They had fought valiantly, as best as they were able. For Queen and country. And now it was over.

Around him he could see corpses, body parts. Torn apart, scattered like cuts of meat. Smoke drifted across the field of Mars, bringing with it the stench of burning flesh. Horses whinnied in their death agonies. Men screamed for their mothers. The victors' shouts were loud in his ears as they roved the battlefield, taking trophies. Blood in his mouth, tasting of copper.

The pain was fading. Not long until it would stop altogether. His mates were all dead. It was nearly his time to join them. Time to lay down his weapons and sleep. *Soon it will be over. Soon I'll join them, all those I knew, all those I loved and who I—"*

"Gabriel?"

"Yes?"

"I said you can get up now."

Gabriel blinked. He got to his feet. Bev was holding out a grey flannel dressing gown for him. He put it on.

"That was impressive. You were down there for an hour. You didn't move. Not even a twitch. Were you meditating? Eli said you were highly skilled in Eastern mysticism. Well, not her words precisely, but close enough."

Gabriel looked round.

"Where is she?"

"Oh, she got bored, I'm afraid. She went home."

"To answer your question, no, I wasn't. Meditating, I mean. I don't know what happened, really. I just let myself be your fallen warrior."

Bev frowned. She came a step closer and looked up into his eyes. Hers were a blue-grey and flecked with hazel.

"You've been there, haven't you?"

"Where, Aegina? I told you."

"You know perfectly well what I mean. You virtually disappeared from the studio, leaving your body behind. Where did you go?"

"I'll tell you some time."

"I'll hold you to that. Maybe you'd let me buy you and Eli dinner one day soon."

"OK. Yes. I'd like that. So, what next? About the picture?"

"I'll do a bit more work on it then, if you're happy with what I show you, I'll ask you to come back and sit, well, lie – for me again. Deal?" she asked, sticking out a charcoal-smudged hand.

"Deal," he said, grasping it in his own.

For the rest of his few days in Aldeburgh, Gabriel and Eli sailed, talked, read, drank, made love, cooked meals – all the things ordinary, everyday couples did. They barely discussed their work. Gabriel arranged a meal out with Bev and asked her to take a photo on his phone of him and Eli.

They grinned, arms around each other, drunk on good white wine, while Bev made a production of arranging the lighting and asking a nearby table to "pipe down" so she could concentrate. And then, all too soon, Friday rolled around.

Gabriel was up, showered, shaved and dressed by 6.30 a.m. He ate a couple of slices of toast and washed them down with instant coffee, went upstairs to kiss Eli goodbye and was sitting behind Lucille's steering wheel ten minutes later. He pointed the big car's nose north and drove through the sleeping town on the way to the A12.

Four hours and five minutes later, he was driving through the centre of Carshalton. He had fifteen minutes before his meeting with Jack Yates.

59

CARSHALTON, SURREY

Here was another of the many similar towns, once part of the county of Surrey, now subsumed into the vast and growing sprawl that was Greater London. The houses were a hodge-podge of Victorian and Edwardian terraces, thirties villas and boxy houses from the fifties and sixties where the local council had rushed to fill in derelict sites as quickly and as cheaply as possible. Plenty of trees, at least, though most were beginning to lose their leaves as October marched on.

Gabriel found Rochester Road. At the far end of the street, where it split in two at a T-junction, he parked outside Yates's house. Late Victorian was Gabriel's guess, the double-fronted house's terracotta pantiles layering the upper half like fish-scales. He walked up the front path and rang the doorbell.

He heard steps almost immediately, and wondered whether Yates had been waiting for him. He'd certainly sounded eager on the phone the previous afternoon, when Gabriel had called to fix up the meeting. A chain rattled, then came the unmistakeable sound of a key opening a mortice lock.

The door opened. Here was the man from the photograph. Older now, though still in good shape for a man of his age. Up close, Gabriel could see that the lustrous black hair, what was left of it, was kept that way by dye. Every strand was the same, uniform dark shade. As they shook hands, he wondered briefly whether Yates dyed his eyebrows or whether they had been the source of the colour match.

"Terry?" Gabriel nodded. "Come in, come in, don't stand out there all morning, you'll catch your death, though looking at you, you look fit enough," he said, the words tumbling over each other as he ushered Gabriel into a wide hallway tiled in a black-and-white chequerboard pattern. "Tea, coffee, something stronger, although it's bit early, even for me, so what, then, tea? Coffee?"

"Coffee, please."

Gabriel found himself in a spacious kitchen. The units, carved pine stained a vibrant orange, looked as though they had been there a long time. Clean, but dated. Matching brown-and-cream glazed jars bore printed names: sugar, coffee, tea.

"How was the golf?"

"It was good! Yeah, good. My game's not what it was. I used to play off eight not so long ago. You'd have to double that now." He winked. "Triple it, if I'm being honest."

While Yates busied himself grinding beans and boiling the kettle, Gabriel wandered over to the window. A large, well-kept garden ran down to a brick wall, on the other side of which there appeared to be a yard of some kind. The building at the far end wasn't residential. It looked like a small, brick-built industrial unit.

"Ah," Yates said, looking up. "You've spotted the enemy, have you? Bloody car mechanics, singing and shouting, playing Radio-bloody-One all hours of the day and night. I've had a word with their boss but he's bloody Polish or something. One of the Eastern European countries, anyway. Says he'll have a word with his lads and never does a bloody thing. I've been onto the council too, mind, but them? Huh! About as much use as an inflatable truncheon."

Having delivered himself of this tirade against his neighbour, Yates assembled the coffee things onto a tray, added a plate of biscuits and jerked his chin at the door.

"Lead on, Macduff. The lounge is through there."

Furnished with matching slate-grey velour armchairs and sofa, and a wall full of bookshelves, the sitting room faced the road. Gabriel took an armchair and sat forward, clearing a couple of boating magazines from the coffee table so Yates could put the tray down.

"Do you sail?" he asked.

"Me? Chance would be a fine thing. Not at the moment. It's the dream, though. To have my own boat. Or it was until the wife cleaned me out when she left. Still, I got the house, didn't I, so didn't do too badly out of the divorce." Then he seemed to realise he was gabbling. He coughed. "God, sorry. No bloody sooner have you got through the door than I'm burdening you with all my domestic trouble. Here, have some of this. Colombia's finest. Coffee, obviously. I keep the marching powder for special occasions."

Colombia. Cartels. El Nuevo Medellín. Tatyana. Novgorodsky. Britta. No! Block it out!

Gabriel picked up the mug and took a cautious sip. The coffee was revolting. Bitter, yet weak at the same time. Yates had barely given it time to brew. He covered up his wince with a cough.

"Good. But too hot!"

He put the mug down on a coaster Yates slid towards him from a short stack, like one of Fang's croupiers at the Golden Dragon.

"On the phone, you said you were looking into one of my old cases," Yates said. "Chrissie Chu put you onto me, is that right?"

"That's right."

"Great copper, Chrissie. I knew her when she was a wet-behind-the-ears cadet, fresh out of the police college. What rank is she now?"

"Detective Chief Inspector."

Yates's eyes widened.

"Is she now? A DCI! Well, good for Chrissie, that's what I say. Good for her. You know, the weird thing is, even though we were out there, you know, in Hong Kong, there was a lot of prejudice against the Chinese on the Force. She had the double burden of being Chinese and a woman. Or three, if you count being bright. But I always reckoned she'd do well for herself. Like a terrier, she was, when she got a hold of a lead, you'd as soon shake off a python as DS Chrissie Chu," he finished, with a mixed metaphor that had Gabriel smiling at the thought of a Jack Russell-python hybrid.

Yates clearly wanted to talk. *Needed* to talk. And, having waited this far, maybe a whole lifetime, Gabriel felt he could wait a few minutes more.

"How old were you when you joined the Force, Mr Yates?"

"Mister? Call me Jack. My mates always did."

"Jack, then."

"Let's see," Yates said, looking upwards. "I joined the Met in sixty-seven. Spent seven years there, all in uniform except for the last two when I made DC, that's—"

"Detective Constable."

"Exactly. So, DC in seventy-two. Then they were holding this recruitment drive in seventy-four for the RHKP and I put my name forwards. I was young, no ties, maybe had a bit of wanderlust. Never been out of Tooting before, except for the old week at the seaside, so, you know, it was a pretty big deal. Halfway round the bloody world on me own? Well, I had to try, didn't I? Anyway, I got in. Sailed in November, no way someone on my salary could afford a plane ticket. Things were like bloody gold dust back then, not like nowadays when kids just go backpacking all over." He hesitated for a moment. "What was your question again?"

"How old were you when you joined the Force?"

Yates became animated again.

"Yes! Well, eighteen when I joined the Met and twenty-five when I joined the RHKP. My thirty came up in ninety-seven, which seemed sort of fitting, what with the handover and everything. The governor, Mr Patten, he was a proper gent. Lost his seat in ninety-two 'cos he was managing the election campaign for the Tories so he came over to be the governor. I met him once, at an official function. Lovely man. Posh, you know, like they all are, but down to earth with it. No side."

"You must have seen a few changes during your time."

"Changes? Don't get me bloody started. Some were good, like more girls on the Force. I was never one of those who said they couldn't hack it. Look at Chrissie. But it was the way people started losing their respect for us. That hurt. But I'll tell you why, Terry. It was graft. I never liked it. Too many dirty cops in Hong Kong when I was there. It was like a bloody epidemic. Not all of them, of course. Plenty of decent coppers doing the right thing. But it wasn't a case of one bad apple spoils the barrel. Sometimes it felt like if you weren't a rotten apple, *you* were the outsider. They were rooting them out by the time I got there, but I tell you, it could get really nasty at times."

Gabriel put his coffee cup down and clasped his hands between his knees as he leaned towards Yates.

"Do you think we could talk about the reason I'm here, Jack? Your old case?"

"What? Oh, yes, of course. Good God, you must think I've lost me marbles, the way I rattle on. Tell me, then. What brings you all the way from Hong Kong to my humble abode in Carshalton?"

"My sister. Her name was Tara Wolfe."

60

The effect on Yates was electric. He sat bolt upright in his chair and gripped the arms. He swallowed convulsively, so that his prominent Adam's apple leaped in his throat.

"Tara Wolfe. Wait. Your sister? Then you're—"

"Gabriel. I'm sorry I gave a false name on the phone. I wasn't sure you'd want to see me."

Yates stood and rounded the coffee table and did something that took Gabriel by surprise. He crouched in front of him and hugged him, tight, before releasing him and resuming his place in the other armchair.

"Want to see you? Oh my God. You poor lad. You were just three years old last time I saw you. I was a DC, a year into my stint working in the DATS. Sorry, the District Anti-Triad Squad."

"I've seen your files. I got copies from Chrissie Chu. Did you really turn up nothing?"

"Not while I was out there, no. But things changed, funnily enough, when I left Hong Kong."

"What happened?"

"After I came back to England, I soon got tired of playing golf or pottering about the house so I applied for a job at the Met again."

"And you got back in?"

"It was easy. They had manpower shortages, like always, and with my background they welcomed me with open arms. My mate John Evans was on a team that raided an unlicensed casino in the West End this one time," Yates said, sipping coffee. "Must have been about 2003 or 2004. Turned out the dominos and mahjong were just a front for a massive drugs operation. One of the scumbags they picked up was a Four-Point Star triad employee named Ronald Bao Dai, aka "Donkey". He told John he'd moved to the UK from Hong Kong in 1984."

"He talked?"

"Had to. They had him bang to rights. He was facing a list of charges as long as your arm and supporting evidence that would send him down for more time than he wanted to think about."

"And he decided to deal?"

"Bao Dai asked for immunity and a new identity in return for a story about a missing baby girl. A very important baby girl."

"Tara."

"Exactly. When John told me about it over a few jars one evening, I had a feeling straightaway it was Tara he was talking about. They got him up to the story of the missing baby and the names and details of a dozen or more of his confederates, at which point he began talking.

"Bao Dai was just the muscle and, from what John said, not the sharpest chisel in the box. The guy who planned the whole thing was still in his teens, believe it or not. A man Bao Dai knew only as Snake."

"How did they do it?"

"After taking Tara, they put her inside a padded top-box on a pizza delivery moped and drove her to the house of a couple named Kwok, employed by the Four-Point Star triad. The wife had just had a baby of her own. The plan was that she should nurse Tara until your parents paid the ransom."

"So why did the trail go cold?"

"The husband, Dennis, was an enforcer for the Four-Point Star triad. Four days before the deadline for the handover, he was killed in a brawl outside a brothel under the supposed protection of the Four-Point Star triad. At that point, Rita fled with the two babies."

"Did John ask Bao Dai whether Tara was still alive?"

"He said he had no idea. Honestly? He had no reason to lie. And, anyway, why give us a loose end? It made his currency less valuable to us."

"Where is he now?"

"No idea. I don't want to sound flippant, but that's the thing with new identities. There's a department that deals with all that witness protection stuff, but you'd be better off trying to break into the Bank of England."

Gabriel felt mixed emotions swirling in his breast. Joy that he had the middle part of Tara's story. How two kidnappers managed to spirit her away and ensure she disappeared from under the noses of the police. But also frustration that, once again, he seemed to have hit a brick wall.

"That's really good of you to tell me all that, Jack," he said. "At least it explains why nothing happened even after my parents put the ransom money together. I just wish the trail was a little warmer."

"Ah, well, here's the thing. Maybe it is. While I was in Hong Kong, I turned up nothing I felt I could act on. Although we knew in our bones it was the triads, we couldn't get anyone to talk and there wasn't anything in the way of physical evidence we could use."

He paused, and even after their short time together, Gabriel sensed not only a "However..." coming, but Yates's need to be prompted.

"You said nothing you felt you could act on. Does that mean there was stuff you *couldn't* act on?"

Yates's eyes widened and he nodded.

"Smart boy. That's exactly what I meant. Remember I said there were a lot of dirty cops in Hong Kong back then?"

"Yes."

"There was one in Special Branch when I was working out

there. His name was Steve Ponting. A sergeant. Big bugger. Boxed for the RHKP. Heavyweight. He was on the take. I mean, really on the take. He'd transferred in from Vice and there were rumours he was running girls of his own. Started off shaking them down for a few dollars here and there, then moved up to acting as a full-blown pimp. If there was dirty money around, you could bet Ponting would have his hand out. Both hands, most of the time. Anyway, I got to wondering whether he knew something about your sister's kidnapping. You know, a copper's feeling."

Gabriel could feel his pulse hammering in his chest. He was closer now than he'd ever been. What was Yates on about? What feeling?

"And when you said you had a feeling?" he prompted.

"It was more than a feeling really. I had a snitch back then. Knew all the London triad guys at the lower levels. The 49ers and the Blue Lanterns. He told me Ponting passed information about your parents to his paymasters. Helped set it up. I made a few discreet enquiries about him, and I mean *really* discreet, and I was basically warned off. Told in no uncertain terms he was protected. If I went after him, I'd end up in pieces in the harbour."

"But how could he know they'd be out on that particular night?"

"Put it together, lad! Special Branch? Diplomatic protection duties? He was your parents' personal protection officer. He practically *lived* at your house."

Gabriel was about to reply that he had no recollection of this Ponting character when he realised that was the problem. He had so few memories of home that there could have been a whole brigade of coppers camped out in the back garden and he might have forgotten them all.

"What was he going to get out of it?" he asked, suspecting he already knew the answer.

"Ten per cent of the ransom. My snitch said that was the usual cut for cops helping set up jobs. What was the ransom demand again?"

"A million Hong Kong dollars."

"Good God, yes. A million cold. So that would be, er, what now?

In 1983, the exchange rate was, um, yes, about eleven to the pound. So just north of ninety thousand pounds. Ponting would have been in line for a nine grand payday for helping triads kidnap your baby sister."

Gabriel felt a sudden, overpowering surge of rage against a man he hadn't met. It was worse than the cold anger he'd directed at Max Novgorodsky. That had been personal. But this was family.

"Apart from what your snitch told you, did you ever get any hard evidence against Ponting?"

"I tried, believe me. But he was too much of an old hand at the game to leave anything incriminating behind him. But my guy was solid. I threatened him with a good hiding if he was lying to me but he swore on his grandmother's grave he wasn't and, well, you know what they're like for their ancestors. I believed him then, and I believe him now. It was Ponting set it up. After that, I did what I could to find out what happened to poor little Tara, but it was just one dead end after another. I kept on going back to the case in my spare time, even after they wound up the investigation. Then, in the end, my thirty came up and I was tired of it all and just came home. Kept my files though, well, copies."

"What happened to Ponting? Was he still there when you retired in ninety-seven?"

Yates shook his head.

"No. He was my age so he still had plenty of years to put in before his thirty, but he left the year after it happened, in 1984."

"Do you know where he went?"

"Sorry, Gabriel. He went back home to England, but the last I heard of him, he'd moved to Spain."

It was disappointing news, but it wasn't the end. Gabriel had a name, and a location. After a little more small talk, Gabriel stood. He sensed Yates's disappointment that he couldn't stay for longer, but pleading his appointment at MHD Forensics, and promising he'd let Yates know if he "solved" the case, he left the neat sitting room, shook hands at the front door and was heading back towards London a minute after that.

61

RICHMOND

Gabriel parked Lucille in a visitor parking spot outside the headquarters of MHD Forensics, a low, modern-looking affair in sand-coloured bricks and a great deal of reflective, film-coated plate glass. The roof prickled with antennae and satellite dishes. The building occupied a riverside site overlooking the Thames as it curved away from the town towards Teddington and Kingston. Beyond the edge of the car park he could see tall trees waving in the breeze.

He passed the five-minute wait in the comfortably-furnished reception area skimming a magazine article about gene-editing, and taking in nothing beyond the idea that 'designer babies' were closer than anyone thought. His belly felt as if it were filled with insects, all skittering and fluttering around in there, trying to get out. Breathing deeply and evenly, he closed his eyes and practised one of Master Zhao's calming mantras.

"Gabriel?"

He opened his eyes and stared up into the bespectacled gaze of a man in his late fifties, wearing a white coat and carrying a clipboard. His hair had receded to the point that all he was left with was silver tufts at the sides of his head. Short of carrying a flask of smoking green liquid, there was nothing more he could have done to say "Mad Scientist" with his appearance.

Gabriel stood and they shook hands.

"I'm Malcolm Eaton. We spoke on the phone. Welcome to MHD Forensics."

"Thanks for seeing me."

"To be honest we don't get very many individuals. It's mostly corporations and the government in all its many guises. I admit I was intrigued by your story. Let's go to my workspace."

Eaton's 'workspace' was part office, part laboratory. Glass walls separated it from a large open-plan area inhabited by a couple of dozen white-coated scientists and technicians. Gabriel could see plenty of Macs, and a handful of pieces of equipment he remembered from school chemistry lessons, but the vast majority of the kit on display, clearly very expensive kit, was alien to him.

Rather than sitting behind the desk, a functional affair in battered wood with a much-scratched top, Eaton walked over to a stainless-steel table on which a large white-bodied microscope rested.

"What have you got for us, then?" he asked.

Gabriel handed over the forensics bag containing the fabric scrap from the kidnapping, along with his handkerchief, enclosed in a Ziploc bag. Eaton took both items and placed them reverently on the table.

Gabriel pointed to each of them in turn.

"The small one is a scrap from the clothing of the person I believe kidnapped my sister in 1983. The handkerchief has blood and saliva on it. I'm not sure why I brought it. The man it came from might have been involved in setting up the whole thing. Anyway, I hope to find out a little more about him."

"As I said on the phone, we can't go further than give you a profile. You're OK with that?"

"Yes, perfectly happy."

Eaton brought out a magnifying glass from a pocket in his lab coat. He picked up the bag containing the fabric scrap and turned to Gabriel.

"May I?"

"Be my guest."

Eaton unsealed the bag, slitting the red tape with a scalpel he picked out of a silver case lined with blue velvet.

He laid the scrap of black fabric with its minute rust-red stain on the table, pulled a lamp down closer and bent over it, magnifying glass to his eye. Without taking his eye off the fabric he murmured to Gabriel, "Yes, well that's definitely blood. Or if it isn't, I'll be mightily surprised. When did you say this was collected?"

"1983."

"Hmm. DNA-testing was in its infancy in those days in the UK. I'm not sure whether they had it in Hong Kong. But even in forces which were using it, you needed big samples. This would have been much too small. Things have moved on a great deal since then. We can test right down to specks you can only see under a microscope. The other one should be fine," he added, straightening. "It's recent, and it's there in quantity, so child's play, basically."

"What sort of turnaround can you offer?"

"Well, that depends to a great degree on your appetite for speed and the depth of your pockets. A normal profile, unprioritised, takes a week and costs five hundred pounds. For another two hundred and fifty pounds, we can shorten that to forty-eight hours."

"How about twenty-four hours?"

"Ah. Well." Eaton cleared his throat. "That would be what the credit card companies like to call the Platinum service. It's a thousand pounds, I'm afraid. Per sample."

Eaton seemed almost embarrassed to be discussing money. Gabriel felt he was face to face with a pure scientist, thrust by his firm somewhat unwillingly into the role of salesman.

"So two thousand for both samples, with the results by, what," Gabriel checked his watch, "eleven tomorrow morning?"

Eaton blinked.

"Yes. Absolutely. Or maybe even a little earlier."

They discussed the finer points of admin and payment – credit card or cash. Gabriel opted for the latter, handing over the money in crisp fifties in return for a receipt and the promise of an invoice marked "Paid" the following day.

Gabriel checked into a hotel in Richmond. Nothing to do but wait.

———

At 10.45 a.m. the next day, as he sat on a bench by the river watching a couple of swans escorting two kayakers, his phone alerted him to an incoming email.

> From: j.eaton@mhdforensics.co.uk
> Subject: DNA profiles
> Attachments: GWolfe/DNA-sample/1.pdf; GWolfe/DNA-sample/2.pdf; invoice-no. 20001765
>
> Dear Gabriel,
>
> Please find attached your two DNA profiles and receipted invoice in the amount of £2,000.00.
>
> Although, as I said, we are unable to cross-reference them to the NDNAD without a police operation name and reference number, what I can tell you is that they come from the same person. This person is male and of Han Chinese ancestry.
>
> I hope this is of use to you.
>
> Best regards,
> Malcolm Eaton
> Deputy Laboratory Director
> MHD Forensics

Gabriel sat back against the bench's hard wooden slats, staring at the far bank where the swans were now harassing a couple walking along the footpath. He didn't need to re-read Eaton's email. It was written in plain English and its meaning, to Gabriel, was inescapable.

Thirty-six years earlier, Fang Jian had kidnapped Gabriel's sister. Then, after leaving her with a couple called Kwok, had contrived to lose her.

And in their subsequent meetings, first with Master Zhao and then without him, Fang had looked Gabriel in the eye and smiled, and joked, and drank, and belched, and sworn and given favours, and requested them, and said absolutely nothing at all. Not. A. Fucking. Word.

He could have come clean but instead he'd preferred to trade favours, enmeshing Gabriel in a web of obligations that ended with Gabriel nearly being blown to shreds by Comrade Liu's RPG-wielding henchmen.

He waited for two women clad in fluorescent Lycra running gear to jog past him, then he stood. He resettled his jacket on his shoulders and pocketed his phone.

Twenty minutes later, he was back in his hotel room. His breathing was steady and he felt determination running through him like taut steel wire. Fang had escaped justice last time by the skin of his teeth. Next time he wouldn't be so lucky.

He called Eli and told her he'd be away for a few days. Then he returned to his hotel and logged onto the BA website.

62

HONG KONG

Somewhere over the Pacific, on either the previous or current flight, Gabriel's body clock had resigned its commission. He slept for two or three-hour stretches wherever and whenever he could. He ate when he was hungry, got up when he awoke, and used exercise and meditation to prevent himself from going mad.

The meetings in London, with Penny, Yates and Eaton, the brief rendezvous in Aldeburgh with Eli, seemed as though they might have happened in a dream. Or they would have done had he not had emailed DNA profiles on his phone proving that Fang Jian had kidnapped Tara. And a name. Steve Ponting. The architect of her kidnapping.

Ponting was in the wind. Gabriel would find him in time. And then there would be a reckoning. Of the final and most bloody kind. But that was for another time. Here in Hong Kong, now, there was only one man in Gabriel's cross-hairs. And his finger was tightening on the trigger.

After landing, Gabriel avoided his own house, figuring Fang would have it under surveillance, either personal or electronic. Either way, he wasn't prepared to take the risk. Instead, he checked into the Sheraton under a false name, using one of his Department-supplied IDs. So it was that the attentive desk clerk had welcomed "Mister Hocking" at just after 6.00 p.m.

But Mister Hocking had a problem. His firearm was locked in a safe two miles away in a house he felt it unwise to return to. Fine. *We'll do it old school.*

Later that evening, he left the Sheraton and walked for half an hour through the Yau Ma Tei district to the Chan Chi Kee knife shop on Shanghai Street in Kowloon. Tourists expecting some fancy kitchen shop with artful displays of the merchandise would be sadly disappointed.

CCK's, as locals called it, was utilitarian to the point of being more of a wholesaler than a retailer. Bunches of long stainless-steel skewers hung from hooks, waist-high stacks of polythene-wrapped woks teetered at the ends of aisles, bamboo steamers were piled up to the ceiling. Gabriel ignored all of these, heading to a counter along a side wall where the knives were displayed.

In the past he had bought cleavers, boning knives and chef's knives from the young women who staffed this corner of the store. Today he was after something at the heavier end of the product range. When he reached the front of the short queue he pointed at a rectangular-bladed cleaver in carbon steel.

"That one, please," he said, thinking back to the tuna he'd beheaded at Master Lo's.

A thousand Hong Kong Dollars lighter in the back pocket, but with the weight more than replaced by the cleaver, he strolled out of the shop, the brown-paper-wrapped package weighing down a plain white carrier bag.

On the way back to the Sheraton, he stopped in at a costume shop and emerged after ten minutes wearing a short wig and droopy moustache in matching black nylon, and a pair of plain-lensed glasses with thin, gold-wire frames. Mister Hocking had disappeared.

Figuring that the last place Fang Jian would be expecting to see him was at the Golden Dragon, that's exactly where Gabriel headed. He reached the rear of the casino at 9.00 p.m. Using the same route as before, and ready this time for the heart-stopping lurch on the fire escape's fifth landing, he made his way up to the roof and then across the sticky bitumen to the hutch with the doors down to the interior.

This time, though, the door wouldn't budge. He shook the handle and was rewarded with the sound of something solid and metallic clonking against the wood on the inside. A padlock. *Talk about shutting the stable door.*

He reared back and kicked the door just below the handle. The wood around the lock splintered and the door flew inwards, leaving the padlock securely locked onto the hasp, which now swung uselessly from a couple of remaining screws in the door jamb.

On soft-soled shoes, he crept down the corridor, ears pricked for the slightest sound. Hearing nothing, he rounded the dogleg and moved onto the carpeted portion of the hallway that led to Fang's office.

He willed his pulse to steady.

Filtering out the sounds from downstairs, he placed his ear to the door. From the other side he could hear voices. It sounded like just two. Deep and resonant. He ran through his plan one final time.

Get inside, hit the muscle hard. Isolate Fang. Rush him. The office is fifteen feet across, max. If he's armed, he won't have time to think straight enough to shoot. Check him for weapons. Tell him why I came back. Kill him. Leave.

Placing his left hand on the door knob, he held the cleaver aloft in his right. He took a deep breath, turned the handle and pushed through into Fang's office.

The adrenaline heightened his senses. He smelled Fang's aftershave. Heard a shocked gasp from the casino manager who'd twisted round in his chair. Saw the gold teeth in Fang's mouth as he snarled at the intruder who'd just burst into his private domain.

63

He closed the gap with the casino manager, and knocked him out with a crushing blow to the side of the head. Fang lurched back in his chair, knocking over a pair of aluminium crutches leaning against the wall behind him. As Gabriel rushed him, he rocked forwards again and snatched open one of the desk drawers.

Gabriel launched himself across the smooth mahogany surface and closed the fingers of his left hand on Fang's right. He brought the cleaver overhead in a slicing arc that would end up separating Fang's right hand from his wrist. But Fang was strong, and used his upper body strength to jerk his hand away, which came free grasping the butt of a small, silver semi-automatic pistol. With a loud clunk, the cleaver buried itself an inch-deep in the desk.

Having lost his weapon, Gabriel slithered backwards as Fang was levelling the pistol. But it was too late. Fang had the muzzle of the stubby little gun pointing straight at him.

"Stop!" Fang yelled.

Gabriel stopped. What choice did he have? Now it was a question of keeping Fang talking until he could make a move on the gun. And that would only happen if he could tempt him out from behind the desk.

Fang squinted at Gabriel, who saw the precise moment his disguise failed.

"You!" he hissed, panting for breath. "Mei, search him."

Gabriel hadn't realised there was anyone else in the office. He'd been too focused on Fang. He now realised he should have looked behind him as he rushed the triad boss. He felt hands, swift, strong and sure, patting him down, squeezing his sleeves and running down his legs, inside and out.

"He's clean, master."

She kept out of his eyeline, not giving him an opening to counter-attack.

"If he moves, run him through," Fang said, reaching down and behind him to retrieve one of the crutches, then heaving himself to his feet with a grunt and threading his left forearm through the grey plastic cuff.

Gabriel felt a prod from something hard and sharp in-between his shoulder blades.

Fang manoeuvred himself out from behind the desk and made his way around it, wincing with each step. Gabriel glanced down at his left knee. The trouser leg was tight there, from the bandages, Gabriel assumed. *Good, I hope it still hurts.* When he was standing face to face with Gabriel, Fang leaned in closer. And smiled. It was an evil grin, devoid of any genuine good humour. The expression of a man about to deliver a beating and knowing he's going to enjoy it.

Keeping the gun pointed at Gabriel's midsection, Fang slapped him hard across the face, knocking the glasses clean across the room. He closed his left fist on the crown of the wig and dragged it off, dropping it to the floor. Finally, with exaggerated care, he peeled the moustache away.

He stepped back, out of range of a fist or a foot.

"Well, well, well. You came back. Despite what I told you last time. Here to kill me, I suppose?"

"Would you like to know why?"

Fang took a couple more halting steps backwards until he reached the edge of the desk. He rested the crutch against it, cupped his right elbow in his left palm and nodded.

"Surprise me."

"After I left you here, I went back to the UK. I took your blood and saliva to a lab. I got it tested, a DNA profile. And it turns out it was identical to another profile. One they pulled from a scrap of black fabric found caught in the trellis at my parents' house back in eighty-three. Which means you kidnapped my sister. I came here to kill you because not only did you take her from us, you lost her."

Fang said nothing. Then he smirked. And at that moment Gabriel knew that if he could just wipe that grin from Fang's face, preferably for good, he could die happy. *I'm sorry, Eli. I think we were good for each other.*

"I lost her. Is that what you think? No. I did not lose her. After Dennis was killed, Rita took off with the two babies. She went to the mainland. Raised both girls there. My plan failed so I moved onto bigger and better things. But I always wondered what happened to the little English baby. One day, I thought to myself, Fang, you have things running sweetly here, why not go and find her? I went to the mainland and I did some asking around. And guess what? I found Rita in a crappy little village outside Shenzhen, living with her cousin. I told her the girl was mine, and left with her, as simple as that. She was fourteen.

"I brought her back to Hong Kong and I thought, now what do I do with this little girl? Do I put her on the street? She is pretty enough. Maybe I should send her to school and university. Get her trained up in business administration. But then I thought to myself, no, too much money. Finally, I had it. She could work for me right away. As a lotus blossom."

Fang's words faded as Gabriel processed the last two. *Lotus blossom.* He felt the pressure in his back lessen fractionally. And he realised the source of the connection he felt with Wei Mei. Without taking his eyes off Fang, he spoke to her.

"You didn't kill me at Max's dacha *because you couldn't.*"

Fang guffawed, a raw, ugly sound.

"You just worked it out, eh, Wolfe Cub? My beautiful plum is your kid sister. Tara's standing right behind you, and at a word from me she'll stick that sword right through your guts."

Gabriel's heart was racing. His vision was so sharp he could see individual loose strands of gold thread dangling from the cuff of Fang's dinner jacket.

And then the pressure in his back disappeared altogether.

64

He rushed at Fang, left fist swinging inside Fang's gun arm and knocking it wide. The gun clattered onto the desk top and skittered across it to vanish over the far edge. Before he had a chance to react, Gabriel had chopped him in the throat with his right hand. But it was a poorly aimed blow and caught Fang's chin, robbing the strike of much of its power.

Fang wasn't done yet. He rolled sideways, out from under Gabriel's fist, and lashed out sideways, delivering a huge punch into Gabriel's left kidney. As he clutched his wounded side, feeling a wave of nausea threatening to engulf him, Gabriel saw Fang's hand dart into his trouser pocket and emerge holding something that flashed and glittered in the lamplight.

The knife came up in a short upwards curve. Gabriel felt the stab as more of a punch than a cut, hitting him under the left armpit. He groaned and fell backwards. Fang righted himself and advanced on Gabriel, who could feel the blood soaking into his shirt. With a triumphant grin, Fang straddled Gabriel's supine body and sat heavily on his ribs, knocking the breath from his lungs. He waved the knife back and forth in front of Gabriel's face.

"You know, after you shot me last time, I made elaborate plans to have you fetched back from whichever rat-hole you'd bolted to. I was going to follow through on my threat. I even chose the method. Master Lo was going to provide the necessary equipment. But now that you've saved me the time, trouble and expense, I'm going to make it easy on you. I'm going to take your face off and show you what's left in a mirror, and then I'm going to cut—"

It took a moment for Gabriel to understand what happened next.

Fang stopped talking and his mouth dropped open. An oddly melodic groan issued from between his slack lips, followed by a thin string of saliva and then a thicker rope of blood. He looked down, and Gabriel looked up, at the same spot, between Fang's third and fourth shirt buttons. Emerging from the gap in the white silk, curved a nine-inch length of glinting steel, its sides smeared red.

Behind Fang, Mei stood in a half-crouch, her hands gripping the cloth-bound handle of the sword. She jerked the long blade backwards. It came free with a sucking sound. Eyes rolling upwards in their sockets, Fang toppled sideways and fell to the carpet with a thump, blood issuing freely from the holes in his back and chest.

"Stay down," she said. "He stabbed you."

She cut Gabriel's shirt away with the sword, wadded it into a ball and pushed it, hard, into his armpit. She took his hand and placed it over the improvised field dressing.

"Apply pressure, yes? As hard as you can manage."

Feeling lightheaded, Gabriel complied, letting his head thump back onto the carpet. He watched as Mei went to the desk and picked up the phone. His hearing warbled and for a moment he felt black curtains swinging shut over his vision. Then it cleared. Mei was by his side.

"I called an ambulance. They won't take long. Not when it's one of *his* places," she added, jerking her head in the direction of the dead gangster.

"What are you going to do with the body?" Gabriel murmured.

"Not your problem. I will call Master Lo."

Gabriel saw the tuna again. The cleaver. Remembered something Lo had said about a cat food factory.

He raised his head off the carpet, ignoring the nausea that rolled over him.

"Mei. You're, you're Tara. You're my sister. I'm your—"

Then the curtains closed properly.

65

Gabriel woke up in a white room. Registered the smell of disinfectant. Heard beeps. He looked around. *OK. Another hospital. This is getting to be a habit.* Moving cautiously, he ascertained that he was connected to monitors and drips by at least half a dozen wires and tubes.

"You're awake."

He turned to his left. His sister was sitting in a chair by his bedside, a book on her lap. She was dressed in jeans and a grey sweatshirt, her hair tied back in a ponytail, her rosebud mouth curved upwards in a smile.

"Tara."

"I find that name uncomfortable. I have never known it. Please call me Mei."

"Mei, then. Thank you for saving my life. Twice."

She smiled.

"It was the least a sister could do for her big brother, don't you think?"

Now it was Gabriel's turn to smile. He reached out for her hand. She took his, and they intertwined fingers. He felt a sense of euphoria. After all the sadness that had dogged his memories of his family, here, finally, was something good. Something genuinely, unequivocally good. If he could just hold on, it might lead him away from the dark thoughts that still plagued him. About Michael, about his parents, about Smudge and the boys, and Britta. He had a living sister, and a girlfriend back home. He had reasons to take care of himself. Reasons to live well, and happily.

"I want to get to know you," he said.

"And I, you. But you have to understand, this is all strange for me. You knew you had a sister. You were looking for me. I did not know I had a brother. All I've known was my life with Mummy Rita and then Uncle Jian. They raised me, one after the other. He trained me to do what I do."

"What do you want, then?"

"I need to think. Fang's gone. Properly gone, I mean. Nobody will ever find him. Though some pampered pussycats might enjoy a little piece of him. But the White Koi will elect a new leader. I cannot just walk away from them. That's not how it works."

"But if there *was* a way, would you take it?"

"Yes. I want to do something else now. I want to have a life of my own. But it's not that simple."

"So you'll stay working for them?"

"For now. I have to. But you don't have to worry. You're in the clear. Nobody saw you arrive at the Golden Dragon and I put your disguise back in place before the paramedics arrived."

"What did you tell them?"

"That there'd been an accident in the kitchen."

"And they believed you?"

"When they get called out to the Golden Dragon, they know better than to ask questions. Same with the cops."

"Can we meet? When I'm out of here?"

She smiled.

"Of course we can. Maybe we can even spar together in your dojo. As long as you fight better than you did against the dummy!"

Mei stayed for another hour or two. The two Wolfe siblings carried on talking, building shared memories out of separate stories.

That their lives had taken similar turns in adulthood surprised neither of them. Without being able to say why, or not precisely why, they agreed that the events of their childhoods had prepared them for a way of living most ordinary people would find impossible to follow.

Suddenly feeling tired, Gabriel laid his head back on the pillow. Against his will, he felt his eyes closing, heavy-lidded. He let them. There would be time for talking, for telling stories, for getting to know each other. Time for them to visit Michael's grave and their parents'. Time for her to meet Eli. Time for everything. But for now, he needed to recover. To sleep. Resisting the downwards drag of his eyelids, he had a final question for Mei.

"Why did you come to see me that day? You know, early in the morning. In the dojo."

"I don't know. Not exactly. I just had this feeling about you. That there was something I should investigate. Now I know what it was."

"Thanks, Mei," he whispered. "I love you."

"I love you, too."

In the morning, Gabriel called Penny Farrell.

"Hi. Where are you?"

"I'm back in Hong Kong."

"Really?" The surprise was evident in her rising inflection. "I thought it might be a bit too hot for comfort out there for you."

"That's why I'm calling. It's cooled down. All the way."

"Is Fang dead?"

"Yes. He's dead."

"And when you say dead...?"

"He met with an accident."

"You killed him."

"No, I didn't."

"Come on, Gabriel. Remember what I said to you. You can't kid a kidder."

"I do remember. And I'm not kidding. I didn't kill him."

"Shit!"

"No, wait. I've been thinking, The White Koi are leaderless. At least for now. In the confusion, you might be able to do something. Get someone in there. On the inside."

"Oh, what, and you have someone in place, do you? Just waiting for my call?"

"I might have. I'll come and see you when I'm back in the UK."

And then he called Eli. To tell her about Mei. To ask her to come out to Hong Kong and meet his kid sister.

———

A few days later, Gabriel discharged himself from the hospital. Vowing to the medical staff and, more importantly, to himself that he would stay out of trouble, he retreated to his house. He invited Mei to dinner. After they had washed up together, he turned to her.

"Go and sit down. I have something for you."

She sat at the dining table.

Gabriel left the room and went to his office. He unlocked the safe and pulled out the cash tin he'd received from John Chang. Returning to the dining room, he placed it in front of Mei.

"Open it," he said. "It's not locked."

He watched as she opened the lid and took out the contents, one item at a time. She read the christening cards then placed them in a neat pile along with the red gift envelopes. One after the other, she unsnapped the tiny brass catches on the red leather boxes and flipped open the lids. She smiled as she withdrew the two tiny silver animals. The horse. And the rabbit. That left the photograph.

She picked it up by its edges and examined it. Then she turned it over and read aloud from the reverse.

"Gordon Lu Photography, Wan Chai, Hong Kong. Gabriel, 2, and Tara, 3 months."

Brother and sister sat quietly for a while after that. Then she got up to leave. Gabriel accompanied her as far as the front door. They hugged, promising to meet again soon, and then Mei broke away.

Reaching the pavement, she turned and waved.

THE END

ACKNOWLEDGMENTS

As with every book I write, the finished story has been shaped by a team of talented and dedicated people whom I now have the opportunity to thank.

My first readers, Simon Alphonso, Sarah Hunt and Sandy Wallace.

My editor, Nicola Lovick.

My proofreader, Liz Ward.

My "sniper spotters": OJ "Yard Boy" Audet, Ann Finn, Yvonne Henderson, Vanessa Knowles, Nina Rip and Bill Wilson.

My cover designer, Stuart Bache.

The members of my Facebook group, The Wolfe Pack.

The serving and former soldiers whose advice helped me to keep the military details accurate: Giles Bassett, Mark Budden, Mike Dempsey and Dickie Gittins.

A special thank-you to ex-Para Dave Bedford, who helped me land the parachuting and Afghanistan scenes safely.

And, as always, my family.

Any and all mistakes are mine alone.

Andy Maslen

Salisbury, 2019

ALSO BY ANDY MASLEN

The Gabriel Wolfe series
Trigger Point
Reversal of Fortune (short story)
Blind Impact
Condor
First Casualty
Fury
Rattlesnake
Minefield (novella)
No Further

The DI Stella Cole series
Hit and Run
Hit Back Harder
Hit and Done
Let the Bones be Charred

Other fiction
Blood Loss - a Vampire Story

Non-fiction
Write to Sell
100 Great Copywriting Ideas
The Copywriting Sourcebook
Write Copy, Make Money
Persuasive Copywriting

ABOUT THE AUTHOR

Andy Maslen was born in Nottingham, in the UK, home of legendary bowman Robin Hood. Andy once won a medal for archery, although he has never been locked up by the sheriff.

He has worked in a record shop, as a barman, as a door-to-door DIY products salesman and a cook in an Italian restaurant.

As well as the Stella Cole and Gabriel Wolfe thrillers, Andy has published five works of non-fiction, on copywriting and freelancing, with Marshall Cavendish and Kogan Page. They are all available online and in bookshops.

He lives in Wiltshire with his wife, two sons and a whippet named Merlin.

AFTERWORD

To keep up to date with news from Andy, join his Readers' Group at www.andymaslen.com.

Email Andy at andy@andymaslen.com.
Join Andy's Facebook group, The Wolfe Pack.